Critical acclaim for
Oscar Wilde and the Candlelight Murders

'One of the most intelligent, amusing and entertaining books of the year. If Oscar Wilde himself had been asked to write this book he could not have done it any better'
Alexander McCall Smith

'Genius . . . Wilde has sprung back to life in this thrilling and richly atmospheric new novel . . . The perfect topography for crime and mystery . . . magnificent . . . An unforgettable shocker about sex and vice, love and death' *Sunday Express*

'Gyles Brandreth and Oscar Wilde seem made for one another . . . There is much here to enjoy . . . the complex and nicely structured plot zips along' *Daily Telegraph*

'Very funny' *Independent on Sunday*

'This is to be a series and if they're all as enjoyable as the first, they'll all be surefire best-sellers . . . Fabulous . . . The plot races along like a carriage pulled by thoroughbreds . . . So enjoyably plausible' *Scotsman*

'Both a romp through *fin-de-siècle* London . . . and a carefully researched portrait of Oscar Wilde . . . Very entertaining' *Literary Review*

'Brandreth has the Wildean lingo down pat and the narrative is dusted with piquant social observations. A sparkling treat for fans of Wilde and Sherlock Holmes alike' *Easy Living*

OSCAR WILDE

and the
Candlelight
Murders

Gyles Brandreth

JOHN MURRAY

First published in Great Britain in 2007 by John Murray (Publishers)
An Hachette Livre UK company

Paperback edition 2008

1

© Gyles Brandreth 2007

A CIP catalogue record for this title is available from the British Library

ISBN 978-0-7195-6930-2

Typeset in Monotype Sabon by Servis Filmsetting Ltd, Manchester

Printed and bound by Clays Ltd, St Ives plc

John Murray policy is to use papers that are natural, renewable and recyclable
products and made from wood grown in sustainable forests. The logging and
manufacturing processes are expected to conform to the environmental regulations
of the country of origin.

John Murray (Publishers)
338 Euston Road
London NW1 3BH

www.johnmurray.co.uk
www.oscarwildemurdermysteries.com

To SRB

What a lurid life Oscar does lead – so full of
extraordinary incidents. What a chance for the
memoir writers of the next century!

Max Beerbohm (1872–1956)

From the previously unpublished memoirs of Robert Sherard

France, 1939

My name is Robert Sherard, and I was a friend of Oscar Wilde. We met in Paris in 1883, when he was twenty-eight and already famous, and I was twenty-one and quite unknown. 'You must not call me "Wilde",' he said to me at that first encounter. 'If I am your friend, Robert, my name to you is Oscar. If we are only strangers, I am Mr Wilde.' We were not strangers. Nor were we lovers. We were friends. And, after his death, I became his first – and his most faithful – biographer.

I knew Oscar Wilde and I loved him. I was not by him in the poor room of the poor inn where he died. I had not the consolation of following to the nameless grave the lonely hearse that bore no flowers on its pall.

But, as many hundreds of miles away I read of his solitary death, and heard of the supreme abandonment of him by those to whom also he had always been good, I determined to say all the things that I knew of him, to tell people what he really was, so that my story might help a little to a better understanding of a man of rare heart and rarer genius.

I am writing this in the summer of 1939. The date is Thursday 31 August. War looms, but it means nothing to me. Who wins, who loses: I care not. I am an old man now, and sick, and I have a tale I need to tell before I die.

I want to complete the record, 'finish the portrait', as best I can. As in a forest of pine-trees in southern France there are great black, burnt-up patches, so too in my memory. There is much that I have forgotten, much that I have tried to forget, but what you will read in the pages that follow I know to be true. In the years of our friendship, I kept a journal of our times together. I promised Oscar that for fifty years I would keep his secret. I have kept my word. And now the time has come when I can break my silence. At last, I can reveal all that I know of Oscar Wilde and the Candlelight Murders. I must do it, for I have the record. I was there. I am the witness.

The good die first,
And they whose hearts are dry as summer dust
Burn to the socket.

William Wordsworth (1770–1850)

31 August 1889

On an afternoon ablaze with sunshine, at the very end of August 1889, a man in his mid-thirties – tall, a little overweight and certainly overdressed – was admitted to a small terraced house in Cowley Street, in the city of Westminster, close by the Houses of Parliament.

The man was in a hurry and he was unaccustomed to hurrying. His face was flushed and his high forehead was beaded with perspiration. As he entered the house – number 23 Cowley Street – he brushed past the woman who opened the door to him, immediately crossed the shallow hallway and climbed the staircase to the first floor. There, facing him, across an uncarpeted landing, was a wooden door.

Momentarily, the man paused – to smile, to catch his breath, to adjust his waistcoat and, with both hands, to sweep back his wavy, chestnut-coloured hair. Then, lightly, almost delicately, he knocked at the door and, without waiting for an answer, let himself into the room. It was dark, heavily curtained, hot as a furnace and fragrant with incense. As the man adjusted his eyes to the gloom, he saw, by the light of half a dozen guttering candles, stretched out on the floor before him, the naked body of a boy of sixteen, his throat cut from ear to ear.

The man was Oscar Wilde, poet and playwright, and literary sensation of his age. The dead boy was Billy Wood, a male prostitute of no importance.

I was not there when Oscar discovered the butchered body of Billy Wood, but I saw him a few hours later and I was the first to whom he gave an account of what he had seen that sultry afternoon in the curtained room in Cowley Street.

That evening my celebrated friend was having dinner with his American publisher and I had arranged to meet up with him afterwards, at 10.30 p.m., at his club, the Albemarle, at 25 Albemarle Street, off Piccadilly. I call it 'his' club when, in fact, it was mine as well. In those days, the Albemarle encouraged young members – young ladies over the age of eighteen, indeed! – and gentlemen of twenty-one and more. Oscar put me up for membership and, with the generosity that was typical of him, paid the eight guineas' joining fee on my behalf and then, year after year, until the very time of his imprisonment in 1895, the five guineas' annual subscription. Whenever we met at the Albemarle, invariably, the cost of the drinks we drank and the food we ate was charged to his account. He called it 'our club'. I thought of it as his.

Oscar was late for our rendezvous that night, which was unlike him. He affected a languorous manner, he posed as an idler, but, as a rule, if he made an appointment with you, he kept it. He rarely carried a timepiece, but he seemed always to know the hour. 'My friends should not be left wanting,' he said, 'or be kept waiting.' As all who knew him will testify, he was a model of consideration, a man of infinite courtesy. Even at moments of greatest stress, his manners remained impeccable.

It was past 11.15 when eventually he arrived. I was in the club smoking room, alone, lounging on the sofa by the fireplace. I had turned the pages of the evening paper at least four times, but not taken in a word. I was preoccupied. (This was the year that my first marriage ended; my wife Marthe had taken an exception to my friend Kaitlyn – and now Kaitlyn had run off to Vienna! As Oscar liked to say, 'Life is the nightmare that prevents one from sleeping.') When he swept into the room, I had almost forgotten that I was expecting him. And when I looked up and saw him gazing down at me, I was taken aback by his appearance. He looked exhausted; there were dark, ochre circles beneath his hooded eyes. Evidently, he had not shaved since morning and, most surprisingly, for one so fastidious, he had not changed for dinner. He was wearing his workaday clothes: a suit of his own design, cut from heavy blue serge, with a matching waistcoat buttoned right up to the large knot in his vermilion-coloured tie. By his standards, it was a comparatively conservative outfit, but it was striking because it was so inappropriate to the time of year.

'This is unpardonable, Robert,' he said, as he collapsed onto the sofa opposite mine. 'I am almost an hour late and your glass is empty. Hubbard! Champagne for Mr Sherard, if you please. Indeed, a bottle for us both.' In life there are two types of people: those who catch the waiter's eye and those who don't. Whenever I arrived at the Albemarle, the club servants seemed to scatter instantly. Whenever Oscar appeared, they hovered attentively. They honoured him. He tipped as a prince and treated them as allies.

'You have had a busy day,' I said, putting aside my paper and smiling at my friend.

'You are kind not to punish me, Robert,' he said, smiling too, sitting back and lighting a cigarette. He threw the dead match into the empty grate. 'I have had a disturbing day,' he went on. 'I have known great pleasure today, and great pain.'

'Tell me,' I said. I tried to say it lightly. I knew him well. For a man ultimately brought down by gross indiscretion, he was remarkably discreet. He would share his secrets with you, but only if you did not press him to do so.

'I will tell you about the pleasure first,' he said. 'The pain will keep.'

We fell silent as Hubbard brought us our wine. He served it with obsequious ceremony. (God, how he took his time!) When he had gone, and we were once more alone, I expected Oscar to pick up his story, but instead he simply raised his glass in my direction and gazed at me with world-weary, vacant eyes.

'How was dinner?' I asked. 'How was your publisher?'

'Dinner,' he said, returning from his reverie, 'was at the new Langham Hotel, where the decor and the beef are both overdone. My publisher, Mr Stoddart, is a delight. He is American, so the air around him is full of energy and praise. He is the publisher of *Lippincott's Monthly Magazine*—'

'And he has given you a new commission?' I conjectured.

'Better still, he has introduced me to a new friend.' I raised an eyebrow. 'Yes, Robert, I have made a new friend tonight. You will like him.'

I was accustomed to Oscar's sudden enthusiasms. 'Am I to meet him?' I asked.

'Very shortly, if you can spare the time.'

4

'Is he coming here?' I glanced at the clock on the fireplace.

'No, we shall be calling on him – at breakfast. I need his advice.'

'Advice?'

'He is a doctor. And a Scotsman. From Southsea.'

'No wonder you are disturbed, Oscar,' I said, laughing. He laughed, too. He always laughed at the jokes of others. There was nothing mean about Oscar Wilde. 'Why was he at the dinner?' I asked.

'He is an author, too – a novelist. Have you read *Micah Clarke*? Seventeenth-century Scotland has never been so diverting.'

'I've not read it, but I know exactly who you mean. There was a piece about him in *The Times* today. He is the coming man: Arthur Doyle.'

'Arthur *Conan* Doyle. He is particular about that. He must be your age, I suppose, twenty-nine, thirty perhaps, though he has a gravitas about him that makes him appear older than everybody's papa. He is clearly brilliant – a scientist who can play with words – and rather handsome, if you can imagine the face beneath the walrus moustache. At first glance, you might think him a big game hunter, newly returned from the Congo, but beyond his handshake, which is intolerable, there is nothing of the brute about him. He is as gentle as St Sebastian and as wise as St Augustine of Hippo.'

I laughed again. 'You are smitten, Oscar.'

'And touched by envy,' he replied. 'Young Arthur has caused a sensation with his new creation.'

' "Sherlock Holmes",' I said, ' "the consulting detective". *A Study in Scarlet* – that I have read. It is excellent.'

'Stoddart thinks so, too. He wants the sequel. And between the soup and the fish course, Arthur promised him he should have it. Apparently, it is to be called *The Sign of Four*.'

'And what about your story for Mr Stoddart?'

'Mine will be a murder mystery, also. But somewhat different.' His tone changed. 'It will be about murder that lies beyond ordinary detection.' The clock struck the quarter. Oscar lit a second cigarette. He paused and stared towards the empty grate. 'We talked much of murder tonight,' he said quietly. 'Do you recall Marie Aguétant?'

'Of course,' I said.

She was not a lady one was likely to forget. In her way, in her day, she was the most notorious woman in France. I met her with Oscar in Paris in '83 at the Eden Music Hall. We had supper together, the three of us – oysters and champagne, followed by *pâté de foie gras* and Barsac – and Oscar talked, and talked, and talked as I had never heard him talk before. He spoke in French – in perfect French – and spoke of love and death and poetry, and of the poetry of love-and-death. I marvelled at him, at his genius, and Marie Aguétant sat with her hands in his, transfixed. And then, a little drunk, suddenly, unexpectedly, he asked her to sleep with him.

'*Où? Quand? Combien?*' he enquired.

'*Içi, ce soir, gratuit,*' she answered.

'I think of her often,' he said, 'and of that night. What animals we men are! She was a whore, Robert, but she had a heart that was pure. She was murdered, you know.'

'I know,' I said. 'We have talked of it before.'

'Arthur talked about the murders of those women in Whitechapel,' he went on, not heeding me. 'He talked about them in forensic detail. He is convinced that "Jack the Ripper" is a gentleman – or, at least, a man of education. He was particularly interested in the case of Annie Chapman, the poor creature who was found at the back of Dr Barnardo's children's asylum in Hanbury Street. He said Miss Chapman's womb had been removed from her body – "by an expert". He was eager to show me a drawing he had of the wretched girl's eviscerated corpse, but I protested and then, somewhat foolishly, attempted to lighten the mood. I told him – to amuse him – of the forger Wainewright's response when reproached by a friend for a murder he had admitted to. "Yes; it was a dreadful thing to do, but she had very thick ankles."'

'Was he amused?' I asked.

'Arthur? He barely smiled, while Stoddart roared. And then, with great earnestness, he asked me whether I believed that I could ever commit a murder. "Oh no," I said. "One should never do anything one cannot talk about at dinner."'

'He laughed then, I trust?'

'Not at all. He became quite serious and said, "Mr Wilde, you make jests of all that you fear most in yourself. It is a dangerous habit. It will be your undoing." It was in that moment that I realised he was my friend. It was in that moment that I wanted to tell him about what I had seen this afternoon . . . But I did not dare. Stoddart was there. Stoddart would not have understood.' He drained his glass. 'That, my dear Robert, is why we shall return to see my new friend in the morning. I must go now.'

The club clocks were striking twelve. 'But, Oscar,' I cried, 'you have not told me what you saw this afternoon.'

He stood up. 'I saw a canvas rent in two. I saw a thing of beauty, destroyed by vandals.'

'I don't understand.'

'I saw Billy Wood in a room in Cowley Street.'

'Billy Wood?'

'One of Bellotti's boys. He had been murdered. By candlelight. In an upstairs room. I need to know why. For what possible purpose? I need to know who has done this terrible thing.' He took my hand in his. 'Robert, I must go. It is midnight. I will tell you everything tomorrow. Let us meet at the Langham Hotel, at eight o'clock. The good doctor will be having his porridge. We will catch him. He will advise us what course to take. I have promised Constance I will be home tonight. Tite Street calls. You are no longer married, Robert, but I have my obligations. My wife, my children. I want to see them sleeping safely. I love them dearly. And I love you, too. Goodnight, Robert. We have heard the chimes at midnight. We can at least say that.'

And he was gone. He swept from the room with a flourish. He had arrived exhausted, but he appeared to depart refreshed. As I emptied the rest of the bottle into my glass, I pondered what he had told me, but could make no sense of it. Who was Billy Wood? Who was Bellotti? What upstairs room? Was this murder a fact or merely one of Oscar's fantastical allegories?

I finished the champagne and left the club. To my surprise, Hubbard was almost civil as he bade me goodnight. There were cabs in the rank on Piccadilly and, as I had sold two articles that month, I was in funds, but the night was fine – there was a brilliant August moon – and the streets were quiet so I decided to walk back to my room in Gower Street.

Twenty minutes later, on my way north towards Oxford Street, as I turned from a narrow side-alley into Soho Square, suddenly I stopped and drew myself back into the shadows. Across the deserted square, by the new church of St Patrick, still encased in scaffolding, stood a hansom cab and, climbing into it, illuminated by a shaft of moonlight, were a man and a young woman. The man was Oscar; there was no doubt about that. But the young woman I did not recognise; her face was hideously disfigured and, from the way she held her shawl about her, I sensed that she was gripped by a dreadful fear.

2

1 September 1889

'You are late, Robert! You should have taken the twopenny tube as I did.'

I was late and I was troubled. I was perplexed by what I had witnessed in Soho Square the night before; consequently, I had slept fitfully and risen later than I had planned; and then, foolishly, I had allowed myself to be distracted by yet another impertinent letter from my estranged wife's solicitor.

Oscar, by contrast, was ebullient and seemed not to have a care in the world. I found him and Conan Doyle hidden behind a cypress tree in the farthest corner of the Langham Hotel's labyrinthine palm court. They were seated close together, side by side, like the Mad Hatter and the March Hare, at a long linen-covered table, the debris of breakfast all about them. Oscar – dressed, I noticed, in the same suit as the night before, but with a fresh shirt and necktie – was on song. Conan Doyle – younger, slighter, more pink-cheeked than Oscar's description had led me to expect – was evidently already under the sorcerer's spell. When Oscar introduced us, Doyle smiled at me with a certain reticence, but barely glanced my way again. He was wholly absorbed by the magic of the master.

Oscar summoned fresh coffee on my account. 'You are too late for breakfast, Robert, but in time at least to hear my story and take note of Arthur's advice. I will be brief, for our new friend is anxious to take his leave of us and of London – "that great cesspool", as he calls it, "into which all the loungers of the Empire are irresistibly drained". We are the loungers, Robert.'

Doyle made a vain attempt to protest, but Oscar's flow would not be staunched.

'No, no, believe me,' he went on. 'Arthur wants to get away at once. His train departs within the hour. He has his ticket and scant means to buy another. He is strapped for cash, Robert. Like you, money is a perpetual worry to him. Unlike you, he pays his bills on time. Besides, it is his wife's birthday and he is eager to hasten back to her, bearing gifts.'

Oscar paused to sip his coffee. Doyle was gazing at him, wide-eyed with admiration. 'Mr Wilde, you are amazing,' he said. 'You are correct in every particular.'

'Come, Arthur, no more "Mr Wilde", please. I am your friend. And I have studied your *Study in Scarlet*. This was scarcely a three-pipe problem.'

Doyle pinched his lower lip with pleasure. 'Give me your methodology,' he said.

Oscar was happy to oblige. 'Well, Arthur, I surmised that you might be short of funds last night because of the alacrity with which you accepted Stoddart's invitation to write for him and then enquired how soon you might be able to expect payment. This morning, when I arrived at the hotel, it was not yet eight o'clock and yet you were already at the desk, settling your account. I saw your cheque book. It was brand-new, but the cheque you were using was the last one in the book. As yesterday was the last day of the month, I thought to myself, The good doctor is a man who likes to pay his bills on time.'

'I am impressed,' said Doyle, laughing.

'I am not,' said Oscar, affecting a sudden earnestness. 'Those who pay their bills are soon forgotten. It is only by not paying one's bills that one can hope to live in the memory of the commercial classes. I further surmised that you were planning to catch an early train because why else would you settle your account before breakfast and have your luggage already brought down into the hallway?'

'But how did you know that today is my wife's birthday?'

'Your luggage includes a bouquet of fresh flowers with card attached, and a lady's hatbox. I do not yet know you well, Arthur, but I know you well enough to be certain that these are not gifts intended for some passing fancy. However, I was troubled by the hatbox—'

'I am anxious about that hat,' Doyle interjected. 'I may have made a poor choice.'

'A hat for a lady is always a poor choice,' said Oscar, holding the moment as he stirred his coffee and considered his next thought. 'In ancient Athens there was neither a milliner nor a milliner's bill. These things were absolutely unknown, so great was the civilisation.'

Doyle was shaking his head in delight and disbelief. 'And how do you know I have already purchased my railway ticket?' he asked.

'Because I see it sticking out of your left breast pocket!' Oscar replied.

Conan Doyle laughed and banged the table with so much pleasure that the teaspoons rattled in their saucers.

'Arthur.' Oscar turned to Doyle and looked into his eyes with sudden intensity. 'I am glad to have made you laugh, for soon I shall make you weep. The words of Mercury are harsh after the songs of Apollo. If you have tears to shed, prepare to shed them now.'

Doyle returned Oscar's gaze and smiled the reassuring smile of a kindly country doctor. 'Unfold your tale,' he said. 'I am all ears.'

'I will tell you the story as simply as I can,' said Oscar. 'In truth, it can be simply told.' As he spoke, he lowered his voice. I recall every word precisely – I made a note of it that night – but I recall, too, having to lean across the table to hear him.

'Yesterday afternoon,' he began, 'at some time between half past three and four o'clock, I presented myself at the door of number 23 Cowley Street in Westminster. I had an appointment there and I was late. I knocked sharply at the door, but there was no reply. I rang the doorbell – still nothing. Impatiently, I knocked again, more loudly. I rang the bell once more. Eventually, after what must have been several minutes, I was admitted by the housekeeper. Because I was late, I did not wait to listen to her excuses. Immediately I climbed the stairs, alone, and let myself into the first-floor sitting room. I was utterly unprepared for the scene that awaited me. It was a scene of horror, grotesque and pitiable.'

He paused, shook his head and lit a cigarette. 'Go on,' said Conan Doyle.

Oscar drew on the cigarette and, his voice barely above a whisper, continued. 'There, lying on the floor, his feet towards me, was the body of a boy – a young man named Billy Wood. His torso was soaked in blood, blood that glistened like liquid rubies, blood that was barely congealed. He could have died only minutes before. He was naked, quite naked. The blood was everywhere, except for his face. His face was untouched. I recognised his face at once – though his throat had been cut from ear to ear.'

Conan Doyle's gaze remained fixed on Oscar. 'What did you do then?' he asked.

'I fled the scene,' said Oscar, lowering his eyes as if in shame.

'Did you question the housekeeper?'

'No.'

'Did you call the police?'

'No. I walked along the embankment, towards Chelsea, towards my house in Tite Street. I must have walked for an hour, and as I walked, and watched the sunlight glinting on the black sheen of the river, and passed by other walkers intent on the pleasures of an afternoon stroll, I began to wonder whether what I had seen had been but a figment of my imagination. I reached my home and greeted my wife and kissed my boys, but as I sat in their nursery and read to them their goodnight fairy tale the picture of the body of Billy Wood would not leave my mind's eye. He was innocent, as they are. He was beautiful, as they are . . .'

'But this Billy Wood,' Conan Doyle interjected, 'he was not a relation?'

Oscar laughed. 'By no means. I doubt that he had any known relations. He was a street urchin, a waif and stray, an uneducated lad of fifteen or sixteen. He had few enough friends. I am sure he had no relations.'

'But you knew him?'

'Yes, I knew him – but I did not know him well.'

Doyle looked perplexed. 'Yet you had gone to Cowley Street to meet him? You had an assignation.'

Oscar laughed again and shook his head. 'No, of course not. He was a street urchin. I barely knew him. I had a professional appointment in Cowley Street – nothing to do with this matter.' Doyle's eyes widened, but Oscar went on, with energy: 'Nothing to do with this matter, Arthur, I assure you. Nothing. My appointment was with a pupil, a student of mine. I found the boy there quite by chance.'

'But you were familiar with the house? You had been there before?'

'Yes, but I had not expected to find Billy Wood there – alive or dead. I had not seen him for a month or more.'

Arthur Conan Doyle pressed his broad fingertips against his moustache and murmured, 'Oscar, I am confused. You went to Cowley Street to meet a "student" of yours who, you tell me, has nothing to do with the case. Where was this "student" when you arrived in Cowley Street?'

'Unavoidably detained. There was a note waiting for me at Tite Street when I got home.'

'And in the room where you had expected to find your "pupil", in his place you found the body of a street urchin, a boy barely known to you, apparently the victim of a brutal attack—'

'A brutal murder, Arthur,' said Oscar, with emphasis. 'A ritual murder, I believe.'

'A ritual murder?'

'Billy Wood's body was laid out as though on a funeral bier: his arms were folded across his chest. There were lighted candles all around him and the smell of incense was in the air.'

Conan Doyle sat back, with arms folded, and appraised his new friend. 'Oscar,' he said kindly, 'are you sure you have not imagined all this?'

'Do you doubt me?'

'I don't doubt that you believe that you saw what you say you saw. I don't doubt your word, not for a moment. You are a gentleman. But you are also a poet—'

'Enough!' Oscar pushed back the table. He rose to his feet. 'This is not a poet's fancy, Arthur. Come! We shall go to Cowley Street. We shall go now! I will show you what I have seen. You, too, shall be a witness. It is no hallucination, Arthur, though it be the stuff of nightmares. Waiter, our bill! Robert, will you come also? Arthur is wary of mad poets – rightly so. You may be his chaperone.'

'But, Oscar,' Conan Doyle protested, 'if all you tell me is true, this is a matter for the police, not a country doctor. I must return to Southsea. My wife is expecting me.'

'And she shall have you, Arthur. We will take you to Waterloo Station by way of Cowley Street. You will miss one train; you may miss two; but we shall have you in Southsea in time for tea, I promise.'

Conan Doyle continued to protest, but he protested in vain. Oscar got his way. Oscar always got his way. The poet, William Butler Yeats, a fellow Irishman, to whom Oscar introduced me that same year, wrote later of Oscar's 'hard brilliance', of his 'dominating self-possession'. Yeats recognised – as few did in Oscar's lifetime – that our friend's outward air of indolence masked an inner will that was formidable. 'He posed as an idler,' Yeats said, 'but, in truth, he was a man of action. He was a leader. You followed him you knew not quite why.'

Conan Doyle and I trooped out of the Langham Hotel in Oscar's wake. He strode ahead of us, *en prince*. He was neither grand nor arrogant, but he was magnificent. He was never handsome, but he was striking, having the advantage of height and the discipline of good posture. Waiters bowed instinctively as he passed; other guests – men and women alike; even, in the hotel forecourt, a King Charles spaniel – looked up and acknowledged him. None of them may have known precisely who he was, but all of them seemed to sense that he was *somebody*.

Some minutes later, as our four-wheeler turned from the main thoroughfare of Abingdon Street into the warren of cobbled lanes and alleys leading to Cowley Street, Conan Doyle enquired, 'This Cowley Street – is it a reputable address?'

'I do not know,' answered Oscar, with a smile. 'It is very near to the Houses of Parliament.'

Conan Doyle, intent on looking out of the cab window, did not seem to register the jest. Oscar, so earnest when he rose from the breakfast table at the Langham Hotel, suddenly appeared not to have a care in the world. It was often like that with him. He was a man of deep emotions, yet frequently he hid his feelings behind a mask of insouciance. He did it deliberately, I believe, the better to be able to observe the reactions of those around him. Now, blithely, he continued, 'Abraham Cowley himself came to a disreputable end, as is the way with minor poets. He was found in a field after a drinking bout and died of the fever. He is buried in Westminster Abbey and has this street as his memorial. Do you know his work, Robert? According to the literary critics, his poems are marred by elaborate conceits and artificial brilliancy. I have always found them simple and affecting. He was a child prodigy. He composed an epic romance at the age of ten – the perfect age for epic romance! – and published *Poetic Blossoms*, his first volume of verse, when he was just fifteen. Whoa, cabby, whoa! We are here. And look, gentlemen, there's a poetic blossom of a sort awaiting our arrival.'

The hansom cab pulled up immediately outside number 23 Cowley Street. Seated on the doorstep, resting wearily against the shiny black front door, was a stout woman of riper years, more overblown fuchsia bush than poetic blossom. Her appearance was both arresting and preposterous: her boots were blue-black, her skirt was brown, her jacket was striped Lincoln green and vermilion. I felt that she would have done credit to a Drury Lane pantomime: her cheeks were excessively rouged, her lips were scarlet, and her extraordinary ensemble was completed by a plum-coloured toque perched precariously on top of a mass of vivid orange curls. At her side was a large carpet-bag; in her lap was a sheaf of papers and a small bundle of keys.

'Is this the lady who admitted you yesterday?' Conan Doyle enquired of Oscar as we clambered out of the cab.

'Nothing like her,' said Oscar, bowing towards the unlikely-looking female who was now struggling to her feet. 'I think we can take it that today is this good lady's first day at number 23.'

'Indeed, sir,' said the woman, dropping a curtsey towards us and revealing a small ostrich feather in her toque as she did so.

'Well done, Oscar,' said Doyle. 'Sherlock Holmes would be proud of you.'

'I think, Arthur, that even Dr Watson would have sur-mised as much. The lady has pages torn from a gazetteer in one hand and in the other a set of keys with which she is obviously unfamiliar. It is the first of the month, 1 September, or, as she thinks of it, the feast of' – here Oscar turned towards the lady who immediately mumbled the words 'St Giles' before curtseying again – 'her first day in her new employment, hence the hat, her best hat. The lady wishes to make a good impression on her first day. Am I not right, Mrs O'—'

'O'Keefe, sir,' said the good lady, bobbing down before us for a third time.

'Do you know this lady?' asked Conan Doyle.

'I know nothing of her,' said Oscar, lightly, 'beyond the obvious fact that she is a widow, recently arrived from Dublin, who, having worked in the theatre, as dresser to some of Ireland's most distinguished leading ladies, is now set to try her fortune in the capital of the empire. She will do well here, do you not think? She is evidently a woman of spirit, though understandably wearied by her long walk from Ludgate Circus this morning.'

Mrs O'Keefe and Arthur Conan Doyle gazed at Oscar Wilde wide-eyed in amazement.

'This is beyond belief, Oscar,' said the doctor. 'You must know her, you must.'

Oscar laughed. 'Come, Arthur, this is elementary stuff – basic observation and deduction. I am merely fol-lowing the rules of the master. Please understand: now that I have met you, Holmes is where my heart is!'

I was equally amazed. 'How did you do it, Oscar?' I asked. 'Tell us.'

'We must not let daylight in on magic, Robert. The conjuror's trick once explained seems very common-place.'

'Tell us, Oscar,' I insisted.

'I believe you are a mind-reader, sir,' whispered Mrs O'Keefe, her voice hushed in astonishment.

'No, dear lady,' said Oscar, amiably, 'would that I were. However,' he continued, turning towards her, 'I come from Dublin also, so I recognised your accent right away. I noticed, too, the small crucifix around your neck, which suggested to me that yours is a good Catholic soul. I sur-mised, therefore, that you would know your saints' days and I was certain you would not leave your husband unless he had been taken from you by God himself. Your fine clothes, interestingly juxtaposed, suggested to me theatrical costumes handed down to you by others – the leading ladies for whom you worked as a dresser – and your lively make-up hinted also at a theatrical way of life. You are more accustomed to dressing for night than for day.'

'But how did you know I'd come here from Ludgate Circus?'

'Messrs O'Donovan & Brown of Ludgate Circus are London's leading suppliers of domestic staff from the emerald isle. They have supplied several maids for us in Tite Street. I guessed that you had collected the keys for this address from them first thing this morning and had then walked here, getting a little lost along the way.'

'Amazing, Oscar, simply amazing,' muttered Conan Doyle, clapping his hands in admiration.

'But, Oscar, how did you know the lady's name?' I asked.

'I didn't,' he replied, revealing his uneven yellow teeth in a broad smile. 'I made a stab at the initial letter, that's all. More than half the surnames in Ireland begin with an O. The odds were with me . . .'

'Are you a mind-reader?' repeated the awe-struck Irishwoman who had now taken up an attitude of semi-genuflection before us.

'No, dear lady,' said Oscar, adding, to our further amazement, 'I am a musician and accustomed occasionally to using the first-floor sitting room at this address to rehearse chamber works with colleagues. Dr Doyle and Mr Sherard here are new members of my trio and have come to inspect the premises. We are working on Mozart's Divertimento in E flat major. Would you be so kind as to admit us?'

As Mrs O'Keefe fumbled with the keys, Conan Doyle said, 'Oscar, you astound me. I do not begin to understand you.'

Oscar laughed again, more loudly than before, but his laughter was bleak. 'I astound myself,' he said. 'I am here on the pavement playing games, indulging in childish charades, when I am about to confront you with unparalleled horror. I do not understand myself at times.'

3

23 Cowley Street

Number 23 Cowley Street was a two-storeyed, single-fronted, red-brick house built in the 1780s as part of a terrace of modest dwellings originally intended for clerks and choristers attached to Westminster Abbey. The exterior of the house had a certain unassuming dignity; the interior, airless and box-like, and seemingly unfurnished, was curiously without character. Mrs O'Keefe, having found which of the keys fitted which of the locks, admitted us to an incommodious entrance hallway, little larger than a sentry box. Immediately ahead of us lay a steep wooden staircase, narrow and uncarpeted.

'Shall we go up?' suggested Conan Doyle.

'If Mrs O'Keefe will allow us,' said Oscar.

'Oh yes, sir,' said the good woman, semi-genuflecting once more and pointing us towards the stairs. 'You make yourself at home now. You know the way. I'll find the gas lamps.'

'No need,' said Oscar, 'there's light enough.'

A gentle beam of sunshine shone through the fanlight above the front door, illuminating the dust that hovered in the air above the stairs.

'Come,' said Conan Doyle, 'let's get the business done.'

We climbed the stairs and quickly reached the landing.

'Is this the room?' asked Doyle.

'It is,' said Oscar.

'Very well,' said Conan Doyle, calmly. 'We are pre-pared. After you . . .'

Slowly, carefully, Oscar turned the handle and pushed open the door.

We adjusted our eyes to the gloom. The curtains, of heavy velvet, bottle green, were drawn closed against the windows facing us, but a rim of warm sunlight fil-tered across the floor below them. The floorboards were bare. The walls were bare. Other than the curtains, there were no furnishings of any kind to be seen. No lamps, no candlesticks, nothing; the room was empty, utterly so.

'They've taken him,' exclaimed Oscar.

'Was he ever here?' asked Conan Doyle.

'On my word, Arthur—'Oscar started to protest, but Conan Doyle raised a hand to silence him.

From the moment we had left the hotel, half an hour before, Oscar had been in command of the situation. He had led the way, full of energy and enterprise. Now he was at a loss. The energy was gone, the enterprise con-founded. Without demur, the metropolitan man of the world let the young provincial doctor take control. As Conan Doyle stepped briskly across the room and drew back the curtains, Oscar, deflated, stood by the doorway in silence, staring at the floorboards.

'Do you smell incense?' Doyle asked.

'No,' I said, sniffing the air. 'If anything, beeswax.'

'Yes,' he said, 'the floorboards have been newly pol-ished. They gleam.' He paced around the room, as though marking out its size. 'No bloodstains on the floor, no signs of guttering candles.'

'There was a carpet, a Persian rug,' murmured Oscar, as if to himself. 'His feet were here, his head was there . . . There was a knife . . . I recall a blade, a glistening blade . . .'

Conan Doyle appeared to pay him no heed. He was busy examining the walls, running his fingers slowly across the grimy, green and black, Regency-stripe flocked wallpaper. He stood for a moment by each wall, studying it intently. There were no visible nails or hooks, no sign that pictures had ever been hung on the walls, no marks to indicate where furniture might once have stood. On the back of the door, there was a small brass coat-hook: nothing else. The room was bare and you felt that it had been so for some time.

'Very well,' Conan Doyle announced at last, 'we have seen what we came to see. Our work is done. I must catch my train.' He placed a kindly hand on Oscar's shoulder. 'Come, my friend, let us be on our way.'

Seemingly in a daze, Oscar allowed himself to be led back down the stairs. Mrs O'Keefe was hovering by the front door, eager to make a further obeisance. 'Was everything satisfactory?' she asked. 'Will the room suit? I have found the kitchen and a kettle if you gentlemen are wanting refreshment.'

'No, thank you kindly,' said Conan Doyle, producing a sixpenny bit from his coat pocket and handing it to her. 'We're much obliged to you, but we must be going now.'

'Much obliged,' repeated Oscar, vacantly, as if half the world away. Then, recollecting himself, he bowed towards Mrs O'Keefe and extended his hand. She took it and kissed his ring, as though he were a bishop.

'Bless you, sir,' she said, 'I'll pray for you.'

'Pray to St Jude,' murmured Oscar, 'the patron saint of lost causes.'

'I'll pray to St Cecilia, too,' added Mrs O'Keefe, crossing herself as she bustled after us out of the house and into the street. 'She takes a special care of musicians, doesn't she now? She'll look after you.'

In the cab, as we trundled back along Abingdon Street towards Westminster Bridge, the silence was strained. I said nothing because I could think of nothing to say. Oscar was lost in melancholy thought, gazing unseeingly out of the cab window. Eventually, as we entered Parliament Square, Conan Doyle spoke. 'I didn't realise you were a musician, Oscar,' he said. 'What instrument do you play?'

'I'm not. I don't,' replied Oscar. 'My brother, Willie, is the family musician. He plays the piano—'

'And he composes,' I added, in the hope of sustaining the conversation. 'Willie Wilde creates the wittiest musical parodies and pastiches.'

'Yes,' said Oscar, still staring out of the window. 'Caricature is the tribute that mediocrity pays to genius.'

Conan Doyle laughed. Oscar turned sharply towards him.

'You are right, Arthur. That was unkind of me. When it comes to my elder brother, I am often uncharitable. It is wrong of me, I know – unchristian. It's just that I'm not entirely sure that Willie's "improved" endings for Chopin's Preludes fulfil their promise.'

Conan Doyle smiled. 'I learnt to play the tuba once,' he said, evidently determined to keep Oscar from reverting to his sombre reverie.

'Did you?' asked Oscar, suddenly clapping his hands. 'Did you really?' The notion of the Southsea doctor with the mournful eyes and the walrus moustache puffing on a tuba lifted Oscar's spirits instantly. 'Tell us more, Arthur. When was this? Why was this?'

'Years ago, at school.'

'At Stonyhurst?' cried Oscar. 'The English public school system has something to commend it after all!'

'No, Oscar,' riposted Doyle, laughing genially, 'not at Stonyhurst. When I was seventeen, before I began my medical training, I spent a year at school in Austria, with the Jesuits.'

Oscar could barely contain his delight. 'Tuba-playing Jesuits,' he exclaimed. 'Heaven be praised!' For a moment, he seemed his customary self again and leant towards Doyle, touching him on the knee. 'Arthur, I think I know you well enough to tell you this. When I was at Oxford, I once spent an evening in the company of a troupe of Tyrolean yodellers.' He lowered his voice conspiratorially: 'The experience changed me for ever.'

Doyle and I laughed out loud, and Oscar sat back, resting his large head against the leather bolster at the back of the cab. We looked at him and smiled. He turned his head to look out of the window again and, as he did so, we saw two small tears trickle down his face.

'What is wrong, Oscar?' asked Doyle, suddenly concerned and not yet accustomed to Oscar's mercurial changes in mood.

'I am thinking of Billy Wood,' said Oscar, quietly. 'I loved the boy.'

There was an awkward pause. 'He was not quite a stranger to you then?' said Doyle, narrowing his eyes and raising an eyebrow.

'No,' said Oscar, turning to face the doctor. 'I misled you there. I apologise. Billy Wood was no stranger.'

'You loved him?'

'I loved him,' said Oscar. 'Yes. I loved him – as a brother.'

'As a brother?' repeated Doyle.

'As the younger brother I might have had,' said Oscar. 'We were friends – best friends. We were good companions. I had a younger sister once. While she lived, she was my best friend. But I lost her too. She was just ten when she died.'

'I am sorry,' said Doyle, 'I did not know.'

'It is a long time ago now,' said Oscar, reaching for his handkerchief and, unselfconsciously, wiping his eyes, 'more than twenty years.' He smiled. ' "The good die first," ' he said. 'Isola was ten. Billy was barely sixteen. "The good die first, and they whose hearts are dry as summer dust burn to the socket." ' He looked out of the cab window onto the river. We were halfway across Westminster Bridge. 'You recognise the line, Robert?'

To my shame, I did not. 'Is it Shakespeare?' I asked.

'No,' he said, reprovingly, 'it is not. It is your great-grandfather, Robert.' He turned to Conan Doyle to explain: 'Robert is the great-grandson of one of the few poets laureate worthy of the honour: William Wordsworth.' Arthur responded with the grunt of awe that is the inevitable reaction, it seems, to this particular piece of information. Oscar continued: 'Robert is reticent about his distinguished forebear because Robert is a poet himself. But given where we are – on Westminster Bridge – and the nature of the morning – "silent, bare" – I hope he will forgive me . . .'

Before Conan Doyle could embark on the train of questions that I knew – from a lifetime's experience – would be prompted by the mention of my Wordsworth connection, I intervened to change the subject. 'Arthur, do you have children?' I asked.

Conan Doyle was a decent man – quick and sensitive – and he recognised at once that I was not eager to encourage a discussion of the Wordsworth–Sherard family history. 'Yes,' he answered readily, 'just the one – a daughter, Mary. She is nine months old this very week. She is plump and full of life, with pretty blue eyes and bandy legs. I love her very much.'

'Children are a joy,' said Oscar. 'My little boys are three and four, and full of hope. I fear for them dreadfully.'

'I understand,' said Arthur, gently. 'Once upon a time, I had a younger sister, too. She also died.'

'I did not know,' said Oscar.

'How could you?' asked Doyle.

'I did not think to ask,' said Oscar. 'That was thoughtless. Pray forgive me, dear friend. I can call you my friend, can I not – even though our acquaintance has been so brief?'

'I am honoured to be your friend, Oscar,' replied Conan Doyle, and I sensed, as he spoke, that he was moved. (As I got to know him better, I noticed that whenever he spoke intimately, or of matters that touched him deeply, his Edinburgh accent, usually almost imperceptible, became quite pronounced.)

'Love is all very well in its way,' said Oscar, 'but, to me, friendship is much higher. I know of nothing in the world that is either nobler, or more rare, than true friendship. Shall we be true friends, Arthur?'

'I hope so,' said Doyle earnestly and, as if to seal the compact, he turned towards Oscar and shook him vigorously by the hand. If Oscar winced – as he might have done: Doyle's was a fist of iron – he did so inwardly. The two men beamed at one another, then turned towards me, and the three of us laughed together. The air had cleared.

' "A timely utterance gave that thought relief," ' I said, adding, awkwardly, by way of explanation, 'my great-grandfather—'

'I know,' said Conan Doyle. 'We learnt the poem by heart at school.'

'In Austria?' cried Oscar.

'No, Oscar! At Stonyhurst. It is my favourite English poem. It contains some of the loveliest lines in the language. "To me the meanest flower that blows can give thoughts that do often lie too deep for tears."'

'If I were to live again,' said Oscar, 'I would like it to be as a flower – no soul, but perfectly beautiful.'

'And what flower would that be, Oscar?' I asked.

'Oh, Robert, for my sins I shall be made a red geranium!'

As we laughed once more, Doyle glanced out of the window and saw the steps of Waterloo Station in the distance. He said, with sudden urgency, 'Oscar, may I ask you something?'

'Anything.'

'About 23 Cowley Street?'

'Anything.' Oscar was now at ease again.

'Who owns the house?'

'Number 23 Cowley Street? I have no idea.' Oscar answered the question quite casually.

'But you have rented rooms there?' Conan Doyle began his line of questioning gently, as a friendly family doctor might elicit details of his patient's symptoms, but gradually the comfortable, coaxing bedside manner gave way to something less cosily avuncular and more akin to a courtroom cross-examination.

'Yes,' replied Oscar, 'I have rented rooms there – now and again, not often.'

'But you are unaware of who is the owner of the property?'

'Entirely. I was introduced to the house through O'Donovan & Brown of Ludgate Circus.'

'They act as agents?'

'Indeed. They charge four pounds a month for the house as a whole, if I recollect aright – or a guinea a week, or four shillings *per diem*, all found. Are you thinking of opening a London practice, Arthur?'

Conan Doyle ignored Oscar's joke. His brow furrowed. 'All found?' he repeated.

'Yes,' said Oscar. 'There is usually a good soul such as Mrs O'Keefe on hand to provide creature comforts.'

'But I don't understand, Oscar. You have a house full of rooms in Tite Street. Why do you need another in Westminster – especially one at four shillings a day?'

'Half-days are possible, Arthur. O'Donovan & Brown are at pains to be accommodating. I believe there is a doctor who takes the house every Monday morning for half a crown. I have not met him. I am told that those who call upon him are young women in the main. I understand he is not entirely respectable.'

'Oscar,' said Conan Doyle, 'you have not answered my question.'

'There is no mystery here, Arthur,' Oscar replied, without rancour. 'Now and then, when I have a pupil to teach, or need a room in which to write, I rent Cowley Street for a day or two. It is as simple as that. At Tite Street I have a wife and children and servants – and importunate friends and impertinent tradesmen calling at all hours, whether invited or not. It is only by entire isolation from everything and everyone that one can do any work. Doctors, I know, require their waiting rooms to be full; poets, on the other hand, require theirs to be empty. Poetry, as Robert's forefather taught us, is emotion recollected in tranquillity. There is no tranquillity in Tite Street.'

The hansom cab had now pulled up at the railway station, but Conan Doyle was not yet done. 'Is it writers mainly who take rooms at Cowley Street?' he asked.

'Writers – and musicians. And artists, also. All sorts, in fact. I once encountered a clergyman there, a suffragan bishop. He was working on a series of sermons – on the theme of sorrow and the seven deadly sins, as I recall. Members of Parliament occasionally use the house as well. They come to play cards – with the artists, and their models.'

'And was it at Cowley Street that you first met Billy Wood?'

'Yes,' said Oscar, simply.

'And he was an artist's model?' suggested Conan Doyle.

'Yes,' said Oscar, surprised. 'How did you guess?'

'You said he was beautiful.'

'He had the beauty of youth. And I have a passion for beauty – as Wordsworth had. As Robert has. As I doubt not, Doctor, you have, too. Poetry is the spontaneous overflow of powerful feelings. A passion for beauty is merely the intensified desire for life. I knew Billy Wood and I loved him. He had youth and beauty – and such spirit. In his company, I was glad to be alive.'

'You told us he was a street urchin.'

'Indeed,' said Oscar, looking his interrogator directly in the eye. 'He was quite uneducated; he could barely read; he could write his name, but not much more. But he had native intelligence – an enquiring mind and a remarkable memory. And an ability to concentrate that I have not come across before in one so young. He was hungry to learn – and I was happy to teach.'

'You taught him?' said Conan Doyle.

'I taught him poetry. I took him to the theatre. I encouraged his talent. He had talent. He was a natural actor. On the stage, he might have gone far.'

'And you say that yesterday you saw this young friend of yours, this Billy Wood, in the upstairs room at Cowley Street, his naked body awash with blood, his throat cut from ear to ear.'

'I do, Arthur. And you do not believe me.'

'Oh, Oscar,' said Conan Doyle, 'I believe you. I believe you completely.'

4

Simpson's in the Strand

Waterloo Station on that close September morning was hot and crowded. The station clock had failed; there was chaos on the concourse.

As Arthur Conan Doyle stepped down from our four-wheeler, I handed him his case, his travelling bag, and the hatbox and bouquet of summer flowers intended for his wife. As he stood there, laden, smiling, bidding us farewell, he had about him an air of trustworthiness and decency that was utterly compelling. In my life, I have known many remarkable men – poets, pioneers, soldiers, statesmen – but I have known few better men, and none more straightforward, than Arthur Conan Doyle.

Oscar, still seated in the cab, was feeling in his pockets for money with which to pay the fare. Arthur called to him, 'Let me pay my share, Oscar, but keep the cab. I want you to go directly to Scotland Yard. I can see myself off well enough.'

'To Scotland Yard?' said Oscar.

'Yes,' said Doyle, firmly, moving close to the open cab door and adopting his best bedside manner. 'This is a matter for the police, Oscar. That boy was murdered – I have no doubt of that. If he was lying with his head towards the window, as you describe him, and his feet towards the door, then I suspect his throat was cut from right to left in a single, savage slice. The carotid arteries leading to his brain will have been severed instantly. He will have died in a matter of moments. Given his youth, the immediate loss of blood must have been considerable.'

Oscar was silent.

'How do you know this, Arthur?' I asked. 'There was no sign of blood in the room.'

'Not on the floor, nor on the skirting,' said Doyle, 'but some five feet up the right-hand wall, as you face the window, I noticed the tiniest traces of blood – not smears, but minute splashes. I imagine that when the internal jugular veins burst, for an instant a stream of the boy's blood spurted high into the air and left its tell-tale mark.'

Suddenly, impulsively, Oscar reached out towards Conan Doyle with both hands. 'Stay, Arthur,' he beseeched him, 'stay and help me find who has done this terrible thing.'

'No, Oscar, I must get home. Touie is expecting me. It is her birthday, remember.'

'Will you return tomorrow?' Wilde implored.

Conan Doyle shook his head and smiled. His sharp blue eyes were ever mournful, but he had a quick and merry smile. 'Oscar,' he laughed, 'I am not a consulting detective. I am a country doctor. Sherlock Holmes is a figment of my imagination. I cannot help you and neither can he. You might as well ask the Happy Prince or one of the other heroes of your fairy tales to assist you. Go to the police. Go to Scotland Yard. Go at once.'

'I cannot,' said Oscar.

'You must,' said Doyle. 'I have a friend at Scotland Yard – Inspector Aidan Fraser. Mention my name and he will give you every assistance. You can trust him. He is from Edinburgh.'

Oscar wanted to protest – absurdly, he held out supplicating arms! – but Conan Doyle would have none of it. Gently shaking his head, he began to back away from us, disappearing into the throng, calling as he went: 'You will like him, Oscar. Tell Fraser everything – and follow his advice. Robert, make sure he does! Go now! Go at once!'

We watched and waved, as our new friend, laden with his bags and bouquet, turned his back on us and vanished amid the confusion of passengers bustling between platforms. 'He is golden,' murmured Oscar, 'and he has gone.'

As I climbed back into the four-wheeler, I called up to the driver, 'Great Scotland Yard, cabby,' but Oscar countermanded me at once.

'No,' he said, coolly. 'No. It is after twelve o'clock, Robert, and I have a fancy for oysters and champagne.'

'But—'

'But me no buts, Robert. Simpson's in the Strand, driver, if you please.' Oscar sat back and looked at me appraisingly. 'I need to think. And to think I must have oysters and champagne.'

Oscar got his way. Of course. Oscar always got his way. We were driven to John Simpson's Grand Divan Tavern in the Strand. But when we arrived at the restaurant and were seated (at the 'best' table, on the ground floor, in the far left-hand corner, the one table that commands the room as a whole), to my surprise, Oscar waved away the proffered menu and announced our order. 'We shall have potted shrimps and a bottle of your finest Riesling to begin with,' he told our waiter. 'And then, from the trolley, I shall take the saddle of mutton and Mr Sherard

will have his customary roast beef – pink and cut slant-
ingly to the bone – with your freshest horseradish sauce,
your heaviest Yorkshire pudding, and some lightly boiled
cabbage, served, if you please, unexpectedly hot. With
the roast meat, we will take whatever red Burgundy the
sommelier recommends. I am in the mood to live dangerously.'

When the young waiter, smiling, had gone about his
business, I said to Oscar, 'What happened to your fancy
for oysters and champagne?'

'That was a quarter of an hour ago,' he replied, 'when
we were south of the river. I have changed my mind since
then. Consistency, as you know, is the last refuge of the
unimaginative. Besides, I have done my thinking. I have
decided we should do as Arthur advises. We shall go to
meet Inspector Fraser – after lunch.'

'Why did you not go to the police at once – yesterday
– as soon as you had discovered the body?'

Oscar, frowning, unfurled his napkin and tucked a
corner of it into the top of his waistcoat. 'I had my
reasons . . .'

I looked at him expectantly. Carefully, he arranged the
napkin across his ample stomach and sat gazing at me in
silence. I waited. He said nothing. I tried to coax him.
'And?' I said.

' "And" what?' he countered.

'Your reasons,' I said, 'what were they?'

He leant towards me and smiled. 'Have you ever met a
policeman, Robert?'

I thought for a moment. 'I'm not sure that I have,' I said.

'Well, Robert, the more blessed is your state.
Policemen are not as we are, Robert. We are poets. We

consider the lilies. We wear silk slippers. The language we speak, the world we inhabit, the company we keep: all these are foreign to your run-of-the-mill Metropolitan police officer. He lives his life in prose, and hobnail boots, and anything that is not utterly prosaic – anything that smacks even slightly of the poetic; anything unpredictable, original, unorthodox – will alarm him, will make him suspicious . . . My intended business at 23 Cowley Street was wholly honourable, but I know that some of what goes on at that address tends towards the colourful. I was not certain that your everyday English bobby would entirely understand. Perhaps Arthur's Inspector Fraser will be different.'

'You think by involving the police you run a risk?'

'A risk of being misunderstood – that is all. But, as I told our charming waiter, I am in a mood to live danger-ously. Besides, I do not think there is any alternative if we are to achieve justice for Billy Wood.'

'And why is that so important to you, Oscar?'

He looked at me sharply. 'What do you mean, Robert?'

'You said yourself Billy Wood was just a street urchin—'

Suddenly he banged the table with alarming ferocity. I blanched. Diners at nearby tables turned towards us. 'Is it only "gentlemen" who are to receive justice?' he barked. 'Is not the meanest street urchin entitled to justice as much as the grandest duke? You amaze me, Robert.'

'You misunderstand me, Oscar,' I protested.

'I trust I do, Robert,' he said, more calmly, as the waiter laid our potted shrimps before us. 'I trust I do, for it behoves us, Robert, you and I – who have so much – to do all we can for those, like Billy Wood, who have so little. We must be friends to the friendless, Robert. If we, poets who want for nothing, are not to care for the Billy Woods of this world, who will?'

The waiter proffered Oscar a basket of crisp toast. Oscar looked up at him and smiled.

'Thank you, Tito,' he said. He looked towards me and, for a moment, placed his hand on mine. His moods were so mercurial. 'You are looking wan, Robert.' He smiled. 'Pallor is attractive in an undergraduate of twenty, but unbecoming in a married man of thirty. I am glad I brought you here. We must put some colour in your cheeks. It is evident you need feeding; you are not eating properly.'

'I cannot afford to,' I said, happy now to change the subject. 'I received another uncivil communication from Foxton this morning.'

'Foxton?' Oscar raised an eyebrow.

'My estranged wife's solicitor. If I am to secure this divorce, it will cost me every penny I possess.'

'Forget the divorce, Robert.'

'Would that I could,' I said, plaintively, 'but Marthe is determined upon it. There is no turning back. And, besides, until I am divorced from Marthe, I cannot marry Kaitlyn.'

'Why marry Kaitlyn?' he asked, skewering a buttery shrimp with his fork. 'She will only go the way of Charlotte, and Laura, and Anna, and that charming little Polish girl to whom you introduced me – the dancer – what was her name?'

'Anelia,' I said, wistfully. 'I loved her.'

'Of course you did, Robert – at the time.' He popped the shrimp into his mouth. 'One should always be in love. That is the reason one should never marry.'

'You mock me, Oscar,' I said.

'No, Robert,' he replied, suddenly in earnest, 'I envy you. Yours is a life of romance – and romance lives by repetition. Each time that one loves is the only time that one has ever loved. We can have in life but one great experience at best, and the secret of life is to reproduce that experience as often as possible. You have the secret of life, Robert. I envy you.'

'And you have Constance, Oscar. I envy you.'

'Yes,' said Oscar, glancing towards the sommelier who was now hovering with our wine. 'I have Constance and in her I am blessed. Life is a stormy sea. My wife is my harbour of refuge. And '86 is the only year for Riesling.'

The wine was certainly outstanding and Oscar Wilde was indeed blessed in Constance Lloyd. She was his truest friend and staunchest ally. The world should know that even in his darkest hours – throughout his term of trial, during his imprisonment and beyond, even unto her untimely death, twenty months before his own – his wife did not fail him. Constance Lloyd loved Oscar Wilde for better, for worse, in sickness and in health. She was ever faithful to her marriage vows.

And Oscar loved Constance: I know that to be true. At the time of his engagement, in November 1883, before I had met her, when I was living mainly in Paris, he wrote to me (I have the letter still), describing her 'matchless beauty'. He called her his 'violet-eyed little Artemis' and spoke of her 'slender, graceful figure', of 'the great coils of heavy brown hair which make her flower-like head droop', and of her 'wonderful ivory hands which draw music from the piano so sweet that the birds stop singing to listen to her'.

Oscar loved Constance. (It bears repeating.) They were married in London, at St James's Church in Paddington, on 29 May 1884. On the same day they travelled by boat and train to Paris for their honeymoon. On the morning following their wedding night I called on them at the Hôtel Wagram on the rue de Rivoli to offer my congratulations. I found them on one of the upper floors of the hotel, in a small suite of rooms overlooking the Tuileries gardens. Constance was no longer a child – she was then twenty-six – but she had about her still the bloom of adolescence and, on that morning, the glow of love awakened.

'Is she not exquisite?' asked Oscar.

'She is perfection,' I replied.

I remember we left her to rest and took a stroll together along the rue de Rivoli towards the Marché St Honoré where Oscar stopped and rifled a flower-stall of all its loveliest blossoms and sent them, with a word of love on his card, to the bride whom he had quitted but a moment before. I recall, too, how eager he was to tell me of the delights of their love-making and how I stopped him, saying, 'No, Oscar, *ça, c'est sacré* – you must not speak of that to me.'

That day the three of us then lunched together and, all at once, I understood completely why Oscar had fallen so deeply in love with his little Artemis. She was beautiful, but she was well educated, widely read and wonderfully intelligent, too. And she had known sorrow. Her father – whom she adored – had died when she was sixteen and her relationship with her mother had been strained. She had the pretty look of a girl, but the wisdom of a woman. She spoke French and Italian fluently – and was learning German to please Oscar. She flattered me by asking after my work and she made me jealous by telling me that her entire life was now dedicated to pleasing her husband. 'I will hold him fast with chains of love and devotion so that he shall never leave me or love anyone else,' she said.

After we had dined, we drove out in an open fiacre – it was a perfect *après-midi d'été* – and, as we were turning into the Place de la Concorde, all of a sudden I said, 'Would you mind, Oscar, if I threw my stick away?'

He said, 'Don't be absurd, Robert. It will cause a scene. Why do you want to throw it away?'

I answered, 'It is a swordstick and, I don't know how it is, but for the last minute I have had a wild desire to pull out the blade and run it through you. I think it's because you look too happy.'

Constance laughed and took the stick from my hand. 'I shall keep this,' she said, 'I shall keep this always.'

At John Simpson's Grand Divan Tavern, over the potted shrimps, we raised our glasses of Mr Simpson's finest Riesling to 'Mrs Oscar Wilde'. 'Bless her,' said Oscar.

'Amen to that,' said I.

Over our roast meats, we raised our glasses of Burgundy (a glorious Gevrey-Chambertin, 1884) to 'Mrs Arthur Conan Doyle'. 'May she enjoy many happy returns of the day,' said Oscar.

'Indeed,' said I.

For a moment I hoped that the mention of Arthur's wife might lead our conversation naturally back to the drama of the morning's events, but it did not. And I knew better than to attempt to steer my friend along a conversational course that was not of his choosing. One of the rules of friendship with Oscar Wilde was that he set the rules.

That afternoon at Simpson's, as he ate and drank – and drank some more, and pondered out loud whether or not we might allow ourselves dessert *and* savoury *and* Stilton (with wines to match) – he talked of many things: if not of murder, nor of shoes and ships and sealing wax, certainly of cabbage (Simpson's one culinary failing) and of kings (Oscar was much taken with the news of the accession of Alexander as the 'boy king' of Serbia). What was remarkable about Oscar's conversation, always, was its scope and unpredictability. At that luncheon, in rapid succession, he spoke of love and literature, of William Morris's dream of a socialist commonwealth, of Chabrier's opera, *Le Roi malgré lui*, of his fondness for daisies, of his horror of Bayswater (and the colour magenta), and of the thirteen-storey Tacoma Building in Chicago, the world's first 'skyscraper'. 'Pity the Americans, Robert,' he said. 'As their buildings rise, their morals will fall – you can depend upon it.'

I always laughed in Oscar's company, but I did not always feel at ease. I was always happy to be with him, yet I was often apprehensive. His mood – like his conversation – was unpredictable. He was aware of his own temperamental changeability and recognised that it did not make him the easiest companion. 'I am a fellow o' the strangest mind i' the world,' he would say. 'Forgive me.'

At three o'clock that afternoon, Simpson's clock struck the hour and, suddenly, out of the blue, Oscar put down his spoon and fork and pushed his plate away.

'What are we doing here, Robert? What madness is this? A young friend of mine has been murdered, his throat cut from ear to ear. Now his body is missing – and I am at lunch! I talk of justice while gorging myself on *tarte aux poires au chocolat courant*. I am a disgrace – and a coward. I did not go to the police yesterday because I was fearful . . . Now that I am half drunk I have the courage.' He pulled his napkin from his waistcoat, threw it on the table and got to his feet. 'Come, Robert, we must make our way to Scotland Yard without delay.' He steadied himself with a hand on my shoulder. 'I'll get the bill. We'll hail a cab in the street. We must do now what we should have done three hours ago. We must meet this Inspector Fraser, whatever the consequences. We must throw the dice, however they may fall.'

5

Fraser of the Yard

Through my friendship with Oscar Wilde, I encountered many remarkable men. None, I think, made a more profound impact upon my life than Aidan Edmund Fettes Fraser.

On the day that Oscar and I first met him, 1 September 1889, Fraser had just turned thirty-two. Despite his hooded, sunken eyes, he looked much younger than his years. He was clean-shaven, with clear-cut features, all proportionate, a complexion as white as chalk and a high forehead as smooth as alabaster. He wore his dark, near-black hair swept back, without a parting, and a touch longer than was the fashion. He was, by any account, extraordinarily striking: tall, slim, athletic, angular. He put Oscar in mind of Rossetti's painting, *Dante Drawing an Angel on the Anniversary of Beatrice's Death*. (It was one of Oscar's favourite pictures; almost any handsome, pale-faced youth reminded him of Rossetti's Dante!) In his appearance, Aidan Fraser put me more in mind of my notion of Conan Doyle's creation, Sherlock Holmes.

Fraser was now a Metropolitan Police Inspector – the youngest of the twenty-two inspectors in 'the Met' – but he had been born a gentleman. According to Conan Doyle, who knew him and his family well, Fraser's late father had inherited a banana plantation in the West Indies and his great-uncle (Fraser's father's mother's brother) had been the noted Scottish entrepreneur and philanthropist, Sir William Fettes, whose benefaction had made possible the founding of Fettes College, in Edinburgh, in 1870. When the school opened, Aidan Fraser had been among its first pupils. Apparently, he was an exemplary student: courteous, conscientious, achieving – captain of cricket, captain of rugby and, in due course (and to none of his contemporaries' surprise or resentment), captain of school.

It was only after Fettes that an element of the unexpected was introduced to Fraser's curriculum vitae. He might have gone, as a scholar, to Balliol College, Oxford, to read law. Instead, he chose to stay closer to home and study natural sciences at the University of Edinburgh. There it was that he met Arthur Conan Doyle, two years his junior (though Doyle was always taken for the older of the two), and the pair became 'best friends', for three years near-inseparable, boon companions.

According to Doyle, their friendship was founded on a mutual admiration for the controversial writings of Professor Thomas Huxley (the biologist known as 'Darwin's Bulldog') and fostered (less controversially) over many hours on the golf links. Huxley is credited with coining the term 'agnostic', and Fraser and Conan Doyle – to the dismay of the traditional true-believers in both their families – became outspoken and enthusiastic champions of 'agnosticism'. Quite as alarming to his family was Aidan Fraser's startling announcement, which he made shortly after his twenty-first birthday, at which he had come of age and, as his late father's only son, inherited a fortune in excess of forty thousand pounds. Upon graduation, he said, he proposed not to follow in the Fraser and Fettes tradition of a career in commerce, but, instead, to leave Edinburgh, go to London and join the recently formed Criminal Investigations Department of the Metropolitan Police.

Fraser claimed that he had been drawn to the CID both by its reassuring address (Great Scotland Yard) and by the prospect of doing 'something real, something useful in life', applying to police work the philosophy he had learnt from Professor Huxley. 'Science,' said Huxley, famously, 'is nothing but trained and organised common sense.'

To become a detective in the CID, Fraser had first to serve as a constable on the beat. He had the necessary qualifications. He was over twenty-one and under twenty-seven at the time; he stood a clear five feet nine inches without shoes or stockings; he was able to demonstrate that he could 'read well', 'write legibly' and had 'a fair knowledge of spelling'; he was judged to be 'generally intelligent' and seen to be 'free from any bodily complaint'. Unsurprisingly, given his advantages of education and upbringing, Fraser rose effortlessly through the ranks, gaining a promotion or accolade of some kind in every year of his service. The day that we met him was the first day of his latest appointment. He was now the detective inspector responsible for coordinating all CID operations in five of the Met's seventeen divisions: A (Whitehall), B (Chelsea), C (Mayfair and Soho), D (Marylebone) and F (Kensington). (He had hoped – 'if only for reasons of alphabetical neatness', he explained – to secure E division also, but, as he put it, 'with a logic at odds with all the best traditions of the Met', E (Holborn) had been grouped with G (King's Cross) and N (Islington) under the command of his friend and fellow Scot, Inspector Archy Gilmour.)

When Oscar and I were shown into his office, on the third floor of the new building at Scotland Yard, it was a little before four o'clock. We discovered Fraser standing, alone, behind his desk, with his back to us, apparently gazing out of a narrow window onto the Thames Embankment below. 'Please,' he said, turning sharply as he heard us enter, 'I was not looking idly out of the window, I assure you. I was examining your cards. This is my first day in this office. It's a brand-new building and the architect is Scottish, but the light is terrible in here. I apologise.'

The room was indeed dark, cramped and inhospitable, but Fraser's welcome was as warm and sunny as we could have wished for. He shook our hands; he clapped his own; he beamed upon us.

'Welcome,' he said. His mouth was quite small, but his smile was remarkable because his teeth were so perfect. They were white and even, and gleamed like newly polished, mother-of-pearl shirt-studs.

'Welcome,' Fraser said again, seating himself on the edge of his bare wooden desk while inviting us to 'take a pew'. There were just two hard, upright chairs ranged side by side against the office wall. Oscar eyed them suspiciously.

'We apologise for troubling you,' he began, perching himself, somewhat awkwardly, on one of the chairs.

'You do not trouble me,' said Fraser, cordially. 'You honour me. Any friend of Conan Doyle's is a friend of mine.' His face was so white, his skin so smooth, his eyes so dark, that the ebullience of his manner, by contrast, and the dazzle of his smile, were quite disconcerting. 'This is my first day in a new job and you are my first visitors. May I offer you both a cup of tea?'

'No – thank you,' said Oscar quickly, fearing, no doubt, that the quality of the tea would be consonant with the comfort of the furnishings. 'Let me introduce myself—'

Fraser interrupted him. 'You do not need to, Mr Wilde. I know your reputation. I admire your work. I have done so for several years, since chancing on one of your early essays when I was an undergraduate, in fact.'

'Oh,' said Oscar, gratified. 'May I ask which one?'

' "The Truth of Masks",' Fraser replied, slowly switching his steady gaze from Oscar's eyes to mine. 'And Mr Sherard,' he went on, 'I was reading your article on the great Emile Zola in *Blackwood's Magazine* only this weekend. You are a social reformer, sir – as I hope to be.'

Aidan Fraser charmed us and disarmed us. He put us completely at our ease and, having done so, invited us to tell our tale.

Oscar told it. He told it well, in detail, but without embellishment. Fraser listened. He listened intently, his eyes glancing between us, occasionally nodding assent or gently tapping his chin with his forefinger to indicate that he was following Oscar's narrative in every particular, but never interrupting. He listened carefully and, when Oscar was done, he allowed a prolonged silence to fall before he spoke.

'Gentlemen,' he said, eventually, leaning towards us, his eyes narrowed, his smooth brow almost furrowed, 'we have a problem.'

'A problem?' Oscar repeated.

'Yes, Mr Wilde, a problem . . . You see, a murder where there is no body is indeed a mystery—'

'But I saw the body!' Oscar exclaimed.

'Yes,' said Inspector Fraser calmly, 'so you tell me. Twenty-four hours ago you saw a body – but the body has disappeared.'

'I saw the body,' Oscar repeated, plaintively.

'And you recognised the body . . .' Fraser continued.

'It was Billy Wood—'

'– whom you knew, but did not know well?'

'I knew the boy, but I . . .' Oscar hesitated. He waved his right hand in the air in a sort of dismissive gesture. 'I knew him, but I did not know him . . . intimately.'

Fraser observed Oscar's awkwardness. He let another silence fall. 'Did you know the housekeeper?' he asked.

'No.'

'Did you recognise her?'

'No.'

'Could you describe her for me?'

'No, I paid her no attention.'

'What was her age? What was her height? Had she no distinguishing features?'

'None that I recall.' Oscar hesitated. 'There was a touch of red about her, I think – a flower perhaps, a kerchief, I don't know. I brushed past her. I paid her no heed.'

The inspector glanced in my direction and spoke as if soliciting my support. 'You see the problem? So many questions, so few answers.' He looked steadily at Oscar. 'You tell me that there was a housekeeper at the scene of the alleged crime, Mr Wilde, but you cannot describe her. You tell me that there was a body, but it seems that it has disappeared. You tell me that this body was that of a boy you knew, but did not know "intimately" . . . Why, I wonder, have none of those who did know him intimately – his family, his friends, his contemporaries – not come forward to report him missing? Where is his body now? Where, in short, is the *evidence* of murder?'

'There is the blood on the wall!' Oscar protested.

'Which you saw?' asked Fraser.

'Which Doyle saw,' said Oscar.

'Ah, yes,' murmured Fraser, almost to himself, 'Arthur's tiny spots of blood . . .' He clapped his hands and got to his feet. 'Those we must investigate,' he said, emphatically. 'That we can do. I will send a man to Cowley Street directly – this afternoon. Number 23, you say? If we find evidence we can make a start, but without evidence, Mr Wilde, without a body—'

'The body must be found!' cried Oscar.

Fraser was now standing behind his desk, resting his long thin fingers upon it. 'Our resources are meagre, I fear,' he said, almost dolefully. 'We have thirteen hundred men to patrol a city of five million. We cannot go out looking for bodies like needles in haystacks, Mr Wilde. And the sad truth is that, even when we stumble upon them, even when we come face to face with the bloodiest evidence imaginable, we are still, all too often, unable to solve the mystery . . . Do not raise your hopes, Mr Wilde. Think of those unfortunate women in Whitechapel.'

For months on end the previous year, the notorious 'Jack the Ripper' case had filled the pages of the popular press.

'There was another one found recently, was there not?' I said.

'Yes,' said Fraser, 'six weeks ago, in Castle Alley. Alice McKenzie. We have her body – or what remains of it. We know her history. We know of her movements in the hours leading up to her death. We have tracked down and interviewed all those closest to her, those who saw her last. We have a mountain of evidence – we even have a letter purporting to come from her killer – and still we are nowhere near a solution to the crime . . . It is possible we never shall be.'

'Was her throat not cut?'

'It was,' said Fraser, 'but do not get carried away, Mr Sherard. Her abdomen was mutilated too. The Whitechapel murderer preys on women in dark alleys, not young men in candlelit rooms.'

It was clear that our interview was coming to an end. Fraser stepped from behind his desk and moved towards the door. Oscar and I got to our feet. As he stood up, Oscar swayed for a moment and looked pale. John Simpson's fine wines and Aidan Fraser's airless room had taken their toll. The police inspector put out a hand to steady him.

'I am sorry if I disappoint you, Mr Wilde,' he said. 'I do not want to promise more than I can deliver. But, rest assured, I will do what I can. I will send a man to Cowley Street this afternoon.'

'Will you let me know the outcome?' asked Oscar.

'Of course,' said Fraser, retrieving our cards from his waistcoat pocket. 'I will send a wire to Tite Street, without fail.'

'To my club, if you don't mind,' said Oscar, quickly.

'Of course,' said Fraser. 'The Albemarle, is it not?'

'You know?' said Oscar, surprised. 'Are you a member?'

'No,' said Fraser, revealing a line of perfect teeth. 'I am a detective.'

Oscar, regaining his colour, laughed softly and shook Fraser by the hand. 'Thank you for your time, Inspector. Thank you for listening. I hope you do not think I have acted amiss in coming to see you today.'

'Quite the opposite,' said Fraser. 'You have done your duty – you have reported a suspected crime to the proper authorities. You have acted entirely correctly, as a gentleman should.' He paused for a moment and looked directly at Oscar. 'I am only surprised that you did not call upon us yesterday, immediately after you made your discovery. Is there a reason why you waited twenty-four hours before coming forward?'

Fraser smiled slyly as he asked the question. To my surprise, Oscar was not discomfited. 'I am the prince of procrastination,' he said. 'It is my besetting sin. I never put off till tomorrow what I can possibly do – the day after.'

Fraser laughed. 'Well, you've done your duty now, Mr Wilde, and, having done your duty, sir, take my advice: leave well alone. Murder is a sordid business. It is a matter for the police, not for the prince of procrastination, nor yet the fastidious champion of aestheticism. You have done all you can in this matter. You have done well. I salute you.'

The sun was still shining brightly when we reached the street, but the air was cooler. Oscar turned back towards the building and looked up to the third floor. At a narrow latticed window we saw Inspector Aidan Fraser gazing down upon us. Oscar raised his hand and waved. Fraser inclined his head and waved back.

'What now?' I asked.

'Now,' said Oscar, 'I need to clear my head. I shall walk home, along the river – by way of Cowley Street, I think.

I have a favour to ask of Mrs O'Keefe.' As I began to speak, he raised a finger to silence me and then, with both hands, straightened my tie and lightly brushed my shoulders as he might have done to his sons as they readied themselves to go to school. 'And you, my dear Robert,' he said, 'need to go home to clear your desk. There is work to be done, a mystery to be solved, and I shall be grateful for your assistance – and your company. Meet me at the club at eleven, or a little after. Meantime, return to your room and finish whichever of your unfinished articles is nearest completion. And wire your wife's solicitor. Tell him a divorce is out of the question just at present. You are currently engaged in a matter much more pressing: murder. He will be baffled by the truth. The mediocre always are.'

At 11.15 that evening, as arranged, I met Oscar at the Albemarle. I found him alone in the library, drinking champagne and reading Wordsworth.

'Your great-grandfather is a great man,' he declared. 'He teaches us to accept the "burthen of the mystery", "the heavy and the weary weight of all this unintelligible world" – does he not?'

I was spared the challenge of summoning up a suitable response by the arrival of Hubbard. The club servant stood obsequiously by the door, holding a small silver salver in his hand. 'A telegram for you, Mr Wilde,' he said.

'It will be from Fraser,' said Oscar, picking up the small yellow envelope and passing it to me. 'What does he say?'

I tore open the envelope and read out the communication. 'SEARCH COMPLETE STOP NO EVIDENCE FOUND STOP REGRET NO FURTHER ACTION POSSIBLE AT THIS STAGE REGARDS FRASER.'

Oscar said nothing. Hubbard was still hovering at the door. He gave a little cough, like a butler in a stage comedy, and murmured, 'And there's a person to see you, sir. In the entrance hall.'

Oscar was galvanised. 'Come, Robert, come,' he said, throwing down the Wordsworth and sweeping us past Hubbard into the hallway. 'The game's afoot.'

The person who had come to see Oscar was waiting nervously in the club's outer lobby, by the porter's lodge. I recognised her at once. It was Mrs O'Keefe. As we appeared, she made her deep obeisance. Oscar raised her by the hand and said simply, 'Well, madam?'

'I did exactly as you instructed, Mr Wilde. I did not leave 23 Cowley Street until your cab came to collect me at eleven o'clock. Nobody has been near the house since you last called by. No police, nothing – nobody, nobody at all.'

'God bless you, Mrs O'Keefe,' said Oscar.

'And you, sir,' said Mrs O'Keefe. 'I'll pray for you.'

'Let us pray for one another,' said Oscar, handing her a sovereign.

6

2 September 1889

The following morning, at eleven o'clock, as instructed by Oscar, I presented myself at number 16 Tite Street, off the Chelsea Embankment, the house that he and Constance had shared since the start of their marriage five years before. From the outside, it was a handsome house: tall, brick-built, solid. Inside, it was exquisite. As Oscar's friend and neighbour, James Whistler, the painter, who had assisted with the decoration, often said: 'The exterior is thoroughly dependable; the interior is wholly Wilde.'

The decoration reflected Oscar's taste and Constance's fortune. At the time of their marriage, Constance inherited five thousand pounds from her grandfather; every penny – and more – went into Tite Street. Everything in the house was of the best, and everything in the house – well, almost everything – was of just one colour: white. In the drawing room the curtains were white, the walls were white, the floor coverings were white, even the furniture was white. In the dining room, also, everything was white, with the exception of a cherry-red lampshade hanging from the ceiling in the centre of the room, immediately above a terracotta statue that stood on a diamond-shaped red cloth in the middle of a white table. It was all picture-perfect.

My friend William Yeats, the poet, had spent Christmas with Oscar at Tite Street the year before – I was in Paris at the time, in pursuit of Kaitlyn – and he wrote to me, describing the day, and Tite Street, and 'the perfect harmony' of Oscar's life there, 'with his beautiful wife and two young children'. Yeats said it suggested to him 'some delicate artistic composition'. Yeats also told me that he had embarrassed himself that day by wearing yellow shoes. Undyed leather was then the fashion, but the moment that he set foot inside the house, Yeats realised that the livid ochre of his festive footwear – he had bought the shoes specially for the occasion – was completely out of keeping with the snowscape whiteness of Tite Street. When he saw the shoes, Oscar started visibly, and, throughout the day, he kept glancing at them surreptitiously, wincing on each occasion.

Yeats, I think, felt uncomfortable in Tite Street. I always felt easy and at home there. Perhaps that was because Constance made me feel so welcome.

That sunny September morning when Constance Wilde opened the door to me I had never seen her looking lovelier. She was dressed in white, with a violet ribbon in her hair and a matching ribbon around her waist. She held the door wide open and smiled at me. 'Welcome, Robert,' she said. 'It has been too long.' Her figure was fuller than I remembered; she seemed taller, too, and older, I suppose. She was thirty-one, but her face was not careworn; she looked happy, confident and gay. She shook my hand and then, with her knuckles, fleetingly caressed my cheek. 'It is so good to see you,' she said. 'I think of you often.' In the hallway, she pointed to the umbrella-stand and said, 'Look, I have your swordstick still. It is here to protect me.'

I said, without thinking, 'Constance, I will protect you always,' and, as I said it, I blushed.

She laughed, took both my hands in hers and squeezed them tightly. 'You are such a romantic, Mr Sherard,' she said. 'I am not surprised that Oscar is planning to take you on a great adventure. He tells me you are going to play Dr Watson to his Sherlock Holmes.'

'You have read *A Study in Scarlet*?' I asked.

'Indeed,' she replied. 'Oscar insisted. And I enjoyed it. Oscar has become quite obsessed with "Mr Holmes" and his powers of observation and perfect reasoning. To be truthful, I think Oscar may be a little jealous of Arthur Doyle and his creation. Let us go and find him.'

She took me by the hand and led me, like a playmate, through the house in search of Oscar. We found him in his Moorish smoking room, where nothing was white except for the narrow plume of smoke rising from his carefully held cigarette. He was lying back on a divan, with his eyes half closed. He must have heard us coming – he must have heard me arrive at the front door – but he did not stir. As we came into the room, languidly he lifted his cigarette into the air and, gazing on it, rolling it around deliberately between his thumb and forefinger, observed, 'Cigarette smoking is the perfect type of perfect pleasure, is it not? It is exquisite and leaves one unsatisfied.'

Constance smiled; I laughed; Oscar sat up and turned towards us. 'Constance has told you of the plan, I trust?' he said. 'She is leaving us, Robert. She is taking the boys with her. She is going to North Yorkshire, to the moors, to stay with her little friend, Emily Thursfield.' Needless to say, Constance had told me none of this. Oscar turned to his wife and added, conspiratorially, 'Do not introduce Robert to Emily, my dear. She is far too pretty. He will fall in love with her at once and be unable to sleep for a fortnight. I don't believe he has slept at all since he first met you.'

I blushed once more. Oscar got to his feet, laughing, and placed his hands upon my shoulders.

'Constance is going on holiday, Robert, and we are going to work. We are going to unravel this mystery, Robert. We are going to solve this crime, with or without the assistance of Inspector Fraser.'

'Oscar has told me of the horrible murder he stumbled upon,' said Constance, seriously. 'I feel for the poor boy – and for his family, whoever they may be.'

'We shall begin with his family, Robert,' said Oscar, extinguishing his cigarette. 'That is where we shall start.'

I was puzzled. 'But, Oscar,' I said, 'I thought you said that the boy had no known relations. Isn't that what you told Conan Doyle and the police?'

Oscar offered me a half-smile, but no answer.

'I cannot understand why the police will not help,' said Constance.

'Constance has seen Fraser's outrageous telegram,' Oscar said. 'I have given it to her – for her collection.' I looked at him, uncomprehending. 'She has a special box in which she stores such items,' he explained. 'She began the collection on our wedding day, with the telegram Whistler sent to us at the church: "FEAR I MAY NOT BE ABLE TO REACH YOU IN TIME FOR THE CEREMONY. DON'T WAIT." Fraser's missive is less amusing, I grant you, less well phrased, but I want it kept. I believe it may prove of interest in the fullness of time.'

58

'Why did Mr Fraser say he had searched for evidence when he had not?' asked Constance.

'Why indeed?' asked Oscar.

I thought it was most likely that Inspector Fraser felt that the body of Billy Wood was a figment of Oscar's imagination and that he was disinclined to use scarce police resources in the pursuit of a phantom murderer, but I kept my thought to myself and said instead, 'If we are to find the family of Billy Wood, where do we begin?'

'At the roller-skating rink, if I'm not much mistaken,' said Oscar. The carriage clock on the mantelpiece – a trophy from his American lecture tour – struck the half-hour. 'Come Robert, our carriage awaits.'

Oscar had ordered a two-wheeler. It was waiting for us in the street below. Oscar thought nothing of keeping carriages waiting for him at all hours. He was wantonly extravagant. On hansom cabs and amusements – flowers, champagne, luncheon, dinner, supper and the rest – he could spend in a day what I might earn in a month. Even with the income that Constance brought with her to the marriage, and even when he was at the height of his powers, with two plays running simultaneously in the West End, Oscar lived beyond his means – dangerously so. At the time, I had no idea that his financial position was as fragile as it turned out to be. From the moment of his marriage, I took him to be a moderately wealthy man. Had I known the truth, I trust that I would not have permitted him to be as generous towards me as invariably he was. The first inkling I got of the parlous state of his affairs was some three years after this, at the time of his brilliant success with *Lady's Windermere's Fan*. From that play alone, in one year, he earned more than seven thousand pounds in royalties. That was the year I recall being told by Gertrude Simmonds, the boys' governess, that 'things were not so prosperous' in Tite Street, that the butcher had 'refused to send a joint until the account was settled' and that 'Mr Wilde himself had to drive round in a hansom to settle up'.

However, there were no clouds apparent in the blue sky above Tite Street on the morning of 2 September 1889. Annie Marchant (bustling, busy Annie Marchant), the boys' nursemaid, had brought her young charges out onto the pavement to bid their papa farewell. Oscar loved his boys. He kissed each of them fondly. To Cyril, who had turned four that summer, he said, 'Take care of your mother, young man. The Yorkshire moors are perilous and a mother is a precious thing. You are granted only the one.'

'Hush, Oscar,' said Constance, anxiously. 'You will frighten him.'

'No, my dear,' said Oscar, 'these are wise children. Remember who their parents are.' He turned to Constance, who now had little Vyvyan in her arms, and kissed her gently on the forehead. He looked closely into Vyvyan's round and smiling face and said solemnly, '*Sunt lacrimae rerum et mentem mortalia tangunt.*'

Vyvyan, who was not yet three, gurgled appreciatively and pulled his father's nose. Oscar turned to me proudly. 'Their English is developing slowly, but when it comes to Virgil these boys don't miss a trick.'

Laughing, we climbed aboard the two-wheeler. Constance, Annie Marchant and the two young children, all smiling, all so happy, waved us on our way.

'Take care, Oscar,' Constance called out, as our driver (a dour sort) cracked his whip. 'I will see you in a month, my darling. I will be back for your birthday, have no fear.'

'With you as my wife, I have no fear,' said Oscar, blowing her a kiss.

As the cab turned right from Tite Street into Christchurch Street on its way towards the King's Road, Oscar, adjusting the cuffs of his lemon-coloured linen jacket – he was now properly dressed for the season – sat back and said, 'I have a good wife, do I not?'

'You do, Oscar,' I answered, with feeling.

'And darling children?' he added.

'Indeed,' I replied.

'And we,' he said, suddenly clapping his hands together, 'have the excitement of a new venture in hand. Ennui is the enemy, Robert! Adventure is the answer. We shall find the murderer of Billy Wood. If Conan Doyle's friend cannot help me, Conan Doyle's example can. Oscar Wilde masquerading as Sherlock Holmes: why not? A mask tells us so much more than a face . . .'

It took us no more than ten minutes to reach our destination: the Dungannon Cottage Marble Rink at Knightsbridge. Yet another skating rink! London in the 1880s was awash with them. But the Dungannon was different. In the aftermath of Professor Gamgee's success in transforming the floating swimming bath by Charing Cross Bridge into the 'Floating Glaciarium' – an indoor rink that used 'manufactured' ice – another enterprising 'professor of physical culture', Colonel Henry Melville, had created a new marvel in Knightsbridge. His all-weather, all-year-round ice rink dispensed with ice altogether, offering skaters instead a 'marble' surface on which to skate – a surface, according to Colonel Melville, the smoothness of which was 'unrivalled save by the clearest sheet of ice to be found within the Arctic circle'.

'I did not know that you favoured roller skating as a sport, Oscar,' I said, laughing, as we entered the Dungannon's crowded foyer.

'I do not,' said Oscar, coldly, 'but Billy Wood did and Gerard Bellotti does. It is Bellotti we have come to find.' He glanced towards me. 'Did I mention Bellotti to you?'

'You did, Oscar,' I said, 'just the once. But you did not mention him to Conan Doyle or Inspector Fraser, I noticed.'

'I am glad you noticed, Robert. A good detective notices everything.' His eyes were now scanning the crowd.

'Might I ask,' I said, '*why* you didn't mention his name to Fraser?'

'If Inspector Fraser deigns to take an interest in the case, he will come across Mr Bellotti soon enough. He may even be familiar with him already. I imagine Gerard Bellotti is not unknown to the police.' Oscar's gaze had moved from the rink and its surround to the refreshment tables adjacent to the bandstand. 'There he is,' he cried suddenly, pointing his cane.

Gerard Bellotti was not a prepossessing sight, nor did he have the appearance of a natural roller skater: he was grotesquely corpulent. Although he was seated a distance away, with his back to us, he was immediately remarkable, not only because of his fleshly bulk – he gave the impression of a toad that sits and blinks, yet never moves – but because of his gaudy apparel. He was wearing an orange checked suit that would have done credit to the first comedian at Collins' Music Hall and on the top of his onion-shaped head of oily hair, which was tightly curled and dyed the colour of henna, he sported a battered straw boater.

'Who is Gerard Bellotti?' I asked.

'Not a man of refinement, I fear,' said Oscar, as we pushed our way through the crowd. It was midweek, but the Dungannon Cottage was packed. All human life was there (of a certain class, at least): courting couples, solitary loungers, mothers and grandmothers with children, servant-girls on holiday, young men bent on pleasure.

'How do you know him?' I called above the din. The noise was oppressive. Everyone was shouting to be heard above the music of the band and the relentless low roar of roller skates on marble.

'He works for Messrs O'Donovan & Brown of Ludgate Circus, London's leading suppliers of domestic staff from the emerald isle,' Oscar called back. 'Bellotti is one of their recruiting sergeants – he scouts for lads who might be suitable as bootblacks and page-boys. That's what he does here.' Oscar paused and put his face close to my ear. 'And, as a sideline, he runs an informal luncheon club for gentlemen.'

' "For gentlemen"?'

Oscar laughed. 'Well . . . Members of Parliament and the like. He offers cold cuts and companionship. He will supply an MP with a partner at cards – or an artist with a model. I know he has a marquess on his books – an amateur pugilist, who needs lads to wrestle with.'

'Mr Bellotti sounds interesting,' I said, amused.

'No,' replied Oscar, seriously, 'Bellotti is complex, without being interesting.'

We had reached his table. Bellotti neither looked up nor even turned to look at us. As we sat down, with a pale plump hand he pushed away from him what appeared to be a cup of cold tea and spoke immediately. 'Ah, Mr Wilde, how are you? I recognise your scent.' His voice was more melodious than I had expected, his accent more refined. 'Canterbury Wood Violet, is it not? Always your favourite. Alsop & Quilter are still looking after you, I trust. And who is your friend? Is he in search of entertainment or employment?'

'Neither,' said Oscar. 'Mr Sherard and I have come to you in search of information.'

'Indeed.'

Oscar leant his cane against the table's edge and then, discreetly, pushed a sovereign beneath Bellotti's saucer. 'When did you last see Billy Wood?' he asked.

'Billy Wood? What a delightful boy. So bright, so breezy. One of your favourites, Mr Wilde – one of your enthusiasms.'

'When did you last see him?' Oscar repeated the question.

'Yesterday,' said Bellotti.

Oscar leant towards him urgently. 'Are you sure?'

Bellotti pondered. 'Perhaps the day before?' he said. 'Yes, the day before. He came to one of the club lunches. We're meeting in Little College Street now, you know. You must come, Mr Wilde. It is too long since we have had the pleasure of your company. He was in excellent form. Billy is always a delight. Why do you ask after him? Is he in trouble?'

'I fear so,' said Oscar, bleakly.

'Oh dear,' muttered Bellotti. 'He'll have run away then. They do. Am I right? Has he disappeared?'

'Yes.'

'He'll have gone to his mother in Broadstairs. That's what happens. That's what they all do. In time of travail, they turn to their mothers.'

'Do you happen to have her address?' asked Oscar.

'The Castle, Harbour Street. The property does not quite live up to the address, but as seaside guest houses go, it has all the essential amenities. I stayed there two summers ago. That's how I met young Billy Wood. He was waiting at table. I sensed at once you'd like him, Mr Wilde. I encouraged him to come to town, partly on your account.'

'Thank you,' said Oscar, and we got to our feet. Bellotti did not move.

As we pushed our way back through the crowd, I asked, 'Is he blind?'

'He may be,' said Oscar. 'He appears to be. But I would not count upon it. With a man like Bellotti, you can never be quite sure of anything.'

Back in the street, our two-wheeler was waiting. We were about to clamber aboard when, simultaneously, both Oscar and I lurched forward and let out an involuntary cry of pain. A blow, like the lash of a whip, had been struck across the backs of our calves. Oscar fell forward against the carriage. I turned around angrily. Standing immediately behind us was a small figure in a page-boy's uniform. I was about to cuff the lad across the ear when I realised that our assailant was not a boy at all, but a dwarf. His body was diminutive but not misshapen; his large head was both unnatural and grotesque. His face was heavily lined; his skin was sallow and weather-beaten. There was a sneer on his lips and in his hands the cane that he had swiped across our legs to attract our attention. I saw at once that it was the swordstick that I had presented to Constance on her honeymoon, and I realised at once that Oscar must have left it at Bellotti's table.

The dwarf held out the cane towards Oscar, who, recovering his balance, took it. To my astonishment, he then reached into his pocket and found a coin to give to the man. 'For God's sake, Oscar!' I protested.

The dwarf grabbed the money and backed away, laughing at us contemptuously. Oscar climbed into the cab. 'Pleasure and pain,' he said, 'they've both to be paid for, one way or another.'

'Did you know him?' I asked, as I followed Oscar into the two-wheeler.

'He's a creature of Bellotti's,' he answered. 'He is unpleasant, I grant you, but I pity him his deformity.'

'What does he do for Bellotti?' I said.

'His bidding,' Oscar replied, with a wan smile.

'He is a nasty piece of work,' I said, rubbing my calves, which were still sore from the unwarranted assault.

'It needs not a ghost come from the grave to tell us that, Robert. He is ugly and vicious, so put him out of your mind. The less said about life's sores the better. Think happier thoughts. Think: tomorrow, we shall be going to Broadstairs and perhaps I shall buy you a boater when we are at the seaside . . .'

The two-wheeler took us from Knightsbridge, down Piccadilly and through Soho towards my room on Gower Street. When we reached the side-street by Soho Square where, two nights before, I had seen Oscar with the young woman – the stranger with the disfigured face – abruptly my friend called to the cab to stop. 'I will alight here,' he said. 'You go on home, Robert. The fare is paid.'

He climbed down from the carriage and turned to me. 'Yes, Robert,' he said, 'I have an assignation – in a slightly disreputable part of town. And you have curiosity. Both, I trust, will do us credit.'

7

3 September 1889

What was Oscar's assignation in that slightly disreputable part of town? He did not volunteer the information, and I did not press him for it.

It is curious how men who are good friends, close friends, true friends, who may have been on the most intimate and familiar terms over any number of years, can nevertheless know next to nothing of one another's love lives.

I knew Oscar Wilde well, but I did not then know the secrets of his heart.

In Paris, in the cloudless spring of 1883, when we first met, we dined together, time and again, at Foyot's, at Voisin's, at Paillard's, at all the best tables; we strolled together, hour upon hour, through the gardens of the Tuileries, through the Palais du Louvre, along the banks of the Seine; we dined and we talked; we walked and we talked; and when we talked, we talked of everything beneath the sun and moon, of art and literature, of music and revolution, of life and death, and, yes, of love. But when we talked of love, I realise now, it was always in the abstract.

Once, I told Oscar how at Oxford, when I was twenty (before I was sent down), I had visited a prostitute.

Immediately, he reciprocated and told me how at Oxford, when he was twenty (before he won the Newdigate Prize), he, too, had visited a prostitute, but he told me no more of the experience than that. In Paris, memorably, we had been together at the Eden Music Hall on the night on which he met – and shared the bed – of the celebrated Marie Aguétant. Following that first encounter, I know that he called upon her more than once and later, after her brutal murder, I recall him saying, 'I think of her often, Robert,' but what he thought of her – and why – he did not tell me.

In London, in Soho, on occasion, I visited a brothel and enjoyed the dubious delights on offer there. Did Oscar also? Before his marriage, and after, several of his closest friends were actresses. Not all were ladies. He flirted with them outrageously. Did he lie with them also? He told me he loved Lillie Langtry 'with a passion' – but said no more than that. He called her 'Lil'; he kissed her upon the lips (I know; I saw it happen); but did he share her bed? I cannot tell. He loved Constance – of that I am certain – but did he love others too? Did he betray his wife with other women? And was the girl I had seen him with in Soho Square one such? And if he did, and if she was, was it truly betrayal? Or did he believe – as I did; as I do – that you can love more than one person and keep faith with both?

Travelling with him, first class, on the train to Broadstairs, early in that September of 1889, he seemed to read my thoughts. We were alone in the carriage, seated opposite one another, and a silence had fallen between us. I was gazing at his tired eyes and wondering whom he had met the night before – and why – and what had passed between them. I was thinking of Constance, whom I loved, and of my promise to protect her. Did she have cause to be jealous? Could she depend on Oscar's fidelity? And, if she could not, would the truth, if ever she learnt it, be very painful to her?

I was in a kind of reverie, slowly turning over these questions in my mind, when I realised that my friend was speaking to me.

'Fidelity is overrated, Robert,' I heard him say. 'It is loyalty that counts – and understanding.'

'Indeed,' I murmured, unsure of where our conversation might be leading.

'Take my mother, for example. Such a feeling as vulgar jealousy could take no hold on her.' I nodded, but said nothing. With Oscar, I often nodded and said nothing. 'My mother was well aware of my father's constant infidelities, but simply ignored them. Before my father died, he lay ill in bed for many days. And every morning a woman dressed in black, and closely veiled, used to come to our house in Merrion Square, in Dublin. Unhindered either by my mother or anyone else, she used to walk straight upstairs to my father's bedroom, sit down at the head of his bed, and so remain there all day, without ever speaking a word or once raising her veil.

'She took no notice of anybody in the room, and nobody paid any attention to her. Not one woman in a thousand would have tolerated her presence, but my mother allowed it, because she knew that my father loved this woman and felt that it must be a comfort to have her there by his dying bed. And I am sure that she did right not to judge that last happiness of a man who was about to die, and I am sure that my father understood her apparent indifference, understood that it was not because she did not love him that she permitted her rival's presence, but because she loved him very much, and died with his heart full of gratitude and affection for her.'

He smiled at me and brushed what might have been a tear from the corner of his eye. 'We have mothers on the mind, do we not, Robert? It is understandable. We are on our way to meet the unfortunate mother of poor Billy Wood – a mother who has lost her child and does not yet know it.'

'Are we to tell her?' I asked.

'If she does not already know,' said Oscar, 'we must.'

'But if there is no body—'

'I saw the body of Billy Wood, Robert. He is dead. Mrs Wood will not see her boy again. And he was her only child.'

'You know that?'

'He told me so. He spoke often of his mother. He loved her dearly. He told me that his mother did not understand him, but that she understood herself well enough to know she did not understand him. He was a clever boy. And kind. He told me he had come to London to make his fortune so that one day he could care for his mother as she had once cared for him. And he would have made a fortune, Robert . . .'

'You think so?'

'I know so, Robert. He had no education to speak of – he could barely read – but when I read Shakespeare to him, he would memorise the words almost at once and then declaim them with an instinctive authority, intelligence and feeling that were remarkable. He was perhaps the most gifted young actor I have ever known. We were working on *Romeo and Juliet* when he died. I had planned to introduce him to my friend Henry Irving at the Lyceum. Irving, great actor-manager that he is, would have recognised Billy's gift. Billy Wood had the makings of what they call "a star". He was luminous. He shone. He would have gone far, Robert. He would indeed have made a fortune. I was proud to be nurturing his natural talent. His loss to me is grievous. His loss to his mother will be terrible.'

'What sort of woman is she?' I asked. 'Do you know?'

'I have dark forebodings about her, Robert,' Oscar replied, blowing his nose and mopping his mouth with his handkerchief. He shifted in his seat. 'I am not optimistic. You must remember, she lives in Broadstairs.'

'What does that mean?' I asked, sensing that Oscar's mood was moving rapidly from the elegiac to the playful.

Oscar shook his head, muttering with a sigh, 'Broadstairs . . . ah me!'

'What is wrong with Broadstairs?' I ventured. 'Is it not one of Queen Victoria's favourite watering holes?'

'Her Majesty is not the problem, Robert. It is Dickens who is the difficulty.'

'Dickens?'

'Dickens! Yes, Robert, Charles Dickens, the late, lamented. Broadstairs was his favourite holiday retreat. It was Dickens who put Broadstairs on the map. He wrote *David Copperfield* there – in a cliff-top villa that, naturally, now glories in the name of Bleak House. If you are so inclined, you may visit it. There is a twopenny tour. And if you take it, when you reach the room that used to be the great man's study you will learn of the legend that says, "Leave a note for Mr Dickens in the top drawer of his writing desk and he will come in the night to read it . . ." Oh, yes, in Broadstairs the spirit of Dickens is every-where – *he* is everywhere. You cannot escape him, try as you might, because, by way of unconscious tribute to their most celebrated visitor, the good people of Broadstairs have each and every one transmogrified themselves into characters from their hero's oeuvre. The stationmaster looks like Micawber, the town crier *is* Mr Bumble, the benevolent landlady at the Saracen's Head takes her cue from Mrs Fezziwig . . .'

'You exaggerate, Oscar.' I laughed.

'Would that I did,' he sighed. 'Our Mrs Wood, I fear, poor Billy's mother, will be playing her part like all the rest. She will be Mrs Todgers, I imagine, "affection beaming in one eye, calculation shining out of the other" – or, more likely, Mrs Gummidge, a lone, lorn creature for whom "everythink goes contrairy". Broadstairs is not as other towns are, Robert, mark my words.'

To my astonishment, when we alighted from the train, it seemed that Oscar was right. It must, of course, merely have been the power of his suggestion, but, as we walked the short distance down the hill from the railway station towards the centre of the town, every passer-by appeared to be a caricature of humanity, decked out in elaborate period costume, playing a role in a vast Dickensian pageant. We passed an obsequious muffin-man who touched his cap to us ('Uriah Heep,' murmured Oscar); a fair-haired, shoeless, ragged boy to whom Oscar tossed a halfpenny ('Oliver Twist?' I asked); a beaming, bon-homous, bespectacled gentleman who raised his hat to us unbidden with a 'Capital morning, is it not?' ('Mr Pickwick!' we whispered merrily, together and at once);

and several more. But the game stopped – the game was forgotten – the moment we reached The Castle, Harbour Street.

The house itself was tall and narrow, running to three floors. It took its name from the castellated design of the decorative brick-and-flint work above the ground- and first-floor windows and the front door. The Castle looked to be what it was: a small seaside hotel that had known better days. The dilapidation was evident: the curtains at the unwashed windows were faded and ill hung; the stone front steps were chipped and badly worn; the boot scraper was broken; the brickwork was weather-beaten and discoloured; and the paint was peeling on the hanging sign that announced the hotel's name as well as on the wrought-iron railings and the gate that led to the area steps.

It was on these steps that we first encountered the man who, we later learnt, was Edward O'Donnell.

Had we still been playing Oscar's game, we might, in unison, have cried, 'Bill Sikes!' for the man – unshaven, unkempt, and unsteady on his feet – was clearly a brute and a drunkard. Nevertheless at that moment I do not believe that either Oscar or I gave Dickens a moment's consideration. Edward O'Donnell inspired fear, not playfulness. He was not young – he might have been fifty – but he had the build of an ox and there was madness in his eyes.

As we approached the house, he lurched from the area steps onto the street and stood before us, confronting us, blocking our way. We froze, quite terrified. With one hand outstretched he steadied himself on the iron railings; with the other he gesticulated wildly towards our faces, jabbing his extended forefinger close to Oscar's eyes first, then to mine. 'Have you come for her?' he bellowed. 'Have you come for the bitch, the slattern? I wish you joy of her – and her beloved boy. God rot them both. She is the devil's whore. God knows, I've always hated her. *La putaine!*'

As he finished his vile utterance, he turned suddenly and spat into the gutter, and then, pushing himself away from the railings, muttering oaths and obscenities, he rolled away from us along the street towards the harbour.

We stood in silence and watched him go. High above us, a seagull screamed. I turned to Oscar. 'Let us leave this place now,' I implored him. 'This is not for us.'

'Oh,' said Oscar simply, 'but I fear that it is. That, I take it, was Mr Wood. Billy never mentioned him. I am not surprised, are you? I had taken it for granted that Mrs Wood was a widow. It seems I was mistaken.'

Lightly, Oscar climbed the three front steps and, unhesitating, knocked firmly three times on the hotel's front door. Reluctantly, I joined him. We waited, side by side, saying nothing. Oscar knocked again and, as he did so, from behind the door we heard the turning of a key in the lock and the pulling back of one bolt and then another. Slowly the door opened and a thin, pale woman, dressed all in grey, stood before us. Her face was white, but her eyes were red and rimmed with tears. She trembled as she spoke. 'We've no rooms,' she said, barely above a whisper. 'The hotel's closed.'

'We don't wish for rooms,' said Oscar, gently. 'We have come to call on Mrs Wood.'

'I am Susannah Wood,' she said.

'My name is Oscar Wilde,' said Oscar, making a small bow as he spoke, 'and this is my associate, Mr Robert Sherard.'

'What do you want?' said Mrs Wood, sharply. 'Who sent you?' She looked beyond us into the empty street. 'Who sent you?' she repeated, more loudly. 'Was it him? *Was it him?*'

'Nobody sent us,' said Oscar. 'We have come of our own volition. We have news – grave news – about your son.'

'About Billy?' she cried. 'Is he in trouble? What has happened? Has he come to harm?'

'I fear so,' said Oscar, solemnly. 'Madam, may we come in?'

We stepped across the threshold of The Castle as Mrs Wood backed away from us, alarmed. 'What is it?' she cried. 'What has happened? Tell me. Tell me!'

Quietly Oscar closed the door behind us. He turned back to Mrs Wood and removed his hat. He said, 'Billy is dead, Mrs Wood. He has been murdered. I am so sorry.'

'No,' shrieked the poor woman. 'No. It isn't so. It can't be.'

'I fear it is,' said Oscar, stepping towards her. 'God have mercy on his soul.'

He put out his hands as if to take her in his arms, but, violently, she pushed him away, shrieking through her sobs, 'Who are you? Why do you come here? Why do you tell me these lies?'

'These are no lies, dear lady. I was Billy's friend, believe me, and on Tuesday last, in London, I found his murdered body, by candlelight, in an upstairs room.'

'It wasn't Billy,' she sobbed. 'It can't have been.'

'It was,' said Oscar.

'I don't believe you!' she cried.

'You must,' he said. 'I bring you proof.' He handed me his hat and, reaching into his coat pocket, he produced a tiny paper package. He placed it in the palm of his hand and unfolded the paper to reveal a thin gold wedding band, smeared with blood.

'My wedding ring!' she cried.

'I know,' said Oscar. 'Billy told me. He wore it always. When I found his body, I took it from his finger to bring it to you.'

8

The Secrets of The Castle

Susannah Wood snatched the wedding band from Oscar's hand and pressed it to her lips.

'My boy,' she whimpered, 'my boy is dead . . .'

'I fear he is,' said Oscar, placing both his arms about the poor woman's shoulders.

'Why?' she wailed. 'Why? Who has done this to my darling boy?'

'I do not know,' said Oscar, now holding the bereaved mother close to him, 'but as I was Billy's friend I will be your friend, also. I will discover the truth, Mrs Wood. I promise you that.'

Suddenly, she pushed herself away from him. 'I must come to London at once,' she cried. 'I must see his body. I must see his beautiful face one last time. Is my boy dead? How was he killed? When was this? On Tuesday, you say – by candlelight? In an upstairs room? Why? Why?' She sobbed as she spoke and began to toss her head violently from side to side.

'Be calm, dear lady,' said Oscar, 'I will answer for you what questions I can. Be calm, I beseech you.'

'Forgive me,' said the distraught woman, taking a deep breath and attempting to contain her grief. 'He was my only joy.' Slowly, she brought her hand up close to her face, opened it and gazed upon the bloodied wedding band. She leant forward and kissed the ring once more before slipping it onto her third finger and pushing it up against the wedding band that she already wore. She looked up at Oscar. 'Who are you?' she asked. 'How did you come to know my son?'

'I am a writer,' said Oscar, 'and a teacher. I met your son by chance.'

'In London?' she asked.

'In London,' he said, 'about a year ago. I liked him at once. He was a bright boy – and eager to learn. He hoped to become an actor, you know.'

'I know,' she said.

'We met, perhaps once a month, sometimes more often. I gave him lessons in "spoken English". We read Shakespeare together. He was a quick student and, in truth, he had not much need of me. He was blessed with a natural gift: an athletic voice, an easy grace and such a sparkle in his eye! Above all, he had energy – boundless energy – and energy is the secret of all worldly success.'

'I realise who you are now,' she said, touching his hand. 'Billy spoke of you. He called you "Oscar".'

'We were friends.'

'He was grateful to you, Mr Wilde, I know,' she said. 'He spoke very little of his life in London, but he spoke of you. He trusted you.'

'I am glad of that,' said Oscar.

'May I get you some tea?' she asked, wiping the tears from her face.

'That would be a kindness,' said Oscar. 'Let us have tea – and let us talk. If I am to help you, Mrs Wood, if I am to find who has murdered your son, you must tell me everything – about yourself, about Billy, about the man we met in the street just now . . .'

She nodded. 'And you must tell me all you know of Billy's death,' she said.

'I will tell you what I know,' said Oscar.

In the dimly lit, faded front parlour of The Castle, seated at a table laid for breakfast some weeks before, over many cups of hot, sweet tea – the beverage that only the English turn to in times of sorrow – Oscar told Susannah Wood all he knew of the circumstances of the death of her son. It did not take long. And when he had finished, he asked her: 'Did Billy have enemies, Mrs Wood? Can you imagine who would have wished to take his life in this horrible way?'

The poor woman sat in silence, staring blankly at the table. Eventually, she spoke. 'I knew virtually nothing of his life in London,' she said, 'I am so ashamed.'

Oscar took her hand in his. 'Tell me of your own life,' he said, gently. 'Tell me your story, and Billy's story, too. Tell me everything.'

'Actors are so fortunate,' Oscar wrote to me in a letter once. 'They can choose whether they appear in tragedy or in comedy, whether they will suffer or make merry, laugh or shed tears. But in real life it is different. There are no choices. All the world's a stage, but we must play as we are cast.'

As she told her story, told us of the part that real life had thrown her way, I sensed that Susannah Wood had waited a long time to unburden herself. She spoke fitfully, but with an apparent openness that was disarming. As she spoke, occasionally her grief came crashing in upon her like huge waves upon a beach. When a wave struck, suddenly she sobbed uncontrollably and clung to Oscar as she might have done to a beloved father; when the wave had broken and the water had crept back across the sand, she dried her eyes and spoke fluently and fast as though desperate to say what she had to say before the next wave should overwhelm her. She directed everything she said to Oscar – only to Oscar – but as I listened to her tale and, at Oscar's behest, took written notes of the essential points, I believed it all.

Oscar had been mistaken about her: she was neither a Mrs Todgers nor a Mrs Gummidge. To begin with, she was only thirty-four years of age and she was handsome. She was not blemish-free – her copper hair was flecked with grey; her pale green eyes were bloodshot; there were tight lines around her mouth and a livid red birthmark on her neck – but she had a dignity and grace about her that I would not have expected to find in the landlady of a small seaside hotel. Despite her coarse-grained, work-aday grey dress, she had the figure of a lady, not a drudge. She was especially striking, also, because she was of above average height and, even in her sorrow, held her head high.

She told us she had been born in 1855, on 11 August – 'Ah,' murmured Oscar, 'the feast of St Susan' – and was the bastard child of a Mr Thomas Wood, a solicitor of Gray's Inn Road, London WC. Her mother, whose name she had never known, had died in childbirth. Her father, who had been born in the year of the Battle of Trafalgar, died at about the time of her fifth birthday, in the summer of 1860. She had been brought up by an elderly couple – Mary and Joseph Skipwith, now deceased – who lived in Bromley, a suburb in south-east London, and who, once upon a time, had worked for her father as cook and gardener.

The Skipwiths were austere, God-fearing folk. They had no children of their own and cherished no particular fondness for Susannah. They did their duty by her, because of their respect for her father and because he paid them to do so. He did not pay them very much – Mr Skipwith made that plain to her – but he paid them 'sufficiently', and in this life (in which, as the Psalmist teaches us, we can expect no more than to be fed upon the bread of tears) a 'sufficiency' must be counted a blessing.

The Skipwiths were devoted to the words of the Psalmist and assiduous in counting their blessings. They required Susannah to follow their example: to read her Bible every morning and every night, and to thank God for her good fortune at every opportunity. As a child, Susannah was never idle. From the age of eight to the age of twelve, she attended the Poor School in Bromley, but, except for those hours when she was in the classroom, or walking to or from school, or in church, or walking to or from church, she was always occupied doing the work that God, and the Skipwiths, had ordained for her: sweeping, scrubbing, mopping, scouring, peeling, shelling, washing, sewing, making, mending. Mrs Skipwith taught her how to run a house. Mr Skipwith taught her how to manage a garden, grow and pick vegetables, light fires, chop wood and wield a knife.

Joseph Skipwith was skilled with a knife. He could slaughter and skin a rabbit or a hare and have it ready for the pot, in a matter of minutes. He was also skilled at woodcarving, and from him Susannah learnt to use a simple kitchen knife and pieces of wood gathered at random – small logs and fallen branches – to craft models of every kind. With Mr Skipwith's help, when she was eleven, Susannah carved a Noah's ark of beechwood – the ark was more than two feet in length – and a complete menagerie of creatures, great and small, to dwell within it. She was fifteen when, one Sunday evening after evensong, Mr Skipwith forced himself upon her, attempting to kiss her on her lips and to place his hands upon her body. When she resisted him, he threw the ark and all the animals upon the fire, railing against her vanity, her arrogance and her ingratitude.

While she lived with the Skipwiths, Susannah wanted for nothing, except happiness. Her life in Bromley was as she expected it to be: a vale of tears. She knew – she had known ever since she could remember – that she would not always live with the Skipwiths, that on her eighteenth birthday it was preordained that her life would change, but she had no notion until the day itself what that change might be. The Skipwiths had told her that, although she was a bastard child, nonetheless her father was an honourable man who recognised that, in this world as much as the next, there is a price to be paid for every sin and that, in consequence, he had provided for her future – and theirs. And so it proved.

On 11 August 1873, from the estate of the late Thomas Wood Esquire, of Gray's Inn Road, London WC, Joseph and Mary Skipwith received an ex gratia payment of three hundred and fifty pounds in final recognition of services rendered. Susannah Wood, his acknowledged natural daughter, received the title deeds to a freehold property known as The Castle, Harbour Street, Broadstairs, Kent, together with an income of eighty pounds per annum guaranteed for life.

Mr and Mrs Skipwith were satisfied with their reward. Mr Skipwith said it was 'sufficient', but he said it, according to Susannah, with an unwonted touch of colour in his cheeks, suggesting to her that the sum exceeded his wildest expectations. Susannah herself was overwhelmed by her inheritance. 'I did not know what happiness was, Mr Wilde, until that moment. Happiness is freedom. My father gave me this house and, in so doing, he set me free. He gave me a home of my own; he gave me an occupation; he gave me an income; he gave me happiness. And I never knew him.'

The Castle was one of several seaside properties owned by Thomas Wood. When Susannah acquired it, it was a dilapidated rooming house. Within two years of her ownership, before the summer of her twentieth birthday, she had transformed it into a respectable residential and visitors' hotel. 'This was my castle, Mr Wilde.'

'And when, one day, a prince came to your castle,' said Oscar, 'for a moment your happiness was complete.'

She laughed through her tears. 'How did you know?' she asked.

'I am myself the writer of fairy tales,' said Oscar. 'I know how they begin. I know how they end. I weep for you. What was he called, your prince?'

'His name? William O'Donnell,' said Mrs Wood.

'William O'Donnell?' repeated Oscar.

'Yes,' she said. 'He was just a boy—'

'But he had beauty?' suggested Oscar.

'Yes,' she said, eagerly, placing her hand on his. 'How do you know all this?'

'I know nothing,' said Oscar, 'but I surmise . . . Your prince was a lighthouse keeper . . .'

Susannah Wood started suddenly and put her hands to her mouth in astonishment.

'He was young,' Oscar went on, 'he was beautiful, he was brave. And he died at sea.'

'How do you know?' she gasped. 'I have told no one.'

I was equally amazed. 'How do you know this, Oscar?' I asked.

Oscar turned to me and smiled. 'Look about you, Robert,' he said. 'What do you see upon the parlour walls? What did you observe as we passed through the hallway?'

I looked around the dingy room. 'Pictures?' I hazarded. Now I saw that the walls were covered with a profusion of framed pictures of various shapes and sizes.

'Yes, Robert, "pictures" – prints, etchings and engravings, lithographs and mezzotints. And do you not see? Mrs Wood has chosen these pictures, not for their artistic merit – the quality of the art is indifferent – but for their subject matter. Have you not noticed that every one of these pictures depicts a similar scene – either that of a lighthouse or that of a shipwreck? Mrs Wood has created a shrine to her secret sadness.'

'No sooner had I found him,' she said, as if to herself, 'than I lost him. And now I have lost my Billy, too.'

Oscar got to his feet and moved closer to the chair where Mrs Wood was seated. He placed his right hand upon her shoulder. 'When we find Billy's body, I promise you this,' he said solemnly. 'If you so wish, Billy, too, shall be laid to rest in the sea – the sea that, as Euripides says in one of his plays about Iphigenia, washes away the stains and wounds of the world.'

Susannah Wood turned and looked up toward Oscar. 'I do not entirely follow you, Mr Wilde.'

Oscar smiled. 'I would be sorry if you did,' he said. 'I imagine Euripides is not much read in Bromley.'

'No,' she said, a little confused, 'but we had the complete works of Dickens in Bromley – as well as the Bible.'

'Indeed,' said Oscar, with a small sniff. 'I am not surprised.'

Suddenly, Susannah Wood clutched at Oscar's hand and began to weep once more. 'Oh, Mr Wilde,' she sobbed, 'will you find whoever has done this terrible thing?'

'I will,' said Oscar. 'You have my word.'

Gently, he broke away from the grieving mother and turned to me. 'Come, Robert,' he said, 'we have work to do. We must leave Mrs Wood to her sorrow and return to London.'

'I must come with you,' she cried, getting to her feet.

'No,' said Oscar, firmly, 'not yet. It is too soon. The time will come, no doubt, but there is nothing you can achieve in London now.'

'But I must help you, Mr Wilde, in every way I can.'

Oscar was standing by the parlour door, examining one of the larger prints of a storm at sea. He turned back and looked steadily at Mrs Wood. 'You can answer me one more question, if you will . . .'

'Gladly,' she said. Her eyes were dry again. Her head was held high.

'Your prince – young William O'Donnell – was the father of Billy Wood?' he asked.

'Yes,' she said.

'But when William O'Donnell died at sea, he did not know that he had a son?'

'No, he did not.' She shook her head. 'Poor William,' she sighed. 'He had no idea. How could he? It was all so sudden.'

Oscar offered her a reassuring smile. 'When did you first meet William O'Donnell?' he asked.

'We met in August – the August that I came here, the August of my eighteenth birthday. I had only been at The Castle a matter of days. He came to call, "to introduce himself", he said. He found me on my hands and knees, scrubbing the front doorstep. I remember his first words to me. "Good morning, Mrs – or is it Miss?" Even then I wore a wedding ring and dressed as a widow; it was a mask I hid behind. It made me feel more secure and older than my years.'

For a moment, Mrs Wood put her hands to her eyes, then she smiled wearily and lowered them again.

'He raised his cap to me. His hair was golden. He told me he was the lad from the North Foreland lighthouse and that he was collecting subscriptions to help fund the lifeboat stationed in Viking Bay. He told me he worked on the lifeboat himself. His smile was wonderful, Mr Wilde. He was so handsome. Willingly, instantly, I promised him a shilling a month for the lifeboat. I invited him into the house, into this room, and offered him a glass of lemonade. We became friends that afternoon and, within days, we had become lovers, also.'

She paused and gazed down at the rings on her finger. 'Who knew of your friendship?' Oscar asked.

'No one. It was our secret. The Castle was our secret kingdom. Yes, we were children, living in a fairy tale of our own making. I was eighteen. He was seventeen. We were so young. We played together. We laughed and sang together. And we lay together. We knew it was a sin, and yet . . . How could it be a sin when it was so natural and it made us both so glad to be alive?'

Oscar was studying the inscription beneath the print on the parlour wall. 'So William died barely five months after your first meeting,' he said, 'on the night of 7 January 1874, in the great storm that drove the *Dolphin* aground on the Goodwin Sands.'

'Yes,' she said. 'Three lifeboats set out to rescue the sloop in that terrible tempest. Five men lost their lives. William was the youngest. I discovered that I was with child three weeks later. I told no one who the father was. I bore the child – and the shame of seeming to be a widow bearing a child out of wedlock – alone. Alone, Mr Wilde. No one knew my secret. No one knows it still, except for you and . . . Edward O'Donnell.' She flinched as she spoke the name.

'The brute that we saw in the street?' I asked, looking up from my notebook.

'Yes,' answered Mrs Wood. 'He does not know the truth for certain. I have admitted nothing. But he has guessed. And he knows he has guessed right.'

'This Edward O'Donnell,' said Oscar, 'he is William O'Donnell's father?'

'No, he is my William's elder brother and, when he is in drink, he is as heartless and cruel as my William was tender and loving. Edward O'Donnell has been my tormentor these past two years.'

'Two years?' Oscar queried.

'When William died and Billy was born, Edward was abroad. He was ten years William's senior. At sixteen, he had joined a French steamer and gone to Canada to seek his fortune. At first he prospered, and then, in Montreal, living among the French, he learnt to drink. Eventually, all but destitute, he found a ship that would bring him home. I did not know of his existence until two years ago.' Suddenly, another wave of grief came crashing down upon her. 'That man has ruined my life,' she sobbed, 'destroyed it. He ruined Billy's life, too. If Billy is dead, it is Edward's doing.'

'Calm yourself, madam,' said Oscar. 'I have told you: whoever is responsible for Billy's death shall be brought to justice.'

'Directly or indirectly, Edward O'Donnell is responsible,' she cried. 'He took him to London. He corrupted him. He introduced him to a man called Bellotti and, through him, to a life of vice. I am so ashamed. Until he came into our lives, we were innocent.'

'Calm yourself,' said Oscar, 'you are innocent still.'

'No, I am not,' cried Mrs Wood. 'I took Edward O'Donnell to my bed. He forced himself upon me and I acquiesced. I acquiesced, Mr Wilde. He said, as William's brother, that he had the right.' She was weeping uncontrollably now. 'He said, if I did not submit to him, he would share my secret with the world. I should have let him. What would the world have cared? Instead, I submitted to him in his rage and in his drunkenness. He came to the house holding a letter that William had sent to him fourteen years before. It was no more than a note, a few lines, but it told him that William had met me – that I was a widow "with a fortune" and "the love of his life" . . . Edward guessed the rest, and took advantage of it. I let him live here with us. I gave him shelter. I gave him money. Because he was William's brother, because he was Billy's uncle, his flesh and blood, I let my poor child fall under his sway. I let him take my Billy to London. Billy wanted to discover the world and make his fortune. I let him go. God has punished me for my weakness, for my *sinfulness*. The Skipwiths were right. God is not mocked.'

Her grief had turned to anger, but, just as swiftly, she took control of herself. Wiping her eyes once more and straightening her dress, she extended a hand to Oscar and said, 'Forgive me, Mr Wilde. You and your friend have come here with good intent and I have laid my sorry, broken heart before you. You must go back to London now. I know that.'

Oscar looked about the room one final time. 'We shall return before long,' he said, 'when we have news. Meanwhile,' he asked, 'will you be safe?'

'Yes,' she said, 'I am of no interest to Edward O'Donnell now. He has done his worst. He cannot harm me further. Besides, he needs me still. Even in his drunkenness, he knows that. He has a room beside the kitchen. He has a key to the basement door. He comes and goes as he pleases. Often I do not see him for days on end. When he first arrived, he was sometimes sober and I grew fond of him because he had something of my William's look about him. He is William's brother. He is Billy's uncle. He has ruined us, I know it – but he is all I have.'

As soon as Mrs Wood had closed the front door of The Castle behind us, Oscar said, 'There is a telegraph office at the railway station, managed, no doubt, by a veritable Mr Jingle. We will send a wire to Fraser before we catch our train. I will confess the matter of the ring to him. We will tell him of O'Donnell – and Bellotti, too. He will have little choice but to see us again now.'

9

A Candle at the Window

But Aidan Fraser did have a choice, and he exercised it.

By the time we reached the Albemarle Club it was gone midnight. The front door was locked and the windows looking onto the street were in darkness, but Oscar rang the bell nevertheless. Almost instantaneously, Hubbard swung open the door and stepped back, obsequiously, to admit us, murmuring as he did so, 'You'll be wanting a nightcap, Mr Wilde?'

'Thank you,' said Oscar, pressing a coin into the servant's hand, 'you deserve one, too.' (I never saw Oscar fumbling in his pockets for change. Effortlessly, like a professional prestidigitator, he appeared always to have precisely the appropriate coin ready between his fingers at the exact moment required.) 'You're closing up, I know. We'll just perch in Keppel Corner. We'll not keep you late, I promise. Any messages for me?'

'Four telegrams, sir,' said Hubbard, with satisfaction. 'I'll bring them to you directly, sir, with the champagne.'

The Albemarle had not yet been equipped with electric light. We sat, in sepulchral gloom, beneath a single gasolier, in Keppel Corner, an alcove adjacent to the club's main staircase. The alcove took its name from the handsome youth – with amused eyes and a pleasing mouth – whose fine portrait, said to be by Sir Godfrey Kneller, adorned the back wall. Aged just nineteen, Arnold Joost van Keppel was brought to England from Holland in the retinue of King William III. He was the king's catamite – reputedly. Certainly, he was one of the sovereign's favourites. Aged twenty-six, in 1696, he was created 1st Earl of Albemarle. Whenever he saw the portrait, Oscar would offer up a small sigh and whisper, 'I was adored once, too.'

Hubbard brought the champagne and the telegrams. Oscar examined the envelopes in turn. 'We shall start with this one, I think,' he said, tearing open an envelope. 'It is indeed from our friend – if that is how we should view him.' Oscar passed the telegram to me. I read it with some incredulity: 'MUCH REGRET CANNOT SEE YOU IMMEDIATELY. WILL MAKE CONTACT IN DUE COURSE. REGARDS FRASER.'

'What is the meaning of it?' I asked.

'And what is the meaning of this?' countered Oscar. He had opened the second envelope. 'A second communication from Inspector Fraser – this one, it seems, despatched exactly an hour after the first.'

'He's had second thoughts?'

'A further thought, in any event,' said Oscar, reading out the policeman's second wire: 'REST ASSURED YOU WILL UNDERSTAND ONCE I EXPLAIN. FRASER.'

'He wishes to reassure us,' said Oscar. 'I wonder why?'

'He fails to reassure us,' I exclaimed, 'utterly! Edward O'Donnell is on the loose. He could commit a further atrocity.'

Oscar put down his glass and gazed at me, wide-eyed. 'O'Donnell is not our murderer, Robert.' He laughed. 'Come now, man, you cannot think that?'

'But I do,' I protested. 'We have seen him. We know what he is like. We have heard Mrs Wood's story—'

'O'Donnell is a brute and a drunkard.'

'Precisely.'

'Robert, whoever murdered Billy Wood was not a drunkard. I found Billy's body lying neatly on the floor, his arms folded across his chest, guttering candles arranged around him. Not twenty-four hours later you visited the scene of the crime yourself – and smelt the beeswax polish on the floor. The body was gone – there was order in the room, cleanliness, and not a shred of evidence to be found, bar the fleck of blood that Arthur discovered high up on the wall. None of this could have been the work of a shambling drunkard such as Edward O'Donnell.'

'But Mrs Wood said he was responsible—'

'Indirectly, perhaps. He may have brought the boy to London on the fatal day. Yes, Robert, O'Donnell may help lead us to the guilty party, but he is not the murderer himself: of that I'm certain.'

'Mrs Wood said it was O'Donnell who had introduced Billy to Bellotti and—'

'Yes,' said Oscar, interrupting, 'I was intrigued by that because Bellotti, you will recall, told us that he had met Billy two years ago when he stayed at The Castle. Do you think Mrs Wood had forgotten Mr Bellotti's summer sojourn at her hotel?'

'Possibly,' I ventured.

Oscar laughed. 'I think not, Robert. A presence like Mr Bellotti's is neither easily overlooked nor quickly forgotten.'

'Are you saying that Mrs Wood was lying to us?' I asked, incredulous.

'I am saying, Robert, that in the matter of murder no one is to be trusted. As the plot thickens, remember that – above all else. Deception is the order of the day. Why, look at me! I took that wedding band from Billy's lifeless finger within minutes of his murder – his hand was still warm, his fingers still soft and pliable. Did I tell Conan Doyle about the ring? Did I mention it to Fraser?'

'You had your reasons,' I said. 'Mrs Wood might not have believed that Billy was dead if you had not produced the ring.'

'Indeed,' said Oscar. 'I had my reasons – just as Susannah Wood has her reasons for telling us it was Edward O'Donnell and not she who introduced her unfortunate son to Gerard Bellotti.'

'We will return to Bellotti, I presume?' I asked. 'We will question him further?'

'In due course,' replied my friend, casually.

'And should we not interview O'Donnell ourselves if Fraser will not?'

Oscar smiled and, languidly, raised his glass of champagne in my direction. 'I do not believe that you or I, Robert – robust as we are – would get very far interrogating a brute such as Edward O'Donnell.'

'Well then,' I said, 'who is your third telegram from? Perhaps Inspector Fraser has decided to come to our aid after all.'

Oscar tore open the third envelope. 'No,' he said, perusing the contents, 'this is from Stoddart – my American publisher. He wants me to write a hundred thousand words – by November! He is absurd. There are not a hundred thousand beautiful words in the English language.'

'Will you do it?' I asked.

'I must,' he sighed. 'I need the money.' He leant towards me with the bottle of champagne and topped up my glass. 'Work, Robert, is the curse of the drinking classes. We must pay for our pleasures. Mr Stoddart is offering me an advance of a hundred pounds.'

I was impressed, but I was envious, too. (I was then working on my study of Emile Zola and was expecting a total fee for my labours in the region of ten to fifteen pounds.)

'I shall start on Stoddart's story tomorrow. I am going to visit my Aunt Jane. I shall take my notebook and sit at the bottom of her garden, beneath the ilex tree.'

'Oscar,' I said, smiling, 'you do not have an Aunt Jane.'

'She is very old,' said Oscar, peering into his glass. 'Come to think of it, she is dead. She died of neglect. People like you never believed in her. The young are so heartless. As I cannot go to stay with Aunt Jane, I shall go to Oxford instead.'

As I came to know, Oxford was a special place to Oscar. In times of travail, when he sought refuge, or comfort, or consolation, and when he felt the need for distraction, or wanted inspiration, he turned to Oxford. It was where, in the 1870s, as a dazzling undergraduate, he had first heard the tunes of glory and tasted the bitter-sweet fruit of national notoriety. Oxford was the well-spring of the myth of Oscar Wilde. Oscar knew it and never forgot it.

What I never forget is that Oscar, while a gentleman, was not an Englishman. He was Irish. He understood English ways (none better!) and spoke the English language as only an Irishman can, but he was not educated at an English public school; he did not have the English feeling for Dickens; he did not play rugby (imagine if he had!) or care for cricket; he neither rode to hounds nor shot nor fished. He did not wear an old-school tie. In England, overall, Oscar was an outsider. In Oxford, uniquely, he felt at ease; he was at home. He liked to say: 'Oxford is the capital of Romance, in its own way as memorable as Athens.' I teased him and told him that he was sentimental about Oxford only because it was where – aged twenty – he had sowed his wild oats. With playful indignation, he reproved me: 'Robert, I have never sowed wild oats. I have planted a few orchids, that is all.'

Oscar claimed to reverence Oxford for its architecture and its intellectual life, but, in truth, what drew him back there, time and again, was the promise and the prospect of youth. He went to Oxford to spend time with the undergraduates and the younger university dons, to be amused by their conversation, to be charmed by their good looks, to be warmed by their admiration. He admitted as much to me that night at the Albemarle Club. 'I see what I want to see of myself reflected in them,' he said. 'I look into their faces as into a looking-glass and, for a moment, I feel young again. Youth! Youth, Robert! There is absolutely nothing in the world but youth!'

I laughed. 'Forty-eight hours ago, Oscar, there was nothing in the world but justice! As I recall, the day before yesterday, fuelled by Mr Simpson's fine wines, you were committed to befriending the friendless. You vowed not to rest until you had achieved justice for Billy Wood. Now, it seems youth is everything and justice is to take a sabbatical while you go floating down to Oxford.'

My friend narrowed his eyes and looked at me sternly. 'I shall not be floating down to Oxford, Robert. I shall be going by train. And when I get there, justice will not be forgotten. Our investigation will go forward, Robert – even without us. I have my methods, Robert.' He tapped the side of his nose conspiratorially. 'I have my spies. Shh.'

Hubbard was hovering. We had finished our champagne. We got to our feet. A touch unsteadily, we left Keppel Corner and made our way across the hallway and out into the street. We stood together in silence on the club's front steps, absorbing the night, listening as the porter, with a heavy hand, laboriously turned the keys in the locks and bolted the door behind us.

The street before us was dark and unwelcoming. There were precious few street lamps in the byways of Mayfair in those days. There was a chill in the night air; the moon was hidden and the sky was overcast.

Oscar put his arm in mine and said, 'Walk me to the cab rank, there's a good fellow.'

'By all means,' I said.

We came down the steps and turned left into Albemarle Street. Slowly, arm in arm, we made our way towards Piccadilly. It was approaching two o'clock in the morning and such was the all-enveloping darkness that it was difficult to see more than a few steps ahead. The deserted street was as silent as a morgue. We heard our own boots clacking on the pavement, but nothing else. Then, quite suddenly, as we passed the Albemarle Hotel, six doors down from the club, I sensed, without seeing it, the presence of a figure standing in the shadows. Oscar breathed, 'Come, Robert, let us walk a little faster.'

We quickened our pace and, as we did so, I heard footsteps behind us. I stopped abruptly; the footsteps stopped also. Immediately, Oscar pulled me forward. 'Come!' he hissed. My heart beat faster; my mouth was dry. As we moved on, now half walking, half running, the figure kept pace behind us. I made to turn my head to look over my shoulder, but Oscar muttered 'Don't!' and pulled me on.

Out of the corner of my eye, I had glimpsed a cloaked figure. It was a man of medium height and heavy build. I could swear to no more than that. I wanted to look again, but Oscar stopped me. 'Is it O'Donnell?' I whispered.

'No,' said Oscar. 'It is no one.'

We had nearly reached Piccadilly. There were lights ahead of us. Oscar's pace was slackening. 'I believe it is O'Donnell,' I persisted.

Oscar stopped in his tracks. 'It is no one, Robert,' he said, 'no one at all. Look.'

We turned back and stared down the darkened street behind us. There was no one to be seen. The man had disappeared. The street seemed utterly empty and then, suddenly, we heard scampering feet. 'What's that?' I cried.

'Nothing,' said Oscar, 'just a boy.'

Running down the road away from us, vanishing into the darkness, was a small figure with a large head. 'It's Bellotti's dwarf,' I said.

'I think not,' said Oscar, chuckling. 'Come, let's find a cab.'

A young policeman was standing at the corner of Piccadilly and Albemarle Street. He touched his helmet as we approached. Oscar nodded to him: 'Goodnight, officer.'

'Goodnight, gentlemen,' said the young constable. 'It's a cold one, for the time of year.'

We crossed Piccadilly to the all-night cab rank that once stood on what is now the site of the Ritz Hotel. As we waited for a cab to appear, Oscar took the sheaf of telegrams from his coat pocket and began to place them neatly inside his wallet. 'Tomorrow I shall send a note to Fraser from Oxford,' he said. 'I will tell him what we have learnt today from Mrs Wood. I will tell him, too, what we know of Edward O'Donnell. I will omit no detail.'

'I'm glad of that,' I said.

'And the moment I get further word from Fraser, have no fear, Robert, I shall let you know.'

I observed that Oscar had left the last of the telegrams unopened. 'You have not read the final telegram, Oscar,' I said. 'Perhaps it is yet another message from Fraser?'

'No,' he answered, holding up the unopened envelope. 'This comes from Yorkshire. It is from Constance.'

'You have not opened it.'

'There is no need. I can read her thoughts.'

Playfully, I took the envelope from him. 'What does it say then?' I asked.

'If you must know, Robert, it says, "I love you, always."'

'May I?' I enquired. He smiled and nodded. I tore open the telegram. It read precisely as Oscar had predicted: 'I LOVE YOU. ALWAYS.'

' "Always"!' he cried. 'That is a dreadful word, Robert, is it not? It makes me shudder when I hear it. Women are so fond of using it. They spoil every romance by trying to make it last for ever.'

A two-wheeler appeared. Oscar pocketed his wallet and clambered in. 'Goodnight, Robert,' he said. 'It has been an eventful day – even to the last. Note it all in your journal. Remember, you are my Dr Watson now.'

'Goodnight, Oscar,' I said. 'Take care!'

As I watched him go, a second cab arrived at the rank and, on the spur of the moment, suddenly fearful for my friend, I decided to follow him, to see him safely home. As I climbed aboard, I said to the driver, 'Follow that cab, if you please – but at a distance.'

'Right you are, guv,' said the cabman, without expression, as if trailing other cabs through the West End of London in the early hours of the morning was a routine occurrence. Perhaps it was. He did it expertly. At a discreet distance of around a hundred yards, our hansom followed Oscar's as it made its way, not, as I had expected, south towards Chelsea, but north, towards Soho. We travelled along Piccadilly, across the circus and into what was then London's newest thoroughfare: Shaftesbury Avenue. There was little traffic on the road and, on the pavements, not much by way of humanity: a few luckless women of the night, mostly in pairs, still plying their trade; small clusters of what we used to call the 'Won't go home till morning boys' in search of one more drink; the odd, solitary Pall Mall clubman, pondering the possibilities ahead. The gap between our carriages closed a little as we passed the new Lyric Theatre – where the young Marie Tempest was then appearing – and turned sharply left into Frith Street. I began to realise whither we were bound and, as Oscar's hansom trundled into Soho Square, I called to my cabman, 'Whoa! Stop!'

Oscar's cab halted in the square itself. I watched my friend as he clambered out and stood on the pavement gazing up at a tall, narrow building on the east side of the square. The building was cloaked in darkness, but for one small circle of light that stood out against the black, like a pale carnation in a buttonhole. Up on the third floor there was a window and, standing at it, holding a candle in her hand, was the girl with the disfigured face. In the street below, Oscar stood staring straight towards her. The moment she saw him, she started and then raised her hand in what seemed a kind of greeting. Oscar raised his hand towards her by way of answer, and as he did so, she leant towards the candle and blew it out. The window was in darkness. Immediately, Oscar climbed back into his two-wheeler and set off once more.

'Drive on,' I said to my cabman. 'Follow him.' We did – north out of Soho Square, west along Oxford Street, south down Bond Street and into Albemarle Street, to the front door of the Albemarle Hotel, six doors along from the Albemarle Club, which Oscar and I had left together but forty minutes before. Oscar sometimes stayed at the Albemarle Hotel. I knew that, but because I had not anticipated that his cab would come to a halt there, when his hansom stopped, mine, unfortunately, was immediately behind.

Oscar stepped up to the hotel door and rang the bell. A moment later, the door swung open and the night porter admitted him. As he crossed the threshold, Oscar paused, half turned towards the street and called out, 'Goodnight, Robert. I am quite safe, as you see.'

The following morning, Oscar went to Oxford and began to write the story that would become *The Picture of Dorian Gray*. I heard nothing from him for six weeks.

10

16 October 1889

I next saw my friend, Oscar Wilde, on 16 October 1889, the day of his thirty-fifth birthday. We met, at his suggestion, by the flower-stall that stands at the entrance to Sloane Square underground station. He had proposed 4.30 p.m. for our rendezvous and had urged me to be on time – and, for once, I was. I was eager to see him. I had missed him greatly.

I was somewhat startled by his appearance, however, for though he looked well – his head was held high and his customarily pallid cheeks were a healthy pink – he was dressed, from top to toe, in deepest mourning. His coat was black, his tie was black, and in his black-gloved hand he held a black top hat complete with silk mourning bands. More curiously still, though dressed in mourning, he was wreathed in smiles.

'Youth smiles without any reason,' he said as we shook hands. 'It is one of its chiefest charms. I smile because I am happy to see you again, Robert, very happy.'

'And I am happy to see you, Oscar,' I replied, 'though alarmed to find you dressed like this.'

He looked down at his funereal garb and explained: 'This happens to be my birthday, Robert, and on each of my anniversaries I mourn the flight of one year of my youth into nothingness, the growing blight upon my summer . . . *Tempus fugit inreparabile!*' He put his hand on my shoulder. 'But I have not wasted time these past six weeks, though time has wasted me. I have made positive progress with my story for Stoddart.'

'I'm glad to hear it,' I said.

'And negative progress with our investigation into the murder of poor Billy Wood.'

' "Negative progress"?' I repeated. 'What does that mean?'

'It means,' he said, turning his attention from me to the flower-stall, 'that I have eliminated all sorts of distracting possibilities – spared us the time and effort of exploring profitless cul-de-sacs ourselves by sending others in our stead.' He stood contemplating a bucket filled with scarlet-coloured roses. 'For example, over the past six weeks my spies have called upon every one of the house-keepers lately on the books of Messrs O'Donovan & Brown of Ludgate Circus – and none of them appears to have been in the vicinity of 23 Cowley Street on the day of poor Billy's murder.'

I laughed. 'Who are these "spies" of yours, Oscar?'

He looked at me. 'They are secret agents, Robert. If I told you who they were, that would rather ruin the point of them, would it not? But, believe me, they are good fellows and to be relied upon. While I have been scribbling away in Oxford, they have been roaming the streets of London and Broadstairs – keeping an eye on your prime suspects. You will be disappointed to learn, Robert, that, in our absence, neither Edward O'Donnell nor Gerard Bellotti has behaved in the least bit suspiciously. Were they guilty of murder, you might think that they would have left the country or attempted to do so . . . In fact, according to the reports I have received, each has gone about his seedy business in his customary fashion.'

'And Mrs Wood?'

'I have corresponded with Mrs Wood,' he said, contemplating the bucket of roses once again and carefully selecting a single stem. 'Her sorrow is profound and unfeigned. I do not believe she is our murderer, but neither do I believe that she is yet telling us all that she might.'

I frowned at my friend. 'So, six weeks on and we are no farther forward?' I said.

'We are much farther forward, Robert,' said Oscar, threading the rose stem into my buttonhole. 'This autumn bloom is named in honour of the Black Prince. Well worth the sixpence, don't you think? We are *much* farther on, *mon ami*. We have eliminated all sorts of possibilities – and we have secured an audience with Inspector Fraser of the Yard!'

'Goodness,' I exclaimed, 'we are going to Scotland Yard?' I was suddenly alarmed at the thought of how Oscar's funereal appearance might be received by the less imaginative members of the Metropolitan Police.

'No,' said Oscar, moving away from the flower-stall and leading us into the square, 'we are going to number 75 Lower Sloane Street – just here on the left. Fraser has summoned us to his home. He said that to meet him there "might be wiser". He even advised me to come incognito – and unaccompanied.'

'Hence,' I said, chuckling, 'your sombre apparel . . .'

'. . . And your invaluable presence, Robert! We are in this together. I have no secrets from you, my friend.'

'I'm glad to hear it,' I said with feeling, adding at once,

'indeed *proud* to hear it,' for I was proud of our friendship, proud to be the acknowledged true friend of the most brilliant man of his day. I was proud, too, of the unacknowledged trust that I sensed there was between us, though puzzled – I admit – both by the way in which Oscar had offered me no explanation of his nocturnal assignations with the strange girl with the disfigured face and by my own reluctance to cross-question him on the matter. I pondered this as we crossed into Lower Sloane Street – slipping between a dog cart and a chimney sweep on a bicycle – but I said nothing. Oscar – delighted to be crossing the path of a chimney sweep; he was superstitious to a degree – squeezed my shoulder in comradely affection and said, 'I think generosity is the essence of friendship, don't you?'

Number 75 Lower Sloane Street was a handsome house, built of red brick and Portland stone, with a pillared portico and marble steps, not the natural habitat of a detective inspector of police. The house, we later learnt, was part of Fraser's Fettes inheritance. We climbed the steps and Oscar rang the bell. We waited. We listened. We could hear nothing from within. Oscar rang the bell again and, as he did so, Fraser himself – not a servant – opened the door. He was as I remembered him – tall, slim, angular, clean-shaven, well-favoured, with a haunting face as white as frost – but his manner had changed. At our first encounter, he had been effortlessly engaging. Now he appeared fretful, anxious and preoccupied. He was thrown by Oscar's appearance and my presence.

Oscar, removing his black top hat, said at once, 'Do not be alarmed, Inspector. Mr Sherard's discretion can be assured – and I am only in mourning for my lost youth.'

Fraser seemed further confused.

'I do not mean poor Billy Wood,' said Oscar, realising the misunderstanding that his turn of phrase might have caused, 'though, indeed, I mourn for him – I mean the days before my present decrepitude.'

Fraser said nothing, but hesitantly stepped back, allowing us to enter the hallway.

'To win back my youth,' Oscar continued, unabashed, 'there is nothing I would not do – except, of course, take exercise, rise early or give up alcohol.'

Fraser said, starkly, 'I think we should talk before we take any refreshment.'

'Indeed,' replied Oscar, hanging his hat on the hallway hatstand and carefully aligning the silk mourning bands. 'I am sure you have found, Inspector, that while alcohol, taken in sufficient quantities, produces all the effect of intoxication, the only proper intoxication is conversation. I am looking forward to ours.'

'I hope you will not be disappointed,' said Fraser. 'Come into the drawing room, if you will.'

He led us across the hallway and into a large and graciously appointed reception room. There, at the far end of the room, standing in front of an ornate white marble fireplace, dressed in pepper-and-salt country tweeds, with an unlit pipe in his hand, was the reassuring figure of Arthur Conan Doyle.

His demeanour was far from reassuring, however. 'Oscar, Robert,' he mumbled awkwardly, by way of greeting, as we entered.

Oscar's ebullience would not be checked. Oscar, when most anxious, often appeared least so. 'You are looking very serious, Arthur,' he said, reprovingly.

'I have serious matters to relate,' Fraser interjected. 'I felt it would be best if Arthur were here – since he is a friend to us both.' He gestured towards a quartet of upright armchairs that were arranged either side of the fireplace. 'Gentlemen, let me get to the point. Please be seated.'

We did as we were bidden. The armchairs were French and uncomfortable. The atmosphere in the room was uncomfortable too, airless and oddly musty for the time of year. Fraser talked directly to Oscar, occasionally glancing towards Conan Doyle for encouragement. Not once did he look in my direction.

'I have asked you here,' he began, smiling for the first time since our arrival, 'precisely because you are a friend of Arthur's. He is an admirer of yours, Mr Wilde – as am I, of course. The truth is, I have a warning I need to give to you – and a piece of advice.'

Oscar smiled too. 'I have found people are very fond of giving to others what they most need themselves,' he said, removing his gloves and laying them neatly on the walnut side table that stood beside his chair. 'It is what I call the depths of generosity.'

Conan Doyle leant forward and said to Oscar earnestly, 'Listen to Aidan, Oscar. Be guided by him.'

With a raised eyebrow, Oscar inclined his head towards Fraser and said, 'I am listening.'

Fraser was calmer now. His nervousness was gone. He smiled again, revealing his extraordinary white teeth, and said, with some of his old charm, 'Thank you. And thank you for calling on me here today. And thank you, too, for being patient these past few weeks. I have not been in touch with you before for a reason, and the reason is this . . .' He paused and with a delicate thumb and forefinger lightly pinched his lips, looking briefly towards Conan Doyle who nodded to him to go on. 'Mr Wilde,' he asked, 'are you familiar with the address, 19 Cleveland Street?'

'No,' said Oscar.

'It's between Regent's Park and Oxford Street—'

'I am aware of the location of the street,' said Oscar. 'You asked whether I was familiar with the address. I am not.'

Fraser persisted. 'You are familiar with Lord Henry Somerset?' he enquired.

'I know whom you mean,' said Oscar. 'He is the son of the Duke of Beaufort. I have read his poetry. I have reviewed it. He has nothing to say and says it.'

'You have met?'

'Possibly. He lives in Florence, does he not?'

'He *fled* to Florence – to avoid a public scandal.'

Oscar sighed and with his right hand lightly brushed his trouser leg. 'Scandals used to lend charm, or at least interest, to a man. Now they crush him.'

Fraser continued, 'A scandal involving a young man by the name of Harry Smith.'

'That I do not recall,' said Oscar, emphatically.

'Do you know Lord Henry's younger brother, Lord Arthur Somerset?'

' "Podge"?' said Oscar. 'I know Podge a little. He is an equerry to the Prince of Wales.'

'And an habitué of 19 Cleveland Street.'

'Who?' exclaimed Oscar. 'The Prince of Wales?'

'No, Mr Wilde, not the Prince of Wales, though it is possible that his son, Prince Albert Victor, may be.'

Oscar laughed. 'Prince Eddy? You surprise me.'

Fraser pounced. 'So you do know 19 Cleveland Street and what goes on there!'

'I do not know 19 Cleveland Street,' cried Oscar, slapping his hand on the table. 'I have no idea what goes on there. I have no idea what you are talking about. I have no idea what you are driving at. You are talking in riddles, Inspector. I am still listening, but I am confused.'

Conan Doyle shifted in his chair and said, 'Go back to the beginning, Aidan.'

Oscar glanced in my direction and murmured, *sotto voce*, 'Yes, with a fairy tale, the beginning is always the best place to start.'

'Very well,' said Fraser. 'Three months ago, on 15 July to be exact, in the course of a routine investigation into a series of petty thefts alleged to have taken place at the Central Telegraph Office, one of my constables interviewed a fifteen-year-old telegraph boy by the name of Charles Swinscow.'

'I do not know him,' said Oscar, lightly.

'I am glad to hear it. At the time of the interview, this boy was found to have eighteen shillings in his pocket – four times his weekly wage. When accused of stealing the money, Swinscow denied it. He claimed he had "earned" it. When pressed as to how he had earned it, Swinscow said he was paid it for "going to bed with a gentleman". When asked who this "gentleman" was, he said he did not know his name. When asked where the incident had occurred, he said 19 Cleveland Street.'

Oscar leant towards Fraser and enquired, exasperation in his voice, 'Why are you telling me all this?'

'Because a scandal is about to break, Mr Wilde,' Fraser replied, coolly, 'and several of those involved are known to you. Lord Arthur Somerset—'

'I have met him, he is an acquaintance.'

'Lord Euston—'

'I know the name.'

'Prince Eddy—'

Oscar smiled. 'I know his father. With the growth of the empire, so many do.'

'There are to be arrests,' said Fraser.

Oscar burst out laughing. 'You are arresting the eldest son of the heir apparent?' he jeered.

'No,' said Fraser, solemnly. He paused. 'Too big a fish would break the line,' he said, as if in explanation. 'But tomorrow,' he continued, 'a warrant will be issued for the arrest of Lord Arthur Somerset. Lord Arthur knows it. He will leave the country tonight, by the boat-train. And it is his escape from justice that will cause the public scandal. Over the past six weeks, we have kept 19 Cleveland Street under constant surveillance. It is a resort for sodomites. It is a male brothel. It is a den of iniquity.'

'It is appalling, I agree,' said Oscar, leaning back in his chair with hands outstretched, 'but what has it to do with me? What has it to do with Billy Wood?'

Conan Doyle turned towards him. 'Do you not see, Oscar?'

Oscar looked at his friend. 'I do not see, Arthur, I do not see at all,' he said. 'All I see, all I know, is that a murder took place at 23 Cowley Street – a brutal murder – which for some reason, unknown to me, the police refuse to investigate.'

Inspector Fraser burst out, 'Do you not realise why, man?'

'No,' said Oscar, calmly, 'I do not. To be candid, Inspector, I am perplexed. There is much here that I do not understand. You told me, for example – in a telegram – that you had sent a policeman to 23 Cowley Street to investigate the scene of the crime, when, self-evidently, you had not. You lied to me, Inspector.'

'I lied, Mr Wilde, to protect you.'

'To protect me? Why?'

'Do you not understand? If I had so much as begun an official investigation, having embarked upon it, I could not have stopped it – wherever it might have led.'

'You do not need to protect me, Inspector. I have nothing to hide.'

'Are you sure, Mr Wilde? Number 23 Cowley Street and 19 Cleveland Street – were they not both, equally, dens of iniquity, houses of corruption? And Billy Wood – whatever has become of him – was he not, like Harry Smith and Charles Swinscow, a lad who sold his body for money, an unfortunate boy caught up in a vicious and degrading trade?'

Oscar got to his feet, gazed for a moment at his own reflection in the looking-glass above the fireplace, liked what he saw, and then – having deliberately run his finger along the mantelpiece as if to inspect it for dust – turned round and, with his back to the fireplace, deliberately addressed Aidan Fraser and Arthur Conan Doyle.

'Gentlemen,' he said, 'I thank you for your kind intentions, however misplaced. You have meant well, I can see. But let me assure you both of one thing: my conscience is clear. When I called at 23 Cowley Street on 31 August last,

I went on business that was entirely honourable. I went, by appointment, to meet a friend, but my friend was detained elsewhere – and instead of finding my friend there, as I had expected, I found, to my astonishment and horror, the body of poor Billy Wood.'

'Your friend?' asked Fraser. 'Is this another young man? May we know his name?'

'You are too quick to jump to conclusions, Inspector. As it happens, my friend is a young lady, but you do not need to know her name. She has no bearing on the case. She did not visit 23 Cowley Street that day. Do not concern yourself with her, Inspector. Concern yourself with Billy Wood—'

Conan Doyle interrupted, 'But Billy Wood—'

Oscar turned sharply towards him, 'Yes, Arthur, I loved Billy Wood. I loved him because he was young and open, carefree and full of joy. I loved him, too, because he had a talent that was rare – a talent that I was proud to nurture. I loved him as I might have loved a younger brother or a son. I give you my word of honour as a gentleman that in my relationship with Billy Wood there was nothing sordid, nothing immoral, nothing corrupt or underhand.' He paused for a moment and then put his hand out towards Conan Doyle. 'I trust you will accept my assurance on this matter.'

At once, the good doctor sprang to his feet and shook Oscar heartily by the hand. 'I accept your assurance – unreservedly.'

Oscar, rescuing his hand from Doyle's crippling grasp, turned back to Fraser who remained seated and impassive. 'And you, Inspector?'

'I do not know what to say.'

'Come, Aidan,' exclaimed Conan Doyle, 'Wilde is a gentleman – he would not deceive us. Take him at his word.' Fraser folded his arms across his chest and looked towards the empty fireplace. The doctor placed his hand on the detective's shoulder. 'We have done as you felt we should, Aidan,' he said. 'We have raised the issue; we have cleared the air.'

Fraser did not appear convinced. Suddenly, Oscar laughed, leant towards him and said, 'Inspector – Aidan – I shall call you Aidan, for we must be friends – I have only just realised why you are in this unpleasant mood. The pickle you had with your cheese at lunch has disagreed with you!'

Startled, the detective sat back and stared at Oscar. Oscar pressed home his advantage. 'You have been irritable and harassed all day, have you not? I believe I know the reason. It has nothing to do with us – and everything to do with a lady. You are expecting a lady to call, are you not? Her visit is causing you some apprehension. She is a strong-willed woman – a lady, I would hazard, who is sufficiently close to you to feel able to reprimand you for your slovenly bachelor habits.'

Fraser gazed at Oscar, with deep suspicion in his eyes. 'How on earth do you know this?'

Oscar shrugged his shoulders lightly. 'Why else, just before Arthur arrived, would you have removed the vase of fading lilies from this side table and hurriedly begun to dust the mantelpiece?'

'Have you been spying on me?' snapped Fraser. 'Explain yourself, please.'

Conan Doyle rubbed his hands together with glee. 'No, no,' he chortled, quite his usual self once more,

'Oscar has been playing at Sherlock Holmes again. How did you do it, Oscar? Tell us.'

'Look at the cuffs of your shirt, Aidan,' said Oscar with a teasing smile. Fraser raised his hands, warily, and examined his shirt-cuffs. 'On the inside of the left cuff what do you see? A small greasy smear that is a combination of dark brown and pale orange in colour, suggesting a right-handed man who has prepared himself a Cheshire cheese and pickle sandwich in something of a hurry. Look at the inside of both cuffs and what do you see? A dusting of rust-coloured speckles. What is it? Rust? No, the dusting is too delicate. Pepper perhaps? Or saffron? Or, look, what have we here on this side table? – a sprinkling of pollen from the stamens of overblown lilies . . . Aidan is leading a bachelor existence, alone, unattended. It is several days since he has been into his drawing room. Today, however, he has visitors and must prepare the room for them. Naturally, were his visitors merely men, he would not rush to clear away a vase of dead flowers. He is a man himself; he knows other men never notice these things. No, Aidan is expecting a lady to visit him – possibly the lady who brought him the flowers and arranged them for him on her last visit.'

Conan Doyle turned eagerly to Fraser and enquired, 'Is he correct?'

Fraser dropped his hands and smiled his perfect smile. 'In every particular,' he said. 'You are a remarkable man, Mr Wilde.'

' "Oscar", Aidan – we must be friends.'

'Oscar,' said the police inspector, getting to his feet and offering Oscar his open hand, 'I accept all that you say – of course I do. I warn you, nonetheless, that you are fishing in dangerous waters. I advise you, nonetheless, to pursue the matter no further. And I tell you again what I have told you already: I can do nothing whatever to assist you without a body.'

Conan Doyle sucked on his empty pipe and said dryly, 'With Oscar's powers of observation and detection I have little doubt that, if he chooses, he can solve the mystery, with or without the assistance of Scotland Yard.'

'Possibly,' said Fraser, still with his hand in Oscar's, still fixing him with his eye, 'but at what cost?'

'And to whom?' asked Oscar, returning the inspector's gaze.

Suddenly, sharply, the front doorbell rang and the tableau by the fireplace broke up.

'Ah,' said Oscar smoothly, 'the lady in the case.'

Inspector Fraser moved quickly towards the door to the hallway.

Oscar went on, 'I am sure she is a beauty. I believe she has red hair.'

Fraser stopped by the door and stared at Oscar with what seemed to me to be fearful eyes. But his laughter belied his look. 'How on earth do you know that?'

From his left waistcoat pocket Oscar pulled out a long strand of fair red hair. He held it aloft between his thumb and forefinger, displaying it to the room as if he were a magician holding out a coloured silk handkerchief before transforming it into a silver-topped cane or a bunch of paper flowers.

'I found this on the coatstand when I was hanging up my hat. Given the length, I took it to be a lady's. I imagine it came from the hat she wore on her last visit here.'

The doorbell rang once more. Fraser stepped quickly into the hallway and opened the front door wide. When his visitor had removed her hat and placed it next to Oscar's on the coatstand, Fraser brought her immediately into the drawing room. The lady he admitted was indeed a considerable beauty, and her hair was Titian red. 'Gentleman,' he said, 'may I present my fiancée, Miss Veronica Sutherland?'

11

Veronica Sutherland

I have to confess that Aidan Fraser's fiancée stole my heart the moment I set eyes upon her. She had a presence that was compelling and a look that took my breath away. Her face was long and lean, yet full of life. Her green eyes were huge and accentuated by the strength of her eyebrows and her aquiline nose. It was a face you would not forget. It was a face that I felt I already knew – and, at the moment of our meeting, I told her so.

As Aidan Fraser presented her to me and I shook her hand for the first time, I found myself saying, quite absurdly, 'I know we have not met before, Miss Sutherland, yet I feel that we have because your face puts me in mind of my favourite painting—'

'Oh!' cried Oscar in a mock-wail. 'Robert is in love again!'

Veronica Sutherland squeezed my hand, laughed and said, 'How thrilling! Which painting? Do tell me!'

'Well,' I stammered, 'several as a matter of fact.'

'Robert!' called Oscar. 'You go too far!'

'All by the same artist,' I said, stumbling on. 'All by Millais – Sir John Millais. Do you know his work? You have the exact look of his favourite model – his sister-in-law, Sophie Gray.'

'Good God,' said Oscar, taking a step towards Miss Sutherland. 'You are right, Robert. The resemblance is uncanny.'

'Really?' said Miss Sutherland. 'I must see this Sophie Gray. Is she beautiful?'

'She is fascinating,' I said, not knowing quite what I was saying, 'entrancing, extraordinary.'

'You shall see her,' said Oscar. 'I shall arrange it. Sir John's studio is not far from here. Robert will take you – won't you, Robert?'

'Indeed.'

'With Aidan's permission, of course.'

Miss Sutherland turned to her fiancé. 'Who are these wonderful people, Aidan? Where did you find them? Why have you not introduced me to them before? All your usual friends are so dull – except for Dr Doyle, of course. I am always happy to see him.'

She had let go of my hand and was now giving her full attention to Conan Doyle. She had put her arm through his and, with her head to one side, with her enormous eyes she was gazing intently at his smiling face.

I looked around the room and saw that, thanks to her, each of us – including Fraser – was now smiling. Billy Wood, O'Donnell, Bellotti, Cowley Street, Cleveland Street: all had been forgotten. Veronica Sutherland had burst into Fraser's drawing room like a gust of fresh air. There was an energy about her that was irresistible. We were invigorated by her presence – and held by it, too. She had a natural authority that belied her years and her gender. She was younger than each of us (she was just twenty-four), yet she was in command of us all.

Still linking arms with Conan Doyle, she glanced about her and said, 'Aidan, fiancé, husband-to-be: no flowers? No refreshments? No tea for our guests? What have you been thinking of?'

She sighed a theatrical sigh, broke away from Conan Doyle, threw down the book that had been tucked under her arm and, shaking her head of glorious red hair, swept out of the room, crying, 'Can men do *nothing* for themselves?'

Minutes later – while we were still standing in a circle by the fireplace, beaming blithely and singing her praises – she returned. She was carrying a large butler's tray, with, on it, three champagne saucers, one wineglass, one sherry glass, and, in a silver ice bucket filled to the brim with fresh ice, a magnum of Perrier Jouët. 'Aidan has a cellar in the basement and an ice house in his garden,' she said by way of explanation. 'The cellar is almost empty and the ice house he never uses. It is probably the only ice house in Chelsea and I doubt that he's been into it once. Has he shown you round the house and garden? He has ten rooms here; he uses three. The kitchen is a disgrace. Do not go. Even the mice find it inhospitable. He's been in residence a year and still there is no furniture to speak of. Have you seen his bedroom? There's an iron bedstead in one corner and a cheval looking-glass in the other – and that's that. There isn't a hook on the back of the door, let alone a wardrobe. He's living out of a suitcase. What am I to do with him?'

Conan Doyle laughed. 'Marry him!'

'If I must,' she replied, laughing, too. 'Open the wine, Aidan. I want to toast your friends. I want to drink to Sophie Gray.' She looked at me and widened her eyes.

'I want Mr Wilde to recite one of his poems for us,' she said turning to Oscar, 'or tell us one of his ghost stories,' adding, 'you see, Mr Wilde, I do know who you are really . . . Aidan has told me all about this mysterious murder that you are intent on investigating. Dr Doyle believes you, even if Aidan still has his doubts.' Her candour was disarming. She turned to Conan Doyle and raised her glass to him. 'I am so happy to see you, Dr Doyle. We can talk of my hero once more, can we not?'

'Are you, too, an admirer of Sherlock Holmes?' I asked.

'No,' she answered. 'I do admire Dr Doyle's writings, of course, but I did not mean Sherlock Holmes.'

'I believe Miss Sutherland is speaking of Dr Joseph Bell,' said Oscar.

'Indeed,' she said, acknowledging Oscar with a pretty tilt of her head. 'How did you know?'

'I saw the book – his book – the one you were reading on the underground train on your way here,' said Oscar, indicating the red-bound volume that she had thrown down on the side table before fetching our champagne.

'How did you know she travelled here by train?' asked Fraser.

Conan Doyle picked up the book and brandished it before us. 'Here is Miss Sutherland's twopenny tube ticket used as a bookmark. Oscar misses nothing.'

'Who is Dr Bell?' I asked.

'A great man,' said Conan Doyle, examining the spine of the volume. 'Not only the author of this definitive text – *A Manual of the Operations of Surgery* – but my mentor. He taught me at the Royal Infirmary in Edinburgh. As a surgeon, he was meticulous. As a lecturer, he had the quality of a mesmerist. As a master diagnostician, I do not know his equal. If anyone is the model for Sherlock Holmes, it is he. Dr Bell instilled in his students the critical importance of the powers of observation. He would have been proud of you, Oscar.'

Oscar smiled contentedly. Oscar was not averse to flattery.

Conan Doyle put down the book and continued: 'Dr Bell made an extraordinary impression upon us at our very first lecture. Almost as he began, he produced a glass vial containing a noxious amber liquid and held it aloft before us.' Conan Doyle picked up his glass of champagne as if it had been Bell's vial. ' "Gentlemen," he announced, in his rich Edinburgh burr, "this vial contains a most potent drug. It is *extremely* bitter to the taste — aye. But I want you to taste it! What, gentlemen? You shrink back?" Bell swirled the amber liquid with a finger, like so.' Conan Doyle, with his champagne, suited the action to the word. ' "Naturally," said Dr Bell, "I do not ask anything of my students that I would not undertake myself. I will taste the liquid before passing it around." The great man brought his hand to his mouth and sucked his finger. As he did so his features contorted as though he had sampled poison.'

As he told the tale, Conan Doyle re-enacted the drama before us.

'After a moment, Bell recovered himself and handed the vial to a student in the front row. "Now," he instructed, "you do likewise." Each of us in turn dipped a finger into the amber fluid and tasted it. It was indeed an awful brew, repellent to the taste. But when the vial had completed its rounds, Bell looked out over the rows of students spread before him and sighed. "Gentlemen," he said, "I am deeply grieved to find that not one of you has developed his power of perception, the faculty for observation that I speak so much of, for if you had truly observed me, what would you have seen?" '

Oscar had the answer. 'That while you placed your *index* finger into the amber liquid, it was your *middle* finger that found its way into your mouth!'

'Correct!' cried Conan Doyle, clinking the side of his glass against Oscar's. 'You do not miss a trick, my friend. You observe everything! I have decided that I am going to give Mr Sherlock Holmes an even more brilliant older brother and, with your permission, he shall be modelled on you! Holmes is based mostly on Dr Bell, but he has something of Fraser about him also. Holmes's brother will be entirely you, Oscar—'

'But I am not like Holmes,' Oscar protested. 'I am not a man of action. I am indolent.'

'Holmes's brother shall be indolent then,' replied Conan Doyle. 'Do not argue with me. I have decided. It is settled.'

As we all laughed and drank our champagne, I noticed that Miss Sutherland was cradling her copy of Dr Bell's book to her chest. 'Why are you reading Dr Bell?' I asked.

'Because it seems that I am never to sit at his feet,' she said.

Conan Doyle explained: 'Miss Sutherland entertained hopes of becoming a doctor. She wished to study at Edinburgh University, but it was not to be.'

'You see, I am a woman, Mr Sherard, and women are not fit to be physicians. Women are not fit to be anything!'

'I don't know about that,' protested Fraser in a jocular fashion.

'I do,' said Miss Sutherland, fiercely. 'Aidan, you, and Dr Doyle, and Mr Wilde, and Mr Sherard have all enjoyed the benefits of a university education. Why? Because you are men. I am denied one. Why? Because I am a woman. It is appalling – outrageous. And you do nothing about it – except laugh! The only women allowed within the hallowed walls of our ancient universities are cleaners and concubines. It is *scandalous*, Aidan, and you know it.'

For a moment, silence fell. Oscar broke it by taking the book that Miss Sutherland was clasping to her bosom and asking her, 'So what do you do, Miss Sutherland – by way of occupation?'

'Nothing,' she cried. 'I do nothing – except live off my parents and await the day when I marry, when I shall live off poor Aidan here. You are right, Mr Wilde. I am frustrated in my ambitions. I long to make my mark on the world. Perhaps your friend Sir John will paint my portrait and I shall achieve fame that way. I am determined to join the ranks of the immortals somehow.'

'You might try committing a murder,' suggested Oscar, casually, leafing through Bell's book.

'Come, Oscar,' said Conan Doyle, reprovingly, 'do not make light of murder.'

'I am quite serious,' said Oscar. 'If Miss Sutherland is bent on immortality and the conventional paths are blocked to her, perhaps she should try murder. After all, a hundred years from now, who will be best remembered? Lord Rosebery? Henry Irving? Sir John Millais? Or Jack the Ripper?'

'Oh, Mr Wilde,' exclaimed Veronica delightedly, 'what an amazing man you are! Why are you here? Why are you in mourning? Tell me all about this murder you are investigating. Tell me everything. Do, please.'

Fraser protested, in vain. Conan Doyle mumbled his demurral, to little effect. I stood by, in admiration, sipping my champagne, as Oscar took centre stage and told Miss Sutherland his story – our story: the story of the murder of Billy Wood.

Despite interventions from the detective and the doctor, Oscar omitted none of the salient details. When he had completed his narrative, Miss Sutherland, who had listened with rapt attention throughout, asked, 'This boy, Billy Wood, did you care for him, Mr Wilde? You say he had talent and youth and beauty—'

Oscar interrupted her: 'He had genius, Miss Sutherland. Beauty is a form of genius – is higher, indeed, than genius, as it needs no explanation. It is one of the great facts of the world, like sunlight, or springtime, or the reflection in dark waters of that silver shell we call the moon. It cannot be questioned. It has a divine right of sovereignty. It makes princes of those that have it. Billy Wood was a prince.'

'But did you *care* for him, Mr Wilde?' she repeated. 'You talk of beauty in the abstract and that perplexes me. For all your protestations, I am not sure how much you really loved the boy.'

Oscar smiled at her and said, 'In so vulgar an age as this, Miss Sutherland, it is not wise to show one's heart to the world. We all need masks, do we not?'

Aidan Fraser broke the mood, with some finality. 'At all events,' he said, gathering up the now-empty glasses and returning them to the tray, 'Oscar has decided to ignore our advice. He is pursuing the case, willy-nilly. He is determined to solve it, with or without our help.'

'I must,' said Oscar, 'and not only for poor Billy's sake. After all, if the murderer is not apprehended, may he – or she – not strike again?'

12

16 October–5 November 1889

'Do you truly believe that the murderer may strike again?' I asked, as I walked my friend home that evening, along the Chelsea Embankment towards his house in Tite Street.

'It is possible,' he said. 'Indeed, I think it likely. Few of life's occurrences turn out to be unique. For most of us, whatever we do, once is not enough. The poet does not pen the perfect sonnet and retire. The drinker is never satisfied by a single glass of wine. Having tasted the forbidden fruit, the sinner, inevitably, is hungry for more.'

'But if the murderer is a man like O'Donnell—'

Oscar interrupted me. 'The murderer is not a man like O'Donnell, Robert. If I had found Billy beaten to death in one of the backstreets of Broadstairs, I might have believed a brutish drunkard such as O'Donnell capable of the crime. But Billy's murder was not a random act. It was not a momentary aberration. It was carefully planned and painstakingly executed. I found Billy in an upstairs room, surrounded by candles, lying, as on a catafalque, his arms folded across his chest . . . There was something formal about the manner of poor Billy's murder, something ritualistic even.'

'Are you suggesting he was "sacrificed" in some way?' I asked, incredulous.

'And if he was,' said Oscar, 'how many other sacrificial lambs have been similarly slaughtered and laid to rest we know not where?'

He paused and stood for a moment looking onto the black surface of the river Thames. The tide was high, but the water was quite still. 'Tomorrow,' he announced, 'I shall begin a melancholy journey through all the morgues and mortuaries of the metropolis. There are thirty-seven of them in all, I understand. And in one of them, perhaps, among the unclaimed corpses, I shall find the body of Billy Wood. And – who knows? – I may find, too, the cadavers of other young men killed in a similar fashion.'

'Thirty-seven morgues and mortuaries . . .' I repeated.

'Yes, Robert, death is everywhere. This river alone throws up a hundred nameless bodies a year.'

'But it will take you months to visit every morgue and mortuary in London.'

He shook his head. 'Weeks, not months,' he said. 'I aim to visit three a day. It must be done. There is no alternative.'

'Can you not send your "spies"?' I asked.

'No,' he said, smiling. 'I have to go myself. I know what Billy looked like. My "spies" do not. I enquired of Mrs Wood and there are no photographs of Billy – even as a little boy. If he is to be identified at all, it can only be by someone who knew him personally.'

'I shall come with you, Oscar,' I said. 'At which morgue do we start?'

He laughed and, turning away from the river, put a hand on my shoulder. 'You are very kind, Robert, but, when visiting the dead, I prefer to go alone. It is melancholy work that suits one of my age and disposition. While I go in search of the body of Billy Wood, I suggest you lay siege to the heart of Miss Sutherland. I think you will find it more congenial employment.'

'But she is engaged to Fraser,' I protested.

'Indeed,' said Oscar, now putting his arm through mine as we resumed our walk along the embankment. 'That will add a certain frisson to the enterprise. A romance without a dash of danger is hardly worthy of the name.'

'And I am in love with Kaitlyn,' I said, firmly and with a certain pride.

'Of course you are,' he answered, beaming at me broadly, 'but Kaitlyn is in Vienna, Robert, and you are in London—'

'And am I incapable of fidelity?' I wailed.

'Fidelity fiddlesticks!' cried Oscar. 'You are a man, Robert! You know my rule: the only way to behave with a woman is to make love to her if she is pretty and to someone else if she is plain. What a ridiculous fuss is made of fidelity! Young men want to be faithful, and are not; old men want to be faithless, and cannot. That's all there is to it. Be grateful you are young, Robert. Seize every bit of happiness while you can.'

I did as Oscar counselled (I did not need much persuading!) and I confess that the weeks that followed were among the happiest of my life. On the morning after our first encounter, as Oscar set off for the morgue at Kennington Rise, I wrote a note to Miss Sutherland inviting her to join me for tea at the Cadogan Hotel. By return of post, she accepted my invitation. It was the beginning of what was, for me, a most magical experience.

That autumn and winter, Veronica Sutherland had time to spare, and I had time to give, and we spent it together, hour upon hour, day after day – taking tea, taking lunch promenading, playing (we were in our twenties, still young enough for play), laughing (so much!), and talking (so much!).

We never talked of love; we talked of *life* – and the life of the mind. We spoke of art and drama and science (her interest in medicine was sincere); of Scotland (which she loathed); of Italy (which she loved; she had a passion for Venice); of Conan Doyle (whom she much admired); and, of course, of Oscar (she was fascinated by Oscar's obsession with the death of Billy Wood). She rarely spoke of Fraser; and I never spoke of Kaitlyn or Marthe – or of my divorce. (Foxton, my estranged wife's solicitor, continued to bombard me with communications; I put his existence out of my mind and his correspondence on the fire.)

At our first tête-à-tête – over tea and toasted teacakes at the Cadogan Hotel – Veronica told me her life story. She was the only offspring of elderly parents. By her own admission, she had been a wilful child, disrespectful of her betters, at all times determined to get her own way. Mr and Mrs Sutherland, according to Veronica, were devoted to God and to Dundee in equal measure, so inevitably when, aged twenty-one, she announced her intention to abandon both in order to study surgery in Edinburgh, there was much weeping among the Sutherlands, and even some gnashing of teeth. Her mother threatened to die of shame; her father threatened to cut her off without a penny. (Mr Sutherland did nicely in the jute-importing trade.) In the event a compromise was reached. Neither Edinburgh University nor the Royal Infirmary would entertain her as a student, but her father had a cousin – a married clergyman – who was loosely attached to the university. It was agreed that Veronica could live with him and his family for a year and follow a course of 'reading' under his instruction. This she did, and it was during her year in Edinburgh that she met Aidan Fraser. Almost as soon as she met him, she became engaged to him. Her family was delighted. The Fettes fortune counted for something; indeed, in Dundee it counted for a great deal. When Fraser moved to London to join the Metropolitan Police, Veronica was permitted to follow him. While he acquired his house in Lower Sloane Street, she moved into furnished lodgings with a widowed great-aunt in Bedford Square.

I rarely saw Veronica in the evenings (she was expected to dine with her great-aunt at least four times a week) and almost never at weekends (that was when she saw Fraser) but during the week, from Monday to Friday – when Fraser was about his duties at Scotland Yard and I was 'available', as authors and poets tend to be – Veronica and I spent some time together almost daily. She took a particular delight in our visits to the studios of the eminent artists of the day. Because they all knew Oscar, either personally or by reputation, we had an entrée everywhere, and because Veronica was so beguiling and so full of vitality – which is the secret of glamour – wherever we went we were welcomed and, as often as not, invited back.

On virtually every Friday during the course of our friendship, Veronica and I found ourselves taking luncheon with Sir John Millais. He was a good and decent man, recently turned sixty, a fine painter (a *great* painter, in my view), and celebrated, of course, as one of the founders of the Pre-Raphaelite Brotherhood – though, by this time, he was scorned by younger critics (and most of Oscar's other friends) for having 'sold his genius for a mass of sovereigns' as portrait-artist-in-waiting to the great and the grand of British society. Oscar was invited to these Friday luncheons, but seldom came. 'I have morgues to visit, Robert,' he explained, 'and a story to write. I have not yet found the body of Billy Wood, nor yet finished my portrait of Dorian Gray. Besides, while I admire Sir John, I feel less certain about his cook. No doubt the cod is a splendid swimmer – admirable for swimming purposes – but for eating . . .'

I understood Oscar's reservation. While the Millais mansion was truly magnificent – a huge, square house, situated at Palace Gate, Kensington – lunch chez Millais was a modest affair. We ate in his vast drawing-room-cum-studio, at a covered card table set up by the fireplace. We dined, invariably, on cod and boiled potatoes, surrounded by life-sized portraits (Gladstone, Disraeli, Rosebery, Tennyson, Lillie Langtry in her prime; whom we got varied from week to week), some framed, some unfinished, all fixed on easels, positioned in a semicircle as though the subjects of the paintings were spectators at our feast. As I recall, the walls of the room were mostly covered with heavy eighteenth-century tapestries. There was only one painting on permanent display, hung on the wall to the left of the mantelpiece, above a Chinese lacquer chest: Millais's last portrait of Sophie Gray.

Veronica Sutherland liked Sir John, she said, because 'he is what he is', 'a man without guile, without pretension'.

She enjoyed the way he puffed away at his briar pipe in her presence and, indoors, unselfconsciously sat at table with his deerstalker hat on his head. 'He is honest, Robert, and of how many men can you say that nowadays? And he likes women, he *understands* women. Of how many men can you say *that*?'

Sir John liked Veronica Sutherland because, indeed, she did remind him of his late sister-in-law, Sophie Gray. 'You have her wit and gaiety,' he told Veronica, 'as well as her beauty and intelligence. Her life-force was extraordinary, but in the end it overwhelmed her. She became an hysteric, poor child. She died by her own hand. She flew too near the flame.'

It was late one Friday afternoon at the end of that October, following one of our lunches with Sir John, when Veronica and I were at Tite Street, taking tea with Oscar, and telling him about the picture of Sophie Gray, that Oscar told us he had nearly completed his new story for Stoddart and had decided on its title. 'I shall call it *The Picture of Dorian Gray*,' he announced.

'Do you think Millais will mind?' I asked.

'Why should Millais mind?' answered Oscar, somewhat peevishly. 'The artist in my story bears no resemblance to Millais, none whatsoever. And Dorian Gray, whose portrait is at the heart of my story – and who is perfection itself, who is perhaps what I would like to be in other ages! – knows no kinship to Sophie Gray.'

'But is not suicide one of the elements in your story?' I persisted. 'Does not Dorian Gray take his own life? I am only anxious for Millais's sake because Sophie Gray took hers . . .'

Oscar waved me away airily. 'If Dorian Gray is cousin to anyone,' he said, indicating the discussion was at an end, 'it is to my young friend from the Foreign Office, John Gray. The surname is, of course, commonplace, but John, I assure you, is not.'

John Gray was Oscar's new enthusiasm – the one distraction he allowed himself that autumn. I later learnt that though Oscar had told me, emphatically, that when 'visiting the dead' he preferred to go alone, in fact, on each of his investigative visits to what he called 'the melancholy morgues and mortuaries of the metropolis', he had been accompanied by John Gray.

Gray was twenty-three and worked at the Foreign Office. He was not a diplomatist; he was a clerk in the library, a young man of humble origins who had made his way in the world by dint of his own endeavours. 'His father was a carpenter,' said Oscar; 'we shall assume his mother was a virgin.' Obliged by his parents' penury to leave school at thirteen, Gray had become a metal-worker by day while, by night, continuing his studies at his own expense. To his credit, aged sixteen, he had entered the examinations necessary to secure a clerkship at the Post Office – and passed with flying colours. 'He is a complex, multiform creature,' said Oscar, 'interested in art and music, poetry and languages, postage stamps and me!' Oscar met him for the first time that September – just a few weeks after the death of Billy Wood – at a literary gathering in Chelsea. 'We became firm friends the moment we met,' said Oscar. 'John has the appearance of a Greek god – and only shallow people do not judge by appearances.'

I first learnt of John Gray's existence on that last Friday in October 1889. I met him for the first time a week later, on Bonfire Night, 5 November 1889. Veronica was dining in Bedford Square with her great-aunt, and Oscar and I had arranged to go together to the theatre. (The Irish-American actress, Ada Rehan, was making her debut at the Lyceum.) Oscar had told me he would come to collect me by cab and to be ready and waiting for him at my room in Gower Street at seven o'clock – no later.

I was booted, suited, polished and brushed by 6.45 p.m. I was standing in the street at seven. By seven-fifteen I was anxious. By seven-thirty I was alarmed. Oscar was occasionally late for dinner, but never for the theatre. (Others insulted actors casually, treating them as servants; Oscar never did.) At 7.45 p.m., simply to reassure myself, I decided that I must have misunderstood him and that what he had in fact proposed was that we should go by separate cabs and meet at the theatre. I was reluctant to hire a hansom myself, of course, because what spare funds I had I'd all but spent on cream teas and iced champagne for Veronica, but if I was to have any chance of reaching the theatre by eight o'clock a cab was the only way. With my mind made up, and my forehead throbbing, I peered up and down the gloomy thoroughfare. By rights, Gower Street on Bonfire Night, when the fog is thick and the West End at its busiest, should not be the easiest place to hail a passing cab, but to my amazement, at the precise moment that I needed one, a four-wheeler appeared out of the yellow gloom and drew to an abrupt halt before me.

'The Lyceum Theatre,' I called out to the cabman.

'I don't think so, guv,' he replied, 'I'm going home.'

'Why have you stopped then?' I barked.

The cab door opened and I was answered. Onto the street stumbled two figures: a fair-haired boy in a sailor suit and Oscar Wilde, in dishevelled evening dress, his face blue-black with bruises, his hair matted with blood. 'This is how I found him,' said the boy. 'He told me to bring him here.'

I paid off the cabman and, between us, the boy and I helped Oscar up the stairs and into my room. 'My name is John Gray,' said the boy, who looked fifteen at most. His hair was blond and longer than it should have been. His eyes were blue and watchful; his skin was golden; his lips were pale; his high cheekbones were dusted with freckles the colour of sand. John Gray was indeed a young Adonis in a sailor suit (a French sailor suit, I think) – just as poor crumpled Oscar, with his sagging flesh, his swollen mouth, his eyes half closed (they were too bruised to open), was an ageing Bacchus after a brawl.

We eased Oscar onto my bed. I loosened his collar and tie, and poured what brandy I had into a glass and held it to his lips. He whimpered. He was exhausted and in pain.

'What happened?' I asked.

'I don't rightly know,' said the boy. (He spoke well. He had the manners of a young gentleman.) 'I was crossing Soho Square, on my way to Kettner's restaurant to meet a friend. I saw Oscar standing on the pavement, by the church, talking to a man. They were arguing.'

'What sort of man?'

'I don't know – just a man, in a heavy coat.'

'What sort of man?' I repeated. 'Was he young? Old? Bearded?'

'Not young, not bearded.'

'Was he tall?'

'Quite tall, and well built. He was dark – swarthy, that's the word. He was carrying a stick. Because they were shouting at one another I didn't go too close.'

'What were they shouting?'

'The man said something like, "Keep away! Keep away or I'll kill you!" – and then he began to hit Oscar. He beat him with his stick and forced him to the ground. Oscar fell back onto the steps of the church and the man flung himself on top of him and hit him in the face. He punched him, again and again. That's when I ran towards them, shouting, "Stop! Police!" The man got up and cursed me and ran away.'

'You say the man said, "Keep away or I'll kill you!"'

'Yes, something like *Laisse-la ou je te tue!*'

'What?' I exclaimed. 'He spoke in French?'

'Yes, it was French. I'm sure of that. But the accent was a strange one.'

'It was a man called O'Donnell,' I said. 'He comes from Montreal. He is a brute.'

'He was certainly that,' said the boy,

Oscar said nothing. His head was turned to the wall. His breathing was deep and ragged, but steady. I sensed he was asleep. 'I'll keep him here,' I said. 'Mrs Wilde is not expecting him home tonight in any event. Best not to worry her.'

'Are you sure?' said the boy, straightening the collar of his sailor suit and looking about him for a mirror in which to check his hair.

'I'm sure,' I said. 'I'll look after him. I'm his friend.'

'His "best friend", according to Oscar,' said the boy.

137

'I'm glad of that,' I said.

'Well, I'll be off then,' said the lad cheerily, offering me his hand. 'I'm dining at Kettner's. Did I say? We'll meet again soon, I hope. And Oscar will be right as rain in a day or two, won't he? I love him. We all do.'

And with a half-salute and the hint of a wink, John Gray was gone.

13

6 November 1889–2 January 1890

Oscar stayed in my room for the following three days.

On the morning of 6 November, when I awoke with a stiff neck and a twisted spine (the price of a night on a dilapidated divan), I discovered him sitting up in bed, the pillows well plumped behind him, smoking a Turkish cigarette and reading Baudelaire by candlelight. '*Bonjour, mon ami*,' he said, cheerfully.

His face was still a mass of bruises, but his spirits appeared entirely restored. He professed no recollection of the events of the night before. None whatsoever.

'John Gray in a sailor suit? Are you hallucinating, Robert?'

'Oscar, I assure you—'

'You *are* hallucinating, Robert,' he continued blithely, as I fumbled with a match to light the gas ring to boil some water for our tea. 'Look at you – your hands are shaking! I blame Conan Doyle.'

'Why? What's he to do with it?'

'Ever since Arthur told us of his plans to make Sherlock Holmes a dope fiend, you, Robert Sherard, have been itching to experiment yourself. Admit it. Is it morphine or cocaine you've turned to?'

'Don't be absurd, Oscar,' I said, laughing. 'If anyone's mind is not quite as it should be, it is evidently yours. John Gray rescued you last night when you were attacked by that brute O'Donnell.'

'Whatever may have happened to me last night, I was not attacked by Edward O'Donnell.'

'According to Gray, your assailant was abusing you in French.'

'Ah,' said Oscar, 'that sounds to me like a disappointed poet – they can be so violent. Give a man a poor review and the next thing you know, he is knocking you down in the street – and doing so in French to give his actions the veneer of respectability.'

'If it wasn't O'Donnell,' I persisted, 'who was it?'

'It wasn't O'Donnell, Robert,' he replied, blowing out the candle as I drew the curtain and let in the cold, grey light of morning. 'O'Donnell is not our man.'

'So you say. So you keep saying.'

'Indeed,' he went on, pulling my eiderdown close about him, 'as I have lain here on your most comfortable bed – for which many thanks, old friend – as I have lain here, I have been reflecting that "our man" may, in fact, be a woman – or a man with womanish ways. The scene of the crime was as clean as a whistle when we found it. The floorboards had been polished with beeswax, you'll recall. Beeswax suggests a woman's touch.'

'Or, possibly,' I ventured, 'a man accustomed to household work – a domestic servant? Did you not tell me that Mr Bellotti recruits bootblacks and the like on behalf of O'Donovan & Brown?'

'I did,' said Oscar. 'Well remembered, Watson. You are right. Bellotti is mixed up in this business for certain, but how and to what extent I have no idea. While I have been trawling the morgues of the metropolis, my "spies" have been keeping a close eye on friend Bellotti – and on the brute O'Donnell – and, I am sorry to tell you, they have nothing of interest to report.'

'And what have the morgues revealed?' I enquired.

'Nothing of interest either,' he answered with a smile, 'except that death no longer holds any terror for me. In recent weeks, I have gazed on the faces of the dead *by the dozen* and what I have discovered is quite consoling, Robert. When we die, we disappear. Our spirit escapes we know not where. The shell we leave behind means nothing. A dead body is no more disturbing than a discarded overcoat.'

'How many more morgues have you still to visit?' I asked.

'None,' he said, sitting up and pushing the eiderdown away from him, letting Baudelaire slip to the floor. 'I have exhausted them all. Now, I plan to embark on the dissecting rooms of the London hospitals. Had I thought, I should probably have started there.' With a suppressed groan he pushed himself off the bed and onto his feet. 'According to Conan Doyle, the medical schools are so eager to have fresh cadavers for their students to dismember and dissect that there is now a black market in the mortal remains of the recently deceased. I must get dressed and be about my business.' Suddenly, he caught sight of himself in the mirror above the washbasin and let out a yelp of anguish. 'Mary Mother of God, I cannot be seen in the streets like this! It'll be all over the papers within hours.'

I smiled. 'Fear not,' I said, 'in a day or two, you'll be fine.'

'I am hideous, Robert – deformed!'

'Bruised, that's all. Sit yourself here by the gas fire. Rest, recuperate, recover your strength. Tomorrow, or the next day, will be soon enough to venture out. I'll send a wire to Constance. I'll say you've gone to Oxford for a day or two.' He turned away from the looking-glass with a shudder and slowly, with my help, eased himself into the armchair by the fire. I covered his lap with his overcoat. 'Rest up here, while I go and get us some breakfast.'

'Oh, would you, Robert? You are an angel. And, yes, do send a wire to Constance. And, while you're out, perhaps you could find me a fresh shirt also? Could you bear it? You know my size. Perhaps two shirts, in fact.' He found his wallet inside his coat pocket and gave me a five-pound note. 'Silk shirts,' he added. 'And some nice soap, if you see any. I feel so grubby. Houbigant's if you can get it – either Peau d'Espagne or Sac de Laitue . . . And while you're in the chemist's shop, there's a wonderful thing called Koko Marikopas. It is costly, but the name alone is worth the price and it works miracles. It's a hair tonic – and before my very eyes my hair is turning grey.'

'Don't be absurd, Oscar,' I said, taking his money and putting on my own overcoat. 'You have a strand or two of silver, that is all.'

'Who cares for silver?' he murmured, closing his eyes. 'I care only for gold.'

I was gone an hour. When I returned, laden with groceries, shirts and soap (but without the hair tonic), Oscar was not there. For a moment, I felt infuriated. Oscar was, essentially, a kindly man, generous to a fault, courteous in a way that would seem incomprehensible to a later generation – and yet . . . Let it be said: he was fundamentally selfish; he did as he pleased when he pleased.

As I was pondering what to do with my superfluity of supplies, there was a loud knocking at the front door. I looked out of my window onto Gower Street. There was Oscar, beating on the door with a cane. I ran downstairs to admit him, my resentment waning as I went.

'Where have you been?' I asked.

'In search of life's essentials,' he answered, 'fresh air and cigarettes.'

I laughed. 'And what if you'd been noticed? I thought you were anxious about being all over the papers,' I said.

'You are right, Robert. It is a dreadful thing to have one's name in the newspapers. And still more dreadful not to. I decided to take the risk, but went prepared – with this!'

From behind his back, he produced an ornate Venetian carnival mask and held it before his face. It was a present, given to me by Veronica Sutherland, and given to her by Aidan Fraser. Oscar must have found it on my mantelpiece.

'You are preposterous, Oscar,' I said. 'I'm surprised you weren't arrested – especially carrying that cane.' I had recognised it at once. 'That is my swordstick, the one I gave to Constance, is it not?'

'It is.'

'Where did you find it?'

'Find it? I had it with me last night.'

'Are you sure?'

'As sure as God's in his heaven and all's well with the world.'

I knew full well that Oscar had not had the swordstick with him when John Gray had brought him to my room the night before. I took it that he had lost it at some point during his encounter with O'Donnell in Soho Square. I surmised that he had set out that morning – behind his mask! – to retrieve it from wherever it had fallen. I could have argued all this with him, forced him to admit as much, but to what avail? Oscar told only what he wished to tell when he wished to tell it.

Back in my room, Oscar hung his coat on the peg behind my door, returned the Venetian mask to the mantelpiece and, with some ceremony, laid the swordstick across the washbasin like a sceptre on an altar. He then stood with his back to the fireplace, facing the room, and checked his timepiece. 'Twelve noon – is it to be breakfast or lunch?'

'Brunch,' I declared, using the new portmanteau word just in vogue and proudly unwrapping my range of provisions.

'Brunch,' he repeated. 'Callooh! Callay! Bacon and sausages followed by clear turtle soup and luscious ortolans wrapped in Sicilian vine-leaves . . . And a bottle of wine from the banks of the Mosel. Heaven comes to Gower Street! I would be smacking my lips, Robert, were they not so swollen. You are a true friend and a perfect host.'

When we had feasted, Oscar slept. He slept all day and all night. On the second morning the blue-black of his bruises had turned to muddy yellow and the swelling had subsided. He was still weary, however, and in pain, content, it seemed, to lie upon my bed, dozing, smoking, reading Baudelaire to me out loud – in French – and then inviting me to join him in translating Baudelaire out loud – into Italian! I had recently received a copy of

The Bostonians, inscribed to me by the author, and I volunteered to read it to Oscar. 'No, thank you, Robert,' he said, closing his eyes. 'Mr Henry James writes fiction as if it were a painful duty. If only Arthur had completed his new story, *that* I would enjoy.'

On the third day, he rose, inspected his face in the looking-glass and declared himself both 'fit to be seen' and 'seen to be fit'. 'I must return to Constance and the boys – by way of St Thomas's hospital.' He prepared to depart. 'And you must return to Miss Sutherland, Robert. Another man's fiancée requires so much more attention than one's own.'

'We are just friends, Oscar,' I protested.

He rebuked me, tapping me on the chest with the end of the swordstick as he did so. 'There is no friendship possible between men and women, Robert. Remember that. There is passion, enmity, worship, love, but no friendship.'

I walked him into the street and stood with him on the pavement until a cab came past. We hailed it and then shook hands – as friends.

'In the long run, Robert, you will find a handshake so much more reliable than a kiss,' he said. He climbed into the two-wheeler. 'I will see you soon. Thank you for giving me sanctuary, my friend. John Gray was in a sailor suit, you say?' He sat back, laughing, and waved to me, shaking his head, as the cab took him on his way.

As it turned out, I saw very little of Oscar between then and Christmas. He was busy, completing *Dorian Gray*, entertaining John Gray, placating Constance, and – as he reported to me in mock-despair on the two occasions when we caught up briefly over a nightcap at the

Albemarle Club – running up bills at Kettner's and the Café Royal at the behest of importunate poets ('The more sentimental their sonnets, the more unquenchable their thirst!') and running down blind alleys in vain pursuit of the mortal remains of poor Billy Wood.

I saw very little of Oscar, but I saw a great deal of Veronica Sutherland that November and December, possibly too much. We met each day – we even found ways in which to steal an hour or two to be together at weekends – and then, on the night before she was due to go to Scotland for Christmas and Hogmanay, beneath the Albert Memorial, as the midwinter moonlight filtered between the clouds, we kissed – and kissed again – and I said the fateful words, 'I love you.'

'Thank you,' she whispered as she held me close, 'thank you. It is a dreary thing to sit at home with un-kissed lips.'

Miss Sutherland and her fiancé, Aidan Fraser, departed by train for Scotland on 23 December. They were away for ten nights. Pining, I wrote to Oscar, 'What am I to do?'

By return, he replied, 'Assuming that Kaitlyn is still in Vienna and that your estranged wife is not proposing a seasonal reconciliation, come to Tite Street. Constance will look after you and I promise there will be no readings from *A Christmas Carol*. Tiny Tim is dead! Hallelujah!'

I went. Christmas in Tite Street was wonderful – and curiously Dickensian. Oscar, personally, had decked the hall with boughs of holly, and Constance, assisted by Annie Marchant (bustling, busy Annie Marchant, the boys' nursemaid), had dressed a Christmas tree – quite beautifully – in the German tradition. There were log fires burning in all the rooms (and, from I know not where, the smell of pine kernels and sandalwood). Whenever Constance appeared – long-suffering Constance – she seemed to me to have an angelic smile on her gentle face and in her hands a tray of Christmas cheer: decanters of sherry and Madeira, bowls of rum punch, plates of sweetmeats, nuts and crystallised fruits. It was, as she put it, 'just the family – and you boys': herself and Oscar, Cyril and Vyvyan, Annie Marchant and Mrs Ryan (the cook-cum-maid-of-all-work) – plus John Gray and myself. John Gray stayed as a house guest, sleeping on the divan in Oscar's smoking room. I went home each night to Gower Street to sleep, but returned to Tite Street each day in time for luncheon.

We were the only outsiders, both invited for the whole holiday, from Christmas Eve to Twelfth Night, and both arriving at exactly the same moment (six o'clock in the evening on 24 December), bearing precisely the same gifts for the two young sons of the house: a football for each of them. Oscar was appalled. 'So it has come to this: we celebrate the nativity of the Christ-child with gifts of air-filled leather bladders. Yesterday, there were no footballs in this house; now there are four! Was there no frankincense at Whiteley's?'

Cyril and Vyvyan were delighted with their presents, and Constance thanked us both with kindly kisses and whispered endearments. (She was as warm towards John Gray as she was towards me.) 'Pay no attention to Oscar,' she said, giving him a teasing look of reproof. 'He plays no outdoor games at all.'

'Not so, my dear,' said Wilde. 'If you recall, I have sometimes played dominoes outside French cafés . . .

Football, I concede, I have avoided. It is all very well as a game for rough girls, but it is hardly suitable for delicate boys, now is it?'

There was much laughter in Tite Street that Yuletide. On Christmas Day itself, there was singing too. Willie Wilde, Oscar's elder brother, joined the party and led an hour of communal carol-singing around the piano, followed by an informal (and gently inebriated) recital of his own 'favourites' from the repertoire of Gilbert and Sullivan. Willie joined us again on Boxing Day, when we left the children at home with Annie Marchant and went to Kempton Park for the St Stephen's Day races. 'St Stephen is the patron saint of horses,' Oscar announced as we arrived, 'and Willie is a pagan deity worshipped by turf accountants everywhere. Willie comes to the races almost daily and has a faculty for choosing the loser, which, given he knows nothing about horses, is remarkable.'

On New Year's Eve there was a family dinner, with toasts. Oscar insisted that Cyril and Vyvyan be woken and brought into the dining room in the arms of Annie Marchant and Mrs Ryan to listen to the toasts. 'They'll not understand a word, Oscar,' said Constance. 'Leave them be.'

'They'll hear the music of our voices,' said Oscar, 'it's a start.' He explained to the rest of us: 'When Willie and I were boys in Dublin, Sir William Wilde, our father, allowed us to sit at the large dining-room table in Merrion Square on feast nights such as this . . . That is where we learnt to listen and to look.'

Oscar's toasts – inevitably! – were many and splendid. He toasted the future, he toasted the past; he toasted literature, he toasted art; he toasted new friends (with a nod to John Gray) and true friends (with a nod to me) and absent friends (with a mention of Conan Doyle and, smiling at me, a reference to Veronica Sutherland). With tears filling his eyes, he toasted 'those we have loved and those we have lost' and spoke of his sister, Isola, who had died when she was only ten:

> . . . she is near
> Under the snow,
> Speak gently, she can hear
> The daisies grow.

He invited us to raise our glasses to her memory and that of 'others too young to die, some taken from us during this now-past and bitter year'. He did not mention Billy Wood by name.

For me, Oscar's final toast was the most touching. 'Gentlemen,' he said, 'and this includes you, my sons,' he added, smiling, looking directly at his boys. 'Gentlemen . . . Let us drink to the ladies! Let us give thanks and do honour to the women in our lives. We bless them for their strength and their sweetness and their sacrifice.' He motioned to his brother, to John Gray and to me to rise to our feet. 'I give you womankind,' he said, 'and in particular – and especially – the four ladies gathered in this room tonight.' He lifted his glass to each in turn, starting with the servants, both of whom stood amazed before him with tear-filled eyes: 'Miss Marchant . . . Mrs Ryan . . .' He turned then to his mother and his wife: 'Lady Wilde, so brilliant and so brave . . . and Constance, my wife . . . Constance: was ever a woman more aptly named?'

On 2 January we toasted Constance again. It was her thirty-second birthday and the last formal evening of the Wilde Christmas and New Year 'season'. Willie and Lady Wilde were not in attendance, but there were other guests: Aidan Fraser and Veronica Sutherland, who had returned that very day from Scotland, and Arthur Conan Doyle and his young wife, Touie, up from Southsea.

At dinner, I was seated between Miss Sutherland and Mrs Doyle, and I hope I acquitted myself reasonably. It was not easy: I was at a loss with both of them. I was at a loss with Veronica, because the moment I saw her again my passion for her was rekindled, but her manner towards me, while full of playful charm, gave no inkling of her present feelings about our relationship – or its possibilities. I was at a loss with Touie because her painful shyness made it almost impossible to communicate with her. I learnt that her proper name was Louisa, that her maiden name was Hawkins, and that motherhood was 'agreeable' to her, 'though tiring', but that was about all.

If I acquitted myself reasonably that night, I did so, I suspect, only because the opportunities for doing otherwise were limited. For most of dinner, none of us was talking to our neighbours; we were all listening to Oscar. He was on song! He told a series of fantastic tales, claiming that each one was a true story. He gave each tale a title – 'The Value of Surprise', 'The Value of Character', 'The Value of Presence of Mind' – and said that he had plans to publish the stories as 'moral tracts'. As I recall, he had hopes that the Bishop of London might contribute a preface!

The last of these tales was the most memorable: an account of an extraordinary night at the theatre. 'I forget the title of the play that was being presented,' said Oscar, 'but you will recall the plot: a virtuous heroine rescued from a fate worse than death by a handsome hero . . . You remember it now? Indeed. Well, on the night in question, during the tremendous scene in which the fair flower-girl of Piccadilly Circus – our heroine – rejects with scorn the odious proposals of the debauched marquess – the villain of the piece – a huge volume of smoke and fire poured out of the wings. The audience rose in panic and stampeded towards the exits. Then, suddenly, on stage there appeared the noble figure of the young man who was the true lover of the flower-girl. His voice rang out, clear and strong – "The fire is already under control. The chief danger is from panic. Let all go back to their seats and recover their calm." So commanding was his presence that all in the audience returned to their places. The young actor then leapt over the footlights and ran out of the theatre. The rest were burnt to a crisp.'

As our laughter and applause subsided, we heard a sharp rat-tat-tat on the Tite Street front door. A moment later, Mrs Ryan appeared at the dining-room door bearing a parcel – a box, perhaps one foot square – wrapped in brown paper and tied up with string. 'It is for Mrs Wilde,' she said, 'a birthday present, I assume.'

'How exciting!' said Constance.

'Will it be a hat?' asked Conan Doyle.

'It will be a birthday cake,' said John Gray.

'Pray God it is not another football!' said Oscar.

'Fetch me a knife, would you, Mrs Ryan?' said Constance. She took the package and laid it on the table before her. 'It is quite heavy,' she said.

'It *is* a football!' groaned Oscar.

Mrs Ryan handed Constance a small fruit-knife. Constance cut the string and tore back the paper. Within the brown wrapping was a sturdy cardboard box. Constance leant forward and, bright-eyed with anticipation, with both hands and a flourish, she lifted off the lid.

As she saw the horror within, the blood instantly drained from her face and she let out what seemed at the time to be a never-ending scream. She closed her eyes and, with sudden force, pushed the box away from her. It toppled over and out of it rolled a human head – the severed head of Billy Wood.

14

Billy Wood

It was Conan Doyle who took immediate command of the situation.

He got to his feet at once, while Constance was still screaming, and threw his napkin over the severed head, which had rolled to the centre of the table and come to rest – grotesquely, nose up – against the rim of a silver fruit dish. He looked at his wife and said, quite calmly, 'Touie, take Mrs Wilde to her bedroom.' Mrs Doyle did not move. 'Now, Touie,' he said, '*now*.' Mrs Doyle got to her feet. Her husband looked about him. 'Veronica, you go too, please. Mrs Ryan, would you get some brandy for the ladies? And for yourself, of course. Mr Gray, would you escort the ladies? Thank you.'

People began to move. Mrs Ryan put a comforting arm around Constance's shoulders. Mrs Doyle stood tentatively at her side. John Gray did as he was bidden and began to usher the womenfolk out of the room. As he went, he turned to Conan Doyle. 'Should we not call the police?' he asked.

'That won't be necessary,' said Aidan Fraser.

Everyone was now standing or in motion, except for Oscar who was still seated at the head of the table, gazing fixedly ahead of him, as if in a trance. When the women had all gone, Conan Doyle said, 'Let us leave this room.' He leant across the table and, with both hands, scooped up the head, still covered in his napkin, and cradled it in his arms. 'Come, Oscar, let us adjourn to your study.'

It is worth noting at this point that Oscar was right. The boy was beautiful – there was no doubt about that. The fact of the severed head was shocking and horrific, but the face of the boy was neither. It was perfect.

'He was a god,' said Oscar.

'He was certainly a good-looking lad,' said Conan Doyle.

The country doctor was holding the severed head in his hands, examining it, assessing it as if he had been the curator of antiquities at the British Museum inspecting the latest trophy from the excavations at Pompeii.

The head looked as if it had been lopped from a marble statue: the features were clear and strong; the forehead was broad and smooth; the cheekbones were high; the nose and chin were sharply defined; and the skin was flawless, grey-white in colour, firm and smooth as marble. The one disconcerting element – the one element that served as a reminder that this was not, in fact, an effigy, but the severed head of a human being – was the hair. There was so much of it. It was thick, dark brown and swept back as if newly brushed. He had thick eyebrows too and, on his closed eyelids, long, dark eyelashes, like a girl's. His mouth was set almost in a smile and on his upper lip were the beginnings of a young man's moustache.

'He looks at peace,' I said.

'He has been embalmed,' said Conan Doyle.

'Embalmed?' repeated Aidan Fraser, taking a step closer to Doyle.

'Preserved,' said the doctor, 'with chemicals — most skilfully.'

'Where is the box it came in?' asked Fraser.

'In the dining room still,' I said. 'I'll get it.'

As I came out of Oscar's study to retrieve the box from the dining-room table, I was surprised to find Veronica Sutherland at the foot of the stairs. She had her overcoat in her arms.

'Are you leaving?' I asked.

'No,' she answered.

'How is she?' I asked.

'Mrs Wilde? Disturbed. Understandably. She is weeping. I came to find some smelling-salts for her. She has none.' She indicated the coat in her arms. 'I brought some with me. I was feeling faint myself a little earlier. The train journey from Scotland was exhausting.' She smiled at me. 'How is Mr Wilde?' she asked.

'Shocked,' I said. 'It is shocking. Horrible.' I moved towards the staircase. 'Veronica, my dear, I love you still.'

'Robert, this is not the time.' She turned to mount the stairs.

'Forgive me.'

Burning with embarrassment (in those days I was *such* a fool!) I waited for her to climb the stairs and then made my way to the dining room. The cardboard box and wrapping paper were still at Constance's place at the table. I took them and hurried back to Oscar's study.

Oscar had recovered himself. He was standing behind his writing desk — his famous writing desk: the writing desk that had once belonged to Thomas Carlyle — leaning upon it, supporting himself on his fingertips, addressing Aidan Fraser who stood alone in the centre of the room. 'You wanted evidence of murder, Inspector. I trust a severed head will be sufficient? I believe King Herod would have settled for less.'

Fraser laughed a mirthless laugh. 'Oh yes, Mr Wilde, you will get your investigation now – you need have no fear of that.'

For a moment, as I re-entered the room, I could not see Conan Doyle, so I was startled when he spoke. He was standing away from the others, in a corner, leaning against the wall, still holding the boy's head, but now holding it aloft beneath a gas lamp, examining it minutely through a magnifying-glass. 'Holmes would have been proud of this,' he said.

'What?' snapped Oscar.

'No,' said Doyle, soothingly, 'not my Holmes, Oscar. We are in the real world now, alas. Dr Thomas Holmes, the father of modern embalming. During the American Civil War he received the commission to embalm the corpses of dead Union soldiers to return them to their families. Embalming had been an art. Holmes made it a science.'

Conan Doyle walked slowly to the middle of the room and, having held the severed head close to his nostrils for a moment and sniffed sharply, he carefully placed it inside the cardboard box that I had put down on the writing desk. 'This has been most skilfully achieved,' he said.

'Using formaldehyde?' asked Fraser.

'No,' said Conan Doyle, 'arsenic, I think – which suggests to me the work of a skilled and gifted amateur rather than a professional. Your regular undertaker would not use arsenic nowadays.'

'Do you imagine that the rest of the body has been preserved?'

'Oh, yes. I think the decapitation is recent. Look at the clean cut across the neck. I imagine the embalming took place within hours of the murder.'

'The embalming – could anyone do it?' asked Fraser. 'On their own, I mean, without assistance.'

'Certainly,' said Conan Doyle, 'it's a simple process. If you have the knowledge – and the pump.'

'The pump?' I repeated, involuntarily.

'No more,' said Oscar, 'I beg you.'

Conan Doyle lowered his voice. 'The embalming fluid is forced into the blood vessels, usually via the right common carotid artery, by means of a small mechanical pump. The embalmer has then to massage the corpse to ensure the proper distribution of the fluid. That's where skill and experience play their part. As I say, this has been most skilfully done – though the boy's youth will have helped. As a rule, the older the deceased, the poorer the circulation.'

'You appear remarkably well informed upon the subject,' said Fraser.

'Holmes is something of a hero of mine. He brought comfort to many grieving families. I have studied his work.'

Oscar had now come around his writing desk and was gazing into the cardboard box, looking fixedly at the face of the dead boy.

'Is this how you remember him?' asked Conan Doyle.

'Yes,' said Oscar.

'Is this how he appeared when you discovered the body?'

'Yes,' said Oscar. 'I believe so. It is difficult to recall. There was so much blood. So much. But I believe his face was just as we see it now – serene.'

'Untroubled,' I said.

'Untroubled,' repeated Oscar. 'Exactly.' He looked up at Conan Doyle. 'Might he have been murdered in his sleep?'

'Quite possibly,' said Conan Doyle. 'As you can see, his face has been dusted with powder, like a woman's make-up, but beneath the cosmetic the skin is quite blemish-free. There is no damage to the eyelids, which suggests that his eyes were already closed at the moment of death – and remained so. And while the embalmer has secured his mouth with the assistance of a needle and a ligature, there is no sign of bruising as you might expect. I do not get the impression that the poor boy struggled in death.'

'Thank you for that,' said Oscar, resting his hand lightly on Conan Doyle's shoulder. 'That is something.'

An awkward silence fell, broken by Fraser. In my left hand I was still holding the brown wrapping paper and string that I had fetched from the dining room. Fraser said, abruptly, holding out his hand as if to confiscate contraband from an errant schoolboy, 'Give them to me, if you please.'

As, obediently, I handed them over, there was a rap at the study door and Mrs Ryan entered, carrying a tray bearing a decanter of brandy and four glasses. 'Mrs Wilde is much better, sir,' she said to Oscar as she came in. 'She thought you gentlemen might be in need of refreshment.'

'Thank you, Mrs Ryan, thank you,' said Oscar, turning his back to his writing desk so as to hide the cardboard box from view.

Conan Doyle relieved the cook of her tray. 'You have handled a difficult situation well, Mrs Ryan,' he said. She bobbed a grateful curtsey and started to retreat, when Fraser stopped her in her tracks.

'Before you go – if I may?' he asked, glancing at Oscar. 'When you received the parcel at the door, how did you know it was intended for Mrs Wilde?'

'The cabman said so.'

'It was delivered by an ordinary cabman?' said Fraser.

'Yes, in a two-wheeler. He said he'd been sent from the Albemarle Club. He gave me the parcel. I gave him a tip. And he was gone.'

'What did he say? Precisely?'

'I can't recall, exactly.'

'Try, woman!'

'Inspector,' said Oscar sharply, 'treat Mrs Ryan with some respect. She has endured a hateful experience this evening. We all have.'

Mrs Ryan looked steadily at Inspector Fraser. 'He said, "I've come from the Albemarle Club with a gift – for immediate delivery."'

'That is all he said?' asked Fraser. 'Just those words? Are you sure?'

'Those words, or thereabouts. Yes, that was all he said, I'm sure. Other than "Goodnight". He was a courteous fellow.'

'Thank you, Mrs Ryan,' said Oscar.

'Thank you,' said Fraser. 'Thank you.' As the woman left the room, the detective held out the wrapping paper and asked us to read what was written on it. I read, 'Mrs Oscar Wilde, c/o The Albemarle Club'. Arthur read, 'Mr Oscar Wilde, c/o The Albemarle Club.'

'You see?' said Fraser. 'It could be "Mr" or "Mrs", could it not?'

'I suppose so,' said Oscar, examining the paper. 'Is it material?'

'It might be,' said Fraser. 'Do you recognise the hand-writing?'

'No,' said Oscar, 'not at all. The hand looks uneducated to me. Beyond that . . .' Oscar's voice trailed away as he turned back to the cardboard box and its macabre contents.

'Who would wish to send this to you, Oscar, let alone to Constance?' asked Conan Doyle.

'Who, indeed?' said Fraser. 'I think we should go to the Albemarle at once. There is no time to be lost.'

' "No time to be lost"?' Oscar offered up a hollow laugh. 'It is four months since I first reported this murder to you, Aidan – and now, suddenly, there is "no time to be lost"!'

'There was no body then, Oscar, no evidence of murder . . . Come,' – he said it kindly – 'if your young friend Gray will see Veronica and Touie into a cab, we can go to Albemarle Street now and be back in Chelsea within the hour. Are you happy to leave Constance with Mrs Ryan?'

'Indeed,' said Oscar. 'She will be quite safe with Mrs Ryan. I have found our servants to be among our truest friends.'

I was despatched to give John Gray his instructions. He was to ensure Miss Sutherland's and Mrs Doyle's safe return to 75 Lower Sloane Street, leaving Mrs Ryan to see Constance to bed, while Fraser led Oscar, Arthur and me on what he described as 'the trail of this infamous package'.

It was a trail that ran cold at once. We found a four-wheeler in the King's Road and reached the Albemarle Club within twenty minutes. Hubbard had plenty of information to offer (he was at his most obsequious; club members in general, and Oscar in particular, had been bountiful with their seasonal gratuities), but none that was especially helpful. Yes, he recalled the arrival of the package at about seven o'clock that evening. A nonde-script cabman – not one he recognised, not one whose number he could recall – had brought the parcel to the porter's lodge. The cabman – a south Londoner if he remembered aright, or maybe a Cockney; accents were not his 'strong suit' – had said, 'It's a gift for Wilde for immediate delivery,' or words to that effect.

As soon as the cabman had gone, Hubbard noticed that the package was in fact addressed, as he read it, to Mrs Wilde and, knowing that Mrs Wilde rarely, if ever, visited the club, took it upon himself to order another cab immediately and get the gift sent on to 16 Tite Street straightaway. He had done what he had done for the best. He hoped he had done right. He hoped so most sincerely. Oscar assured him he had indeed done right, thanked him for his pains and gave him half a sovereign (*half a sovereign!*) to ensure that there was no doubt about the fullness of his gratitude.

'What do we do now?' I asked as we stood in silence in a small circle on the club's front doorstep. It was gone eleven and the January night was chill and foggy.

Fraser was still cradling the 'infamous package' in his arms. 'I must take this to Scotland Yard,' he said. 'I suggest the rest of you go home to bed. We can catch cabs in Piccadilly.'

As he spoke, looking down the darkened street to see whether a cab might not be coming our way, I saw the outline of a figure that I sensed I recognised, standing, waiting, by the front step of the Albemarle Hotel, just a few doors away. I sensed that Oscar had seen it too because he turned from it to look at me directly and, as he did so, almost imperceptibly, he shook his head. 'Gentlemen,' he said, quite suddenly, 'we have not yet heard the chimes at midnight – shall we take a nightcap?'

'It's late, Oscar,' said Conan Doyle.

'Come, Arthur, just the one.' Oscar brooked no argument; wasted no time. Ignoring the protests from Conan Doyle and Fraser, he proceeded briskly back into the club. Muttering, still in our overcoats, Fraser still clutching the package, we followed. 'Gentlemen,' said Oscar, once we were ensconced in Keppel Corner, 'Hubbard is at your service. What is your pleasure?'

Though Keppel Corner was deserted and, once Hubbard had served our drinks (iced champagne for Oscar and me; brandy and soda for the detective and the doctor), we were completely alone, for the next forty minutes, incredibly, no one made any mention of the curious and disturbing events of the night. Oscar led the conversation and led it in every direction except that of the murder of Billy Wood. He was, given the circumstances, almost bizarrely playful. He said to Aidan Fraser – who sat in his hat and coat, with the grim package fixed resolutely on his lap: 'If I did not know you,

Inspector, I'd take you for a Fenian on the run. You look exactly like a revolutionary nursing a home-made bomb.' He teased Conan Doyle in particular. 'Is that to be your New Year resolution, Arthur – "Just the one"? You are moderate in all things, are you not? But nothing is good in moderation. You cannot know the good in anything until you have torn the heart out of it by excess. This year may I urge you to live a little dangerously? Make 1890 the year in which you try to cultivate at least one redeeming vice.'

Fraser appeared perturbed by Oscar's banter. Conan Doyle seemed only amused. 'What is your New Year resolution to be, Oscar?' he asked.

'Let old acquaintance be forgot!' said Oscar, without hesitation.

'Surely not?' said Conan Doyle, laughing.

'There will be exceptions, Arthur,' said Oscar, 'and you will be among them. We are friends for life, I know that – I believe that – but why should we not joyfully admit, both of us, that there are some people – other people – we do not wish to see again? It is not ingratitude. It is not indifference. They have simply given us all they have to give and we must move on.'

Conan Doyle raised his glass to Oscar and said, 'I amaze myself, but I think I agree with you.'

'Oh, no!' cried Oscar. 'Please, Arthur, no! Whenever people agree with me, I always feel I must be wrong.'

We laughed.

'And Robert?' asked Fraser, turning to me. 'What is your New Year resolution to be?'

I looked at Aidan Fraser and I thought of Veronica Sutherland. I said, with too much emotion in my voice, 'To follow my heart, wherever it may lead.'

'And where might that be?'

Deftly, Oscar intervened to save me from myself. 'Do not ask, Aidan. Robert does not know the answer, I assure you. But you, Aidan, is this the year in which you and Miss Sutherland will follow your hearts to the altar?'

'I think so. I hope so. I shall be thirty-three this year—'

'On 31 August,' said Oscar.

'Yes,' said the inspector, clearly taken aback. 'How did you know?'

'I think you told us on the day we met – on 1 September, the day following your birthday. Either you told us, or I discovered it when I was reading up on you in the Metropolitan Police Directory.'

Fraser laughed. 'You never cease to surprise me, Mr Wilde.'

Oscar looked at him reprovingly. 'My name is Oscar, Aidan. We are friends . . .'

'Anyway,' resumed the inspector, 'I believe thirty-three is the correct age for a man to marry.'

'There is never a correct age for a man to marry,' said Oscar, teasingly. 'Marriage is as demoralising as cigarettes and far more expensive.'

'Do not listen to Oscar,' said Conan Doyle. 'He is talking nonsense and he knows it.'

Now it was Oscar's turn to laugh. 'I will not argue with you, Arthur. It is only the intellectually lost who ever argue.'

Oscar's conversation was so brilliant that he could make you forget the toothache. That night, we sat in a dark corner of a London club with a dead boy's head in a box before us and for forty minutes thought not a thing about it. (No doubt, the champagne and the brandy helped.)

Eventually, as midnight struck and our glasses were drained, it was Oscar who brought us back to reality. 'Well, Inspector,' he said, looking steadily at Fraser, 'what next? What now? Where do we go from here with this murder inquiry?'

'I hope you go nowhere with it, Oscar. Leave it to me now, please.'

Oscar gave a nod of apparent acquiescence. 'What will your first move be?' he asked.

'I will get some of my men to try to trace the cabman who delivered this parcel. And tomorrow I shall go to Broadstairs. I must meet Mrs Wood. You have told me her story, but I must talk to her myself. And I must show her the boy's head.'

'You cannot!' exclaimed Oscar.

'I must,' said Fraser.

'The shock will kill her.'

'It is a dangerous thing to do, Aidan,' said Conan Doyle.

'Fear not, I will take her to a police morgue. It will be a formal identification. The young man's head will be placed on a slab with, below it, a bolster beneath a sheet to give the impression of a body. She will not know of the decapitation.'

'Is this really necessary, Aidan?' asked Oscar.

'It is essential. We must know for certain whose head this is.'

'It is the head of Billy Wood.'

'So you tell us, Oscar. So you say. But whose word do we have for this – for any of this – other than yours? You are a writer, Oscar, a raconteur, a teller of tales. I am a policeman. This is a police inquiry now.'

15

3 January 1890

'It is a humiliating confession,' said Oscar, extinguishing one cigarette beneath his right foot while lighting another, 'but we are all of us made out of the same stuff.' We were standing at the north end of Baker Street, outside the railway station, about to cross the road. My friend drew on his fresh cigarette with deep satisfaction. 'The more one analyses people,' he continued, 'the more all reasons for analysis disappear. Sooner or later, one comes to that dreadful universal thing called human nature.'

'What is your point, Oscar?' I asked. It was eleven o'clock on the morning after the night of Constance's birthday dinner and my mind was not in a fit state to absorb fundamental truths about the universality of human nature.

'I know who murdered Billy Wood,' he said, blowing a small cloud of grey-white cigarette smoke into the cold January air. 'Or, at least, I think I do.'

I gazed at him, amazed. 'What are you telling me, Oscar?'

'It's all down to human nature. We're all made of the same stuff. We're all motivated by the same impulses: you, me, the murderer—'

'And you know who it is? You know who murdered Billy Wood?'

'I believe I do,' he said, smiling slyly, 'thanks, in large part, to something you said last night, Robert . . .'

'Something I said?'

'But, as yet, I have no proof – and it's proof we're after now.'

'Come, man,' I expostulated, 'spill the beans, spit it out. Whom do you believe the murderer to be?'

'Not yet, Robert—'

'What do you mean, "Not yet, Robert"? You can't leave me in suspense like this!'

'Oh, but I can, Robert, and I must.' We stepped into the busy roadway, Oscar forging a path between a milk-float and an omnibus. 'Suspense is everything!' he cried. 'Only the banal – only the bearded and the bald – live for the here and now. You and I, Robert, we live for the future, do we not? We live in anticipation.' We weaved our way through the traffic, Oscar raising his voice in competition with the rumble of wheels and the clatter of hooves. 'We live for the promise of delights only dreamt of, of sweets not yet savoured, of books as yet unwritten and unread.' At last, we reached the safety of the pavement on the other side. At the kerb's edge, leaning against a lamp-post, was a street urchin – a friendly-faced lad of twelve or thirteen – who raised his cap to us. Oscar nodded to the boy and handed him sixpence. 'We are grateful for our memories, of course. What's past sustains us. But it's what's to come that drives us on.'

'Is it?' I asked, unnerved by our crossing and bewildered by his flow of words.

'It is. It is the *pursuit* of Miss Sutherland that excites you, Robert. The chase is everything. Once you have achieved her, what then?'

I said nothing. Oscar put his arm through mine and turned us northwards, in the direction of Regent's Park. '*Mon ami*,' he said, 'when I am certain who is the murderer – certain beyond doubt – I shall tell you. I shall tell no one before I tell you, I promise. At present, all I am truly certain of is that I shall unravel this mystery before our friend Fraser does.'

'I thought you said last night that from now on you were going to leave the detective work to him.'

'Did I say that? I don't think I did. But if I did, that was then and this is now, and now I'm saying something different. Who wants to be consistent? Only the dull and the doctrinaire – the tedious people who carry through their principles to the bitter end of action, to the *reductio ad absurdum* of practice. Not I!'

'You are on song this morning,' I remarked, marvelling at my friend's energy and resilience. He could have had no more than five hours' sleep.

'Am I?' he said cheerfully. 'If I am, I have you and Conan Doyle to thank for that. Last night was not easy for any of us, but you came up trumps—'

'I did nothing.'

'You did more than you realise. As I said to John Gray at breakfast, "Sherard is a true friend," and there's something about Conan Doyle, despite his hideous handshake, that lifts the spirit.'

'He is a decent man,' I said.

'He is a genius,' said Oscar. 'He left me a copy of the story that he has just completed, *The Sign of Four*.

It is a little masterpiece. Sherlock Holmes is my inspiration!'

I laughed. 'Is that why we have come to Baker Street?'

'No, Robert, we are going to the zoo. We are on our way to interview Gerard Bellotti.'

'At the zoo?'

'It is Monday, is it not? Bellotti is always at the zoo-logical garden in Regent's Park on a Monday morning. He is a creature of habits – few of them good ones.'

'What does he do at the zoo on Mondays?'

'What he does at the skating rink on Thursdays and the Alhambra or the Empire on Saturdays: he scouts for boys.'

As all the world knows, on 25 May 1895, at the Central Criminal Court at London's Old Bailey, Oscar Wilde was found guilty of committing acts of gross indecency with other men and sentenced to two years' imprisonment with hard labour. The trial judge, Mr Justice Wills, described the case as the worst he had ever heard, accus-ing Oscar of being 'dead to all sense of shame' and 'the centre of a circle of extensive corruption of the most hideous kind among young men'.

Bellotti's 'boys' were the type of young men of whom Mr Justice Wills was speaking: that I must accept. What I do not accept, however, is that Oscar was ever the centre of any circle of corruption. He cultivated the company of young men – he revelled in their youth – but he did not corrupt them. He reverenced them. Whether they were always worthy of his adoration is another matter. Several of those who gave evidence against him at his trial were young men whom he had treated as friends – and who repaid that friendship with false testimony bought at a price. (From the spring to the summer of 1895, every one of the prosecution witnesses in the case of *Regina v. Wilde* was paid a retainer of five pounds a week.)

In a conversation with me some time after Oscar's death, Arthur Conan Doyle likened what he called 'our friend's pathological obsession with masculine youth and beauty' to his creation Sherlock Holmes's addiction to morphine and cocaine. 'In my experience,' said Conan Doyle, 'great men are frequently shot through with an obsessive or addictive strain that may seem aberrant – even abhorrent – to the rest of us. It does not diminish their greatness. It may make us more aware of their humanity.'

If, on occasion, in moments of weakness, in the privacy of a darkened room, Oscar succumbed to the sins of the flesh, so be it. It happened. It was his way. It does not make him a corrupter of youth. I knew Oscar from the time he was twenty-eight until the time of his death; you must believe me when I tell you he was a gentleman in the fullest, best and truest sense of the word. As Conan Doyle has written in his own memoir,* 'Never in Wilde's conversation did I observe one trace of coarseness of thought.' Neither did I.

The same could not be said of Gerard Bellotti.

We found Bellotti in the monkey house, eating peanuts. He was cracking open the shells between his teeth and spitting the nuts through the bars into the monkeys' enclosure.

'Bread and bread, these two,' he said, as we approached. He did not turn to greet us. 'I thought they might take a fancy to one another, but they haven't. Fighting like cats. That's monkeys for you.' He uttered a

* *Memories and Adventures*, 1924.

small high-pitched laugh and held out his paper bag of peanuts in our direction. 'Care for one?'

'No, thank you,' I said, 'I've breakfasted.'

'Oho, Mr Wilde, your friend has a lively sense of humour. We like that in a man, don't we?' Oscar said nothing. 'Mr Wilde has a lovely sense of humour,' Bellotti added, shifting his huge bulk slightly, but still keeping his gaze fixed firmly ahead of him. The monkeys – long, lanky, ugly creatures, with low-slung pot-bellies, their shaggy coats grey-haired and moth-eaten – swung wildly around their cage, squealing and screeching as they went. Bellotti's head did not follow their movements, but he seemed to know what they were doing nonetheless. One of the animals came to rest immediately in front of him, lying on its back, scratching itself against the ground. 'Nice pencils they have,' murmured Bellotti. 'I like a well-endowed monkey, don't you?'

'These are spider monkeys,' said Oscar, 'and these are females of the species.'

'Surely not?' said Bellotti, turning in our direction for the first time. There was a milky-white translucent film across his eyes and his blackened teeth were decorated with shards of peanut shell. His sallow skin was faintly pock-marked and, beneath his boater, tight curls of his henna-coloured hair glistened with oil and perspiration. He was not a pretty sight.

'The elongated sexual organ of the female spider monkey is often confused with that of the male. Do not trouble yourself, Mr Bellotti. It is a common mistake.'

I laughed. 'How on earth do you know this, Oscar?'

Oscar smiled. 'I have read *Mycroft on Monkeys*. It is the standard text. My reading extends beyond Sophocles and Baudelaire, you know.'

Bellotti sniffed and stuffed his paper bag of nuts into his pocket. He pinched his nose and closely studied his thumb and forefinger as he rubbed them together lightly. 'I take it you've come about Billy Wood,' he said. 'I've heard the news. It is very sad. He was a bright boy, one of the best. You were especially fond of him, Mr Wilde, I know. My condolences.'

'Who told you?' asked Oscar, moving a half-step closer to Bellotti and at the same time indicating to me that I should take a written note of what was to follow.

'O'Donnell,' said Bellotti, 'the uncle.'

Oscar raised an eyebrow. 'When was this?'

'Just before Christmas. He was drunk – and abusive. Made all sorts of threatening noises. Demanded money, the usual thing. I sent him on his way.'

'Did you give him anything?'

'Advice, that's all. But good advice. I told him to leave the country – return to Canada or go to France. He speaks French of a sort, when he's sober enough to speak at all. I've not heard from him since. Have you, Mr Wilde?'

'No,' said Oscar, quietly. He seemed suddenly distracted, in a reverie, thinking of something other than what Bellotti was saying, though with a brief nod of his head he indicated to me that I should continue to take notes.

'I believe he may have killed the boy himself,' said Bellotti, now peering at a grubby thumbnail as he used it to push back his cuticles, 'though he denied it. And vehemently. With more threats and vile abuse. Of course, he

172

could have murdered the poor boy in a drunken rage and clean forgotten that he had done so.'

'In that case, wouldn't the body have been discovered by now?' I asked.

'Not necessarily. I imagine it happened in Broadstairs. Having killed the boy, he disposed of the body at sea. Or maybe he drowned him in the first place – pushed him off the cliff at Viking Bay or flung him off the end of the pier. I don't know. I do know Billy Wood couldn't swim.'

'How do you know that?' asked Oscar, snapping back from his reverie.

'I took him to the baths in Fulham once, Mr Wilde. With Mr Upthorpe. Billy told me he couldn't swim. He told me he had a horror of water. He got it from his mother, he said.'

'Why did O'Donnell come to you at all?' I asked.

'He came for money. He came for Billy's wages.'

'Billy's wages?' I asked. Gerard Bellotti was slowly pushing ajar a window on a world with which I was entirely unfamiliar.

'The wages go to the guardian. The tips and presents go directly to the boy. Mr Wilde gave Billy a beautiful cigarette case, did you not, Mr Wilde? It carried a charming inscription, I recall. Billy was proud of it, rightly so.'

Oscar said nothing. (I thought nothing of the cigarette case at the time – or later. Oscar was absurdly generous with his gifts. He was particularly partial to presenting his friends with inscribed cigarette cases. Over the years, he gave me three.) 'Was O'Donnell the boy's guardian?' I asked.

'He was his uncle. And his mother's lover, as I understand it. He was the one who first brought the boy to me, in any event. It was just a year ago. I assume he had the mother's blessing. I assume they shared the wages. Billy was properly paid – and enjoyed the work. He took to it. He was a natural, wasn't he, Mr Wilde?'

'I did not realise that you paid him, Mr Bellotti,' said Oscar, coldly.

'Did you not, Mr Wilde?'

'I gave the matter no thought, I am ashamed to say.'

'A labourer is worthy of his hire, is he not, Mr Wilde? And modelling is onerous work, especially when you're working for an artist as particular as our Mr Aston Upthorpe.'

'I'm afraid I don't know his work,' I said.

'You wouldn't,' said Oscar, with a hollow laugh. 'And I don't believe Edward O'Donnell murdered Billy Wood. Why should he – if, as you say, Billy earned him a weekly wage? Why slaughter your own milch cow?'

'I'm not saying he did, Mr Wilde. I'm saying he might have done. He has the temperament. He's a violent man at the best of times, and when he's in drink . . . All I'm saying is it's possible, you'll grant me that? And assuming the boy was already dead when you and your friend came to see me, Mr Wilde – you remember, at the skating rink? – assuming Billy was dead by then . . .'

'He was,' said Oscar.

'Well,' said Bellotti, 'then O'Donnell was, as far as I know, the last man to see the boy alive.'

'What?' exclaimed Oscar. 'What are you saying?'

The monkeys in their cage whooped and screeched as Gerard Bellotti looked up towards us with a devilish smile. He lifted his straw boater, took a yellow handkerchief from his pocket and mopped his brow. He was evidently elated by the effect on Oscar of the intelligence he had just let slip.

'You both came to see me on a Thursday, did you not?'

'Yes,' said Oscar, 'on 2 September.'

'And you asked me when I had last seen Billy Wood?'

'And you told us first it was on the day before,' I said, 'and then corrected yourself and said it was on the Tuesday.'

'It was on Tuesday 31 August, was it not?' asked Oscar. 'You told us Billy had been at one of your "club lunches" and you always hold your lunches on the last Tuesday in the month.'

'That's right, Mr Wilde, you remember. You've been to one or two of them yourself, of course – not for a while, I know, and not since we moved to Little College Street.'

'O'Donnell was not at the lunch, surely?'

'Naturally not,' said Bellotti, with a splutter of disgust. 'But the point, Mr Wilde, is this. Billy left the lunch early in order to meet up with him. At two o'clock, on the dot, Billy got to his feet and asked to be excused. I can see the boy now – in my mind's eye. He was wearing a sailor suit. Very fetching. He said he had an important appointment with his uncle. He told us he was looking forward to it. He said he had shaved especially, I remember. We all laughed at that – given he was so young. He stood at the door and took his leave of us with a little naval salute. He was a lovely lad. That was the last I saw of him.'

'And you say it was two o'clock?'

'On the dot. We heard Big Ben strike.'

'And within two hours the poor boy was dead,' said Oscar, 'murdered in cold blood – not in Broadstairs, but in a perfumed room not two streets away.'

'Now you are telling me what I did not know,' said Bellotti, mopping his face with his yellow handkerchief. The monkey house was hot and airless.

'Who else was at the lunch?' asked Oscar.

'All the regulars – Mr Upthorpe, Mr Tirrold, Mr Prior, Mr Talmage – Canon Courteney, of course – and a couple of other boys.'

'No strangers?'

'No strangers.'

'I must meet them,' said Oscar. He looked at me, indicating that it was time for us to take our leave. 'We must piece together all the details of Billy Wood's final hours. We must talk to those who saw him last.'

'Come to our next lunch,' said Bellotti, holding out his hands, palms upwards, by way of invitation. 'They'll all be there. I'll make sure of that. Bring your friend, Mr Wilde. He'll be most welcome.'

'Thank you,' said Oscar.

'Little College Street, number 22. Any time from twelve. I take it you've still got your key?'

'But you've moved, haven't you?' said Oscar.

'Different address. Same lock. Canon Courteney's idea.' Bellotti raised his boater in my direction. 'It's always the last Tuesday in the month. Be sure to breakfast lightly. We lay on a good spread, don't we, Mr Wilde?'

'Indeed,' said Oscar, without emotion. 'Thank you, Mr Bellotti.'

We made to leave. Bellotti returned his attention to the monkeys, feeling in his coat pocket for his bag of nuts. 'You say they're all females, Mr Wilde?'

'Without question, Mr Bellotti.'

The fat man shifted his bulk uneasily and shook his head ruminatively from side to side. 'Appearances can be very deceptive,' he said, with a small laugh.

'Indeed,' said Oscar. 'Good day.'

As we reached the door of the monkey house, it swung slowly open as if by magic. As we stepped through it, we saw that it was being held open by Bellotti's dwarf. The ugly creature gazed up at us with ill-concealed contempt. Oscar threw a sixpenny piece at his feet.

When we reached the gates of the zoo itself, we found a hansom cab awaiting us, with, standing by it and holding open the cab door, the street urchin with the friendly face who had touched his cap to us in Baker Street an hour before. As we clambered into the vehicle, Oscar turned to the lad and said, 'Continue to keep an eye on them, Jimmy. They're not to be trusted.'

As the hansom set off towards town, the boy stood on the roadside watching us, waving us on our way.

'Who is that?' I asked.

'One of my "spies",' said Oscar. 'One of the best.'

16

'Look at the Postscript'

'Who are these "spies"?' I asked, as our cab rumbled through Clarence Gate, out of Regent's Park and, into Baker Street.

'Good-hearted boys, like Jimmy there,' he said. 'Street boys — ragamuffins, urchins, call them what you will. Their lives may be rackety and irregular by the standards of the sons of stockbrokers and civil servants, but they are good lads, my "spies", hard-working and as honest as the day is long.'

'They work for you? You pay them?'

'I give them the odd sixpence and keep them out of mischief. They run errands for me: carry messages about town, deliver flowers, get me cabs . . .'

'And "spy" on your behalf?'

He smiled. 'When necessary. They are my roving eyes and ears, Robert, and — more to the point — my roving legs. As you've observed, I'm not much given to exercise. I wasn't built for it. These lads are nimble and fleet of foot. They can throw a girdle round the capital in forty minutes. Each one's my Ariel.'

'How many of them do you have, then?'

'Across London? Two dozen perhaps, thirty at the most. I count them among my truest friends. Conan

Doyle has given Holmes a similar band of youthful assistants, but I came up with the idea first. Posterity will give me no credit for it, of course – unless you put the record straight. You are my Recording Angel, Robert. My reputation rests with you.'

Oscar did not keep a diary, but he knew that I did and he encouraged me to continue. He was fond of remarking that he had put his genius into his life but only his talent into his work and he told me, regularly, that he was relying on me and my journal to show posterity where his genius lay.

I took this responsibility seriously. For example, when we parted after our encounter with Gerard Bellotti, the first thing I did on getting back to my room was to write up the record of the morning's adventure. Indeed, it would be true to say that, during the years when Oscar and I were closest, my journal is as much an account of his life as it is of my own. Perhaps that is not so surprising. His life was infinitely more remarkable than mine.

Re-reading my diary of January 1890, what do I appear to have achieved that month? Very little. My days, it seems, were spent in pursuit of Veronica Sutherland. My evenings, until I met up with Oscar at around 11 p.m. for our customary nightcap at the Albemarle Club, were mostly empty. Usually, I dined in my room alone and then wandered the streets of Bloomsbury and Soho for an hour or so. Occasionally, I treated myself to a solitary glass of beer at a public house in Chenies Street. I went to the theatre twice (to the Drury Lane pantomime and, with Oscar, to the revival of an H. J. Byron farce at the Criterion) and one evening, so the record shows, I took a young lady named Lucy (of whom I have no recollection whatsoever) to the Agricultural Hall to witness an American cowboy on horseback racing a French bicyclist on a penny-farthing! (I reckoned the outing 'a costly failure'; the novelty of the entertainment quickly wore thin and Lucy, apparently, spent the entire evening explaining to me that her brother would be most anxious if she were not home by half past ten.)

In the exact same period, by contrast, Oscar, according to my journal, dined out on twenty-six nights out of thirty-one. He spent his evenings in the company of the outstanding personalities of the age – poets, playwrights, politicians, artists and actresses, men and women whose names still resonate half a century later – and his days seated at Thomas Carlyle's writing desk, writing, reading, reflecting. That month, while I wrote not one worthwhile word (and appear to have read nothing of note except, appropriately enough, Jerome K. Jerome's *Idle Thoughts of an Idle Fellow*), Oscar's reading encompassed (to my certain knowledge) Goethe, Balzac, Baudelaire, Plato, Petrarch and Edgar Allan Poe, and his writing included two articles, one lecture, three poems, the outline of a play (for George Alexander) and ten thousand words of *The Picture of Dorian Gray*.

He made light of his industry. (His account of spending a morning deciding to place a comma in a paragraph, and then spending the afternoon deciding to take it out again, was one of his favourite *jeux d'esprit*.) And he made a point when we met of enquiring about my endeavours before giving news of his own. As soon as we had each been served with our eleven o'clock glass of champagne, he would ask, 'How is Miss Sutherland today? Is she still pretty? Is she still pleasing? Is she more pliant?' He gave the impression of being truly interested. Oscar had the charmer's gift of looking you in the eye and making you feel that, in that particular moment, he cared more about you than about anybody else in the world.

Usually, once we had spent five minutes discussing Veronica (and her infuriating ability to both encourage and resist me at the same time), Oscar would throw in a casual reference to Aidan Fraser. Did Miss Sutherland have news of her fiancé?

'No, we never speak of him. He is her fiancé, you understand?'

Of course, of course, but had I chanced to see him?

'In the hallway, in passing.'

Yes – and?

'And nothing, Oscar. He said good day. That was all. He did not ask after you. He did not mention our case.'

' "Our case"!' Oscar would explode. 'It's *his* case now! And he appears determined to keep it to himself.'

One evening towards the middle of January (it was the evening of our outing to the Byron farce at the Criterion) Oscar said to me, 'Do you not think it more than curious, Robert, more than strange, perverse, in fact, that friend Fraser – whom you encounter sometimes twice, sometimes three times a week – makes no reference, no reference of any kind, to his ongoing investigations in the matter of poor Billy Wood? Has he made a forensic examination of the poor boy's severed head? Has he traced O'Donnell? Has he interviewed Bellotti? He knows of your interest in the matter. He sees you, yet he says nothing.'

'I do not think his behaviour either strange or perverse, Oscar,' I said. 'I think it is a matter of professional pride.

He wants to solve the mystery in his own way, on his own terms. Veronica has told me as much.'

He pounced. 'Has she now? I thought you said that you and she never discuss Fraser—'

'It is Fraser-the-fiancé we don't discuss. Occasional references to Fraser-of-the-Yard are permitted.'

Oscar raised a cynical eyebrow. 'Do you not also wonder, Robert, why Fraser tolerates you as a rival for his fiancée's affections?'

Of course, I had wondered about this, but I did not want to admit as much to Oscar. 'I do not think Fraser sees me a rival,' I said quickly. 'He works long hours. He appears grateful to me for keeping Veronica occupied and entertained in his absence.'

Oscar said nothing, but uttered a little murmur, suggesting that he found my answer less than convincing. After a moment of reflection he added, 'All I'll say is that both Fraser-the-fiancé and Fraser-of-the-Yard seem oddly uninquisitive. He doesn't ask you about your intentions towards his bride-to-be. He doesn't ask me about the ring I removed from the body of the murder victim—'

'He keeps his own counsel,' I said.

'Yes,' said Oscar, 'I suppose that's admirable in its own way.' The thought seemed to amuse him. He threw the remains of yet another cigarette onto the smoking-room fire. 'Does Miss Sutherland, at least, make the occasional enquiry about the progress of the case?' he asked.

'She does,' I replied, 'but have no fears. I am circumspect.'

'There is no need to be, Robert. Feel free to tell Miss Sutherland everything – especially if it helps you secure another kiss. I'm pleased to hear of her interest. "Our case", as you call it, has become the unicorn in the corner of the drawing room: all are aware of it, but no one mentions it.' He began patting his coat pockets as if feeling for something. 'I had a ten-page letter from Arthur Conan Doyle today – ten pages! in a neat Edinburgh hand – and not one reference to the case.' He found the letter and brandished it before me. 'Arthur makes extensive enquiries about my "spies", but says not a word about Billy Wood! Two weeks ago, in my house, in his own hands he held the severed head of the murdered boy – yet today he writes to tell me about his plans for a new Sherlock Holmes story and to report, *in extenso*, that the weather in Southsea is surprisingly clement for the time of year! Come, come, Robert, something's up.'

I laughed. 'Are you suggesting a conspiracy of silence, Oscar?'

'I'm not sure,' he said. 'Read the letter for yourself.' He passed it to me. 'It's mostly about the weather, as you'll see, but he mentions you, sends you his kind regards – and hopes that, if you read *The Sign of Four*, you'll notice the quotation from La Rochefoucauld. Entirely your doing, apparently. I am responsible, it seems, for the references to Goethe and Thomas Carlyle, and for Holmes's addiction to cocaine.'

It was my turn to raise an eyebrow.

'Since, as you know, Robert, cocaine has never been one of my enthusiasms, I find this a trifle bizarre, but I have no doubt that it is intended as a compliment. Arthur is, essentially, a good man.'

I was glancing through the letter. Conan Doyle's hand was most precise. 'Much of this seems to be about your father, Oscar,' I said.

'Yes. Sir William Wilde was a distinguished eye and ear man in his day – a pioneer, in fact. Arthur, it seems, wishes to follow in his footsteps. He proposes to specialise in ophthalmology. Some people will do anything to get out of Southsea.'

As Oscar was speaking, my eye had moved on and I was reading the passage of the letter that referred to *The Sign of Four* and Sherlock Holmes's addiction to cocaine. 'I don't see where he says that you are responsible for Holmes's addiction, Oscar,' I said.

'He does not say so explicitly, I grant you.'

'He does not say so at all, Oscar. This is not about you. It's all about Holmes. Arthur simply says that he is anxious that the general reader will not take against Holmes because of the great detective's weakness for cocaine.'

'Read the next paragraph.'

' "It was to guard against this that I put a rebuke of my own into the mouth of Dr Watson." '

'And what does he have Watson say to Holmes? Read, Robert, read!'

' "Surely the game is hardly worth the candle. Why should you, for a mere passing pleasure, risk the loss of those great powers with which you have been endowed?" '

'Do you not see, Robert? Wearing the mask of Dr Watson, Dr Conan Doyle is sending me his own rebuke. A mask tells us so much more than a face . . .'

I scanned the page again. 'I do not see it, Oscar.'

'Arthur does not like the company I keep. I do not mean you, Robert . . . I mean others. He is fearful for me. He thinks, for "mere passing pleasure" I am putting at risk the "great powers" with which I've been endowed. It is well meant, I'm sure.'

'I think you are being over-sensitive, Oscar,' I said.

'Look at the postscript,' he replied.

I turned to the final page of the letter.

'In a letter,' Oscar continued, with the sly smile that he employed when he was about to say something that he hoped you would find amusing, 'what you cannot read between the lines, you will usually find in the postscript. It is like a codicil to a will. It is where you discover the meat of the matter.'

Beneath Conan Doyle's signature, I read his postscript: 'PS. For how long have you known Mr John Gray?'

I folded the letter and returned it to Oscar. 'What do you make of that?' I asked.

'That Arthur did not care for John Gray when they met, which is tedious, for they are both charming, in their different ways. I should have liked them to get on.' Oscar replaced the letter in his coat pocket, tapping it gently as he did so. 'It is an interesting communication nonetheless – as much for what it does not tell us, as for what it does. Why is there no reference to Inspector Fraser? Why is there no allusion to Billy Wood?'

'Have you replied?' I asked.

'I have,' said Oscar, smiling his sly smile once more. 'I have sent the good doctor a detailed report of the weather conditions in the vicinities of Sloane Square, Albemarle Street and the Strand – together with a line from *The Picture of Dorian Gray* by way of a postscript.'

'And the line is?'

' "Nobody ever commits a crime without doing something stupid." '

'Do you believe it?'

'I do. I know it to be true.'

'And you have sent the line to Arthur for what reason?'

'By way of a gentle rebuke of my own. I want him to know that I am still on the case. That is all. He may choose to ignore the unicorn in the corner. I choose not to. I am going to solve this mystery, Robert. *We* are going to solve this mystery, Robert!'

'We are indeed, Oscar,' I said, raising my glass to him. His enthusiasm was infectious – and endearing.

'And I think you will find our next set of interviews especially rewarding,' he continued. 'I am hopeful that one of Mr Bellotti's luncheon guests will supply us with the final clue.'

' "The final clue"?' I expostulated. 'I'm not sure that I yet have the first clue, Oscar!'

'Come, Robert. We are nearly there. Surely you see that? Re-read your notes, consult your journal. And meet me next Tuesday at noon. Shall we rendezvous at Westminster Bridge, on the north side? I am off to Oxford for five days. John Gray is coming with me. I am to give a lecture on "Poetry and Suffering". The truth is that a poet can survive anything but a misprint – but is Oxford the place for the truth? I don't know. All I know is that I shall attempt to inflame the undergraduates with my words and John Gray will then attempt to pacify them with locks of my hair. We shall have fun. Take care while I am gone, Robert.'

Oscar told me – quite clearly – that he was going to Oxford for five days. But four days later – quite clearly – I saw him in a two-wheeler travelling along the Strand.

In fact, it was Veronica Sutherland who saw him first. We had been lunching at the Savoy Hotel – an absurd extravagance on my part, but it was a cold and gloomy day and Veronica had told me that she had a craving for the warmth and excitement of the Savoy's electric lights – and thus it was that we stepped into the Strand at a little after half past three. We stood together on the pavement, arm in arm. I was gazing down the street, pretending to be looking for an empty cab, but hoping not to find one (the train journey from Charing Cross to Sloane Square was both quick and inexpensive), when Veronica suddenly cried, 'Look! Across the road. It's Mr Wilde – with a beautiful young lady. Do you think she is an actress?'

I turned to look in the direction in which Veronica was pointing and, indeed, there in a cab that was turning off the Strand into the small side-street that leads to the back of the Lyceum Theatre was Oscar. It was certainly he. He was extravagantly dressed, in a bottle-green winter coat with an astrakhan collar, and his head was thrown back in laughter. He looked as happy as I have ever seen him. Oscar was certainly Oscar, but the young lady was by no means beautiful. Though I could not see her features distinctly – there was a hood to her cape – I could see enough to know that she was the young woman from Soho Square, the young woman with the disfigured face.

'Do you think she is an actress?' repeated Veronica.

'I have no idea,' I said, 'but I would not call her beautiful.'

'Would you not?' said Veronica. 'Men have such odd ideas about women's beauty. I would say she is very lovely indeed. Mr Wilde has a passion for beauty, has he not?'

'And a horror of ugliness,' I said. 'I have known him cross streets to avoid the sight of someone he considered

ill favoured. He regards ugliness as a form of malady –
which is why I find it strange to see him in the company
of that particular young lady.' The cab had now disappeared from view in the gathering gloom of dusk.

'She is not ill favoured, Robert. If you think she is, you
are the one who is strange.'

'Perhaps all women seem plain to me in comparison
with you,' I said.

'You are very gallant, Mr Sherard,' she said, squeezing
my arm with hers and turning me in the direction of
Trafalgar Square. 'I should enjoy a promenade with such
a gallant gentleman. Would you walk me to Charing
Cross? We can then catch the twopenny tube.'

I leant towards her and kissed her on the forehead.

'Tell me,' she said, as we proceeded along the street, 'I
have been meaning to ask: for how long has Mr Wilde
known Mr John Gray?'

17

25 January 1890

When I met up with Oscar, as arranged, at twelve noon on 25 January 1890 – the last Tuesday in the month – he was looking well. His large face was as pale and pasty as it ever was, but his eyes had an unaccustomed sparkle to them and, even before he was aware of my approach, I saw that he was smiling. His smile, when it flashed at you, could be disconcerting – his teeth were discoloured and slightly protuberant – but, on this occasion, there was nothing forced or fleeting or uncomfortable about it. It was the easy smile of a man in a contented frame of mind. Sometimes, I thought, a face tells us more than a mask.

'You are looking well, Oscar,' I said, shaking him warmly by the hand. He was wearing canary-yellow kid gloves and sporting the green coat with the astrakhan collar that I had seen him wearing in the cab in the Strand two days before. Tied around his neck, he had a yellow jabot fixed with a diamond tie-pin. Tucked under his arm was a slim black cane, like a swagger-stick.

'Is the cane new?' I asked.

'It is,' he said, with satisfaction, giving it a flourish. 'It is a present to myself. I have mislaid your precious sword-stick, Robert. Constance is most displeased. It will turn up in due course, I'm sure. Meanwhile, I have acquired this black malacca cane to keep ruffians and vagabonds at bay.'

'It'll certainly do that,' I said. He preened himself; he was in peacock mode. As I sensed that a further compliment was expected, I added: 'You look quite the young buck about town.'

'I am pleased to hear it, Robert,' he said, tilting his head in acknowledgement of my bouquet, 'and I agree, wholeheartedly! Thank you, my friend. I *am* well. I have rarely been better. I feel fully alive today. To *live* is the rarest thing in the world. Most people exist, that is all. What a waste! I was just telling Old Father Thames here how blessed he is to be a river. Oceans and seas – they come and go. Lakes and ponds – they stagnate. But a river flows, a river makes progress, a river is always on the move.'

As Big Ben struck the last of the hour, we turned from Westminster Bridge and began to walk past the Houses of Parliament towards Westminster Green. Oscar was leading the way. 'How was Oxford?' I asked.

'Exquisite!' he replied, 'Made the more so by the fact that my visit was cut short. John Gray is still there, distributing locks of my hair among the faithful. I returned to town on Sunday.'

'Business or pleasure?' I enquired, as casually as I could.

'Both,' he said. 'I was summoned to see Henry Irving at the Lyceum. He is producing a new play based on *The Bride of Lammermoor*, Sir Walter Scott at his noblest . . . and most lugubrious.'

'And Irving wants your assistance?'

Oscar beamed at me. 'I have made a contribution that I trust will lift the gloom of the proceedings a little. We shall go together to the opening night, Robert. Mr Irving is a great man and a good man, too.'

Irving – the great actor-manager of the Victorian age, the first of his profession to be honoured with a knighthood – was only sixteen years older than Oscar, but Oscar venerated him, almost as a father. I observed them together on several occasions (chiefly in the studio of Sir John Millais; Millais and Irving were old friends) and it was intriguing, because it was so unusual, to see Oscar-the-prince transformed into Oscar-the-courtier. As a rule, Oscar treated all men as his equal, regardless of age or distinction. With Irving it was different. Oscar was in awe of Irving. Irving was his hero. And I sensed that, as a consequence, Irving was a little uncomfortable in Oscar's company.

We crossed Westminster Green and turned into Great College Street. 'Perhaps I should have been an actor, Robert,' said Oscar, still smiling. 'I should have liked to be a member of Irving's company.'

'You *are* an actor, Oscar,' I said.

'Yes,' he replied, suddenly swirling his cane above his head, 'but fated forever to play the same part. I envy Irving. One day he is Romeo, the next Mephistopheles. I am always Oscar Wilde.'

'Romeo touched with Mephistopheles,' I said. He roared with laughter, clearly liking my joke. I had rarely known him quite so merry.

We had reached Little College Street. 'Where is number 22?' he asked. 'I'm already feeling peckish. Bellotti lays on a good spread, as I recall.'

'There is number 22,' I said, indicating the narrow red-brick house immediately facing us. 'It looks identical to 23 Cowley Street.'

'The work of the same builder, I suppose,' said Oscar, looking up at the house as we crossed the road. The curtains at the first-floor window were drawn shut. The window on the ground floor was shuttered from within. The house appeared deserted. The street itself was empty, too. Suddenly, simultaneously, we both noticed how loud our voices seemed.

'Do you have the key?' I asked.

'I have Bellotti's key,' said Oscar, 'but we shall knock. We are visitors on this occasion.' As he drummed a rat-tat on the door, he said, 'See the knocker, Robert, how it gleams. We shall find a good woman in attendance here.'

We waited a moment in silence and then Oscar knocked again. 'There is no one here,' I said.

'There is,' said Oscar. 'She is coming down the stairs, holding a candle. Look.' He directed my gaze to the flecks of light dancing on the coloured glass above the front door. 'And I think we know her . . .'

The door was opened by a stout lady of riper years dressed in a full-length dress of black crêpe and taffeta. Around her waist was a white starched apron and on her head a curiously beribboned white linen mob cap that revealed a fringe of orange curls. I did not immediately recognise her, but Oscar did at once.

'Mrs O'Keefe,' he said, extending his hand towards her, as she bobbed down to genuflect before him, almost setting alight the ribbons of her mob cap in the process. 'The pleasure was hoped for, but not expected. How are you?'

'I am well, sir, bless the Lord,' she said, getting to her feet again, 'and you look well, too.' She held her candle up towards Oscar's face. 'I have been praying for you, as I promised.'

'To St Jude, I trust.'

'Not only him, but to St Cecilia too – come in, come in.' She stood back and beckoned us into the tiny darkened hallway. 'And, of course, to our blessed St Helen of the Holy Cross. I've always found her most dependable.' She had shut the door to the street behind us and we were standing in a tight circle, huddled around the candle. She looked up at Oscar with loving eyes. ''Tis good to see you, sir.'

A voice called from upstairs. 'Are they here? Are they here? Bring them up, Mrs O!'

'That's the canon, bless him. You're expected. He's not a Catholic, poor soul, but St Helen and I are working on that.' She turned to climb the stairs, plunging us – such was her bulk! – into virtual darkness. 'Follow me, gentlemen. You're in for a treat.' Over her shoulder she called to Oscar, 'It is so good to see you again, sir. So good.'

When we reached the top of the stairs, whoever had called for us from the landing was no longer there. The door that faced us was shut. 'You have to knock,' explained Mrs O'Keefe. 'Club rules.' She looked at Oscar with shining eyes. 'You're a member, of course, I know that, but they tell me you haven't been to any of the lunches for a while. Busy with your Mozart and your mind-reading, I imagine.'

Oscar gave her his most beatific smile and, with his cane, beat sharply on the door three times. After a moment's pause, the door swung open and before us, with arms outstretched, stood a diminutive clergyman, aged about sixty, bald, with a face like a monkey, wreathed in smiles. 'Hallelujah!' he cried, in a high-pitched, piping, happy voice. 'The prodigal is returned!'

If Mrs O'Keefe, on first encounter, several months before, had put me in mind of the dame from a Drury Lane pantomime, the tiny cleric who now took Oscar in his arms was no more and no less than the ecclesiastical equivalent of the Lane's mightiest comedian, the immortal Dan Leno – sometime clog-dancing champion of the world, celebrated (and rightly so) as 'the funniest man on earth'. The clergyman was as small and spry as Leno and as delightful. His face was so amusing; his movements were so dainty; and his warmth so true that I would defy you to resist it.

When he had released Oscar from his embrace, he turned to me and with both hands – and the softest fingers – reached up and lightly pinched my cheeks. 'Welcome!' he cried. 'Welcome, young man, thrice welcome!'

'This is Robert Sherard,' said Oscar, presenting me.

'Sutton Courteney,' said the clergyman, shaking my right hand with both of his. 'Canon Courteney – call me Canon, call me Sutton, call me anything you like. The boys all call me Can-Can – because I do!' Still holding my hand in both of his, gently he pulled me farther into the room. 'Meet the boys!' He glanced towards the house-keeper. 'Thank you, Mrs O'Keefe.' Beaming and bowing, with a final simper in Oscar's direction, the good lady backed her way out onto the landing, closing the door as she went.

I looked about the room. It was an extraordinary sight, like a tableau at the waxworks of Madame Tussaud. There were seven figures, all seated or lounging on the floor, each with a lighted candle at his side, and each with, before him or in his hand, a plate of food and a silver wine-cup. They were having a picnic. Only one of the seven was seated on a chair: it was Bellotti, who sat apart, at a small table, in a corner by the window. The rest – four benevolent-looking men (one in his early thirties, the others much older), and two good-looking boys, aged fifteen or sixteen – were lying on rugs and coats spread out on the bare floorboards, resting on their elbows or leaning against one another, back to back. The men were dressed in everyday apparel, suitable to the time of year. The boys, incredibly, were dressed in bathing suits.

'Welcome to our *Déjeuner sur l'herbe*!' cried Canon Courteney. The members of the party looked up towards us and offered assorted greetings. The canon produced two wine-cups for us and filled them with champagne. 'Now, whom do you know?' he asked. 'Mr Bellotti, of course.' He nodded towards Bellotti in the corner, who waved a lobster's claw in our direction. 'And Aston Upthorpe is an old friend of yours, Oscar, is he not?' Mr Upthorpe, apparently the oldest member of the group, began to struggle to his feet.

'Pray, don't move,' said Oscar. 'We will join you. You can see he is a fine artist, Robert. He wears a fine beret.' Upthorpe, his mouth full of ham and mustard, rumbled genially and offered me his hand. Oscar put down his cane, removed his gloves and took off his coat, laying it on the floor, adjacent to the wall. Taking one arm each, the canon and I helped lower him gingerly to the ground, where he sat, resting against the wall, like a beached porpoise leaning against a rock. 'Dear Lord,' he wheezed, 'such exertion. I'll be playing a round of golf with Conan Doyle next.'

'Aston, of course, knew poor Billy Wood best,' continued the canon. 'Billy worked for him. He was his special friend. Of course, Billy was special to us all.'

Oscar had recovered his breath. 'Was everyone who is here today also here at that last lunch – Billy's last lunch, I mean?'

'Yes, indeed, Oscar,' said the canon solicitously. 'Mr Bellotti told me that was what you wanted.'

'Mrs O'Keefe was not your housekeeper on that occasion?'

'Alas, no,' said the canon. 'We had no housekeeper that day. O'Donovan & Brown let us down. Most unlike them. We had to fend for ourselves. Mrs O'Keefe only joined us in September. We like her. She has proved completely reliable.'

'And Mr Bellotti's dwarf?' said Oscar. 'Was he not in attendance that day?'

'Mr Bellotti's dwarf?' repeated the canon, bemused.

Gerard Bellotti looked up from his table in the corner. 'He is my son, Mr Wilde.'

'I am sorry,' said Oscar, confused. 'I did not know.'

'Why should you?' answered Bellotti. 'He's an ugly wretch, with an evil temper. But he was not with me that day. He is never with me on a Tuesday. It is the day when he goes to Rochester. To the asylum. To visit his mother. She is feeble-minded. She dotes on him.'

An awkward silence fell. 'I did not know,' Oscar said again.

'It matters not,' said Bellotti, sucking a shrimp from its shell.

Canon Courteney cleared his throat by way of helping to clear the air. 'Let me complete the introductions, Oscar,' he said, 'and then the stage is yours.' Oscar nodded to him, gratefully. 'The lads you remember, of course – Harry and Fred. Don't ask me which is which. I do know, but I pretend not to.' The two boys in bathing suits waved in Oscar's direction. The canon continued: 'The other gentlemen are all newcomers since your time, I think. They joined us when we moved from Cowley Street. Mr Stoke Talmage, Mr Berrick Prior, Mr Aston Tirrold.' The three men raised their glasses first to Oscar, then to me.

'Yes, another Aston,' said Mr Tirrold, the youngest of the group, the only one with a moustache. 'It can cause confusion, but I believe Can-Can likes a bit of that.' The canon tiptoed past Tirrold, on his way to the picnic hamper, ruffling the young man's thick fair hair as he went.

'What wonderful names you all have,' said Oscar, quietly. 'Names fascinate me terribly.'

The canon was piling a plate high with good things for Oscar. 'You don't do so badly yourself, Mr Oscar Fingal O'Flahertie Wills Wilde.'

'Are those really your names?' asked one of the boys in a bathing suit.

'Indeed,' said Oscar.

'I like Oscar best,' said the other boy.

'I do, too,' answered Oscar, raising his wine-cup to the lad.

The canon was tiptoeing back towards Oscar with his lunch. 'Mr Wilde is Irish,' he explained to the boys as he went, 'and Oscar was the favourite son of Ossian, the fabled Irish warrior-bard. Oscar was killed at the battle of Gabhra in single combat with King Cairbre. It was a terrible day, even by third-century standards. Our Oscar, needless to say, follows in the bardic rather than the battling Irish tradition.'

The canon presented Oscar with a wide dish piled high with oysters and dressed crab, smoked fish and cold cuts, scoops of savoury jellies, slices of game pie, pickles, mayonnaise, mustard, bread and cheese. Oscar smiled up at him and then, under the canon's outstretched arm, in a stage whisper told the boys, 'In fact I'm named for the late King Oscar of Sweden. He was my godfather. My own father was an eye-surgeon and performed an operation on King Oscar for the treatment of his cataract.'

'That's what I need,' muttered Bellotti in his corner. 'When you want the father, you get the son. Isn't that just life?'

'It's such a pity Drayton isn't here,' said one of the other older men. Mr Talmage had a genial, drinker's face, ruddy and worn by life, with rheumy eyes and unnaturally black lank hair. 'Drayton is fascinated by surgery,' he added, by way of explanation. 'You could have described the operation to him. He would have liked that.'

'Who is Drayton?' asked Oscar. 'Is it Drayton St Leonard or Drayton Parslow, by any chance?'

'Drayton St Leonard,' answered the canon, now back at the hamper preparing a luncheon plate for me. 'Do you know him, Oscar?'

'I know the name, that's all.'

'We haven't seen him for a while. He wasn't with us in August, that last day with Billy, or I'd have made sure he was here today. It must be six months since we've seen him. You must meet him, Oscar. You'd like him. He's young – and very handsome.'

'We're all young and very handsome,' said the elderly gentleman with the drinker's face. 'That's one of the club rules.'

When we had laughed at Mr Talmage's joke (and one or two more that he had to offer in similar vein); and when the canon had given me my food and prepared a plate for himself; and after he had ordered the boys to make sure that everyone's wine-cup was properly charged and that those who wished for second helpings had been satisfied; and once the company had settled once more, he clapped his hands and said, 'Gentlemen, boys, Mr Bellotti, may I have your attention, please.' He had closed the hamper and perched himself on the top of it. In the flickering candlelight he looked like a holy hobgoblin seated on a toadstool at the centre of a fairy ring.

'We are gathered here together on a special day, the feast day of the blessed soldier saints, Juventinus and Maximinus, martyred together at Antioch under Julian the Apostate. As we shall recall later, during our service, neither was baptised until he came to manhood – but what a manhood it proved to be!'

The canon paused and in the silence that followed one of the boys in bathing suits suppressed a snigger.

'Hush, Harry!' said the canon.

'It wasn't me, Can-Can,' said the boy. 'It was Fred.'

'Hush, both of you,' hissed the canon. He looked at the boys reprovingly. 'Before we turn our attention to this afternoon's service,' he said, 'we have business to attend to. Mr Wilde and his friend are with us today for a purpose. They are investigating the tragic death of young Billy Wood, whom we all remember with such affection.'

A susurration of sympathy floated round the room. Aston Upthorpe said out loud, 'Billy was wonderful.'

'They believe he was murdered on the afternoon of 31 August last,' continued the canon, 'at 23 Cowley Street, not a stone's throw from where we are all gathered today. They believe that we – we few, the eight of us in this room now – were perhaps the last people to see poor Billy alive, and they want us to tell them whatever we can remember of that fateful day.' He paused and looked about the room. 'Have I got that right, Oscar?'

'You have, Sutton, thank you. Thank you very much. With your permission, my friend Mr Sherard will take notes. Perhaps each could say a word or two in turn?'

Aston Upthorpe spoke first – most eloquently and at greatest length – and what he had to say was echoed by all who spoke after him. Billy Wood was a dear boy, intelligent, honest, capable, devoted to his mother, determined to better himself and, in so doing, in due course, to be in a position to improve her lot as well as his own. He had plenty of friends and no known enemies. On the day that he met his death, he had been as he always was: cheerful. Had he been more cheerful than usual? asked Oscar. One or two of those present thought that possibly he had. He was undoubtedly in great good humour that day – cracking jokes and being playful – and when he announced that he was off to see his uncle he did so, apparently, with a certain swagger.

'He seemed quite pleased with himself,' said Aston Tirrold, 'the little bugger.' He said it not unkindly. 'He told us that he had shaved especially. We laughed at that.'

'He was wearing his Sunday best,' said young Fred.

'And he had your cigarette case with him, Mr Wilde,' said Harry. 'Will you give me a cigarette case too?'

Canon Courteney leant forward and clipped the boy sharply round the ear. He hit him hard. 'Mind your manners,' he said and hit him a second time. The boy yelped and fell silent.

'Thank you,' said Oscar, looking round the room, 'thank you all. That has been most helpful.'

'Is that all?' asked the canon, slipping nimbly off his perch.

'Oh, just one thing more,' said Oscar. 'You say Billy Wood left here at two o'clock—'

'As the clock struck,' said the canon, 'there's no doubt about that. I believe he even said that it was two o'clock and that he had to go because two was the time of his appointment.' There were murmurs of agreement from around the room.

'Indeed?' said Oscar, raising an eyebrow. 'And when he went, did anyone go with him? Or follow him?'

'No,' said the canon.

'I went to the window,' said Aston Upthorpe, 'and watched him go into the street. That was the last I saw of him.'

'And was he alone?'

'Quite alone. The street was empty.'

'And which way did he go? To the left? To the right?'

Upthorpe considered for a moment and then said, 'To the left. He ran off, without a care in the world.'

'And no one followed him? No one left this room?'

'Not until four,' said the canon. 'We all remained here until four. That's when we break up the party. At four, that's the rule. No one left until then – you have my word for it.'

'Thank you,' said Oscar, 'thank you.' He glanced in my direction and indicated that I should put away my notebook.

'Well,' said the canon, cheerily, 'if your business is done, if you have all you need to know, shall we move on? I will enrobe and we will proceed with the service. I trust you'll both stay.'

'Alas, we cannot,' said Oscar, putting out his arms in the hope of being helped to his feet. 'We have a train to catch.'

'Everybody seems in a hurry to catch a train now-adays,' muttered Bellotti from his corner.

'You are right,' said Oscar, giving himself over to the two boys in bathing suits who were easing him upwards, 'it is a state of things that is not favourable to poetry or romance, but there you are.'

'Is it to be a special service?' I asked the canon, as he was being assisted into his surplice by two of the other older gentlemen. His moon-shaped monkey-face appeared through the neck-hole of the surplice and he grinned at me.

'It is to be a baptism,' he said. 'This afternoon Fred and Harry are to follow in the footsteps of Juventinus and Maximinus. They are to be baptised! Today I really must remember which one is which.'

Messrs Prior and Talmage spoke together: 'We are to be godparents.' Aston Tirrold added, 'We all are – these two need all the spiritual guidance they can get.'

Canon Courteney kissed the embroidered crucifix on a white-and-gold silk stole and placed it carefully about his neck. 'This is why the boys are dressed as they are. I hope you did not think they were in bathing suits for amusement's sake. That would be perverse.'

I was bemused. 'Is there a font?' I asked.

'There's a champagne bucket,' said Bellotti from his corner.

'You see,' said the canon happily, 'God has provided. I am sorry you cannot stay, truly sorry. Come next month – the twenty-second. It's always the last Tuesday. It will be the feast of dear St Margaret of Cortona. We always do something very special for her. She was sorely tried, you know.'

Oscar had put on his gloves and coat, assisted by the boys, and retrieved his cane. Now he was passing around the room, stepping between candlesticks and wine-cups, to shake each of the club members by the hand. 'Thank you,' he repeated to each of them. 'Bless you.' He nodded to Bellotti and embraced the canon who, with a finger dipped in wine, anointed his forehead with a sign of the cross.

'Come, Robert,' he said to me, taking me by the arm and steering me towards the door. 'We must leave our friends to their service. Today is a special day.' He looked at the two boys who were hovering close by him. 'Don't worry, gentlemen, I shan't forget you. I shall send you both baptismal gifts. I know spoons are more customary, but I'll make it cigarette cases, if you don't mind – inscribed, of course. One for Fred, one for Harry. You can decide who should have which.'

By now everyone in the room – bar Bellotti – was standing to bid us farewell.

'Thank you once more for your assistance,' said Oscar, with his hand on the handle of the door. 'Thank you, too, for remembering Billy with so much sympathy and affection. Is there anything that was left unsaid?'

As Oscar opened the door, a slight gust of cold air blew into the room and the candles flickered in unison. Aston Upthorpe, the elder of the Astons, the one in the artist's beret, spoke up, quite clearly. 'I think the boy was in love,' he said.

'In love?' repeated Oscar.

'Yes — for the first time in his life. In love. But not with me.'

18

'Where is the Blood?'

'Do we have a train to catch?' I asked, as Mrs O'Keefe closed the door of 22 Little College Street behind us and we adjusted our eyes to the surprising brightness of the world outside. It was a little after half past two. The sky was overcast and there was the sulphurous haze in the air that was common in those days in the streets adjacent to the river, but by contrast with the candlelit gloom of the house, the street was a dazzle of light.

'No,' said Oscar, producing a handkerchief and blowing his nose, 'not today. It's too late today. And tomorrow, I am committed. I shall be attending a rehearsal for Mr Irving's new production at the Lyceum. I am looking forward to it more than I can tell you. But on Thursday, Robert, if you are free, we shall indeed catch a train. We shall return to Broadstairs, first thing. We must find O'Donnell, sober, if we can. We must see Mrs Wood once more. That will be our task for the day after tomorrow. But for now, my friend, since we are here, we shall retrace the final footsteps of poor Billy Wood. This way, I think.'

He pointed his cane across the street and stepped briskly into the empty roadway. Oscar was thirty-five but, to me, he had always seemed older than his years. He was large; he was cumbrous; he was not given to physical exertion. He regularly lamented the passing of the sedan chair. Usually, when he moved, he moved reluctantly, at the pace of the turtle, not the hare. That afternoon, however, in the empty backstreets of Westminster, there was a spring to his stride that I had not known before.

He read my thoughts. 'Yes, Robert,' he said, putting his hand on my shoulder as we crossed the cobbled street, 'we are retracing the final footsteps of poor Billy Wood, yet my spirit is high. I am intoxicated by more than Bellotti's cheap champagne. My mind rebels at stagnation. I abhor the dull routine of existence. The game's afoot – and my heart beats faster. I am exhilarated because in tragedy there is excitement. We thrill to Euripides in a way that we never do to Plautus.'

He paused halfway across the road, turning back to look up at the first-floor window of the house that we had just left. The heavy curtain was partially drawn back and there, at the window, stood Aston Upthorpe, in his absurd artist's beret, gazing down at us. He raised a hand and waved. Oscar waved back.

'Poor man. How he loved that boy. An old man's unrequited love is pitiful, is it not? May we be spared.'

The sudden clip-clop of hooves interrupted this maudlin meditation. A coal merchant's cart turned into the street and trundled towards us. Oscar clutched my arm and we hastened to the safety of the pavement opposite. 'So, Robert, the boy comes out of the house and, according to Upthorpe – our one witness – he turns left and runs across the road. He does not pause to consider which way to go. He knows where he is going. His appointment is for two o'clock, but he does not announce his departure until he hears the clock strike. Why? Because he knows he has not far to run. He reaches the corner of the street, he turns right . . . and immediately right again . . . and he is here.' We were now in Cowley Street. 'The journey has taken us barely two minutes. A boy of sixteen could run the distance in thirty seconds. So, one moment Billy is with his friends at 22 Little College Street and the next – within the twinkling of an eye – he is here, on the doorstep of 23 Cowley Street. *Why?* Why on that day? Why at that time? What was his purpose? Whom had he come to see?'

'That much we do know,' I said. 'He had an appointment with his uncle, Edward O'Donnell.'

'No, Robert, that cannot be; that makes no sense. O'Donnell is a brute and a drunkard – you don't run *to* him, you run *from* him. Billy ran here as eager as a bride. He came newly shaved, in his Sunday best: all our witnesses attest to that. And poor Upthorpe tells us that Billy was "in love" – and not with him . . . Was Billy running to meet his love?'

'You are saying that he could have come here to meet a girl?'

'Yes, Robert, it could have been a girl – or, perhaps, a woman? You have told me often of the woman who stole your heart when you were just sixteen. What was her name?'

'Madame Rostand.'

'And her age?'

'Twenty-seven.'

'And her breasts were like pomegranates . . . I remember.' (Oscar was indeed in high spirits that afternoon.) 'But if it was a woman, Robert, why did the other boys –

Fred and Harry – make no mention of her? Surely they would have known. Could a boy of sixteen keep "the older woman" in his life a secret from his friends? Could you?'

'But, Oscar,' I countered, choosing to rise above his banter, 'what I still don't understand is this: why did Billy say to the others, quite specifically, that he was on his way to see his uncle, if, in fact, he was not?'

'Either because he needed an excuse that would not be questioned, especially by Bellotti, or because – now here's a thought – because he *was* to meet his uncle, whom he feared, but in the company of someone else – someone with whom he felt safe, someone who, he thought, might be able to rid him of his uncle's tyranny . . .'

I was confused and unconvinced. I said, looking up at the house and grabbing at certainty: 'Whomever he came to meet, he came to meet them here.'

'Yes,' said Oscar. 'And within an hour, within an hour and a half at most, he was dead.' He knocked sharply on the door.

'What are you doing?' I asked.

'Hoping to gain admittance.' He knocked again. 'But see the door knocker – how dowdy it looks. Mrs O'Keefe has not been in attendance here for some time. I think we will find the house deserted.' He undid his coat and, from his waistcoat pocket, fetched a small Chubb key. He held it up. 'Bellotti's key,' he said.

'One key,' I said, looking at the door, 'but three locks.'

'And the key,' said Oscar, 'fits all three.' He undid each lock in turn. 'It is a Chubb skeleton key such as house-keepers use to gain entry to every room in an hotel. Bellotti knows his business.' Oscar pushed open the front door. The light from the street spilt into the tiny hallway, but there was darkness beyond.

'Do you have a match?' I asked.

'And a candle,' said my friend, with a smile, producing one from his coat pocket. 'There seemed to be a superfluity in Little College Street.'

He handed me his cane and lit the candle. We closed the front door behind us and stepped towards the stairs.

'Listen!' he whispered. We stopped, in silence. Nothing. We stood close together at the foot of the stairs. He held the candle between us. His eyes were glistening.

'Did Billy Wood have a key?' I asked.

'We can assume so,' said Oscar, 'either from Bellotti or from Upthorpe – but perhaps he did not need one . . . Perhaps it was the housekeeper who admitted him?'

'Was she "the older woman", do you think? Could she have been?'

'It is possible.'

'What was she like, Oscar? What was her age?'

'I cannot tell you!' he said. And as he said it, such was his sigh that he almost extinguished the candle. He turned from me in his exasperation. 'I cannot tell you, because I do not know. I did not look at her – even for a moment. I was late, I was preoccupied. She opened the door. I brushed past. It was so hot that day. I put down my hat and cane and – immediately, without pause – I made my way up these stairs.' He began to climb the staircase, holding the candle high to light the way. 'I was late. I had arranged to meet a pupil here at three—'

'A pupil?' I interrupted him. 'I thought you said it was a friend?'

'Indeed,' he answered impatiently, 'a pupil and a

friend – a student of mine. It really matters not.' He moved on up the stairs. 'The point is that I was thirty minutes late, perhaps more. I was in haste. I gave the housekeeper no attention, no thought whatsoever – fool that I am.'

We had reached the landing and were standing side by side outside the closed door to the room in which Oscar had found the dead body of Billy Wood. He paused.

'Hush!' he whispered. 'Hush! Listen!' I listened. I heard nothing. 'What was that?' he asked, handing me the candle. I waited, and then I heard it – a faint sound from within the room. It might have been the muffled cry of a whimpering child or the distant yelp of a wounded dog. We moved closer to the door. Abruptly, the mewling ceased and after a moment's silence, like a held breath, there was a sudden sharp explosion of scratching and scrabbling, followed by a noise that sounded like a fist pounding at glass. Oscar flung open the door and a tiny bird flew at our faces and then, with a fearful flapping of its little wings, flew chaotically away again. Wildly, it crashed and spun about the room, hitting the floor, hitting the walls and, again and again, throwing itself frantically against the window-pane.

'Oh God!' cried Oscar. 'It is the trapped spirit of poor Billy Wood! We must set it free.' He rushed across the room and, with both hands, pushed the window open wide. He stood back against the wall and, as he did so, the bird flew directly towards the window casement and out into the world beyond.

'Well done,' I said. 'Good man.'

'It was a sparrow,' said Oscar, closing the window.

'God is not mocked.' He fastened the window latch. 'Did we leave the window open when we were here with Conan Doyle?'

'We may have done,' I answered. 'The day was close. I don't remember. Perhaps Mrs O'Keefe opened it when she was here?'

'Perhaps.' He stood gazing about the empty room. 'It is curious how little we remember, even of experiences that seemed so vivid at the time. The mind's eye is not a camera; it is an artist's brush. It provides no photographic record, alas. It can bring back the colour of the day, the feeling of the moment, but the detail is all gone. It's an adequate instrument for poets and painters, but for detectives – useless!'

He walked slowly to the window and peered down into the street.

'What do I recall of the afternoon of Tuesday 31 August 1889? Not enough, Robert, not enough!' He turned and fixed me with his gaze. 'At approximately three-thirty that afternoon, I stood in the doorway to this room, where you are standing now, and what *precisely* did I see?'

'You saw the body of Billy Wood.'

He moved towards the centre of the room. 'He was lying here. His head was where my feet are now. He was naked. His arms and legs were white – so white – but his body was awash with blood. So much blood. Where were his clothes? I don't recall. There was a rug – a Persian rug. That I remember. And candles here, guttering but still alight, in candlesticks, in a half-circle about his head. But how many? Four certainly – possibly six.'

'There was a knife. You said there was a knife.'

'Yes, a small knife. Or it might have been a razor. The

blade shone. It gleamed. I remember that.'

'Is that significant?'

'If it had been the murder weapon it would have been mired in blood.'

'Could it not have been used as the murder weapon and then wiped clean?'

'It could,' said Oscar, 'it could indeed.' He walked around the imagined outline of the corpse and came to stand at my side. He took out a cigarette and lit it from the candle I was still holding. We stared at the bare floor-boards.

'What is your most vivid recollection of the scene that afternoon?' I asked.

As he answered, the cigarette smoke drifted slowly from his mouth and nostrils, forming a grey cloud about his head. 'The horror of it,' he said, 'the purple of the blood . . . and how beautiful he looked, how innocent. His body was soaked in blood, but his face was clean, serene. His eyes were closed. He looked at peace, Robert. He had been butchered to death and yet he looked at peace. How is that possible?'

'And how is it possible that when we returned to the scene of the crime – not twenty-four hours later – there was no trace of any of this horror? It had all been cleaned away.'

'Except for Arthur's spot of blood!' Oscar broke away from me and went to examine the room's right-hand wall. 'Where is it, Robert? Where is the blood?' He scanned the wall with care, running his eyes and hands along it. 'Bring the candle – it is getting dark.' I took the candle to him. We stood where Conan Doyle had stood. 'It was somewhere here, was it not?'

'I believe so.'

'Divide up the wall into squares, Robert – as friend Millais does when planning one of his larger canvases. Now, carefully, consider each square: first vertically, then horizontally. Take your time . . . Where is the blood, Robert?'

'I cannot see it,' I said.

'Nor can I,' said he.

We stood in silence, gazing at the wallpaper. He drew on his cigarette and smiled.

'Hideous, is it not, this wallpaper? So grotesque that I imagine it is the manufacturer's most popular design.' I laughed. He turned to me, still smiling, but with a sweetness in his smile. 'The wall hangings will not have troubled poor Billy. He paid little heed to his surroundings, as I recall. He was happy in himself. Indeed, I now think that he may never have been happier than at the moment of his death. "If it be now, 'tis not to come; if it be not to come, it will be now; if it be not now, yet it will come . . ." Are you ready, Robert? Let us inspect the other rooms and be on our way.'

Oscar took the candle from me and led us out of the room, without a backward glance. He now seemed to be in haste to get away. Our inspection of the rest of the house was almost cursory. There were two rooms on each floor, plus a water-closet, a cloakroom beneath the stairs, and a scullery and washroom adjacent to the kitchen. He opened the door to each, held up the candle, muttered, 'Nothing here,' or words to that effect, and moved swiftly on. The house, from what I could see, was exactly as it had been when we had visited it last: empty, unlived in, almost completely bare.

'When Bellotti's club met here,' I asked, as we came up

from the kitchen and moved back towards the front door, 'was the house unfurnished then?'

'Yes,' he said. 'Bellotti is a travelling showman – he takes his costumes and his properties with him. When you rent a room in a house such as this, it comes as it is: with a table and a chair, perhaps a bare bedstead, a kettle in the kitchen, nothing more. When I came to the house in August, it was as you see it now – except . . . except . . .' We were standing in the hallway, at the foot of the stairs. Suddenly exultant, he spread his arms wide. 'Bravo, Robert!' he cried. I looked at him, uncomprehending. 'Except that here,' he said, 'just here,' – he indicated the wall by the foot of the stairs – 'there was a chest, a long wooden chest.'

'Are you sure?'

'Yes,' he said, kneeling down, with difficulty, to examine the floorboards. 'There are no scratch marks that I can see, but there was a chest just here, I'm certain of it . . .'

'Certain of it?'

'Where else would I have placed my hat and cane? I would hardly have dropped them on the floor, would I?' He got to his feet, helping himself up on my arm. 'Thank you, Robert, thank you! You have unlocked another of the gates along our pathway.'

'Have I?' I laughed.

'You have, my friend. Dr Watson could not have done more. By enquiring about the furniture that is not here, you reminded me of the one piece of furniture that was. When I came into the house that afternoon, I brushed past the housekeeper in my haste, but as I did so, I automatically removed my hat and, as I made to climb the stairs, I laid it down with my cane. And I laid them here – on a wooden chest – the chest in which the Persian rug, the candlesticks and whatever other paraphernalia was required were brought to the house – and in which the body of poor Billy Wood was borne away! I salute your genius, Robert! I shall reward it with tea and muffins at the Savoy – or perhaps a hock and seltzer. What time is it?'

By the time we reached the Savoy Hotel and had been served with tea and muffins, plus buttered crumpets and anchovy toast, not forgetting the hock and seltzer, too, it was after five. On the way, Oscar had halted the cab by the flower-stall at Charing Cross and bought us each a buttonhole: a camellia set against a sprig of fern.

'A really well-made buttonhole is the only link between Art and Nature,' I remarked as he climbed back into the cab. 'A gentleman should either be a work of art, or wear a work of art.'

'Who said that?' he asked.

'You did,' I replied, 'as well you know.'

'Really?' he said, his brow furrowed. 'Are you sure it wasn't Whistler? . . . No doubt it will be.'

He was in exuberant form. And when taking afternoon tea at his favourite table at the Savoy – 'No cakes, Cesari! We are in savoury mood and on the strictest diet!' – he was, in every sense, in his element. 'We have made progress today, Robert,' he said, mopping butter from his chin. He had impeccable manners, but he was not the daintiest of eaters. 'And very soon,' he said with relish, 'we shall make more.'

I pondered what he meant by 'progress'. 'Did you believe Bellotti,' I asked, 'when he said that the dwarf was his son?'

He reflected for a moment before answering. 'Yes,' he

215

said, slowly, putting down his napkin, 'I believed him. I was taken aback, but I believed him. There was no need for him to lie about that.'

'I do not trust Bellotti,' I said.

'And I know it to be true,' Oscar continued, 'that the dwarf visits the women's asylum at Rochester on a Tuesday afternoon. I've had Jimmy and another of my spies follow him there.'

'I do not trust Bellotti,' I said again, with emphasis, 'and I do not like him.'

'He is not likeable,' said Oscar, smiling at me. 'But what did you make of Canon Courteney and his crew?'

'I liked them,' I said.

'I am glad. I like them, too. One's real life is so often the life that one does not lead – the life one imagines, or hopes for, or might have led. Within the confines of their curious club, Canon Courteney and his quaint companions are free to live their lives as they would wish. Between twelve and four on the last Tuesday in the month, they become themselves. They come alive. I envy them.'

'Could one of them be our murderer?' I asked.

'You mean Aston Upthorpe?'

'Yes,' I said. 'He loved Billy Wood, but Billy Wood loved another . . .'

Oscar examined his muffin contemplatively. 'They say each man kills the thing he loves . . . I wonder? He had a motive, that's true. And he had the opportunity.'

'But they all say they were together all the time, so he also has an alibi.'

'Were they all together all the time today, when we were with them?'

'I believe so. Were they not?'

'No. Upthorpe went to relieve himself, twice. So did Bellotti. And Stoke Talmage went once. But you did not notice. Or, if you did, you assumed – rightly – that they were answering a call of nature and thought no more about it. Upthorpe – or any of the others – could have been away from the room for a few minutes on 31 August without anyone noticing. Time enough to cross the street and commit a murder, I suppose.'

He did not sound convinced.

'Tell me about the man who wasn't there,' I asked.

'Drayton St Leonard?'

'You know him?'

'No.'

'But you knew his name.'

'I *guessed* his name,' said Oscar.

'Guessed it?'

'It was not difficult. Aston Upthorpe, Aston Tirrold, Sutton Courteney, Berrick Prior, Stoke Talmage . . . Drayton St Leonard. They are all the names of villages in Oxfordshire, probably in the parish where "Canon Courteney" was rector before he was defrocked. Don't look so shocked, Robert. A *nom de guerre* does not make a man a criminal. Henry Irving's real name is John Brodribb, after all.'

19

27 January 1890

'Moods don't last,' Oscar liked to say. 'It's their chief charm.'

Certainly, the mellow mood in which I had left my friend after our tea together at the Savoy Hotel on Tuesday afternoon had wholly evaporated by the time I joined him on the nine o'clock train to Broadstairs on Thursday morning. He sat in the corner seat of our first-class carriage, huddled in his coat, with the astrakhan collar pulled about his ears, gazing disconsolately at the greasy raindrops as they chased one another down the dirty window-pane. 'This is not cosy, Robert,' he muttered. 'Not cosy at all.'

I realised too late where the problem lay. He had forgotten to bring his cigarettes. I had none either, and our train was on the move.

'There's a tobacconist on the platform at Tonbridge,' I said.

'Tonbridge!' Oscar sighed. 'That's an hour away, longer than Stainer's *Crucifixion*! And as mortifying. I am sorely tried.'

As our train rumbled sluggishly through the suburbs of south London, Oscar drummed his fingernails on the lid of the metal ashtray affixed to the carriage door.

'Divert me, Robert,' he commanded. 'Distract me. Tell me about your divorce.'

'There is nothing to report,' I said.

'There must be *something*!'

'Foxton, the solicitor, has gone quiet. I've heard nothing from him for weeks. Or from Marthe. I am content to let sleeping dogs lie. There really is nothing to report, I'm afraid.'

Oscar sighed once more and closed his eyes. Between Coulsdon South and Nutfield, we travelled in silence. At Godstone, when the train stopped briefly, I had hopes of procuring a cigarette from a young man whom I noticed on the platform. He was dressed in a glengarry cap and cape, and his face was shrouded in an encouraging cloud of smoke. He had just lit a cigarette and was still holding his cigarette case in his hand. At first he looked as if he might be about to join us in our compartment, but when he reached the door and saw us he moved on. As the train juddered out of the station, Oscar stirred. He stifled a yawn and gazed at me reproachfully.

'How long have you known John Gray?' I asked.

'That's a curious question,' he answered, slowly sitting forward. 'Why do you ask?'

'For no reason,' I replied, immediately regretting that I had not broached the subject in a more roundabout way.

'There must be a reason, Robert,' he said, tetchily.

'No reason,' I protested. 'I was just making conversation.'

'Asking after Henry Irving's *Richard III*, or the weather in Dover, or the consequences of the abolition of slavery on the economy of Cuba, is "making conversation",

Robert. Asking when one gentleman met another gentleman is "making enquiries". Why do you ask?'

'It's unimportant,' I said, waving my hands about in front of my face in the hope that they might waft the subject away.

'The answer to the question is unimportant, to be sure,' said Oscar who was now on the edge of his seat and leaning directly towards me, 'but the fact of the question is significant. You ask it in the way that you ask it – directly, unadorned, of a sudden – because it has been preying on your mind. You have been waiting to ask it. I suspect that you ask the question because Aidan Fraser has been asking it, has he not? Am I right?'

I said nothing. I did not wish to lie to my friend.

Oscar began to tap the lid of the metal ashtray once more. 'Inspector Fraser is an odd one,' he said, quietly. 'He is handsome, he is intelligent, he is a friend of Conan Doyle's – he and I should get on so well and yet . . .'

'What?' I asked.

'It's evident that he neither likes nor trusts the company I keep, Robert.'

I began to protest.

'No, Robert, it's true. With the exception of Arthur and yourself – and possibly the Prince of Wales, the prime minister and the poet laureate, and maybe, at a pinch, Mr Irving and Miss Ellen Terry – Inspector Fraser is profoundly suspicious of the associates of Oscar Wilde. He as good as told me so. Were you not there when he tried to warn me off our case? He sees my friends as "the enemy". I believe Fraser despises John Gray because he suspects that he is musical.'

'Is that a crime?'

'Since the 1885 Criminal Law Amendment Act, apparently it is.'

I laughed.

'Why do you laugh?' he asked.

'Is it not a joke?' I said.

'By no means, alas.'

I was puzzled. A silence fell.

'I had no idea that John Gray was musical,' I said, eventually. 'What instrument does he play?'

'He doesn't play an instrument.'

'He is not a composer, surely?'

'No.'

'A conductor, then?'

Oscar smiled. His lips parted and he grinned at me, showing his ungainly teeth. 'Ah, Robert. We are speaking at cross-purposes. You have clearly spent too much time in France. You are unfamiliar with the argot of the English *demi-monde*. To say a man is "musical" is a colloquialism, Robert. It suggests that when it comes to his gross bodily appetites, he may be an apostle of Greek love.'

'Oh,' I said, 'I see.' I blushed. Another silence fell.

I do not believe that the word 'homosexual' was known in 1890. If it was, I never heard it. Nowadays, at any cocktail party, you can hear expressions such as 'homo' and 'queer' bandied hither and yon without embarrassment, but the Victorian age was more discreet — and none the worse for that. Nowadays, what Oscar and his friend, Lord Alfred Douglas, came to call 'the love that dare not speak its name' can be heard bellowing its universal presence from the rooftops, but then it was different. Fifty years ago a man of the world would doubtless have been familiar with the phenomenon of sexual inversion, but it was not a subject that he would have expected, openly, to discuss.

'Well,' I said, after a moment, 'is he musical?'

Oscar laughed. 'John Gray? Yes. And he is troubled by it, poor boy. He is taking "the cure" – cold baths, wet runs, sleeping on wooden boards, praying *incessantly*. The last is a mistake: I have told him. The Almighty loves a sinner, but cannot abide a bore. He won't be gainsaid, however. He wants to be "pure" before he is received.'

' "Received"?' I repeated the word carefully, suddenly anxious that this might be another unfamiliar euphemism. 'Received by whom?'

'The Catholic Church. John Gray has been taking instruction for some months now. He is hoping to be received in a fortnight's time – on 14 February. Under the circumstances, I fear the date is inauspicious.'

'And how long have you known him?' I sensed that it was safe to ask the question now.

'Not long enough. I would like to know him better. I met him at a party in the King's Road, a gathering of poets. He was the only one who was not prosaic. He came over and introduced himself.'

'He sought you out?'

'Yes, I was blessed – for he is beautiful, is he not? Even you and Fraser must be able to see that. He told me that he had secured an invitation to the party with the express purpose of meeting me. He told me that I was his "obsession". He said it most charmingly. I was flattered. Who would not be?'

'And when was this?'

'Several days *after* the murder of Billy Wood. I do not see how you or Fraser could possibly implicate him in this affair.'

'I do not seek to,' I protested, 'not for a moment, but—'

'But what?'

I drew breath before I spoke. 'It is curious that a young man, whom you barely know, whom you have met apparently by chance, out of the blue, suddenly starts turning up at all the key moments in the drama . . . That is all.'

' "Key moments"?' Oscar snapped. 'What "key moments"?'

'When you were attacked in Soho Square, when the head of Billy Wood was delivered to your house—'

'Robert! Robert! Robert!' Oscar rocked slowly backwards and forwards in his seat, gazing at me with baleful eyes. 'Think what you are saying! When the head of Billy Wood was delivered to my house, you, too, were there! So were Fraser and Miss Sutherland – and Constance and the Conan Doyles! Are you telling me that Mrs Conan Doyle is one of your suspects too?'

'No, Oscar, of course not, but I do say that whoever murdered Billy Wood must be someone who knows of your interest in the case – and where you live. The poor boy's head was delivered to your front door.'

'It was delivered to my club, Robert, and the list of those who know of my interest in Billy Wood and of my membership of the Albemarle Club is a very long one indeed. It starts with the unhappy Mrs Wood and the wretch O'Donnell, then stretches from Bellotti and his band of merry men to Fraser and, through him, I imagine, to half the Metropolitan Police – especially, no doubt, those officers involved in what Fraser likes to term "the unsavoury Cleveland Street affair". Even Mrs O'Keefe knows of my membership of the Albemarle. She came to meet me there, remember. Have you got her on the list?'

I was vanquished, overwhelmed by Oscar's torrent of words. I glanced out of the window. The rain was abating. 'We will be in Ashford soon,' I said. 'We change trains there.'

Oscar exploded. 'What happened to Tonbridge?' he demanded. 'I was promised a cigarette in Tonbridge!' It was evident that he could not decide whether to laugh or grumble. He began to cough, a short, dry, hacking cough; but could not shake himself free from it. He leant forward and indicated that I should bang him on his back to beat it out of him. He was now laughing, coughing, wheezing, speaking all at once. 'And, Robert,' he spluttered, 'do not assume that whoever sent the severed head is necessarily the murderer.' He indicated that I should hit him harder. 'The head was sent to tell me something,' he gasped, 'but what?' The cough would not dislodge itself. 'Lower,' he rasped. 'Hit me lower.'

He was now perched on the edge of his seat, bent double, with his head between his knees. I was standing over him, my left leg braced against his, my right kneeling on the seat adjacent to him. I was still beating the small of his back rhythmically with the edge of my clenched fist when the train juddered to a halt at Ashford Station. Abruptly, the carriage door was flung open and a brute of a railway attendant jumped in. With one heave, he pushed me violently to the ground. 'Get off!' he roared at me. He turned to Oscar. 'Are you all right, sir?' He was fumbling in his pocket for a whistle.

Oscar looked up. His lungs had cleared and he smiled at the attendant. 'I'm well, thank you. No need for the police, I assure you. This gentleman is my friend. He was assisting me.'

'What?' growled the railwayman. 'He was beating the living daylights out of you.'

'No, I assure you – I had a cough,' said Oscar, now reaching into his own coat pocket. 'Appearances can be so deceptive.' He found a coin and handed it to his rescuer. 'Thank you,' he said, 'thank you for your kind intention.'

The attendant felt the weight of the coin and muttered, 'Thank you, sir.' He looked at me with disdain, as though he might have spat upon me had a gentleman not been present. I returned his glance and realised that he must have been in his mid-sixties. His face was deeply lined and weather-beaten; the hair beneath his cap was as grey as ash. Oscar got slowly to his feet and allowed the man to help him down onto the platform. 'Anything more you need, sir? A porter or something?'

'A cigarette,' said Oscar, smiling at the man, 'if you have one.' The railwayman took a cigarette from behind his right ear and presented it to Oscar, who reached at once for his coat pocket and handed over another coin. Gingerly, keeping my distance, I clambered out of the carriage after them.

'We need the Broadstairs train,' I said.

'Platform three,' said the attendant, 'at twenty past.'

Oscar presented him with a third and final token of his appreciation. 'Robert,' he said, as the attendant stepped back, touching his cap to Oscar and throwing me one last contemptuous glance as he went, 'do you have a light?'

I was confused. My head and heart were still pounding following the unexpected assault of a moment before, but I reached into my pocket and found a box of matches. My hands were shaking slightly, but Oscar did not appear to notice. 'Will you share this cigarette with me?' he asked. 'We can have half each or take alternate puffs.'

'You have it,' I said. I struck a match and held it cupped between my hands as I lit the cigarette. We were still standing on the station platform, by the compartment from which we had just alighted. Oscar had his back to the train, but, as the whistle went and the train lurched forward, going onward towards Folkestone, over Oscar's shoulder I saw into the compartment that had been adjacent to ours. In the corner seat by the window sat the young man in the glengarry cap and cape. He was no longer shrouded in a haze of cigarette smoke. I could see him quite clearly. It was John Gray.

The train moved noisily forward. Oscar drew on his cigarette with his eyes closed and a look of supreme contentment on his lips. When the train was gone, he opened his eyes and smiled at me. I was unsure what best to say.

I began, 'This is passing strange, Oscar—'

'Yes,' he said.

'Do you know who I have just seen?'

'Yes,' he said. 'Is it a coincidence, do you think?'

'I do not know, but—'

'We shall soon find out. She has seen us. She is coming towards us now.'

I turned and there, hurrying towards us along the platform, half walking, half running, was a tall young woman in a long black coat. Beneath her hat she wore a veil, but as she came close I saw fear in her eyes and tears of desperation on her cheeks.

'Mrs Wood,' said Oscar, throwing his cigarette to the ground and taking her hands in his, 'we were on our way to find you and you, it seems, were on your way to find us.'

'Oh, Mr Wilde,' she said, 'they have taken him. They have arrested Edward, Mr Wilde. He is to be charged. He will be hanged.'

'And he is your husband?' said Oscar.

'He is my husband . . .' she whispered and she fell, fainting, into Oscar's arms.

20

Ashford Station

Susannah Wood hung limply in Oscar's arms. From the far end of the platform my railwayman assailant saw what had occurred and, at once, ran to offer his assistance. Between us, we carried the poor lady to what the railwayman called 'the stationmaster's snug', a dark, low-ceilinged room, the size of a railway carriage, tucked behind the ticket office. There, by a coal fire no bigger than a colander, we propped her in an old armchair and revived her with a cup of sweet tea, fortified with a nip of the stationmaster's 'special reserve brandy'. Oscar accepted a nip for himself. It made his eyes water.

'Reviving, isn't it, sir?' said the railwayman.

'It would bring Lazarus to life,' said Oscar.

When Mrs Wood had recovered herself, Oscar, seated on a hardwood chair facing her, held both her hands in his and said, earnestly, 'Dear lady, hide nothing from me now.' I sat on the corner of the stationmaster's desk and took out my notebook.

She looked piteously into Oscar's eyes and said: 'How did you know that Edward O'Donnell is my husband?'

'He wears a ring of rose-gold on his wedding finger,' said Oscar. 'I noticed it when I first encountered him on

your doorstep and he jabbed his hand towards my face.'
Oscar held Mrs Wood's left hand before him. 'You wear
an identical ring of rose-gold on the third finger of your
left hand,' he said. 'I noticed it first when I returned to
you this other wedding-band of yours, the one that Billy
wore.'

Susannah Wood closed her eyes. 'Will Edward be
hanged?' she asked.

'It is possible,' said Oscar. 'I do not know. Tell me
about his arrest.'

Hesitantly, coaxed by Oscar, she told us what had happened. It was that morning, between five and six, before
the break of day, that the police had called at The Castle.
The noise of their truncheons beating on her front door
had awoken her. She came to the door, she said, 'bewildered, half asleep'. She thought at first that it must be
O'Donnell returning to the house in one of his drunken
rages, but then she recalled that she had heard him
coming in by the basement entrance a few hours before.
As she began to unchain the front door, the beating
stopped. 'There was a moment of sudden stillness,' she
said, 'and in that moment I knew something terrible was
about to happen.' She opened the door and, as she did so,
five or six policeman, all in uniform, all wielding truncheons, rushed past her into the house. As they came, one
of them shouted, 'We've come for O'Donnell. Where is
he? Where is he, woman?'

It did not take the policemen long to find their prey.
O'Donnell, still dressed from the night before, still in his
cap and coat and boots, lay fast asleep, spread out like a
crucified man, on a mattress on the scullery floor. 'That's
where he slept when he was in drink,' said Mrs Wood. As

two of the policemen dragged him to his feet, he barely stirred. When two others slipped handcuffs around his wrists, he opened his eyes and began to curse. Gradually, as the policemen pushed and pulled him up the basement steps, he regained his strength and, uttering terrible oaths and imprecations, struggled to break free. 'He has the strength of an ox,' said Mrs Wood, 'but he was outnumbered. They subdued him with their truncheons. They beat him about the head. They rained blow upon blow upon him until, at last, he fell, unconscious, to the ground. Then they bundled his body into the back of the Black Maria.'

'A Black Maria?' said Oscar, surprised. 'Are you certain of it?'

'Is that not what they are called?' asked Mrs Wood. 'It was a large carriage, all enclosed and painted black, drawn by two horses. It could have carried a dozen prisoners. I took it to be a Black Maria.'

'It must have come from London,' said Oscar.

'Yes. The officer in charge said that they had brought it from London especially. He said they were taking Edward to the police cells at Bow Street. He said Edward would be charged with murder.' Mrs Wood, who had remained calm while recounting her narrative thus far, began to sob. 'He will be hanged, Mr Wilde. I despise him, but he is all that I have left – and he will be hanged.'

'This "officer in charge",' asked Oscar, 'can you describe him?'

'No, not really,' she said, breathing deeply and making a supreme effort to regain her composure. 'It was dark and it was all over in a matter of moments.'

'Was he in uniform?'

'No, but he was evidently in command, though he seemed the youngest of them. He was tall – that I remember. And his face was very pale.'

'Did he give his name?'

'I did not ask him his name.'

'Was he not the same officer who took you to identify poor Billy's body?'

Without warning, Susannah Wood let out a piercing scream and turned violently from Oscar, suddenly raising her fists to her face and beating them against her temples. 'Why do you torture me like this?' she cried.

Oscar leant towards her and whispered to her urgently, 'Believe me, dear lady, I am your friend. I would not hurt you for the world. It was thoughtless of me to remind you of the horror of what you have seen. Forgive me.'

'I have seen nothing!' she shrieked.

'What?' cried Oscar. 'Did the police not take you to the morgue?'

Mrs Wood turned back to Oscar, her tear-stained face now contorted with anguish. 'Are you telling me that Billy's body has been found? Where? Where is it? Where is my boy that I may go to see him? He is dead, I know. I know he is dead,' she wailed, 'but may I not take his body in my arms and cradle him one last time? He was my son.'

The poor woman had struggled to her feet and was pulling her coat about her. Oscar, now utterly confused, had risen to his feet also and put his arms about her to restrain her. 'No, no,' he cried, 'you misunderstand me. I did not mean to raise your hopes. I confused you. I confused myself. I thought a police officer might have called on you to enquire after a likeness of your son – a photograph to help with the identification of his body in the event that it is found . . .' He released his hold upon her. 'In the event that it is found,' he repeated.

Susannah Wood sat down once more. She wiped the tears from her eyes. 'So his body has not been found,' she said.

'No,' said Oscar, seating himself again, 'no. I expressed myself poorly. Please accept my most profound apologies.' Mrs Wood took Oscar's hand in hers and, drawing it to her cheek, held it there.

The railwayman filled the silence that followed by throwing some coals onto the fire and announcing that there was just time for him to brew fresh tea before the arrival of the midday train from Dover Priory.

'Might I be permitted a further nip of your station-master's special reserve?' asked Oscar, lowering his hand from Mrs Wood's cheek and feeling in his pocket for another coin.

After the railwayman had refilled our teacups, he left us to go about his duties. When Oscar had taken several further nips of brandy ('It was vile, Robert, but necessary'), he turned again to Mrs Wood. 'Mr Sherard and I must return to London,' he said. 'We came to find you and to question O'Donnell, but it seems we came too late. We will return to London now and endeavour to discover what is happening to your husband. We will keep you posted. You can trust us. We are your friends.' Susannah Wood, with tears still in her eyes, smiled at Oscar and reached out for his hand once more. 'Will you be able to return to Broadstairs on your own?' he asked.

'Yes,' she said, 'thank you. I will be quite safe. No one can harm me now.'

Oscar got to his feet. 'May I ask you something?'

'Of course, Mr Wilde. You are my friend. Anything.'

'Why did you marry him? Why did you marry Edward O'Donnell?'

Mrs Wood paused before she answered. She turned and gazed at me for a moment. I was embarrassed by the pencil and notebook in my hand. She turned away and looked, not towards Oscar, but into the fire. 'I married him because I had lain with him,' she said. She blushed. The birthmark on her neck turned scarlet. 'I married him because I felt I must.'

'When was this?' asked Oscar.

'Almost two years ago now, not long after his return from Canada. He forced himself upon me. He claimed me as his own. He said I was his – by right. I tried to beat him off. I screamed. I scratched his face. I spat at him. But with one hand he seized my wrists and held them, effortlessly, above my head and with the other he covered my mouth to silence me. I bit his flesh until the blood ran, but I could not fight him. He was too strong. He took me – and, having taken me once, came back, night after night. At first, I resisted him, resisted him with all my might, but then . . . I succumbed, I acquiesced. And strange as it may seem, over time, I even found some comfort lying with the man – brute that he was.' She looked up at Oscar. 'I married Edward O'Donnell because he was William O'Donnell's brother. I lay with Edward and thought of William.'

'I understand,' said Oscar.

'And when he was not in drink – which was not often, I grant you that – there was something about him, about the way he walked, about his laugh, that almost brought my William back to life. I despised him, but I came to love

233

him, too. I despise him still, and yet I love him, even now . . . Can you understand that, also?'

'Oh yes,' said Oscar. 'Often we despise the most what we love the most. And we despise ourselves for loving where we should not, for loving those we know to be unworthy of our love. I understand completely.'

She turned towards me and, smiling, added – as if offering up something that I might also understand, 'I married him, too, for Billy's sake.'

'For Billy's sake?' I repeated, not certain what she meant.

'To protect him,' she said.

'O'Donnell was jealous of Billy?' Oscar asked.

'Insanely so. He was jealous of my love for Billy. Billy was everything to me. I could not hide that – but I thought that if I agreed to marry Edward it might make him less jealous of the boy, it might lead him to leave Billy alone more.'

'And did it?' I asked.

'For a while, yes – but not for long. As Mr Wilde will tell you, Mr Sherard, Billy was an exceptional child. He had the beauty of an angel, but he had the spirit of a boy, and such quickness and such sweetness too. Billy was perfection. I know I am his mother, but it is true! Billy was perfect – that is why Edward sought to corrupt him. He took him to London and sold him into a life of degradation.'

Oscar said nothing. He drained his teacup of the last of the stationmaster's brandy before picking up his hat and cane in readiness to depart.

'Did Billy go willingly to London?' I asked.

'Not at first,' she said. 'A man called Bellotti stayed at The Castle one summer and took a fancy to Billy. He said he'd give Billy work in London. Edward said Billy should go. Billy was uncertain, but Edward forced him. The boy was only fourteen. He had no choice, he was afraid of his uncle. Edward O'Donnell is a violent man, Mr Sherard. Billy went to London in fear, I know that, but, over time, I believe he came to like his life there. He made friends, other boys of his own age, and good men, decent men, such as Mr Wilde . . . and others.'

Oscar, now wearing his hat and gloves, was standing by the door leading from the snug to the ticket office. 'Did Billy ever mention the name Drayton St Leonard to you?' he asked.

'Oh, yes,' she said, 'often. He said Mr St Leonard was like a father to him. He said Mr St Leonard was going to take him on holiday with him.'

'Did he say where?' Oscar enquired.

'No – abroad, I think.'

'And were you happy about that?' I asked.

'I wanted Billy to be safe,' she said, 'and I sensed that with Mr St Leonard he would be. I knew that with Edward – my Edward, my husband, God help me! His own father's brother – he was never wholly safe. If Billy did not do his uncle's bidding, if Billy crossed his uncle even for a moment, Edward would beat the boy.' She closed her eyes at the recollection of it. 'I am so ashamed,' she whispered.

I shut my notebook and got to my feet. 'Mrs O'Donnell,' I said, 'according to your own testimony, your husband is a man given to violence, to insane jealousy, to acts of unspeakable cruelty . . . Could not so violent a man have murdered your son?'

'Yes, Mr Sherard,' she said, 'he could have done so.

Often, I feared that he would. That is why I longed for Billy to escape. That is why I came to think of Mr St Leonard as his saviour. Edward O'Donnell at his best is a pale ghost of his brother William. At his worst, he is certainly capable of murder. But he did not kill Billy, Mr Sherard – that I know.'

'And how do you know it, Mrs O'Donnell?' asked Oscar.

'Because it was you, Mr Wilde, who told me that Billy was murdered on the afternoon of Tuesday 31 August last . . .'

'Yes,' said Oscar, 'that was the fateful day.'

'Is there any doubt about the date?'

'None whatsoever.'

'And there is no doubt either that on the afternoon of 31 August, when my poor Billy was in London being murdered, Edward O'Donnell was with me, in Broadstairs, at The Castle.'

'Are you certain of it?' I asked.

'I am not likely to forget the day, Mr Sherard. As Mr Wilde says, it was a fateful day. It was the day I lost both my children.'

I was about to speak, to say I did not understand, when Oscar raised his hand to silence me. 'You were with child?' he asked.

'Yes,' she said, 'only by a few weeks, but I was with child – with Edward's child, the child of the man I both love and despise.' She looked up at Oscar. 'He did not know it. I had not told him. Had I told him, he might have been gentler with me – who knows? He was in drink that day, at his worst. At his most terrible. We argued.'

'About Billy?'

'Edward said that Billy was going to run away – to leave

the country with another man, a friend of Mr Bellotti's. I said I was glad of it. I said I hoped he would. I said I wanted Billy as far away from Edward as possible. He accused me of loving Billy more than I loved him. I told him it was true. I told him I loved Billy more than all the world. He laughed and told me he would put a stop to that. He threatened to go London to find Billy. He said he would find him – and murder him. And, once Billy was dead, I would be his, properly his. He raved – like a lunatic. It was madness, brought on by drink and jealousy. We struggled on the stairs. He pushed me and I fell. It was a fatal fall. Later that night I lost the baby I was carrying. Edward threatened to kill his brother's child. He threw me down the stairs and killed his own.'

21

27–28 January 1890

O n our return from Kent, we took a cab from the railway station directly to Scotland Yard. There, as we arrived, as we were clambering out of the cab in the yard, we encountered Aidan Fraser's colleague, Inspector Archy Gilmour, a red-headed, red-faced Scotsman, who recognised Oscar at once and greeted us effusively. 'It's good to meet you at last,' he boomed. 'I have heard a deal about you both – and your skills as sleuths.'

I liked Archy Gilmour at once; he had an openness about him that put me in mind of Conan Doyle. Oscar was less certain. 'Men over forty with red hair are a problem,' was a favourite Wildean maxim.

Inspector Gilmour – clearly intrigued to be encountering Oscar; he looked at him as if he were appraising a controversial work of art – told us that if it was Fraser we had come to see we had just missed him. 'He went home not five minutes ago and in high spirits. He's nabbed your murderer, Mr Wilde. Another triumph for our Aidan, the Met's very own "infant phenomenon"!'

Oscar mumbled a cursory pleasantry and ordered our cab to take us on to 75 Lower Sloane Street without delay.

'Why, Fraser?' Oscar demanded the moment the inspector opened his front door to us. 'Why have you arrested Edward O'Donnell?'

'To charge him with murder, Oscar,' said Fraser, calmly. 'O'Donnell killed Billy Wood. I have no doubt of it.'

'Has he confessed?'

'Not yet, but I believe he may – in the fullness of time. And if he does not, no matter. We have evidence enough to convict him.'

'I do not believe you.'

Aidan Fraser smiled at Oscar. 'You will, Oscar. You will . . .' The inspector stepped back and invited us over the threshold. 'Come in now and have a glass of wine. Let us not forget that we are friends.'

He led us through the hall and into the drawing room. It was shortly after six o'clock. There was a light in his eye and an energy in his movements that I had not seen since our first encounter with him all those months before. 'I have wine here with which to tempt you – and we all know, Oscar, that you can resist everything except temptation! It is one of your favourite Moselles, chilled, as you'd say, *comme il faut.*'

'Were you expecting me then?' enquired Oscar, hanging his coat on the hallway coatstand and following our ebullient host into the drawing room.

'No,' laughed Fraser. 'I was expecting Conan Doyle – and it is one of his favourite Moselles also!'

'Arthur is expected?' remarked Oscar, mellowing a little. 'I am glad of that.'

'Alas,' said Fraser, 'he was expected, but it is not to be.' He poured us each a glass of the pale green wine.

'Arthur has just wired me to say that he is detained in Southsea – "pressure of business"; an outbreak of the measles. Bad news for the victims, good news for his depleted bank balance. It is a great pity. He and Touie were due to join us on an expedition to Paris.'

'To Paris?' said Oscar, in amazement. 'You are leaving the country?'

'Only for a week. *Un petit séjour*, that's all. A touch of Paris in the spring.'

Oscar rolled the wine around his mouth. 'Only a Scotsman could think of a rainy day in late January as the spring,' he said.

'We're going because it is Veronica's birthday on Monday,' Fraser added. 'I'm sure Robert has not forgotten.'

I had not forgotten. I had a manuscript copy of one of my great-grandfather's favourite poems to present to her: 'I travelled among unknown men'.

'Miss Sutherland's birthday is 31 January?' said Oscar, as Fraser replenished his glass. I noticed his eyes were darting about the room as he spoke. 'That is a curious coincidence, is it not?'

'A coincidence?' asked Fraser. 'How so?'

'You each have your own St Aidan.'

'I'm sorry,' said Fraser, replacing the Moselle in the wine bucket, 'I do not follow you.'

'Your birthday falls on 31 August, as I recall – the feast day of St Aidan of Lindisfarne.'

'Yes,' said Fraser, 'hence my name.'

'And your fiancée's birthday falls five months later, on 31 January – the feast day of St Aidan of Ferns.'

'Goodness me,' said Fraser, 'a coincidence as you say – but a happy one.'

'Indeed,' said Oscar. 'I am surprised you did not know. They did not teach you your saints' days at Fettes?'

'It's a Scottish school,' said Fraser. 'I imagine we did not have much time for Irish saints.'

'Yes,' said Oscar, 'they are both Irish. At least you knew that much.'

There was a momentary hiatus. All three of us gazed into our empty glasses. 'More wine?' said Fraser, retrieving the Moselle from the wine bucket.

'Oscar has a passion for hagiology that borders on the unnatural,' I said.

'Is there a St Oscar?' Fraser asked.

'Not yet,' said Oscar. 'I am working on it. But it may take some time. I am quite particular when it comes to martyrdom.'

'Is martyrdom essential?'

'By no means, but it helps. Both St Aidans died peacefully in their beds. That's the luck of the Irish for you.'

Fraser laughed and emptied the last of the Moselle into Oscar's glass. 'Let me get another bottle – and then I have a proposal to make to you both.'

Oscar held up his hand. 'No, thank you, no more wine. At least not yet. We have come here on business.'

'I understand,' said Fraser, not unkindly. He took our glasses from us and placed them carefully on the side table. 'Gentlemen,' he said, indicating the chairs by the fireplace, 'shall we be seated? I am all ears.'

Oscar took his seat and lit one of the cigarettes that we had bought that morning at Ashford Station. He smiled at Fraser (not unkindly) and said, 'Aidan – Inspector Fraser – listen to me: Edward O'Donnell is not guilty of the murder of Billy Wood.'

Fraser sat back in his chair and looked directly into Oscar's eyes. 'Surely, Oscar, that will be for the courts to decide,' he said, 'not us. If O'Donnell is innocent, O'Donnell will go free. If he is guilty, he will hang.'

'He is guilty of much,' said Oscar earnestly, 'but he is innocent of Billy's murder. Believe me. Robert and I had an interview with Mrs Wood earlier today. She told us that she was with O'Donnell at the time of the murder. She is ready to swear to it.'

'Of course she is.' Fraser leant towards Oscar, resting his elbows on his knees and placing the palms of his hands together as if in prayer. 'She probably also told you – if you did not already know it – that she is married to O'Donnell. She is not a credible witness, Oscar. She cannot testify on her own husband's behalf. She is lying to protect the man she loves.'

'Is she?'

'She is! Come, man, you must see that!' Fraser slapped the palms of his hands on his knees. 'She is lying to protect the man she loves – and perhaps, also, to protect herself.'

'What do you mean?'

'I mean that she herself may even be implicated in the murder.'

'What?' cried Oscar, flinging his cigarette into the empty grate and rising to his feet. 'You think she may have had a hand in killing her son?'

'She would not be the first mother to have played a part in the murder of her own child.'

'This is preposterous,' exclaimed Oscar. 'This is outrageous.'

'Outrageous, yes,' said Fraser calmly, 'but not, I think, preposterous . . . Who was the housekeeper that day at number 23 Cowley Street? Whoever she was, she was also the murderer's accomplice. Who was she? You saw her, Oscar — who was she?'

'I did not see her,' Oscar protested.

'But you did, Oscar. She opened the door to you. You told me so.'

'I did not notice her. I paid her no attention.'

'But you noticed something about her, Oscar, did you not? When you and Robert first came to see me, you described what happened when you arrived at Cowley Street. You said that you could not describe the house-keeper — except in one particular. You had a recollection of a flash of red about her person. Do you recall?'

'Yes,' said Oscar, 'I do — a red shawl or a scarf, a hand-kerchief or a brooch—'

'Or a livid scarlet birthmark on her neck . . .'

Oscar fell silent and turned towards the looking-glass above the fireplace. On the mantelpiece, resting next to each other, was a pair of Venetian carnival masks, sou-venirs of one of Veronica's expeditions to her favourite city. Oscar ran his finger along the rim of one of them as if checking it for dust. Fraser got to his feet and put his arm around Oscar's shoulder. Oscar looked up. In the looking-glass, they made an unlikely couple: Sir Thomas Lawrence's last portrait of the Prince Regent and Rossetti's painting of Dante, side by side. As their eyes met, Fraser smiled.

'Oscar,' he said, 'let us be friends. Forget this business! Come to Paris! Bring Robert! We have Arthur's tickets.' He turned to me. 'You will come, will you not, Robert? It will please Veronica so much, I know. You will persuade Oscar — if he needs persuasion.' He turned back to Oscar who was still gazing fixedly into the glass. 'Do you need persuading, Oscar? Come, a Scotsman is offering you a touch of Paris in the spring . . .'

Oscar smiled. In that moment, his face to me seemed like a mask. I could not tell what he was thinking – about O'Donnell; about Susannah Wood and the possibility that she was implicated in the death of her own son; about Aidan Fraser and his extraordinary proposal that we should join him and his fiancée on a sudden expedition to Paris.

'Tell me something, Aidan,' he said, in a matter-of-fact sort of way. 'When last we met, you told us that you planned to ask Mrs Wood to identify the severed head of her son – but you did not do so, did you? Why was that?'

'Because I thought better of it, Oscar,' he replied at once. 'Because you and Conan Doyle were of the express opinion that the shock of it might kill her. And because I found that Bellotti – your friend Bellotti – was ready and willing to identify the boy.'

Oscar's eyes narrowed. 'You have interviewed Bellotti?'

'Oh yes,' said Fraser, 'I have interviewed Bellotti. He has talked most freely, most informatively. I have learnt a good deal from Bellotti.'

'And he is ready to give evidence?' Oscar asked, still addressing Fraser via the looking-glass.

'He is, but have no fear. The privacy of the more innocent members of his curious luncheon club is assured. Bellotti hopes to return to business as soon as the court case is concluded – and I have told him that the Metropolitan Police will leave him and his clients to their own devices so long as they avoid causing a public nuisance or creating a public scandal.'

'So Gerard Bellotti is your key witness?'

'Yes,' said Fraser, 'he is not as blind as he pretends to be. You interviewed him, too, I believe.'

'Yes,' Oscar replied.

'Did he, by any chance, reveal to you the identity of Drayton St Leonard?'

'No,' said Oscar.

'I thought not,' said Fraser. 'Drayton St Leonard, according to Mr Bellotti, is the *nom de guerre* of Edward O'Donnell.'

A silence fell.

'Well,' said Oscar eventually, slowly turning away from the looking-glass and addressing us directly, 'that seems to be that.'

He smiled. One mask gave way to another. What he thought, in that moment, of Fraser's revelation, I could not tell, but his immediate mood appeared to lighten. 'Paris in the spring, you say?' He rubbed his hands together. 'Why not? Thank you for inviting us, Aidan. If Robert is free for the next few days, I shall make myself free also.' He seemed, suddenly, inexplicably, exultant. 'Are you planning to whisk us away on the night train, Aidan? Or is there time for that other bottle of Moselle before we depart?'

We did not take the night train. In the event, we lingered at 75 Lower Sloane Street and enjoyed two further bottles of Fraser's fine Moselle wine, before going on to Kettner's for a light supper – lamb cutlets, roast potatoes and spinach: '*En branches*, not *à la crème*,' Oscar instructed the waiter. 'I'm on the strictest diet – I'm off to Paris in the spring!'

It was a little before midnight when we turned in. I walked home from the restaurant. Oscar took a cab.

'Have no fear, Robert,' he said, as he clambered aboard, 'I shall be making no detours tonight. I am going straight home to explain to my ever-patient wife why I am going to Paris for a week without her – and then I am going to bed. À *demain, mon cher*. Our train departs at eight-forty-five. Do not be late.'

I was not. And nor was he. And nor was Miss Sutherland, who arrived at Victoria Station at eight-thirty in the morning, looking – to my eyes at least – like a fairy-tale princess: Perrault's Cinderella crossed with Hans Andersen's Snow Queen. She was dressed in a floor-length coat of black velvet, with cuffs and a collar of white ermine. Her hands were hidden in a silver-grey fur muff and her glorious red hair was piled high on her head beneath a matching fur bonnet. Tall and slender, she held herself proudly, but there was a playfulness in her pale green eyes, a look of merriment, or mischief. As we waited at the agreed rendezvous beneath the station clock and she came towards us, leading a trail of station porters bearing her bags and baggage, she appeared positively imperious. The bustling crowd parted instinctively to let her through. But when she reached us, greeting us each with a smile and a kiss (and, for me, a second kiss!), her manner was disarmingly natural, utterly unforced.

'Where is Aidan?' she asked. 'He is supposed to be our leader and he is nowhere to be seen!'

'I thought I glimpsed him in the distance when we arrived,' said Oscar, 'but I must have been mistaken.'

We looked about the station concourse. A mass of humanity was surging to and fro. From the platforms steam was billowing towards us. Whistles were being blown, ever most insistently. Oscar glanced up at the clock. 'We should board the train,' he said, 'or we shall miss it. Do you have your ticket?'

'I have,' said Veronica, producing it from her muff with a flourish. 'Do you have yours?'

'We do,' said Oscar. 'Aidan kindly gave them to us last night. We are travelling in the names of Mr and Mrs Arthur Conan Doyle . . .'

Veronica laughed. 'Well, that will be something for you to declare when you reach Customs!' she said.

As we followed her and her retinue of porters towards the platform, I realised how deeply I had fallen in love with her. This was not one of my passing fancies. This was a woman who had me wholly in her thrall. When we had found our compartment (and Oscar had tipped and charmed the porters and sent them on their way), she ensconced herself in the seat by the window, laying her muff and her bonnet on the seat beside her. 'You must sit opposite me, Robert,' she said, 'so that I can look into your eyes and, through them, discover the secrets of your soul.'

'Do you believe that there is such a thing as the soul?' asked Oscar, removing his hat, coat and gloves, and placing them carefully in the rack above our seats. 'I thought you surgeons were committed to the corporeal.'

'We have a heart and a mind, Oscar. Who is to say that we do not have a soul? Were I allowed to be a surgeon, I might be the first to uncover its whereabouts!'

'Indeed,' replied Oscar distractedly. He was now at the carriage window, scanning the platform for signs of Aidan Fraser.

'Do not mock me, Oscar,' she continued. 'Our mutual friend John Millais is convinced that the soul is not merely tangible but is located somewhere within the muscles and the membranes of the eye. When he paints a portrait, he claims to be satisfied only when he has captured "the soul within the eye".'

There was a sudden burst of whistles, a whoosh of steam and a grinding and clanking of wheels as the train lurched forward. 'It seems Aidan is not coming after all!' exclaimed Veronica.

'But he is!' cried Oscar, abruptly pushing open the carriage door. There – wild-eyed, pale and perspiring – was Aidan Fraser, running as if his life depended on it. In his arms he was holding his portmanteau. He flung it into the compartment and then, as the train gathered momentum, with a mighty effort he jumped up into the carriage and fell forward onto the floor. He lay with his eyes closed and his mouth open, panting at his fiancée's feet.

'Not a pretty sight,' said Veronica, laughing.

'But one of abject devotion,' said Oscar, slamming the carriage door shut and seating himself in the corner seat diagonally opposite her. 'Did not Sir Edwin Landseer paint a canvas of a Labrador at his master's feet in just such a pose?' Veronica clapped her hands together with delight. 'Of course,' Oscar added, 'Landseer considered the pad of the front paws to be the seat of the soul!'

Fraser, still gasping for breath, opened his eyes and struggled to his feet. 'You may well laugh at me,' he wheezed, as I helped him hoist his portmanteau up onto the luggage rack. 'I overslept. I blame the Moselle. Please accept my profound apologies.' He stood for a moment before us, dusting down his coat and shaking his head as if at his own stupidity. His face was spangled with heavy beads of perspiration. He wiped them away with his handkerchief and then, with both hands, swept back his jet-black hair and slumped, exhausted, into the seat facing Oscar. 'I am so sorry,' he murmured huskily, 'so sorry.'

'No time for lamentation now,' said Oscar, smiling, and patting him on the knee, 'nor yet any cause. You're here. You're safe. We're here. We're happy. All's well with the world.'

All was indeed well with Oscar that day. He was at his most amused – and amusing. From London to Dover, from Dover to Calais, from Calais to Paris, to the very moment of our arrival at the newly opened Hôtel Charing Cross, he was on song. For nine hours – virtually without respite – he entertained us. If our compartment was uncomfortable, or the Channel crossing was choppy (as it must have been!), I cannot tell you. All that I can recall, all that I noted in my journal, was the effulgence of Oscar's discourse throughout that long day. What was most remarkable about his performance (for it was a performance) was the way in which, for so many hours, effortlessly, he commanded our attention.

His secret – his trick – lay, I think, in the way in which he varied both the tone and the content of what he had to say. At one moment he was debating the locus of the soul with Veronica; the next he was describing in forensic detail the operation that his father had performed to save the sight of the king of Sweden. Then, of a sudden, he reduced us to tears of laughter with an outrageous story of one of his brother Willie's drunken escapades. A moment later, he brought different tears to our eyes (and his own) with a whimsical and pathetic tale of the mermaid who lived in Dover Harbour and fell fatally in love with the harbour-master's son.

Apart from a passing reference to Bellotti and 'the loucher members of his luncheon club' ('Are not some of their practices against the law?' asked Veronica; 'We are mid-Channel, dear lady,' Oscar replied, 'I cannot tell you; in England, most probably they are; in France, according to the Code Napoléon, most certainly they are not; what a difference twenty-one miles makes!'), throughout the entire journey the case of the murder of Billy Wood was not raised once.

At Veronica's instigation, Oscar talked much about Paris, which he and I knew well, but which she and Aidan Fraser knew hardly at all. Fraser was eager for us, during our visit, to make a pilgrimage to the city's new sensation: Gustave Eiffel's recently completed tower.

'Spare us Monsieur Eiffel's Tower!' cried Oscar.

'But it is extraordinary,' protested Fraser. 'It rises nine hundred and eighty-five feet above the ground!'

'And still gets you no closer to heaven!' said Oscar. 'Turn your back to the Eiffel Tower and you have all Paris before you. Look at it – and all Paris disappears.'.

'The Tower is a phenomenon, Oscar,' I protested. 'You can't deny it.'

'I don't deny it,' he said, 'and you should not be denied it either. Go to your tower. Enjoy! I'll leave you to it. While you are scaling the heights, I shall take myself off to wander in the foothills of Mount Parnassus . . .'

'And what do you mean by that, Oscar?' Veronica enquired, an eyebrow gently raised. 'Do you have mischief in mind?'

'No,' he answered, easily, 'far from it. I simply mean

that, while you are all busy inspecting Monsieur Eiffel's monstrosity, I shall go to Montparnasse and take a stroll through the cemetery there. I have a grave that I am minded to visit. I shall pay my respects to an old friend. I have been thinking of her much of late – and I have news to share with her. For once the words of Mercury will be sweet after the songs of Apollo.'

22

Paris in the Spring

That night, Oscar talked much of Marie Aguétant.

We reached our hotel – the Hôtel Charing Cross, in the *huitième*, in rue Pasquier – soon after seven o'clock. It was terrifically modern, wonderfully chic. There was a deal of marble on the walls, scarlet carpeting on the stairs and, in the public rooms, ornate electric chandeliers in the centre of every ceiling. Oscar was not impressed. He stood in the foyer, shaking the rain off his shoulders and sniffing the air suspiciously.

'It is very new, Aidan, is it not?'

'It is brand-new, Oscar.'

'It is very shiny – like a new coin. I am always wary of things that are too shiny.'

'Do you want us to look elsewhere?' Veronica asked. 'We will be guided by you and Robert.'

'No, no,' said Oscar. 'We have journeyed far enough and I am sure the facilities here will prove excellent.' He smiled at the hovering bellboy. 'Ignore my foolish prejudice. I'm one of those who warms to a man because his cuffs are frayed. It's not rational, I know. Let us find our rooms and change for dinner. Where shall we eat?'

'I thought we'd dine here,' said Fraser. 'The restaurant is said to be first class.'

'Now, there I do draw the line,' said Oscar. 'It's a rule of life that you must never dine in the hotel in which you are staying. When I dine at the Savoy, I sleep at the Langham. When I sleep at the Savoy, I dine at the Criterion. Between his *digestif* and his pillow, a gentleman should always glimpse the stars. May I propose dinner at the Grand Café? The *soles soufflées à la mousse d' homard* are the best in Paris, and Rigo and his gypsy orchestra never fail to find music to match your mood.'

The facilities at the Hôtel Charing Cross did indeed prove excellent. There was a bathroom attached to each bedroom (a great novelty in those days) and, at the mere turn of a dolphin-shaped tap, an abundance of flowing water, pale brown but piping hot. The food at the Grand Café when we reached it – almost two hours later; neither Oscar nor Miss Sutherland rushed their toilette – was exceptional. I was less certain about Rigo and his gypsy orchestra, however. As we arrived at the restaurant, bizarrely, they were playing a selection from Gounod's *Faust*. As we were shown to our table, they struck up what sounded like a Hungarian funeral march. As we took our seats, I enquired of Oscar, 'What is your mood now?'

He cocked his ear and listened intently to the music. 'Melancholy, it seems. I had not realised. But Rigo never gets it wrong. He has mystic powers.'

We ordered – or, rather, we permitted Oscar to order on our behalf: *soupe au cresson* and *truffes fraîches sous la cendre* to lead into the *soles soufflées*, with *carré d'agneau* to follow ('Let us proceed gently; we must do justice to the *tartes* and *crêpes*'). When the first of several fine wines had been served (a Perrier Jouët, 1880, by way of aperitif – 'I have simple tastes; I am content to settle for the best'), Oscar took his cue from Rigo. He spoke of death. And, in particular, the death of children. He talked of Billy Wood and of the boy's natural sweetness and eagerness to please. He said, contemplating his saucer of champagne as he spoke, 'I imagine poor Billy's desire to please was his undoing. It is for many.' He invited us to raise our glasses and drink to the lad's memory.

He spoke, too, of his own younger sister, Isola, 'taken from us when she was ten – how we loved her!' I knew how much he loved her; he carried a lock of her hair in an envelope in his pocket. 'I can see her still,' he said, 'dancing like a golden sunbeam about the house. She was everything to me . . . Heaven must be a very happy place if Isola and Billy Wood are there.'

As Rigo's mood-music lifted a little (the funeral march giving way to a gypsy aubade), Veronica asked him who was the friend that he proposed to visit in the cemetery at Montparnasse.

'Her name was Marie Aguétant,' he said, tucking his napkin into the top of his waistcoat. 'Robert knew her too – though not, perhaps, so well as I.' He smiled at me knowingly. I answered his smile, but with some awkwardness. Beneath the tablecloth, Veronica, who was seated on my right, had taken hold of my hand and she held it tight. 'Is the soup not to your liking, Robert?' Oscar enquired.

'I am letting it cool a little,' I said, pressing my fingers into Veronica's palm.

'Very wise,' he replied, his smile transmogrifying into a smirk.

Fraser – Veronica's fiancé, God save the mark! – appeared oblivious to what was going on beneath the tablecloth, beneath his very nose. That evening his focus remained, as it had done throughout the day, entirely upon Oscar. 'Marie Aguétant,' he said. 'I know the name.'

'It is notorious,' said Oscar.

'Was she not murdered by her pimp? He was a Spaniard, I seem to recall. Polo? Pablo? Something like that.'

'Yes,' said Oscar, mopping his lips. 'The police did indeed arrest the Spaniard. He was tried. He was found guilty. He was sent to the guillotine. He was quite innocent, of course.'

'Oh, come now, Oscar!' Fraser protested. 'I remember the case. I read all about it. Whatever his name, he was a bad man.'

'Undoubtedly, a very bad man. I knew him. He was evil. But he was innocent of the murder of Marie Aguétant.'

Fraser had turned directly towards Oscar now. He also had abandoned his soup, but for different reasons. 'How do you *know* he was innocent, Oscar? How can you be so certain?'

'Because I have met the murderer of Marie Aguétant, just as I have met the murderer of Billy Wood.'

Beneath the table, Veronica released my hand. 'Oh, Oscar,' she cried, leaning imploringly towards him, 'don't let us speak any more of that tonight. We are in Paris, and this is my birthday treat . . .'

'Quite right, dear lady,' said Oscar, and as he spoke – I may have imagined this, but I do not think so; I noted it in my journal at the time – he glanced towards the *chef d'orchestre* and, the moment his eye and Rigo's met, the orchestra broke into its first mazurka of the night. Oscar reached across the table, took Veronica's hand in his and kissed it. 'Your hand is very warm, my dear,' he murmured.

'But Oscar,' Fraser continued, now using his soup spoon to add emphasis to his argument, 'if you believe that you know the true identity of Marie Aguétant's murderer, you should take the information to the police.'

'No,' said Oscar, shaking his head, 'Marie would not have wanted that.'

'But she is dead,' said Fraser. 'How can you know what she would have wanted?'

'Because she told me before she died,' said Oscar, simply. 'I knew her well. I loved her. We understood one another. She was one of the few human beings who have understood me. I am grateful for that.'

'And yet,' said Veronica, quietly, her hands now held together under her chin, 'she was what Robert coyly calls "a daughter of joy" . . . She was a lady of the night, was she not?'

'A prostitute,' said Fraser.

'A courtesan,' I corrected him.

Oscar appeared quite unperturbed. 'She was indeed — all that and more. But I loved her, not on account of her calling, or of the company she kept, but because of her personality, which was unique. Personality is a very mysterious thing. A man cannot always be estimated by what he does. He may keep the law and yet be worthless. He may break the law and yet be fine. He may be bad, without ever doing anything bad. He may commit a sin against society, and yet realise through that sin his own perfection . . .'

The soup had been cleared away. The truffles were being served.

'And speaking of perfection . . .' Oscar surveyed his plate complacently. The music had stopped; the orchestra had paused between numbers. Oscar looked at each member of our little party. Every one of us was smiling. 'I hope Le Grand Café is to your liking,' he said. 'In some Parisian restaurants, there's a certain surliness about the service. Here, they put themselves out to please.' As he spoke, giving the sommelier a smile and the Burgundy his blessing, across the crowded room, by the doors leading to the kitchen, two waiters collided and there was a mighty crash – like the clashing of cymbals – as a pair of trays piled high with crockery and silver cascaded to the floor. There was a beat of silence in the room, followed by laughter from half a dozen tables and then a general smattering of applause. 'Do you see what I mean? They do that entirely to please their British clientele. They know that an Englishman's idea of a joke is a jug of water balanced on top of a half-opened door.'

We laughed; we tucked into our truffles; we quaffed the Burgundy. Beneath the table, Veronica laid a hand upon my thigh. 'This is wonderful, Oscar,' she said, smiling at our host. 'Thank you.'

'Do not thank me,' he said, 'thank your fiancé. Paris in the spring was his idea. Thank Fraser. And thank France. The English have a remarkable capacity for turning wine into water. Here it is different.'

'It certainly is,' said Fraser, revealing his line of fine white teeth and raising his glass to the room. 'This is a far cry from the officers' mess at Scotland Yard, no doubt about it.'

Oscar smiled and followed Aidan Fraser's eyes as they ranged around the room and came to rest on Rigo. The maestro was playing his violin *con brio*, bobbing up and down in time to the music, looking directly at us as he played. We were being treated now to a selection of lively polkas, interspersed with lyrical gypsy love songs. 'Listen to the music,' said Oscar, 'by turns plangent and rhapsodic. Rigo sees into our souls, does he not?'

Later that night, when Oscar and I were lying side by side in our separate beds ('You may take the bed nearer the bathroom, Robert; that would have been Mrs Doyle's privilege') and, in the heavy darkness relieved only by the burning glow of my friend's last post-prandial cigarette, in hushed tones, like schoolboys telling tales in the dormitory after 'lights out', we were reviewing the pleasures of the evening, I asked Oscar whether I might tell him a secret.

'By all means,' he whispered, comfortingly. 'We are in Paris. In London one hides everything. In Paris one reveals everything. That is the rule.'

'I am in love with Miss Sutherland.'

'And . . ?' he asked, softly, turning his head towards me.

'And?' I repeated. 'And nothing,' I said. 'That is my secret.'

Softly, Oscar began to chuckle. Gradually, his chuckle turned into a rumble and then into a roar. 'Robert, Robert, Robert!' he cried, now coughing and wheezing through his laughter and struggling to sit up in bed to catch his breath. 'That cannot be your secret! All the world knows you love Miss Sutherland! Tonight you missed much of the finest food in Paris because your hands were locked in hers beneath the tablecloth when they should have been above board and about their proper business with your eating irons! That you love Miss Sutherland is no secret!'

I felt very foolish. My face burnt with embarrassment. 'Is it that apparent?'

'If you had hired a balloon from Monsieur Montgolfier and dropped leaflets all over Paris announcing your betrothal, it could not have been more apparent.'

'Do you think she will marry me, then?'

'Robert, you are absurd! You are not yet divorced – and she is engaged to Fraser. Let us face it: your banns are not about to be called.'

'But would she marry me, were I free? Were she free?'

'Ah,' he said, subsiding onto the pillows once more, 'that is a different question, Robert. Now we are delving into Miss Sutherland's secret, not yours.'

'What are her true feelings towards Fraser?'

'A good question.'

'And what are his feelings towards her? Why does he allow her so much freedom – so much *licence*?'

'Indeed.'

Silence fell between us. His raillery ceased. He dropped his glowing cigarette end into the glass of water on the bedside table. There was a tiny hiss and the darkness in the room was complete.

'Do you think she does not love me?' I whispered.

'She is fond of you, I am sure,' he answered, kindly.

'But does she love me? She allows me to make love to her. And tonight it was she who first placed her hand in mine.'

'Yes,' said Oscar, gently, 'she succumbed to that temptation.'

'But why – if she does not love me?'

'Robert, as the poet says in "The Sphinx Without a Secret", "Women are meant to be loved, not to be understood."'

'Which poet is that?'

'Oscar Wilde,' he replied, 'one of our favourites. I think we should let him have the last word, don't you? Goodnight, Robert.'

'Goodnight.'

Oscar slept soundly. I did not. Within minutes of our having exchanged our goodnights, the macabre sound of my friend's snoring – like a never-ending death rattle – filled the night air. I buried my head beneath the pillow and, to distract myself, tried to fill my mind with sensual fantasy. I failed. Where I hoped to see Veronica bringing her soft lips to mine, huge faces – hard and cruel – loomed, unbidden, out of the darkness towards me, like headlamps on an oncoming train. I wanted Veronica's smiling features upon my pillow; instead, I was confronted by Bellotti's blind eyes, O'Donnell's malevolent leer, Fraser's mouth of small white teeth. Eventually, as the hours passed, I fell into a fitful sleep. I can recollect only one dream of that night. It was not of Veronica, nor of Kaitlyn nor of Marthe – nor even of Constance, who, curiously, often featured in my dreams. It was of Conan Doyle examining the severed head of Billy Wood beneath the gasolier in Tite Street.

In the morning, Oscar was up betimes; he had bathed, shaved and dressed even as I slumbered. I awoke to a waft of his favourite scent (Canterbury Wood Violet) and the sight of his large, long face peering down into mine. 'Up, up, my friend,' he cried. 'You've missed the dawn. Soon you'll be missing breakfast too.'

'You're very bright this morning,' I mumbled, pulling the bedclothes over my nose and eyes.

Oscar had drawn the curtains and pushed back the shutters. A sharp white light was filling the room. 'It is St Bathild's Eve,' he declared. 'We must do her due honour.'

'Who on earth is St Bathild?'

'In heaven she ranks among the Almighty's favourites. She was an English girl who became a French queen, a thousand years ago. As a child, she was stolen by pirates and sold into slavery. As a young woman, she caught the eye of King Clovis II.'

'Who was he?'

'The Robert Sherard of the Western Franks,' he cried, pulling back my bedclothes with a mighty sweep. 'King Clovis could not resist a pretty ankle. St Bathild is the patron saint of pretty ankles. You must get up and light a candle at her shrine. She died in Paris – as all the best people do.'

I rolled over and lowered my feet to the ice-cold floor. 'It's too early for this banter, Oscar,' I muttered. 'Where are my slippers?'

'Have you asked St Anthony and St Anne?'

I groaned. 'You and your blessed saints . . .'

He was standing near the window now, adjusting his tie in the looking-glass that was affixed to one of the doors of a large walnut wardrobe. He looked down at my reflection in the glass. 'It's all about saints' days, Robert,' he said, with a smile.

'What is?' I asked, confused. (The wine list of Le Grand Café was beginning to exact its toll.)

'This case of ours,' he replied, turning towards me. 'It's all about saints' days . . . and temptation.' He opened the wardrobe and selected a shirt, coat and trousers for me, casting them on the foot of my bed. 'This has been a profitable night in the matter of the murder of Billy Wood,' he reflected. 'Things I had dimly dreamt of were suddenly made real to me. Things of which I had never dreamt were gradually revealed. Dress, *mon ami*. *Le tout Paris nous attend*.'

It was not much after nine when we found Aidan Fraser in the multi-mirrored breakfast room of the Hôtel Charing Cross. He was seated alone, at a table set for four. 'Veronica has breakfasted,' he said. 'She is taking a walk. She will be back shortly.'

'You look perturbed, my friend,' said Oscar, as we took our seats.

'I am,' said Fraser. 'I have received a wire from London.'

'From Scotland Yard?'

'Yes,' he said, holding up the envelope for us to see, 'from Gilmour.'

'Bad news?'

'The worst,' said Fraser. 'We have lost our key witness.'

'Bellotti?' asked Oscar.

'Yes,' said the inspector, 'Bellotti. Bellotti is dead.'

'Dead!' exclaimed Oscar. 'Did you say dead?'

'Yes,' said Fraser.

'I don't believe it,' said Oscar. He put his hand to his mouth and closed his eyes. 'How is this possible?' he murmured, speaking as if in a daze. He opened his eyes. 'Dead?' he said once more. 'Do you mean murdered?'

'No, not murdered,' replied the inspector, opening out the telegram. 'An accident, it seems – or suicide. He fell under a train.'

'Does Gilmour mention the dwarf?'

'The dwarf?' repeated Fraser, uncomprehending. He stared down at the telegram. 'There's no mention of any dwarf.'

'Well,' said Oscar, with a bitter laugh, recovering his composure and pouring himself a cup of hot chocolate, 'so much for Paris in the spring. We must return to London at once.'

23

29 January 1890

'Must we return to London, Aidan? *Must* we?'

Veronica Sutherland had come back from her early morning walk with colour in her cheek and fire in her eye – and the prettiest feather cap upon her head. She had found us in the hotel dining room and joined us at our breakfast table, but declined to take a seat. In consequence, Aidan Fraser, Oscar and I were standing in our places, clutching our napkins, as if we were errant schoolboys, with slates in hand, being admonished by their governess. 'This is so annoying,' she continued, 'so unfair. We have only just arrived and Monday is my birthday – my birthday! When did we last have any time together, Aidan? You are always working.'

'The world, not the family, gets the fruits of genius,' said Oscar.

Veronica turned on him. 'Oh, do hush, Oscar, *please*. Your never-ending witticisms can be quite wearisome at times.'

'The line was not mine,' said Oscar meekly, 'but Conan Doyle's.'

'The source is immaterial! The point is: we are supposed to be on holiday – this is my birthday weekend – and Aidan is neither a genius nor indispensable. Cannot the case be handled by Inspector Gilmour or some other plodder at the Yard?'

'The case is important,' said Oscar.

'Is it?' she asked, looking him directly in the eye. 'A slut of a boy has been murdered, his pimp has taken his own life, his drunken stepfather is to be hanged. Is the case *really* so important, Mr Wilde?'

I was shocked by the violence of her language. Oscar seemed unperturbed. 'Yes,' he answered, calmly, returning her gaze.

'Oh,' she said, sharply, 'and to whom?'

'It is important to your fiancé, Miss Sutherland, and to his future. He has charged a man with murder – and his principal witness is now dead. How did Bellotti die? Was it suicide? Was it an accident? Or was it, in fact, also murder? The matter cannot be left unresolved, nor can it be handled by Inspector Gilmour. It is Fraser's responsibility, alas! Duty calls.'

Veronica sighed impatiently and looked about her. The dining room was not crowded, but at assorted other tables around the room there were fellow guests affecting to ignore us. I thought to speak – to say that perhaps Oscar and Fraser might return to London while I kept Miss Sutherland company in Paris – but I lacked the courage and I let the moment pass.

'Very well,' she said (her cheeks were paler now, her eyes no longer burnt so brightly), 'I will go to my room to pack. Kindly call me when you are ready to depart.'

'Thank you,' said Fraser. 'We will celebrate your birthday properly at Lower Sloane Street.'

'Indeed,' she said.

'And we can return to Paris,' said Oscar, smiling, 'in the spring!'

She laughed, turned away and swept out of the room.

Within three hours, we were at the Gare du Nord, boarding the Club train for Calais. Fraser and Oscar had no difficulty in exchanging our tickets; the train on each side of the Channel was next to deserted and on board our steamship (the SS *Dover Castle*, 'pride of the line') we were the only passengers to be found in the first-class saloon. The day was a long one, and tedious. Our return to London was not the feast of good humour and fine sentiment that our outward trip had been. If Oscar had shafts of wit in mind (whether his own or those of others), he kept them to himself. For most of the journey home, his nose was buried in a book. We all read, or pretended to. I leafed slowly through my *vade mecum*, my annotated edition of the maxims of La Rochefoucauld. Veronica pored over a scientific journal devoted to Louis Pasteur's work on immunisation against anthrax. Aidan Fraser read Jerome K. Jerome's *Three Men in a Boat*, but not, I think, with close attention. He did not laugh once.

When we were back on English soil, when our train was travelling past the hop fields of north Kent and darkness was falling, Oscar and Fraser, as if by unspoken mutual consent, laid aside their books and, leaning toward one another, in subdued tones, conspiratorially, began to converse about the case.

'When exactly was Bellotti's body found?' Oscar asked. 'Did Gilmour say?'

'Yesterday morning, it would seem.'

'While we were travelling to Paris . . .'

'Yes.'

'And he fell beneath a train?'

'Apparently.'

'At which station?'

'The wire did not specify – but it was not a railway station. The accident occurred on the underground.'

'The accident?' Oscar raised an eyebrow.

'It could have been an accident, Oscar,' Fraser said, with deliberation. 'The man was virtually blind, was he not?'

'That would have made him more careful, I think, not less so. You cannot rule out murder. You must not.'

'But why should anyone wish to murder Bellotti?'

'Because he was your witness, Aidan. You said he told you that Edward O'Donnell and Drayton St Leonard were one and the same man—'

'He did.'

'You are sure of that?'

'Quite sure of it.'

'And he told you, too, that Billy Wood left the lunch party that day to meet up with him?'

'That's what he said. He was ready to testify to that.'

'Very well,' said Oscar. 'If Bellotti was prepared to testify to that, what else might he not have been prepared to say in court? If he was prepared to implicate O'Donnell, what other reputation might he not have been ready to ruin? The moment Gerard Bellotti turned police informer, his days were numbered.'

Fraser laughed and pointed to the slim volume lying on the seat next to Oscar. 'I think you have been reading too much Conan Doyle, Oscar.'

My friend picked up his copy of *The Sign of Four* and turned it over carefully in his hands. 'I am absorbing what lessons I can from Mr Sherlock Holmes,' he said, 'that "perfect reasoning and observing machine".'

Fraser smiled and, settling back in his seat, ran his long thin fingers through his hair. 'It was an accident, Oscar – or suicide. Bellotti realised the game was up and he couldn't face the consequences.' He turned to look out of the carriage window, but night had fallen and he could have seen only his own reflection in the glass. 'You mentioned a dwarf this morning,' he said. 'What dwarf was that?'

'Bellotti kept a dwarf, as a kind of companion, errand-boy, bodyguard . . . I rarely saw Bellotti without the dwarf. He was an ugly creature.'

'If Bellotti was murdered,' suggested Fraser, turning back to Oscar, 'perhaps this dwarf was the murderer.'

'I doubt it,' said Oscar. 'The dwarf was Bellotti's son.'

Fraser turned towards the carriage window once again. 'I did not know about the dwarf,' he said.

'You'll have to find him,' said Oscar.

'Yes,' said Fraser, somewhat distractedly, 'yes, I suppose so. There's much to be done . . .'

'What will you do first?' Oscar asked. 'Interview the members of Bellotti's little luncheon club? They should be able to identify Drayton St Leonard for you, should they not? Of course, unlike Bellotti, they may be reluctant to do so . . .'

'I think I'll begin with Mrs Wood,' said Fraser. Oscar shook his head dismissively. Fraser continued: 'Mrs Wood – or Mrs O'Donnell – or whatever she calls herself: she was your "housekeeper", Oscar, I'm sure of that.'

'She'll deny it.'

'No doubt. Those with blood on their hands are dis-inclined to tell the truth.'

'Will you charge her?'

'Not without a confession, no. Juries don't like to convict mothers of murdering their own. But they'll convict O'Donnell. O'Donnell will hang – and that will be her punishment.'

Our train was now travelling through the outskirts of south-east London. By day, the dreary streets and run-down dwellings that we were passing represented some of the meanest slums of the capital. By night, flickering candles on window ledges and gas lamps on alley walls turned poverty into fairy tale, transforming lines of tawdry tenement buildings into rows of Hänsel and Gretel cottages. Oscar followed my eyes and read my mind. 'Illusion can be a comfort,' he said.

Veronica was waking from a sleep. Her eyes were tired; her skin was pale (the powder had fallen from her cheeks); her hair had become unpinned and was tumbling about her neck. I had not known her look more natural, or more vulnerable. She smiled at me with gently parted lips and held my look in hers. I was overwhelmed by her loveliness.

The train was moving slowly now, as we approached the terminus. Veronica, sitting forward, adjusting her hair and stretching at the same time, turned towards Oscar and said, 'I owe you an apology, Mr Wilde.'

Oscar stood up and bowed to her before reaching up to lift down one of the bags from the rack above our heads. 'You owe me nothing, dear lady.'

'I owe you an apology,' she repeated. 'I was intemperate earlier – and ill mannered. I don't know what got into me. I trust you will forgive me and show that you do so by coming for a birthday drink tomorrow evening.'

'I shall be honoured,' said Oscar. 'Is Robert invited also?'

'He knows he is!' She leant towards me, lifted my hand and kissed it.

'Good,' said Fraser, slapping his knees and getting briskly to his feet. The train had lurched to a stop. 'That's settled then. Six o'clock tomorrow evening at Lower Sloane Street. And now?'

We were all on our feet, gathering our possessions about us.

'I shall return to my great-aunt in Bedford Square,' said Veronica. 'She is not expecting me, of course, and she is not good at dealing with the unexpected, but she will cope. She had her doubts about my travelling to Paris unchaperoned. My early return will give her some satisfaction.'

'I have not had the pleasure of meeting Mrs Sutherland Senior,' said Oscar, pulling on his bottle-green coat with the astrakhan collar. 'I trust she will be joining us tomorrow evening?'

'I think not,' replied Veronica. 'She never ventures out after dark. She's of that generation.'

'Ah,' said Oscar, opening the carriage door and handing a suitcase to a porter on the station platform. 'There are exceptions to every rule. My mother never ventures out by day. She has an aversion to the brutality of strong lights.'

We were now all bathed in the ochre glow of the gas lamps of Victoria Station. Like one of Mr Cook's guides, escorting an expedition through the side-streets of Florence, Oscar strode ahead, cane held high, leading our party (with four porters in tow) to the cab rank in the station forecourt. There was a two-wheeler at the head of the line.

'Would you be so good as to take this young lady to Bedford Square?' said Oscar, handing the driver two shillings. The man examined the coins and grunted. Oscar murmured, 'The vocabulary of the London cabby is terse, but compelling.'

Veronica climbed up into the two-wheeler and looked down at us. I would like to say that, as she departed, she favoured me with her warmest smile – but I cannot. She appeared to regard each of us with equal favour. 'Goodnight, gentlemen,' she said, with a little wave. '*À demain.*'

'Your fiancée is a remarkable woman,' said Oscar, putting his hand on Fraser's shoulder, as we stood watching and waving while her cab trundled away into the night. 'She has fire in her soul. It burns fiercely.'

'I so want to please her,' said Fraser.

'It will not be easy. She has energy and intelligence – the spirit of a man – yet, through an accident of birth, she is fated to play the docile woman's part. It is difficult to be wholly happy in such circumstances.'

The station porters were loading the remainder of our cases into the next cab in line. 'Where now?' cried Oscar. 'A drink? A bite of supper? Buck rarebit and a glass of champagne?'

Fraser was still gazing after Veronica, although her cab had by then disappeared into the traffic. He returned from his reverie. 'I am going to Bow Street to re-examine O'Donnell,' he said.

'What?' exclaimed Oscar. 'Now? It is nine o'clock on a Saturday night!'

'As good a time as any,' Fraser replied.

'A somewhat irregular time for a police interrogation, surely?' said Oscar, looking at the inspector with some puzzlement.

Fraser laughed. 'Come, Oscar, was it not you who urged me to return "at once" to London? I might have left matters to Archy Gilmour, but you said, "Duty calls." You wanted me on the case.'

'Of course,' said Oscar, 'quite right.' He paused a moment and then, with both hands on Fraser's shoulders, facing him, he looked directly into the white-faced policeman's eyes. 'Might I ask a favour, Aidan?' he enquired. 'Might I come too?'

Fraser looked uncertain. 'To Bow Street?'

'Yes,' said Oscar.

'Now, that would be somewhat irregular, would it not?'

'Not to question O'Donnell myself,' Oscar went on, 'that's your job, Aidan, I understand that – but to watch and witness? You believe that O'Donnell is guilty and from what Bellotti told you it seems that there's circumstantial evidence . . . I believe him innocent, but I have never seen the man sober. Perhaps I do not have the measure of him yet. In the cells, he will be sober . . .'

Fraser shook his head. 'Not necessarily,' he said. 'It depends on the sergeant on duty. If O'Donnell has money, he may have been able to obtain liquor, even in his cell.'

'Please, Aidan,' said Oscar, imploringly.

The young detective shrugged his shoulders and sighed. 'It's most irregular, but very well . . . Come,' – he held open the cab door for us – 'come, by all means. It was your case at the start, Oscar. It is right that you should be in at the finish.'

'You think we're at the finish?' I asked as our cab turned into Victoria Street.

'I think O'Donnell will confess,' said Fraser.

We were at Bow Street within a quarter of an hour. As we climbed down from the brougham, Fraser went on into the police station ahead of us while Oscar persuaded our cabman to wait for us with our bags. 'Driver, I fear we could be as much as an hour,' he said. 'If you park across the street, by the stage door to the Opera House, you may catch the last act of *Lohengrin*.'

The driver nodded absently. 'If you say so, sir.'

'I do say so, driver,' said Oscar. 'It is your kind of music – it is Wagner!' The driver looked none the wiser, but nodded again as he pocketed the coin that Oscar had pressed into his hand. 'Wagner's music is better than anybody's,' Oscar persisted. 'It is so loud that one can talk the whole time without people hearing what one says.'

'Very droll, Oscar,' boomed a stranger coming across the street towards us, a small, bald man in evening dress, smoking a large cigar. I did not know him, but evidently he knew Oscar – everyone knew Oscar! – and Oscar, as soon as he registered the man's presence, cried, 'Gus! Gus! *So* good to see you!'

The little man was Sir Augustus Harris, manager of both the Theatre Royal, Drury Lane, and the Theatre Royal, Covent Garden. 'It's not opera tonight, Oscar. It's pantomime – your kind of evening! *Bluebeard* – your kind of show! And all two thousand one hundred and ninety seats are sold! But if you want to join me in my box—'

'No, thank you kindly, Gus. My friend and I are otherwise engaged.'

Sir Augustus Harris looked up at the blue lamp hanging above the entrance to the police station and raised a quizzical eyebrow. 'Your secret is safe with me,' he chortled. 'Goodnight, Oscar.' He nodded to me, 'Good evening, sir.' He crossed back to the other side of the street, waving his cigar grandiosely in the air and calling out to Oscar as he went, 'Irving tells me you've been to his rescue. Bravo! He's grateful. Come and see me soon, Oscar. Let us do something together – so long as it's not your *Salome*!'

'Gus is a good man,' said Oscar, 'a civilised philistine. He represents the survival of the pushing.'

We climbed the stone steps of the police station to find a young constable waiting for us in the dimly lit lobby by the station front door. 'Inspector Fraser's with Sergeant Ritter, sir. They won't be a tick. They're getting the keys.'

'It's very quiet here,' said Oscar, 'sepulchral. One might be in a deserted country church.'

'It'll liven up later, sir,' said the young bobby. 'By midnight, when the pubs and bars have all shut, it'll be as busy as a casbah on novelty night.'

Oscar gazed at the youth in amazement. I could see an elaborate compliment forming in my friend's mind when, suddenly, we were distracted by the sound of clanking keys behind us. We turned and there, in the corner of the empty lobby, in what had given the impression of being a blank wall, we now discerned a narrow door, made of heavy metal, studded with bolts and painted black. Cut into the door, at head height, was an aperture no larger than the mouth of a letter box and through the aperture, brightly lit, we saw the perfect white teeth of Aidan Fraser.

'Are you coming?' he called.

'We are,' said Oscar. He smiled at the young constable regretfully. 'We will meet again, I hope.'

As we reached the metal door, it swung silently inward and, just beyond it, in a narrow, low-ceilinged passageway, we found Fraser, eyes glittering, holding up a paraffin lamp to light our way. 'Step carefully,' he said, 'it's dark and damp down here. I nearly slipped.'

With him was Sergeant Ritter, a middle-aged man, not tall but heavily built, with rheumy eyes, a drinker's nose and a look of defeat about him. He breathed heavily, but said little. When Oscar remarked, solicitously, 'Is your asthma troubling you, Sergeant? It's been a bitter winter,' the sergeant stared blankly at his interlocutor, as though Oscar were a creature from the planet Mars, and offered no response. (Not everyone was susceptible to Oscar's charm.)

'Follow me,' said Fraser, holding his lamp aloft and leading us in single file along the narrow passage, then down a short flight of metal steps to the cells. The place was indeed dark and damp – and claustrophobic. It had a dismal, pestilential feel.

'He's in Cell One,' said Fraser. 'He's our only prisoner tonight. He's still in drink, alas. Ritter thought it best to keep him quiet with liquor. He was not to know we would be coming.'

We were outside the cell door, standing close together around Fraser's lamp. 'It's as quiet as the grave,' said Oscar, 'not a mouse stirring.'

'There may be rats in the cell, Oscar,' said Fraser, with a wintry smile. 'Stay by the door – he could be violent. Let Ritter go in first. We'll see whether he's in a fit state to answer questions tonight. If not, we'll return in the morning.'

Fraser unlocked the door and handed his sergeant the paraffin lamp. It was our only source of light. If its small, flickering flame had been extinguished, we would have been plunged into utter darkness. We stood in silence by the door, at the top of the three steps leading down into the cell. Ritter, breathing heavily, went ahead, holding up the lamp to light his way.

'O'Donnell!' he barked. 'You've got visitors. Get up, man. O'Donnell! O'Donnell!'

But answer came there none.

The cell was no more than four feet wide by eight feet long. At the far end of the cell, immediately facing the door, high up on the wall, just below the ceiling, was an open hole, the size of a brick, that served as an air vent by night and a pathetic window on the sky by day. Across the hole, blocking its passage, was a single metal bar. Hanging from the bar was a leather belt. Hanging from the belt was the body of Edward O'Donnell. His head lolled to one side. His eyes were open wide, wild and staring. His mouth was wide open, too. As Ritter held the lamp up towards O'Donnell's ghastly face, we could see that his chin, beard and shirt were covered with fresh vomit.

'He is dead,' said Ritter, pressing his fingers against the hanging man's wrist.

'I should have known,' said Oscar. 'The fault is mine. I am guilty of this.'

24

29–30 January 1890

Within what seemed like moments – and can, in fact, have been no more than five or six minutes – Oscar and I were back in the two-wheeler being driven along the Strand. My heart was palpitating still, but Oscar, save for a row of tell-tale beads of perspiration across his brow, gave no outward sign of inner turmoil. It was in his nature to remain calm in a crisis. The perspiration was induced by exertion, not anxiety. Oscar Wilde was a man who could – and did – endure, with apparent equanimity, catcalls from a hostile audience, jibes and jeers from an ignorant mob, even his own arrest and imprisonment. The more turbulent the tempest, the more serene he seemed.

From his coat pocket he took out his presentation copy of Conan Doyle's *The Sign of Four* and turned it over carefully in his hands, leafing idly through the pages. 'Holmes is right, Robert. His maxim holds. Once you have eliminated the impossible, whatever remains, *however improbable*, must be the truth.'

'You know the truth of this?' I asked. I was more confused than ever. The hideous image of O'Donnell's dangling corpse filled my mind's eye.

'I believe so,' he said soothingly, caressing Doyle's book and giving me that half-smile that was – to me, at least – the sure sign that he had just conceived a thought that particularly pleased him. 'I believe so, Robert, but I must put it to the test. That I'll do tomorrow . . . And then we're done. Case closed.' He returned the book to his coat pocket.

'Case closed.' Those were the words that Aidan Fraser had used, repeatedly, as he had bustled us out of Cell One at Bow Street Police Station a few minutes before. At the moment of the grim discovery of O'Donnell's body, when Oscar had exclaimed, 'The fault is mine. I am guilty of this,' the inspector had turned on him angrily and hissed, 'Don't be an idiot, Wilde. The man has taken his own life. By his suicide he has confessed his guilt. Case closed.'

Bewildered, appalled by the sight that confronted us, stupidly I exclaimed, 'We must call the police!'

'We *are* the police!' barked Fraser. 'Get a grip, man. The brute is dead, that's all. Case closed.'

The sergeant was still holding up the paraffin lamp towards the face of the dead man. Oscar was gazing directly at the bulging, sightless eyes. He seemed transfixed. 'No time for lamentation now,' he murmured. (It was one of his favourite lines.)

'My apologies, Sherard,' said Fraser, recovering his composure. 'I am as shocked as you are. It is a dreadful thing, though perhaps to be expected.'

'Yes,' whispered Oscar, 'it was to be expected.'

'Forgive me, Oscar,' said Fraser. 'I will not mention your presence here when I write my report. It is not relevant in any event . . . Now you must go. I should not have brought you here in the first place. It was wrong of me. But you pressed me – and you have seen what you have seen. Now go. Go at once and leave us to do our duty.'

Sergeant Ritter stood immobile with the lamp still held high, illuminating the dead body.

'Escort these gentlemen to their cab, Ritter,' Fraser instructed him. 'And retrieve my travelling case while you're about it. I'll not be going home till late tonight.' Ritter came back across the cell towards us. As he stepped nearer, holding the lamp aloft, O'Donnell's body vanished into the gloom and the white light fell onto Fraser's face. 'Make haste, man. I'll wait here to guard the body. On your return bring a knife. We'll cut him down together. Bring the constable with you, too. Now go. Go!'

Neither Oscar nor I spoke.

'Goodnight, gentlemen,' said Fraser, as we turned to depart. 'I will see you tomorrow, at six, as we arranged. Goodnight now. I am sorry you have had to witness this, but at least it's over. The horror is all done. Case closed.'

Sergeant Ritter – saying nothing, though wheezing with every step – led us back along the dank, pestilential passageway to the tomblike police station entrance and out into the lively London street beyond. We left Aidan Fraser in darkness with the dead body of Edward O'Donnell.

'I think I shall go to church tomorrow,' Oscar announced, peering out of the cab window as we passed the entrance to the Savoy Theatre and hotel. The pavement was crowded with noisy playgoers, braying toffs in evening dress, chattering suburbanites in their Sunday best, emerging – evidently well satisfied – from a performance of *The Gondoliers*.

'To pray for the souls of the departed?' I asked.

'Yes,' he answered, 'and to light a candle to St Bathild – and to St Aidan of Ferns. Monday is his feast day, remember.'

'I remember.'

' "Feast days – and temptation", Robert. That's what it's all been about.'

'So you tell me, Oscar, though, for the life of me, I can't see why.'

'You will, Robert, you will.' He smiled at me benevolently. 'St Aidan is another of our blessed Irish saints. There is a bronze reliquary in which his bones are on display in a side-chapel in St Patrick's Cathedral in Dublin. Tomorrow I shall pay his spirit my respects in St Patrick's, Soho Square. It's a new church, but a fine one.'

'It's a Catholic church, Oscar. Are you looking to Rome for salvation?' I asked, bemused at the turn our conversation was taking.

'No, not yet.' He laughed. 'But John Gray is. He is taking instruction at St Patrick's. He speaks highly of the priest-in-charge. And of the aura of spirituality that pervades there. He says it's largely due to the incense they use. He claims it's the richest incense in London and that the young thurifer at St Patrick's spreads it about the church with evangelical zeal.' Oscar clenched his fists one above the other as though grasping the chain of a thurible and, suiting the action to the word, casting his eyes towards heaven, wafted imaginary frankincense about the back of the cab with gay abandon.

I laughed – and then thought back to the grotesque visage of Edward O'Donnell hanging in the police cell half a mile away, and marvelled at Oscar's capacity for turning from tragedy to comedy in what seemed no more than the twinkling of an eye.

Our cab had reached the Haymarket. The West End was busy with Saturday-night revellers. Our progress was slow. Oscar had commanded the driver to take us to Albemarle Street. He had proposed a nightcap. Now he changed his mind.

'Forgive me, Robert,' he said, 'I am suddenly weary – and mindful of the hour. You have your journal to write and I must pen a letter to Susannah Wood. I might yet catch the midnight post.' He called up to the cabman, 'On to Gower Street, driver, by way of Soho Square. We'll drop off my friend, then you can take me on to Chelsea, to Tite Street – if you please.'

His mention of Soho Square triggered a memory, but even as it came into my mind Oscar anticipated it. (Perhaps Mrs O'Keefe was right; perhaps he was a mind-reader.) 'The man who assaulted me that night in Soho Square,' he said, 'the night when John Gray came to my rescue – you recall?'

'I'll not forget John Gray's sailor suit,' I answered. 'I'll not forget that night – or the days that followed.'

'You were convinced that my assailant was Edward O'Donnell, were you not?'

'Yes,' I said, 'though you denied it.'

'And doubtless you thought that the man who followed us in Albemarle Street was O'Donnell, too?'

'You know I did.'

'It was not O'Donnell.'

'Very well,' I said, 'but if it was not O'Donnell, who was it?'

'I will tell you tomorrow, Robert. I think we have both had enough excitement for one day.'

It was early, not yet eleven o'clock, when we parted that Saturday night. It was late the following morning – gone noon, nearer one o'clock – when next I heard from Oscar. I was in my room, lying on my bed, unshaven, reading, when the doorbell rang. It was a boy from the telegraph office with a wire from my friend: 'URGENT. MEET ME AT THE CORNER OF COWLEY STREET AT 3.15 PM NOT BEFORE. OSCAR.'

I reached Westminster at three o'clock. It was Sunday 30 January 1890 and spring was in the air. The London fog had lifted; the sky was eggshell blue; the soft white clouds would have warmed my great-grandfather's heart. I wandered into the garden adjacent to the House of Lords (searching in vain for a host of golden daffodils!) and strolled there idly until I heard the clock on Big Ben strike the quarter. I crossed the road and made my way along Great College Street. I had a spring in my step. I was warmed by the sunshine; I was exhilarated by the prospect of meeting Oscar and discovering what his telegram portended; I was conscious that I was twenty-eight – and glad to be alive. (When I had arrived home at Gower Street the night before, I had found a letter await-ing me from Kaitlyn. She was in London once more; she hoped to see me – 'so much', she said, 'so much!' She had underlined the words.)

I found Oscar part-way down Great College Street, at the turning into Cowley Street, standing by a cab, a two-wheeler, talking with the cabman. He was wearing his bottle-green overcoat with the astrakhan collar and carry-ing his black malacca cane. He greeted me warmly. I could see that he looked well; there was a sparkle in his eye.

'I know I am unseasonably dressed, Robert – but, unlike you, I left the house at dawn. This gallant cabman has been my Sancho Panza since break of day.' From his coat pocket, he produced a coin and passed it to the driver. He fished into his pocket again and this time produced two lumps of sugar, which he held out on the flat of his hand, proffering them to the cabman's horse. 'When England becomes a republic, Robert, and I am emperor, this horse – my faithful Rosinante – will be among the first to be appointed senator. She is what none of our current legislators appears to be: hard-working, discreet and aware of her limitations!'

'You are on song today,' I remarked.

'I have been to early mass,' he said. 'I am refreshed.'

'Your prayers were answered?'

'Prayers must never be answered, Robert! If prayers are answered, they cease to be prayers and become correspondence . . .'

'But the priest-in-charge was all that you had hoped for?'

'He had a fine profile, certainly, but remember, Robert, it is the confession, not the priest, that gives us absolution.' He called up to the cabman. 'What time is it?'

Tied with string to the side of his seat, the cab driver had a clock whose face was the size of a saucer. He peered down at it. 'Now? Twenty-two minutes past, sir.'

'Thank you, cabby,' said Oscar. 'Three minutes to go.'

'And where are we going?' I asked.

'Can you not guess?'

'To 23 Cowley Street, I assume.'

'Yes,' he said, suddenly in earnest. 'Yes, we are to revisit the scene of the crime.'

'Why?'

'To put the truth to the test – as I promised.'

There was nothing playful about his manner now. 'What time is it, cabby?'

'Twenty-five past, sir – just on.'

'Come, Robert. Let us see what we shall see. You shall be the witness.' He called up to the cabman: 'We'll not be long – ten minutes perhaps, fifteen at most. I thank you for your patience. Come the republic, you'll have your reward!' The cabman touched his cap and nodded obligingly. The horse bared its teeth and offered up a snort of appreciation. Oscar tucked his arm into mine. 'Come, Robert, we have reached what I believe our friend Holmes would call "the end-game".'

We had turned into Cowley Street. It looked so pleasant: ordered and peaceful, flooded with pale sunlight. We were standing in the middle of the cobbled roadway, facing number 23.

'Hush!' he whispered. 'Do not speak. Look!' With his cane he pointed to the window on the first floor. 'The sun is shining, but the curtains are drawn. Come. Say nothing. Come.'

We crossed the street and stepped up to the doorway. Oscar stood for a moment gazing at the lintel above the door. 'Are we to ring?' I asked.

'Hush, Robert. Speak not a word.' He put his left forefinger to my lips. 'I have Bellotti's key, as you will recall, but we may not need it.' He spread out his hand and gently pushed at the front door. Slowly, noiselessly, it swung open. 'As you see . . .' he whispered. 'Come.'

Now with his finger held to his own lips, he led me across the threshold. We stood for a moment in the entrance hallway. The house was silent; dust danced in the shaft of sunlight that shone through the window above the doorway onto the stairs ahead. Carefully Oscar closed the front door behind us and, with an inclination of his head, indicated that I should go forward and start to mount the narrow staircase to the first floor. With every step, the boards beneath my feet cracked like rifle shots echoing round a valley and, behind me, as he climbed, Oscar's heavy breathing became louder and more rapid. We'll wake the dead, I thought, but I said nothing. At the top of the stairs, on the uncarpeted landing, we stood together, silently, side by side.

The door facing us – the door to the room where, five months before, Oscar had discovered the body of Billy Wood – was closed. We listened and heard nothing. We stood quite still as Oscar caught his breath. I looked at my friend and smiled. He returned my smile and handed me his cane. With both hands he swept back his thick and wavy chestnut hair. Taking a deep breath, he then lightly, almost delicately, knocked at the door and, without waiting for an answer, opened it wide.

The room was as hot as a furnace and fragrant with incense. We stood in the doorway, adjusting our eyes to the gloom. By the light of half a dozen candles, we saw, stretched out on the floor before us, the naked body of a young man. The young man was John Gray. And standing over him, by his head, was a second man. He was naked, also. It was Aidan Fraser. He held an open razor in his hand.

At our entrance, John Gray rolled over and reached beyond the candles for his clothes. Aidan Fraser threw down the razor and turned towards us with outstretched, supplicating arms.

'Oscar,' he cried, 'this is not as it seems. Let me explain! For pity's sake, let me explain!'

'There is no need,' said Oscar. 'I understand, Aidan. I understand it all.'

Oscar put his hand on my arm and drew me gently from the room.

'Come, Robert, let us reclaim our cab. We have seen all we need to see.' He pulled the door close shut behind him and, silently, led me down the stairs.

25

'Feast Days and Temptation'

'Feast days – and temptation . . . Do you now see, Robert?'

'I fear I do not see at all, Oscar. I am utterly lost. I know I must seem to you intolerably obtuse at times, but I have to confess I am wholly confused by what we have just witnessed – confused and horrified.'

He smiled at me and opened the cab door. 'Your innocence does you credit, Robert.' He called up to the driver: 'Charing Cross Station, if you please, cabby, then on to Bedford Square. What time is it now?'

'Twenty to the hour, sir.'

'Good. Good!' He clambered into the cab after me and settled back into his seat with a look on his large and fleshy face that combined exhilaration with contentment. He patted my knee. 'Don't look so anxious, Robert. We are nearly done.'

'I am bewildered, Oscar, bewildered and appalled. What will Veronica make of this?'

'You must not tell her,' he said sharply, 'not yet.'

I lowered my voice. I felt that what we had witnessed in that upstairs room in Cowley Street was shaming and corrupt, and that by witnessing it we had somehow shared in the shame, tasted the corruption.

'John Gray and Aidan Fraser are lovers . . .' I whispered.

'Or might have been,' he said. 'I fear we have interrupted their first tryst.'

'What does it mean?'

'Mean?'

'Gray lying naked on the floor . . . the candles . . . the incense . . .'

'It means . . .' Oscar was gazing out of the cab window, across the river Thames. 'It means . . . to some, love is a sacrament, I suppose.' He said it casually, almost as though it were a passing thought.

'A sacrament?' I snapped. 'And the razor in Fraser's hand – what part does that play in this sacrament?'

'I do not know. I hazard a guess, that's all. Our friends were acting out a drama of their own imagining: the tale of the priest and the acolyte, perhaps. The priest prepares the acolyte by shaving his body before it is anointed with holy oil. The razor is used in the act of purification . . . The purification is the prelude to the consummation . . .'

'It's barbaric!'

'Barbaric? No, it's very English, Robert – or should I say "British"? They probably played some such game at Fettes when Fraser was a lad.'

'How can you make light of this, Oscar? It is grotesque.'

'It is a playful ritual, Robert, nothing more. The English love ritual. Have you watched a game of cricket? Have you followed a hunt in this country, Robert? The English cannot hunt as other nations do: to bring food to the table. No! The English ride to hounds, in crimson coats, blowing bugles, chasing a defenceless fox. And when they have cornered their prey – and sacrificed it to their own peculiar gods – they smear the blood of the poor creature they have killed onto the face of the youngest child in their midst. It is grotesque, and not to your taste or mine, but to the English it is not a crime – it is a way of life.'

'Oscar, Oscar!' I cried, still in hushed tones, fearful lest the cabman overhear us. 'John Gray and Aidan Fraser were not riding to hounds. They were not playing cricket. They were engaged in unnatural vice. They were naked. They were aroused.'

'Really? I did not notice.' Nonchalantly, Oscar flicked a thread from the sleeve of his coat.

'What we have just witnessed is a scene of degradation. It is abhorrent. It is vile!'

'Is it vile, Robert? Is it really? John Gray is a handsome youth. You have seen him. He is as beautiful as a Greek god, you must acknowledge that. John Gray was a temptation to Aidan Fraser – and Aidan Fraser yielded to temptation. Is it so wrong? Is not the true and certain way to get rid of a temptation to yield to it? Resist it and your soul grows sick with longing for the things it has forbidden to itself. Every instinct that we strive to strangle broods on the mind and poisons us. The body sins once and has done with its sin, for action is a mode of purification . . .'

'Oscar,' I protested, 'are you trying to tell me that we have just been witnessing Aidan Fraser engaged in an act of "purification"? You go too far!'

'I am telling you that what we have witnessed is Aidan Fraser – on the eve of one of his feast days – proving his mortality by succumbing to the temptation of forbidden fruit. That is all. The circumstances may be a little unusual, a trifle baroque perhaps, but the story itself is as old as the Garden of Eden – and they wore no clothes there either, Robert! Indeed, as I understand it, it was years before sailor suits were introduced to paradise.'

'Why do you make light of this, Oscar? Why do you defend their conduct? *Why?*'

I spoke fiercely – and too loudly. For a moment, an uneasy silence fell between us. We looked out of our separate windows, listening to the harsh rumble of the cab's wheels and the steady clip-clop of the horse's hooves. We were passing along Whitehall. Sunday strollers – old soldiers, young men in boaters, women pushing perambulators, a boy with a wooden hoop – were moving to and fro, taking advantage of the unseasonable sunshine.

Oscar turned back to me and touched me on the knee. 'I do not defend their conduct, Robert,' he said quietly, 'I explain it.' He looked me steadily in the eye and smiled. 'It is important to understand others if one is to understand oneself.'

I looked at my friend and marvelled at him. 'You are a phenomenon, Oscar,' I said, 'but sometimes I believe you are too understanding, too generous, too kind.'

'Too kind?' he repeated. 'One can always be kind to people about whom one cares nothing.'

'Do you care nothing for John Gray and Aidan Fraser, then?'

'I care for John Gray. He is my friend. I care for him deeply. I care nothing for Aidan Fraser. Nothing at all. He is a murderer.'

'Whoa!' The cab came to an abrupt halt.

'Oscar! Oscar! What are you saying?' Shocked and astonished at his words, I leant forward urgently, but he held up his hand to silence me.

We had reached the forecourt of Charing Cross Station. Oscar opened the cab door. 'I am alighting here,' he said, smiling. 'I have cigarettes to buy and two trains to meet.'

I tried to hold him back. 'But if Fraser—'

'No questions now, Robert,' he said, closing the cab door. 'I had thought it would all be obvious to you, but if it is not, so much the better. You have work to do.'

He was standing on the pavement looking in at me through the open window of the two-wheeler. My mind was all awry; he appeared at his most self-possessed. 'You are to go to Bedford Square,' he instructed, 'the cab is paid for. You are to collect Miss Sutherland for her birthday party, exactly as planned. Tell her nothing of what has transpired today. Tell her nothing of last night. Nothing, nothing at all. Do you understand me? Talk of Millais, talk of Pasteur, talk of anything – but do not speak of murder. Be with her as you always are. Look into her beautiful eyes and murmur those sweet nothings you murmur so well. Tell her one of your friend Maupassant's short stories: that should keep you both occupied for an hour or two! Go, my friend – and thank you.' He put his arm through the carriage window and shook me warmly by the hand. 'The part you have played in all this has been more valuable than you know. Justice will be done tonight. Go now. Go. Do not let Miss Sutherland out of your sight, Robert – and bring her to Lower Sloane Street at six-fifteen. At six-fifteen, mark, not a minute before. Farewell.'

He stepped back and waved. Then he turned at once and disappeared towards the station concourse as the cabman cracked his whip and the brougham once more set on its way.

I was utterly confused. I was disturbed. I was perplexed. But I did as I was told. Oscar had a natural authority, throughout his life. As a schoolboy, he held sway over his peers; even at the end, after his imprisonment, in his exile (when unkind strangers in false reports spoke of him as 'a crushed spirit' and 'a broken man') those of us who knew him felt the power of his presence barely dimmed. That afternoon, I obeyed him to the letter.

Well, in truth, not quite to the letter . . . Veronica and I did not speak of Millais or of Maupassant that afternoon; we talked of love and of the poetry of love. I spoke of Baudelaire and Byron. She spoke of Wordsworth (to flatter me), of John Keats, and of Mrs Browning. And when we kissed, and kissed again, and kissed once more, she said, as she had said to me once before on that memorable moonlit night beneath the Albert Memorial, 'Thank you, Robert, thank you. It is a dreary thing to sit at home with unkissed lips.'

'I love you,' I told her. 'You are extraordinary!'

It was the strangest afternoon. Our behaviour, under the circumstances, was singularly inappropriate. It was like a flirtation at a funeral: unreal (unseemly, in fact), unexpected, and the more thrilling because of it! For me it was an afternoon of enchantment: intoxicating and unforgettable. In all its detail, in all its glory, and in spite of everything, I remember it still, half a century on! I was more daring with Veronica that afternoon than I had ever been before. I yielded to temptation, with Oscar's words running pell-mell about my mind. Perhaps – though this I only half acknowledged to myself at the time – I felt that what I had seen that day in Cowley Street, and what Oscar had said as we parted at Charing Cross, meant that Veronica would soon be free of Aidan Fraser altogether and I was emboldened as a consequence. I knew as I held her in my arms that ours was still an illicit love, that there was something *wrong* in what we were doing, and yet I could not help myself. I was entranced by Veronica Sutherland, and the act of love between us – let me admit it – gave to my spirit a sense of freedom, a sense of release, that was quite wonderful. 'The body sins once and has done with its sin, for action is a mode of purification . . .'

We did not leave Bedford Square until six o'clock. It was a Sunday evening at the end of January; darkness had fallen and the streets were quiet. Nevertheless, despite the best endeavours of our patient cabman and his faithful horse, it took us nearly forty minutes to reach Chelsea. I was anxious because of Oscar's admonition that I should bring Veronica to the house at six-fifteen exactly; I was less troubled than I might have been, however, because each additional minute alone in Veronica's company was a joy to me. She was so beautiful.

We neither of us paid any heed to the route that our brougham was taking and, even as we turned out of Sloane Square into Lower Sloane Street, we scarcely glanced out of the cab window. It was only as I alighted from the carriage and helped Veronica down onto the pavement that, suddenly, forcibly, I was reawakened to reality and realised, in the instant, that what Oscar had called 'the end-game' was indeed upon us.

The scene that greeted us in Lower Sloane Street was wholly unexpected. Three other vehicles were drawn up in line with ours. Just ahead of where our cab had stopped, immediately outside 75 Lower Sloane Street, was another hackney carriage, a two-wheeler, with its blinds drawn closed. In front of it was a second, larger carriage, a four-wheeler – a police growler, with two uniformed police constables standing at its side. At the front of the line was the largest vehicle, enclosed and windowless, with a single door at its rear. It was the police wagon for prisoners known as the Black Maria.

'What is the meaning of this, Robert?'

'I have no idea,' I said – and said it truthfully.

The door to number 75 was open wide and standing on the doorstep, side by side, looking towards us – as if awaiting our arrival – were two men. One was a police sergeant, a thickset fellow of indeterminate age and blank expression. The other was John Gray, in a sober suit, but with a playful smile upon his face.

'Welcome,' he said as we approached. 'We meet again.' I said nothing, but shook his outstretched hand. Veronica swept past him into the hallway. Another policeman, a young constable, was standing at the foot of the stairs.

'What is going on?' she cried. 'Will someone tell me?'

'Oscar will explain,' said John Gray, amiably. 'He is expecting you. He is in the drawing room. May I take your coat?'

'No, thank you.' She spoke coldly, with anger in her eyes.

'This will not be easy for you, I know,' said John Gray and he pushed open the drawing-room door. To our astonishment, the room was full, brightly lit (the gasoliers were turned up high; there were also lighted candles on the mantelpiece), and crowded with people, talking, laughing, chattering – or so it seemed. Mrs O'Keefe, in her black crêpe and taffeta dress, carrying a tray of drinks, was bustling to and fro. Oscar was centre stage, standing by the fireplace, with several others grouped around him. As we entered the room, the hubbub faltered and all eyes turned upon us.

'Ah,' said Oscar, glancing at me reprovingly, 'you are here.' He came towards us and took Veronica solicitously by the hand. 'Miss Sutherland,' he said, bowing to her.

'Is this my birthday party?' she enquired, looking at him with unhappy eyes.

'Alas, no,' he said. 'Your birthday, I fear, Miss Sutherland, has been overshadowed by the death of Billy Wood – as was Mrs Wilde's birthday, you will recall, only a few weeks ago. You remember my wife, don't you?' He turned and indicated Constance who was seated alone by the fireplace, gazing into the empty grate. (Constance was not dressed for a party; she was wearing a workaday hat and coat, as though she had been disturbed on her way to the post office. On her lap she was nursing a small parcel, wrapped in brown paper, tied with string.)

'Those who joined us that night in Tite Street,' Oscar continued, 'that night when we received poor Billy's severed head: they are all gathered here again this evening.' He looked about the room. 'John Gray you've met already. Dr Doyle, of course, you know.' Conan Doyle stood near the mantelpiece with his back to us. I caught his eye in the looking-glass. He looked tired but, beyond that, his expression betrayed nothing. 'Arthur has forsaken the measles sufferers of Southsea to be with us,' said Oscar. 'I am grateful.'

'And Mrs Doyle?' I asked.

'Touie?' said Oscar. 'Yes, she is with us also – and doing good work, as ever. She is outside, in the street, in the two-wheeler parked by the front door – with Susannah Wood, Billy's mother. I collected Mrs Wood from Charing Cross Station this afternoon and brought her here myself, but she needed a woman's consolation. She is suffering greatly, as perhaps you can imagine. Touie is giving Mrs Wood what comfort she can. They may join us later.'

'Why have you brought Mrs Wood here?' I asked.

'To fulfil a promise I made to her,' he said.

Veronica looked into Oscar's eyes and hissed at him: 'What are you doing, Mr Wilde? What cruel game is this?'

'Oh,' he exclaimed, 'this is not a game, Miss Sutherland! Were it a game, I doubt the police would be here in such numbers.' He took my beautiful mistress by the hand and led her towards an empty chair beneath the window. 'You know your fiancé's colleague, Inspector Gilmour, don't you? The young man with the perfect profile is his assistant, Sergeant Atkins. He comes from Broadstairs also – as chance would have it.' He pressed her to be seated. She acquiesced. I stood behind the chair, perplexed, my hand resting on her shoulder. She glanced up at me and I saw terror in her eyes.

'Whom don't you know?' Oscar went on, blithely. 'Ah, yes . . .'

Stooping over Mrs O'Keefe's tray, returning an empty glass with one hand while, with the other, carefully picking up a full one, was an elderly gentleman who appeared to have wandered into the room from the pages of a book of eccentric fairy tales. He was Doré's painting of Rumpelstiltskin combined with Tenniel's drawing of the White Knight in *Through the Looking-Glass*. White-haired and bent, he was dressed in a shabby velvet suit of midnight blue, with knee breeches, silver stockings, buckled shoes and, on his head, an absurd, oversized artist's beret. He trembled as he walked.

'His name is Aston Upthorpe,' said Oscar. 'He loved Billy Wood – not wisely, but too well.'

Mrs O'Keefe was bobbing across the room towards us with her tray. 'Would you care for some refreshment, Miss Sutherland?' Oscar asked.

'No,' she answered, 'thank you. What I would care for, Mr Wilde, is an explanation . . . What is happening here? What is going on?'

'I will tell you,' he said, quietly. 'I will tell you now. It will not take long.' Oscar smiled at her, but it was a cold smile. He glanced at me and at my hand upon her shoulder. 'Do you have your notebook, Robert? There may be details that are new to you.' He stepped away from us and returned to his position before the fireplace – centre stage. 'Ladies, gentlemen,' he announced, 'if I might have your attention for a moment . . .'

The room fell silent. For the next several minutes, no one moved. Inspector Gilmour and Sergeant Atkins stood sentinel together by the drawing-room door. Mrs O'Keefe cowered in a corner. John Gray and Aston Upthorpe sat, uncomfortably upright, on a French settee. Conan Doyle stood behind Constance Wilde, with his hand resting on her shoulder as mine rested on that of Veronica Sutherland. Oscar held us in his thrall.

'Thank you,' he began, 'thank you all for being here this evening. I imagine you have guessed the purpose of our gathering . . . In her dealings with man, Destiny never quite closes her accounts, but we have reached the final act of this particular drama – the tragedy of Billy Wood – and since each of us in this room has played a part in its unfolding, I felt it only right and proper that we should all be here, together, to witness the curtain fall.'

'But we are not all here,' said Veronica, looking about the room in a sudden state of agitation. 'Aidan is not here. Where is he? Where is Aidan? Where is my fiancé?' She made to move, but I restrained her.

'He is not joining us, Miss Sutherland,' said Oscar, looking not at her but at the room as he spoke. 'Aidan Fraser will not be with us this evening. He is a ruthless murderer – as you know.'

26

The End-Game

The room was still.

Veronica Sutherland gazed at Oscar with unflinching eyes. I pressed my fingers into her shoulder. She put her hand onto mine. It was as cold as ice.

'Last night,' Oscar continued, 'not yet twenty-four hours ago, Aidan Fraser murdered Edward O'Donnell – murdered him in a police cell in Bow Street – during the second act of *Bluebeard*, as fate would have it. It was easily done. To kill a man takes only a moment, if you have the courage.'

'How is this possible, Oscar?' I protested.

'We made it possible, Robert,' he said. 'We gave Fraser his opportunity, I am ashamed to say.'

'I don't understand,' I said.

'When you and I were idling in Bow Street, Robert, exchanging pleasantries with the cabman, making small-talk with Sir Augustus Harris, Fraser seized his moment. He went alone to O'Donnell's cell, found the brute in a drunken stupor, removed his belt, strung it about his neck and, with the strength that the gods give to desperate men, hoisted his victim up against the wall and strapped the belt around the cell window's iron bar. Aidan Fraser hanged Edward O'Donnell. O'Donnell was dead within three minutes, asphyxiated by his own vomit, strangled with his own belt.'

In the corner of the drawing room, Mrs O'Keefe emitted a small cry. At the time, I thought it a cry of anguish. Later I came to realise that it had been a murmur of appreciation. Mrs O'Keefe was a woman of feeling, but she was a woman of the theatre, too. Oscar had a way of telling a tale that was greatly to her liking.

'For O'Donnell there was no escape,' he said. 'If it had not been last night, it would have been some other time. Aidan Fraser needed to contrive Edward O'Donnell's apparent suicide. If O'Donnell had lived to stand trial for the murder of Billy Wood, too much would have been revealed, and – who knows? – a jury might well have found him guilty. On the other hand it might not. Inspector Fraser dared not take the risk. But if O'Donnell, charged with murder, took his own life, his suicide would be seen as an admission of guilt, an apparent confession from beyond the grave.'

Oscar paused to light a cigarette from one of the candles on the mantelpiece. He glanced towards Conan Doyle.

'So far, so elementary, eh, Arthur?' he said. 'I had my doubts about Fraser from the start, of course. I was struck by his wonderful appearance, I was taken with his charming manner, but I was puzzled by him, also. Why was he so reluctant to investigate the case? Why did he not take me to task when I confessed to removing the ring from Billy Wood's dead finger? Why did he tolerate my friend Sherard's devotion to Miss Sutherland? You also had your doubts about your friend Fraser, did you not, Arthur?'

Conan Doyle was silent. He covered his mouth with his hand and buried his fingers in his walrus moustache.

Oscar went on, 'Do you recall, Arthur, the line that I sent you from my story of *Dorian Gray*?'

' "Nobody ever commits a crime without doing something stupid," ' replied Conan Doyle.

'Exactly.' Oscar looked at Dr Doyle and smiled. 'The line lacks the poetry of some of Sherlock Holmes's axioms, but I hold to it. Aidan Fraser was shrewd in his choice of Edward O'Donnell as the putative murderer of Billy Wood. O'Donnell had a plausible motive: jealousy. O'Donnell had a vile reputation – as a drunkard and a brute. O'Donnell was capable of murder, all the world might acknowledge that. In choosing O'Donnell as the man to accuse, Fraser made a shrewd choice. In choosing Gerard Bellotti as his principal witness, he made a stupid one. He forgot that I knew Bellotti so much better than he did.'

'Poor Bellotti,' muttered Aston Upthorpe.

'Indeed,' said Oscar, 'poor Bellotti – obese, half blind and murdered for something he never said.'

I let go of Veronica. 'Murdered by whom?' I asked. 'Not by Fraser. Bellotti died on Friday, surely, while we were in France?'

'No, Robert. Bellotti died on Friday morning, at Victoria underground station, moments before our train departed for Dover, from Victoria railway station. Gerard Bellotti and Aidan Fraser knew one another. They were friends – of a sort. They met on Friday morning by arrangement. They stood together, talking, at the edge of the underground station platform and, as a train approached, Fraser pushed Bellotti to his doom. It was easily done. To kill a man takes only a moment – if you have the courage. And how much courage was needed anyway? The deed was done on a crowded platform filled with smoke and steam. A score of men and women died on the twopenny tube in 1889. What would one more matter?'

On the far side of the room, Archy Gilmour stirred. 'This is guesswork on your part, isn't it, Mr Wilde?'

'It was, Inspector, but it is no longer. There was a witness to what happened: a dwarf, Bellotti's misbegotten son. He was on the platform, too, keeping his distance, as he always did. He was not close enough to save his father, but he saw what happened – and, in the chaos that ensued, panic overcame him. Without his father, he was suddenly adrift. He didn't know where to turn. He didn't know what to do. So, poor, pathetic creature that he is, he went to Rochester, to the asylum where his simple-minded mother lives out her days. One of the lads whom I call my "spies" went to find him there this morning. He brought the unfortunate wretch to Charing Cross to meet me this afternoon. Bellotti's hapless son will confirm to you, Inspector, the time and place of his father's demise. Aidan Fraser killed Gerard Bellotti on the underground platform at Victoria at around eight-forty on Friday morning last. Minutes later, at eight-forty-five, Fraser established his "alibi" when, running for his life, he joined us above ground on the boat-train to Dover.'

Aston Upthorpe was seated with his head in his hands. He rubbed his eyes slowly and looked up at Oscar. 'I don't understand, Oscar. You say that Gerard Bellotti and this Aidan Fraser were friends. I knew Bellotti, as you did. I knew him better than you did. I tell you, Oscar, that in my hearing Bellotti never mentioned an Aidan Fraser – or any name like it.'

'Possibly not,' said Oscar, 'but Bellotti knew Fraser nonetheless – and liked him. And trusted him. As you did, too, Aston . . .'

'I've drunk too much,' said Upthorpe, picking up John Gray's glass and slowly draining it. 'I'm lost.'

Oscar looked towards Conan Doyle once more. 'Inspector Fraser's stupid mistake was this. He told me that Gerard Bellotti had sworn to him that Edward O'Donnell and Drayton St Leonard were one and the same man. I knew that could never be. Bellotti would not have countenanced a common drunk like O'Donnell as a member of his luncheon club. Besides, when Robert and I questioned the other members of the club, they told us that Drayton St Leonard was young and handsome – and O'Donnell, coarse and life-worn, a man in his fifties, was hardly that.'

Conan Doyle now had both his hands on the back of Constance's chair. He stood like a preacher in the pulpit reflecting on the lesson of the day. 'You knew that O'Donnell could not be Drayton St Leonard . . .'

'Yes,' said Oscar, 'and I knew that Bellotti would never have suggested that he was. It was an absurd invention on Fraser's part – unnecessary, ruinous – and even as he spoke the lie he knew how stupid his mistake had been.'

'But having made Bellotti his false witness, Fraser than had no alternative but to silence him—'

'Precisely. Exactly so. I should have seen it at once, Arthur – as Holmes would have done! Instead, I allowed myself to be distracted. I neglected Gerard Bellotti in my eagerness to uncover the true identity of Drayton St Leonard. Drayton St Leonard, I sensed, was key to the case.'

'But, Oscar,' I interrupted, 'Drayton St Leonard did not attend the luncheon club on the day of Billy's murder. He wasn't in Little College Street that day.'

'No, Robert, he wasn't in Little College Street for lunch that day because he was in Cowley Street, around the corner, in an upstairs room, lighting candles, burning incense, preparing a bridal bed for Billy Wood . . . Drayton St Leonard met Billy Wood through Gerard Bellotti. Drayton St Leonard fell in love with Billy Wood. He worshipped him.'

Oscar lit a second cigarette, drew on it slowly and then passed it to Aston Upthorpe, who took it gratefully and smiled up at Oscar with red-rimmed eyes.

'But, Oscar,' I persisted, 'Mr Upthorpe told us, Bellotti told us, Canon Courteney told us that Billy Wood, when he left Little College Street, at two o'clock that day, said openly, clearly and without equivocation, that he was on his way to meet his uncle.'

'Indeed!' Oscar replied, triumphantly. 'Absolutely! That's what he said – and it was true! Drayton St Leonard *was* his "uncle"!'

'What?' I exclaimed.

'The euphemism is an old one,' said Oscar, smiling. 'We are all familiar with it, are we not, Mrs O'Keefe?' The good woman bobbed up and down with suppressed delight at being thus involved in Oscar's narrative. 'A young lady with a mature admirer will often describe the older man as her "uncle". So it was with young Billy Wood and Mr Drayton St Leonard . . . And if, as they

304

had planned, they had gone to France — as Billy told his mother they might do — doubtless they would have travelled as "uncle" and "nephew". It is more discreet. Even on the Continent, I understand, landladies and hoteliers prefer it that way. Drayton St Leonard was Billy Wood's "uncle" . . . And Aidan Fraser was Drayton St Leonard. "Drayton St Leonard" was Aidan Fraser's *nom de guerre*.'

Oscar surveyed the room, his eyes glistening. He was revelling in the drama.

'When did you realise this, Oscar?' asked Conan Doyle.

'Within moments of his telling me that Bellotti had told him that O'Donnell was St Leonard. It was such a stupid lie — and, even as he uttered it, he knew it. That's why he pressed me to come with him to Paris. He needed to keep me out of the way. He knew that I knew Bellotti and, given time, that I would speak to Bellotti and discover the truth.'

'But he got to Bellotti first,' said Conan Doyle.

'Yes,' said Oscar. 'Fraser wanted me in Paris so that he could stall my investigation — and perhaps find out how much I knew. I agreed to go to Paris so that I could keep Fraser under observation. It never occurred to me that, between Thursday night and Friday morning, Fraser would contrive an encounter with Bellotti and murder him. It never occurred to me that Fraser would do something so irrational.'

'Why irrational?' asked Conan Doyle. 'Fraser silenced Bellotti because Bellotti would not corroborate his lie.'

Oscar laughed. 'It was a hopeless lie! And a pointless murder. Fraser killed Bellotti, but Bellotti's death solved nothing. If ever O'Donnell had come to trial, one or other of the members of Bellotti's little luncheon club would have come forward to tell the world that Edward O'Donnell was not Drayton St Leonard and never could have been. When that awful truth dawned on Fraser – and I think it came to him during our return journey from Paris – he knew that his only hope was to despatch O'Donnell and make it seem like suicide. He seized the moment the moment that he could.'

Oscar turned to the mantelpiece to find his glass. In the reflection, through the flickering candlelight, he caught my eye. He was my friend, but in that moment he seemed a stranger to me. 'Mr Wilde,' said Archy Gilmour from across the room, 'it is now seven o'clock.'

Case Closed

The clock on the mantelpiece struck the hour.

'Fear not, Inspector,' said Oscar, smiling. 'I will keep my word.' He turned to Mrs O'Keefe who stood attendant at the policeman's side. 'Mrs O, would you be so kind as to go into the street and have a word with Mrs Doyle and Mrs Wood? You will find them in the hansom outside the front door. Assure them: they will be kept waiting no more than a quarter of an hour now, twenty minutes at most.'

'At most,' Gilmour echoed, sternly.

'Supply them with a cup of tea, would you, Mrs O? And, with the inspector's permission, furnish his men with refreshment as well.'

The red-headed police inspector nodded curtly to Mrs O'Keefe, who bobbed up and down, then man-oeuvred herself sideways and backwards out of the room. Sergeant Atkins secured the door after her departure.

'Mr Wilde,' said Gilmour crisply, 'you have set out your case against Aidan Fraser, as we agreed—'

'And I will lead you to him within the hour, as I promised, Inspector. Indulge me a moment more, I pray you. We are nearly done.'

Both my hands were resting on Veronica's shoulders.

Her head was bowed. I felt her body tremble as, silently, she began to sob.

'You weep, Miss Sutherland,' said Oscar, 'and I know the reason why. Once upon a time, you loved Aidan Fraser – but that was long ago, before you learnt his secret, before you discovered that the true love of his life was "a slut of a boy".'

Veronica looked up at Oscar with unconcealed contempt in her eyes. He gazed at her steadily as he spoke.

'The violence of your language in Paris yesterday morning rather gave the game away.'

Aston Upthorpe stirred and said softly, more to John Gray at his side than to Oscar who was standing directly above him: 'I loved Billy Wood. I loved that boy.'

'I know,' said Oscar, kindly, 'I know.' He returned his glass to the mantelpiece and looked at the policemen standing on the far side of the room. 'Aidan Fraser killed Edward O'Donnell and Gerard Bellotti to keep his secret from the world. He killed them to keep a second secret, too, another's secret. Aidan Fraser is a murderer: of that there is no doubt. But Aidan Fraser did not kill Billy Wood: of that there is no doubt, either.'

The silence was heavy in the room.

'So,' said Conan Doyle eventually, 'it was the housekeeper?'

'Yes,' said Oscar, 'it was the housekeeper. Even at the outset I suspected a woman's involvement. When we went to the scene of the crime, it was so spotless. The floorboards were scrubbed – polished with beeswax, you'll recall. This was woman's work – and the work of a woman whom I met within moments of her having carried out the crime. Who was she? Susannah Wood, driven to murder her own child? Unlikely. Mrs O'Keefe? Impossible. She was newly arrived from Ireland – what would her motive have been? And then I thought, perhaps it is not a woman but a man with a woman's ways . . . One of Bellotti's crowd, obsessed with the boy, driven to madness, dressed *en travestie*?'

Arthur Conan Doyle shook his head and emitted a country doctor's grunt of disbelief. Oscar looked at him, with a sly smile.

'Stranger things have happened, Arthur. Canon Courteney, I understand, conducts "marriages" between men, and even Shakespeare – your beloved Shakespeare! – was not above using a plot device that turned on a boy playing a girl masquerading as a boy . . .'

'Mr Wilde!' Inspector Gilmour brought Oscar to order. 'We are not in the theatre now. This is a murder investigation. We have indulged you sufficiently, I think.'

Oscar turned to Conan Doyle in mock indignation. 'Arthur, tell me: did Sherlock Holmes have to endure treatment such as this?'

'Come, Oscar,' said Constance, 'it was you who assured Miss Sutherland that this was not a game. I think it only fair to her – and to the rest of us – that you bring this sorry business to its conclusion.'

'You are quite right, my dear – as always.' He smiled at his wife, who averted her eyes from his and, in her awkwardness, let slip the brown paper parcel from her lap. Conan Doyle bent down at once to retrieve it for her.

Oscar turned back to address Inspector Gilmour: 'I will do as you would have me, Inspector, and come to the point. You have come to arrest the murderer of Billy Wood.'

'I have,' replied the inspector coldly.

'Well,' said Oscar, 'here she is . . .'

Oscar Wilde turned towards Veronica Sutherland and presented her to the room as if she were a prize lot at an auction. Her back stiffened; she threw off my hands from her shoulders; her eyes blazed, but she spoke not a word.

'To commit a murder,' said Oscar, 'is easily done – even when you are a woman. To kill a boy takes only a moment – if the boy is asleep and you have a surgeon's knife at your disposal. Veronica Sutherland learnt of her fiancé's infatuation with Billy Wood and determined to put an end to it. She chose her fiancé's birthday because she knew that was a day on which Aidan and the boy – "the slut of a boy" – had arranged one of their secret assignations. She had her own key to 23 Cowley Street. Indeed, I learnt from Messrs Chubb & Sons of Farringdon Street that she had the key copied in the last week of June. She had been planning this murder for some time. She acquired the surgeon's scalpel that she used – the one recommended by Arthur's old teacher, Dr Bell, in his celebrated *Manual of Surgery* – from Messrs Goodliffe & Stainer, suppliers to the medical profession, on 1 July. This crime was well planned – and precisely executed.

'On the morning of Tuesday 31 August last, Veronica Sutherland made her way to number 23 Cowley Street and lay in wait for the two men whose lives, in different ways, she sought to destroy. I do not believe it was her intention to confront Fraser and his catamite together. I think her plan was more malign that that. She wanted to kill the boy – the young seducer – and force Fraser to live on without him. The boy meant nothing to her and everything to him. Kill the boy – and let Fraser live on, with an empty hole where once had lain his heart.

'Between two and three that afternoon, in the upstairs room at Cowley Street, Aidan Fraser anointed Billy Wood as he might have done his bride. Surrounded by candles, perfumed with incense, they lay together – and when they were done, they parted. Fraser left the house alone. He had business to attend to. He was a newly promoted inspector at Scotland Yard, after all. But Billy stayed behind – and Billy was young and carefree and had taken wine. He fell asleep where he lay, on a rug on the floor at Cowley Street, with a seraph's smile upon his red-rose lips and guttering candles all about him. That was how Veronica Sutherland found him. That was how he was when she cut his throat from ear to ear.

'And then the doorbell rang and I appeared, rushing in and rushing out! When I arrived I was in haste. When I departed I was distracted. When she admitted me, I barely glanced at Miss Sutherland. She was half-hidden behind the door in any event. I noticed nothing, beyond a flash of her red hair. She was not expecting me, of course – she was expecting Fraser. And when she saw me and not Fraser, she immediately pulled open the door and hid herself behind it as I hurried across the hall and up the stairs. Later, of course, Fraser did return to Cowley Street, as she expected he would. He returned, I imagine, sometime after six o'clock, at the end of his working day. He returned, with a hansom cab, to collect the boy he loved – and instead he found the woman he had once loved with the butchered body of the boy who had taken her place in his affections.

'What could poor Fraser do? If he went to the police, his life was over. At best he would be imprisoned as a corrupter of youth. At worst he would be hanged as complicit in the murder. He had no choice in the matter. He did his fiancée's bidding. He became his fiancée's prisoner.

'Together, I imagine, they finished cleaning up the scene of the crime. They did a thorough job, leaving not a trace of evidence behind. You would not expect them to: Fraser had been trained by the Metropolitan Police. Together, I imagine, they loaded poor Billy's body into the chest in the hallway and conveyed the chest by cab to this house. Together, I imagine, they stowed the chest in the ice house in the garden.'

Immediately Inspector Gilmour and Sergeant Atkins began to move towards the door. Oscar laughed.

'The chest will wait upon you, gentlemen. It has been there for five months, undisturbed. Besides, it no longer holds the body of poor Billy Wood.'

'Do you know then where we will find the body?' asked Gilmour.

'Yes,' said Oscar, 'I believe I do. Aidan Fraser loved Billy Wood and wanted him, even after death. It was Aidan Fraser, alone, who embalmed the body of Billy Wood. He had seen how the job was done in the morgue at Scotland Yard. One night, he visited the morgue, took embalming fluid, borrowed the small hand-held pump that the task requires and brought them home. He embalmed Billy Wood as a sacrament, with reverence and adoration, as the priests of ancient Egypt embalmed the boy kings of the Nile.'

Oscar turned sharply towards Veronica.

'Where did you find the body, Miss Sutherland?' She made no reply, but gazed steadily at Oscar with cold contempt in her eyes. 'You will not tell me? Well, then, let me hazard a guess. Was it in his bed? Was it in the bridal bed that was once your due? Was it? *Was it?*' She turned from him slowly and looked at Constance Wilde. 'I thought it was, Miss Sutherland,' Oscar continued. 'Even after death, Aidan Fraser took Billy Wood to his bed. Even after death, the boy was beautiful.'

Aston Upthorpe hunched forward and hid his face in his hands. John Gray put an arm of consolation about his shoulders. Veronica turned her gaze from Constance and bent it on the two men seated on the French settee. Suddenly, violently, she spat at them.

'Is it contempt? Is it scorn? Is it fear?' cried Oscar. 'Women defend themselves by attacking, just as they attack by sudden and strange surrender.'

Veronica turned back to Oscar and sneered, 'What do you know of women, Mr Wilde?'

'I know what Congreve knew:

> Heaven has no rage, like love to hatred turned,
> Nor Hell a fury, like a woman scorned.

'I know that Aidan Fraser so loved Billy Wood that he took him to his bed even after death – and that drove you mad. Having murdered Billy once, you killed the boy again. You cut off his head, his beautiful head . . . You bought a surgical saw for the purpose from Messrs Goodliffe & Stainer on 23 December at three o'clock in the afternoon – I have inspected their sales ledger – and to hurt and humiliate Fraser further, you had the head delivered on such a day, at such a time, in such a way that you knew it would arrive at my house in Tite Street when

Fraser was seated, apparently at his ease, surrounded by his friends.

'But "Nobody ever commits a crime without doing something stupid," Miss Sutherland. And that night, the night of Constance's birthday, you did something stupid. You stole a swordstick from my house. It was there at the beginning of the evening. It was gone when you left. And I noticed. You took it, hidden beneath your coat. Robert, poor boy, did not realise it when he came upon you in the hallway a moment after you had removed it from the coatstand.

'You thought – wrongly as it happens – that it was my swordstick. It was, in fact, Robert's, a present he gave to Constance some years ago. But you took it, thinking it was mine. Somehow you had decided that you wanted to implicate me in this affair. My talk of Billy's youth and beauty sickened you. You thought – wrongly as it happens; appearances can be deceptive – but nonetheless you thought, possibly because of what Fraser had told you about the sorry, sordid "Cleveland Street Affair", that I was – as others are – as Fraser was: a lover of men, a frequenter of male brothels, a sodomite . . .'

Conan Doyle cleared his throat. John Gray shook his head. Gilmour called across the room, 'It is gone seven-fifteen, Mr Wilde. You promised to deliver the two murderers into my hand within the hour. That was our understanding.'

'And I will keep my word, Inspector. Here is Miss Sutherland. Take her – she is yours.'

'And Fraser? Where is Fraser?'

'He is upstairs, in the room above us, lying on his bed, with the head and body of Billy Wood at his side.'

'Atkins!' barked the inspector, pulling open the drawing-room door. 'Go – go now.'

Oscar called after him, 'He will wait until you come, Sergeant. He is dead. Aidan Fraser took his own life at some point between four and five o'clock this afternoon. I think you will find that he killed himself with the swordstick that Miss Sutherland presented to him for the purpose.'

Suddenly everyone in the room began to move. Gilmour came straight towards Veronica. She stood and faced him with her head held high and her hands out-stretched towards him. She turned to me as he closed a pair of handcuffs about her wrists.

'Goodbye, Mr Sherard,' she said.

'I love you,' I whispered. 'I love you still.'

'You are a fool,' she answered, 'as all men are. So vain and so stupid.'

Oscar was standing with his arm about Constance's shoulders. 'It has been a trying afternoon for you, my dear, but I thought it best that you should see and hear the worst of it at first hand.'

'I understand,' she said. 'I had guessed some of it, not all. This business has filled your mind for many months. I am relieved it is all over now. The children will be, too. They need to see more of their papa.'

'You can blame Arthur for getting me involved in the first place,' said Oscar, smiling benevolently at the country doctor who had now taken out his pipe and was sucking upon it thoughtfully.

'What?' he protested. 'You brought the matter to me, Oscar. It was your affair, not mine.'

'I know you better than that, Arthur. Come now, man, admit it.'

'Admit what?'

'I brought the death of Billy Wood to your attention – but you sent me to meet your friend Aidan Fraser at Scotland Yard. You had your suspicions about him, did you not? Suspicions, but no proof. You could not question him yourself – he was your friend. So you set me about the case, you unleashed me as your bloodhound. And to put the scent in my nostrils you even discovered the first "clue": the tiny drops of blood upon the wall. Those specks of blood: no one saw them but you. No one needed to see them. Whether they were real or imagined, they served their purpose.'

'You amaze me, Oscar,' said Conan Doyle. 'I believe you must be one of the most remarkable men of our time.'

'Well, if you think that of me, I know you will oblige me with a favour.' He looked towards the doorway. Veronica Sutherland had gone. Policemen were moving to and fro. 'When Inspector Gilmour has removed Fraser's body, I have one last duty to perform. I promised Susannah Wood that she would see her son today and she shall. Let us – you and I – lay Billy's body beneath clean sheets, with a cloth about his neck, and let us take her to see her boy one last time.'

'Very well,' he said.

'Sherard and I will then escort the poor woman back to Charing Cross. In the fullness of time, Billy is to be buried at sea – the sea that "washes away the stains and wounds of the world".'

'Euripides?'

'Indeed. You are a credit to the University of Edinburgh, Dr Doyle. And, this afternoon, Mrs Doyle has earned her place among the angels! When we're done, will you and Touie be so kind as to accompany Constance back to Tite Street? I would be so grateful.'

'By all means.' Doyle was about to shake Oscar by the hand but thought better of it and, instead, with a clenched fist, tapped him gently upon the shoulder. 'Well done, my friend. Case closed.'

'And John—' Oscar turned to John Gray who was standing by the curtained window with Aston Upthorpe. 'Would you see Mr Upthorpe home?'

Oscar took the parcel that Constance had been holding and handed it to the elderly artist. 'What's this?' Upthorpe enquired.

'Christening gifts,' said Oscar, 'for Fred and Harry. You remember? Cigarette cases. Would you present them to them for me? – with my love.'

28

Postscript

'I am a fool, Oscar.'

The clocks of the Albemarle Club had struck eleven. My friend and I were seated, facing one another, either side of the fireplace in the smoking room; the fire was burning low; the crackle and smell of the burning wood was comforting; the chill of the champagne was comforting, too. It was Sunday night and the club was all but deserted. Hubbard had served us, as obsequiously as ever, and – taking his cue (and a half-sovereign) from Oscar – had withdrawn, pulling the smoking-room doors closed behind him.

'She did not love me, Oscar.'

'She did not love you, Robert.'

'And yet today, only today, this very afternoon – in her room in Bedford Square, I lay in her arms. It was a fairy tale.'

'Indeed.'

'A fairy tale come true! It was real. It happened. Her love-making, Oscar . . . it was exquisite!'

'I have no doubt. The fact of a poet being a poisoner is nothing against his verse.'

'But she did not love me – I see that now. She used me. These past five months, she has been using me . . .'

He lay back in his chair, examining the purple plume of smoke as it rose from his Turkish cigarette. 'She has,' he said, smiling at me kindly through half-closed eyes. 'Poor Robert!'

'But today, this afternoon, when we lay together – was it not different? Was she using me then?'

'In England,' said Oscar, reflectively, 'a woman who is with child cannot be sent to the gallows . . .'

'Surely,' I cried, 'surely you do not think—'

'But I doubt that she will hang ,' he went on, paying me no heed. 'She is a woman, after all, an unfortunate woman brought low by the betrayal and depravity of the man she thought she loved. She killed her fiancé's catamite and down at the Old Bailey, that's hardly a capital offence. Some might say she has done the state some service!'

'She has done me a service, at least,' I said, leaning toward him fervently. 'I have learnt my lesson. I shall not love like that again.'

'Oh, Robert,' he cried, 'you shall and you must! Keep love in your heart – always! A life without love is like a sunless garden when the flowers are dead. The consciousness of loving and being loved brings a warmth and richness to life that nothing else can bring. A man should always be in love, Robert. Always.'

'But I see now that what happened this afternoon – what I thought was love, was not . . .'

'Yes,' he said, 'there is an important distinction to be made between the act of love and the sins of the flesh. Love is all and the sins of the flesh are nothing . . . My friend John Gray appears to be an expert on the distinction. Perhaps you should take his counsel.'

I drained my glass. 'Don't speak to me of John Gray,' I exclaimed. 'I do not begin to understand him. How he and Fraser . . . Words fail me.'

Oscar threw his cigarette into the fireplace and immediately set about lighting another. 'When it comes to John Gray and Fraser, Robert, I fear I am the guilty party.'

'What do you mean – "the guilty party"?'

'I needed to prove to myself that Fraser was indeed a lover of men. And I wanted you to be my witness. This morning, you recall, I attended mass at St Patrick's in Soho Square. I confess: I did not go solely for the good of my soul. I went because I knew that I would find John Gray there – and so I did. And I asked John Gray if he would do my bidding – and I knew he would.'

'Your bidding?'

'I asked John Gray to seduce Aidan Fraser.'

'What?' I shook my head in disbelief.

Oscar offered me his teasing half-smile. 'I guessed it might be easily done,' he continued, 'and it was. When he awoke this morning, Aidan Fraser felt a sense of freedom that he had not known for many months. Bellotti was dead, O'Donnell was dead – the case was closed. He could move on, at last. It was a day for celebration – and the eve of the feast of St Aidan. When I met John Gray at mass I asked him to send an immediate note to Fraser, inviting Fraser to join him at Cowley Street at two o'clock this afternoon. I asked John Gray to take candles and incense with him in the hope that Fraser might be tempted to recreate with John Gray the sacrament that he had enjoyed with Billy Wood . . .'

'And he did as you asked? He did your "bidding". Why?'

'Because he worships me!'

'He worships you?' I repeated, incredulous.

'It is bizarre, I agree, Robert, but it is true!' He laughed and sat forward in his chair. From his coat pocket he produced a letter, which he passed to me. 'Read,' he said, 'read, Robert! It is from John Gray, addressed to me, given to me by him in Tite Street on New Year's day. The ink is violet, the paper cream, but the sentiments are anything but vulgar. Read!'

I read. 'From the moment I met you, your personality had the most extraordinary influence over me. I was dominated, soul, brain, and power, by you. I worshipped you. I grew jealous of everyone to whom you spoke. I wanted to have you all to myself. I was only happy when I was with you.'

There was much more – much more! – in the same vein. I handed the letter back to my friend, who folded the paper carefully and kissed it lightly before returning it to his pocket. 'It is beautifully phrased, is it not? With John's permission, I propose to include it, word for word, in the story I am writing for friend Stoddart. My hero, Dorian Gray, was "made to be worshipped". According to John Gray, so am I!'

'He is a most peculiar young man,' I muttered, taking a deep sip of my champagne.

'He is handsome and idolatrous, Robert. He sought me out to worship me! And once he had found me, he would not let me go. You recall my visits to the thirty-seven morgues and mortuaries of the metropolis? They were not the solitary expeditions that I led you to believe, Robert. John Gray was my constant companion. And, bless the boy, as he travelled about with me and as he learnt of my determination to achieve justice for Billy Wood, he resolved to prove his own passionate devotion to my cause by solving the crime himself – single-handedly! It was to be his gift to me, an offering to be laid at my shrine.'

'Is this possible?'

'Oh, yes, Robert, in the sere and yellow days of my decrepitude I shall be able to say, "I was adored once too"! When you caught sight of John Gray at Ashford railway station, lurking in the carriage next to ours, he was on his way to Broadstairs to interview Susannah Wood. He was conducting his own, independent, investigation. Of course, we forestalled him. We encountered Susannah Wood first. John Gray's secret mission came to naught. He saw on us the platform with Mrs Wood and dared not leave the train for fear of giving the game away. Poor boy, he was obliged to stay put and travel on to Folkestone – to no avail!'

'And today he was ready to commit the act of darkness with Fraser – all on your account?'

'Indeed, though he confessed to me that he was strangely drawn to Fraser in any event. They shared a mutual weakness for candles and for incense – for transubstantiation and for Rome. They were, as Bellotti would have put it, "bread and butter".'

'"Bread and butter"?'

'In point of fact, given John Gray's humble origins, I believe the correct phrase is "bread and dripping". What I mean, Robert, is that they were "compatible". John Gray was more than willing to play the boy Beatrice to Fraser's Dante!'

'Yes, Oscar,' I said, refilling his glass and then my own, 'I take your meaning.'

'I am happy to know John Gray, and I am not sorry to have known Aidan Fraser. It was you, Robert, you know, who led me to an understanding of Fraser and of this case . . .'

'Me?'

'Yes, you, Robert Sherard, my friend – when you told me that your New Year resolution was to follow your heart, wherever it might lead. That is what Fraser did, quite literally. In this life, nothing is serious except passion and Aidan Fraser was passionate in his love for Billy Wood. I have learnt many lessons these past five months. No, Robert, I am not sorry to have stumbled upon this case . . .'

'Oscar,' I said, sitting back in my chair, nursing my glass of champagne, pondering whether or not I dared ask the question that I had long wanted to ask, 'you still have not told me how you came to be visiting 23 Cowley Street that afternoon at the end of August.'

His brow furrowed. 'But I have told you, Robert, several times. I had an appointment with a pupil, a student of mine, a young lady . . .'

'A young lady?'

'A young lady. My god-daughter, in fact.'

'Your god-daughter? I did not know you had a god-daughter! Is this the truth, Oscar? Or is this god-daughter another figment of your extraordinary imagination, like so many of your sundry aunts?'

'My god-daughter is real, Robert, and very special – and very dear to me. She is a golden ray of sunshine, full of life and energy and warmth. She is as gifted as she is lovely. She is only fifteen, but already she is a talented actress.'

'Why have I not met this paragon?'

'Because, poor darling, she has been in hiding. She is French—'

'French?'

'Yes, Robert, *une jeune française très belle*. She came to England to escape her father but he pursued her. I gave her sanctuary as best I could. I found her a room in Soho Square. I gave her money. I gave her lessons. I have been teaching her English – and drama! She has a natural gift. Sometimes I taught her and Billy Wood together. They were of an age. She could play Juliet to his Romeo. To see them together was extraordinarily affecting.'

'You taught her Shakespeare – in Cowley Street?'

'I taught Billy Wood there also. I taught them together. Billy Wood had expected to come to Cowley Street on 31 August for one of our lessons – we often met at Cowley Street on a Tuesday afternoon. But, a few days earlier, I saw Billy and told him I was cancelling our appointment for the thirty-first. I did not tell him why. I simply said that on that afternoon I now found that I would be "otherwise engaged". The truth was that I needed to see my god-daughter alone. She had a special audition to prepare for and I wished to give her my undivided attention. I did not mention my god-daughter's audition to Billy because I feared he might be envious. That was a mistake – as it turned out, a fatal one. Because I had cancelled my lesson with him, simply saying I was other-wise engaged, Billy assumed, naturally enough, that I would be elsewhere on 31 August – and consequently he reckoned 23 Cowley Street would be unoccupied that afternoon and so, unexpectedly, available for other purposes, different delights . . . I do not know – I cannot know – but I surmise that it was Billy who proposed to his "uncle" that they should meet that afternoon in Cowley Street. Billy, of course, had a key.'

'And Fraser had a key?'

'Indeed. And, customarily, I had a key also. But on 31 August I had lent my key to my god-daughter. That's why I had to knock on the door to gain admittance.'

'You gave your god-daughter lessons in Cowley Street. You found her a room in Soho Square. You gave her money. Yet you did not take her home to Tite Street?' I asked. 'You did not offer her sanctuary there?'

'I did not, Robert,' he said sternly, 'and for a reason. I felt it would be asking too much of Constance.'

'Ah,' I said. 'And why is that?'

'Because my god-daughter's family history is not entirely respectable. My god-daughter is the child of what you would term "a daughter of joy".'

'Forgive me, Oscar, I do not follow you.'

'My god-daughter is the child of Marie Aguétant.'

'By all that's wonderful—' I gasped. 'Perhaps you are her father, Oscar?'

'Would that I were, Robert! But I am not. The child's father is a brute by the name of Bertrand Ramier. He was once a soldier – a man of action and a man of valour, by all accounts – but when he left the army he turned to drink and then to crime. It was about twenty years ago, with some of his ill-gotten gains, that he bought himself a share in the Eden Music Hall – and it was there that he met Marie Aguétant. They became lovers. They had a child. And then, one day, in a drunken rage, he murdered his mistress. Another man was charged with the murder and was executed for the crime. But it was Ramier who killed Marie Aguétant. I know. Odile saw it happen.'

'Odile?'

'That is my god-daughter's name – or was, until she came to England. Now she is called Isola. She has been rechristened, after my sister.'

'And her father?'

'He is the man you saw following us down Albemarle Street. He is the man who attacked me that night in Soho Square. He is the reason she has been in hiding – moving about London, from one set of digs to another, under cover of darkness or hidden behind a mask.'

'Behind a mask?' I repeated.

'Yes,' he said, 'a grotesque carnival mask. Did you not glimpse it when you were keeping watch on us, Robert?' I looked down into the bottom of my glass. 'Oh, Robert! Did you mistake the mask for the face? You cannot have done! You know how I abhor ugliness!'

I blushed and he read my mind.

'You are not a fool, Robert. You are my friend – and a truer friend no man could ask for. I am so glad I persuaded Hubbard to bring us two bottles of champagne tonight. We have much cause to celebrate.'

'Do we?' I asked, as he poured me more wine, spilling a little on my knee.

'We do, Robert! "The case is closed" – and we are alive and well and beautiful, after our fashion . . . And we are friends . . . And we are free!'

'And Isola?'

'My little sister? She is free and with the angels. She is one of them, I'm sure.'

'I meant your god-daughter . . .'

'Ah, yes, Isola O'Flahertie . . . That is her stage name. Striking, is it not? She is free also, I am happy to say. Her father has been returned to France, courtesy of Inspector Gilmour of Scotland Yard. There is more substance to these red-headed men of forty than I realised, Robert. Archy Gilmour is a good man. I promised to deliver Aidan Fraser and Miss Sutherland to his safe-keeping – and in return he promised to deliver Bertrand Ramier to the Paris *préfecture*. We have both kept our word. For Billy Wood, justice has been done. And my little god-daughter is free, and safe at last.'

'Am I to meet her?'

'You are, Robert, and very soon. I hope you will come to her opening night.'

'Her opening night?'

'Did I not tell you? I took her to meet Mr Irving at the Lyceum. I think you caught sight of us on our way there, did you not? He is producing a new play based on *The Bride of Lammermoor* – I am sure I told you this. He sought my help. He was in need of a gifted and beautiful girl to play the ingenue and I proposed Isola. She auditioned for him and he was entranced. Think of it, Robert – my god-daughter is to be Henry Irving's leading lady!'

'Congratulations!' I said.

'I want you to come to the first night,' he said. 'I have tickets!'

'It will be a pleasure, Oscar.'

'It is in two weeks' time – on Monday 14 February, the feast of St Valentine.'

'I will be there,' I said, raising my glass to him. 'I will be there, Oscar. It will be an honour, my dear, good friend.'

'And bring Kaitlyn!' he cried, clinking his glass against mine. 'You told me she had returned to London, did you not? Bring Kaitlyn. Bring her, Robert. A man should always be in love!'

Biographical Notes

Oscar Wilde

Oscar Fingal O'Flahertie Wills Wilde was born at 21 Westland Row, Dublin, on 16 October 1854. He was the second son of Sir William Wilde, an eminent Irish surgeon, and Jane Francesca Wilde, *née* Elgee, a poet, author and translator, who wrote under the pseudonym 'Speranza'.

Oscar Wilde was educated at Portora Royal School, Enniskillen, at Trinity College, Dublin, and at Magdalen College, Oxford, where he achieved a double first and, for his poem 'Ravenna', won the Newdigate Prize for Poetry. On leaving Oxford, he settled in London and embarked on a career as a professional writer, critic and journalist. His play *Vera* was privately published in 1880 and his *Poems* appeared in 1881.

In 1881, Richard D'Oyly Carte presented the Gilbert and Sullivan operetta, *Patience*, satirising Oscar and his fellow 'aesthetes'. Its success, and Wilde's celebrity, led D'Oyly Carte to invite the young author to undertake an extensive lecture tour of North America at the beginning of 1882. In 1883, Wilde spent several months in Paris, working on his play, *The Duchess of Padua*, and meeting, among others, Victor Hugo, Paul Verlaine, Emile Zola and Robert Sherard. On 29 May 1884 he married Constance Lloyd, the daughter of a distinguished QC, and set up home at 16 Tite Street, Chelsea. Their sons, Cyril and Vyvyan, were born in June 1885 and November 1886.

Oscar Wilde's collection of fairy stories, *The Happy Prince and Other Tales* , appeared in 1888, followed more controversially, by 'The Portrait of Mr W. H.' in 1889 and *The Picture of Dorian Gray* in 1890. The first of his successful social comedies, *Lady Windermere's Fan*, was produced in London in 1892, followed by *A Woman of No Importance* (1893), *An Ideal Husband* (1895), and *The Importance of Being Earnest* (1895).

In 1891 Oscar Wilde met Lord Alfred Douglas, the third son of the 8th Marquess of Queensberry. In 1895, Queensberry left a card for Wilde at the Albemarle Club accusing him of 'posing Somdomite' (*sic*) and provoking Wilde to sue Queensberry for criminal libel. The failure of the libel action led to Wilde's own prosecution on charges of gross indecency. On 25 May 1895, he was found guilty and sentenced to two years' imprisonment with hard labour.

Released from gaol on 19 May 1897, Wilde travelled immediately to France and spent the rest of his life on the Continent. His poem, *The Ballad of Reading Gaol*, was published in 1898, and *De Profundis*, his confessional letter to Lord Alfred Douglas, was published posthumously, in 1905. Constance Wilde died in Genoa on 7 April 1898, following an operation on her spine. Oscar Wilde died in Paris on 30 November 1900. He was buried at Bagneux Cemetery. In 1909, his remains were moved to the French national cemetery of Père Lachaise.

Arthur Conan Doyle

Of Irish-Catholic descent, Arthur Ignatius Conan Doyle was born at 11 Picardy Place, Edinburgh, on 22 May 1859. He was the second of Mary Foley Doyle's ten children, of whom seven survived. His father, Charles Doyle, was an artist and alcoholic who died in a mental hospital near Dumfries. His grandfather, John Doyle, left Dublin, aged twenty, to become a successful portrait painter in London. His uncle, Richard Doyle, was a celebrated caricaturist and illustrator. From his great-uncle, Michael Conan, a noted journalist, Arthur received the compound surname of Conan Doyle.

Arthur Conan Doyle was educated at Stonyhurst College in Lancashire, at a Jesuit school in Feldkirch, Austria, and at Edinburgh University, where he studied medicine and became the surgeon's clerk to Professor Joseph Bell whose diagnostic methods he acknowledged as the model for the science of deduction perfected by his most famous creation, 'the consulting detective', Sherlock Holmes.

After serving briefly as a ship's medical officer (on board a whaler bound for the Arctic Circle), he settled on the south coast of England, in Southsea, where he established his own medical practice in 1882. It was while waiting for patients that he began to write fiction. Sherlock Holmes first appeared in *A Study in Scarlet* in 1887. *The Sign of Four* was published in 1890, followed by *The Memoirs of Sherlock Holmes* (1894), *The Hound of the Baskervilles* (1902), *The Return of Sherlock Holmes* (1904), *The Valley of Fear* (1915), *His Last Bow* (1917) and *The Case-Book of Sherlock Holmes* (1927).

In due course, his success as an author enabled him to give up his medical career and, beyond the Sherlock Holmes stories, his many popular books ranged from historical romances, such as *Micah Clarke* (1889) and *The Exploits of Brigadier Gerard* (1896), to science fiction, such as *The Lost World* (1912) and *The Poison Belt* (1913). In 1899, he volunteered to serve as a medical officer in the South African war and he published *The Great Boer War* in 1900. For his services to his country, he received a knighthood in 1902. In his later years he became deeply interested in psychic phenomena and published *The History of Spiritualism* in 1926.

In 1885, Conan Doyle married Louisa 'Touie' Hawkins. They had two children: a daughter, Mary, and a son, Alleyne Kingsley. Touie died of tuberculosis in 1906. Alleyne Kingsley, weakened by injuries received on the Somme, died of influenza in 1918. Conan Doyle married Jean Leckie in 1907 and they had three children. Arthur Conan Doyle died at Crowborough in Sussex on 7 July 1930.

Robert Sherard

Robert Harborough Sherard Kennedy was born in London on 3 December 1861, the fourth child of the Reverend Bennet Sherard Calcraft Kennedy. His father was the illegitimate son of the 6th and last Earl of

Harborough, and his mother, Jane Stanley Wordsworth, was the granddaughter of the poet laureate, William Wordsworth (1770–1850). Robert was educated at Queen Elizabeth College, Guernsey, at New College, Oxford, and at the University of Bonn, but he left both Oxford and Bonn without securing a degree. In 1880, having quarrelled with his father and lost his expected inheritance, he abandoned his 'Kennedy' surname.

In the early 1880s, Robert Sherard settled in Paris and set about earning his living as an author and journalist. He cultivated the acquaintance of a number of the leading literary figures of the day, including Emile Zola, Guy de Maupassant, Alphonse Daudet and Oscar Wilde. He published thirty-three books during his lifetime, including a collection of poetry, *Whispers* (1884), novels, biographies, social studies (notably *The White Slaves of England*, 1897), and five books inspired by his friendship with Oscar Wilde: *Oscar Wilde: The Story of an Unhappy Friendship*, 1902; *The Life of Oscar Wilde*, 1906; *The Real Oscar Wilde*, 1912; *Oscar Wilde Twice Defended*, 1934; and *Bernard Shaw, Frank Harris and Oscar Wilde*, 1936.

He was three times married and lived much of his life in France, where he was made a Chevalier de la Légion d'honneur. He died in England, in Ealing, on 30 January 1943.

In 1960, in *Oscar Wilde and His World*, Vyvyan Holland, Wilde's younger son, gave this assessment of Robert Sherard: 'When they first met they felt that they had nothing in common and disliked each other intensely; but they gradually got together and became life-long friends. Sherard wrote the first three biographical studies of Wilde after his death . . . On these three books are based all the other biographies of Wilde, except the so-called biography by Frank Harris, which is nothing else but the self-glorification of Frank Harris. Sherard got a great deal of his material from Lady Wilde when she was a very old lady and was inclined to let her imagination run away with her, particularly where the family history was concerned; and Sherard, a born journalist, was much more attracted by the interest of a story than by its accuracy, a failing which we can see running through all his books. But where his actual contact with Wilde is concerned, he is quite reliable.'

Gyles Brandreth

Gyles Brandreth was born on 8 March 1948 in Germany, where, in the aftermath of the Second World War, his father, Charles Brandreth, was serving as a legal officer with the Allied Control Commission and counted among his colleagues H. Montgomery Hyde, who, in 1948, published the first full account of the trials of Oscar Wilde. In 1974, at the Oxford Theatre Festival, Gyles Brandreth produced the first stage version of *The Trials of Oscar Wilde*, with Tom Baker as Wilde, and, in 2000, he edited the transcripts of the trials for an audio production starring Martin Jarvis.

Gyles Brandreth was educated at the Lycée Français de Londres, at Betteshanger School in Kent, and at Bedales School in Hampshire. Like Robert Sherard, Gyles Brandreth went on to New College, Oxford, where he was a scholar, President of the Union and editor of the university magazine, and then, again like Sherard, embarked on a career as an author and journalist. His first book, *Created in Captivity* (1972), was a study of prison reform; his first biography, *The Funniest Man on Earth* (1974), was a portrait of the Victorian music-hall star, Dan Leno. More recently he has published a biography of the actor, Sir John Gielgud, as well as an acclaimed diary of his years as an MP and government whip (*Breaking the Code: Westminster Diaries 1990–97*) and two best-selling royal biographies: *Philip and Elizabeth: Portrait of a Marriage* and *Charles and Camilla: Portrait of a Love Affair*.

Robert Sherard's forebears included William Wordsworth. Gyles Brandreth's include the somewhat less eminent poet, George R. Sims (1847–1922), who wrote the ballads 'Billy's dead and gone to glory' and 'Christmas Day in the workhouse'. Sims was also the first journalist to claim to know the true identity of 'Jack the Ripper'. Sims, a kinsman of the Empress Eugénie and an acquaintance of both Oscar Wilde and Arthur Conan Doyle, was arguably the first 'celebrity columnist'. He was also well known in his day for his endorsement of an 'infallible cure for baldness': 'Tatcho – The Geo. R. Sims Hair Restorer'.

As a broadcaster, Gyles Brandreth has presented numerous series for BBC Radio 4, including *A Rhyme in Time*, *Sound Advice* and *Whispers* – coincidentally the title of Robert Sherard's first collection of poetry. He is a regular guest on *Just a Minute* and *Countdown*, and his television appearances have ranged from being the guest host of *Have I Got News for You* to being the subject of *This is Your Life*. On stage he has starred in an award-winning revue in the West End and appeared as Malvolio in a musical version of *Twelfth Night* in Edinburgh. With Hinge and Bracket he scripted the TV series, *Dear Ladies*; with Julian Slade he wrote a play about A. A. Milne (featuring Aled Jones as Christopher Robin); and, with Susannah Pearse, he has written a new musical about Lewis Carroll, *The Last Photograph*.

Gyles Brandreth is married to the writer and publisher, Michèle Brown. They have three children: a barrister, a writer and an environmental economist.

Acknowledgements

I am grateful to my late father, Charles Brandreth, for giving me his copy of the 'enlarged edition' of *Memories and Adventures* by Sir Arthur Conan Doyle, published by John Murray in 1930. It was in reading this book, in the 1990s, that I first discovered, to my surprise, that Arthur Conan Doyle and Oscar Wilde were friends. I am grateful, too, to Merlin Holland, Wilde's grandson, for giving me a copy of his edition of *The Complete Letters of Oscar Wilde*, published in 2000. It was in reading this book that I first became intrigued by the friendship between Oscar Wilde and Robert Sherard. My chief debt, of course, is to Wilde, Sherard and Conan Doyle, whose lives and works I have plundered to create this story and its sequels.

Over the years, many friends and acquaintances have made a contribution to this endeavour. Oscar Wilde died in a small, first-floor room at L'Hôtel d'Alsace, 13 rue des Beaux-Arts, in Paris, at 1.45 p.m. on 30 November 1900. One hundred years later, on 30 November 2000, at the same time, in the same hotel room, at the invitation of my friend Robert Palmer, my wife and I were among a small group who gathered to mark the centenary of Oscar's passing. Forty years earlier, as a boy at Bedales School, my friends included Robert Booth, who, even as a teenager, had an encyclopaedic knowledge of Wilde and his contemporaries, and Simon Cadell who, under my direction, aged thirteen, played a definitive Sherlock Holmes in my school production of *A Study in Sherlock*. At Bedales, too, I was lucky enough to be befriended by the school's founder, J. H. Badley (1865–1967), who, over a series of Wednesday afternoon games of Scrabble at his home in the school's grounds, provided me with vivid accounts of Oscar Wilde's manner and conversational style, including Wilde's habit of trying out on his family and friends lines that would later resurface in his stories and plays. John Badley was a friend of Oscar and Constance Wilde, and their elder son, Cyril, was a pupil at Bedales at the time of Wilde's arrest.

Oscar Wilde had his reservations about publishers. 'I suppose publishers are untrustworthy,' he said. 'They certainly always look it.' But Wilde wasn't published by John Murray in the United Kingdom or by Simon & Schuster in the United States – nor was he represented by the world's finest literary agent, Ed Victor. I am truly grateful to Ed Victor and his team, and to Roland Philipps and Caroline Westmore, among others, at John Murray, as well as to Trish Grader and Meghan Stevenson, among others, at Simon & Schuster. I am most especially indebted to my copy editor Celia Levett and, above all, to my publisher and editor, Kate Parkin. Her care and kindness, attention to detail and skilful editorial guidance, as well as her consistent enthusiasm, have been invaluable to me.

G. B.

Available soon in hardback

Oscar Wilde and the Ring of Death
Gyles Brandreth

The second in Gyles Brandreth's acclaimed series of Victorian murder myseries featuring Oscar Wilde – playwright, poet, wit, raconteur, detective . . .

'And each man kills the thing he loves . . .'

The Cadogan Hotel, London, May 1892. Oscar Wilde – at the height of his fame and fortune – cannot know what he has begun when, at a gathering of the Socrates Club, he proposes a game of 'Murder'. Wilde invites each of his distinguished dinner guests to name a person they would most like to destroy. It is only a game, or so it seems, until within hours the chosen 'victims' begin to die, one by one . . .

Wilde and his confidantes, Robert Sherard and Arthur Conan Doyle, realise that the murderer is among their party. In a race against time, Wilde must take action before he becomes the next victim.

Featuring a cast of brilliantly realised characters from Lord Alfred Douglas to Walter Sickert, *Oscar Wilde and the Ring of Death* tells a compelling story of passion, deceit and multiple murder set against the contrasting worlds of late-Victorian high society, the church, the theatre and the boxing ring.

Now read on . . .

www.oscarwildemurdermysteries.com

The Fortune Teller

It was Sunday, 1 May 1892. The day was cold, though the sun was bright. I recall in particular the way in which a brilliant shaft of afternoon sunlight filtered through the first-floor front window of Number 16 Tite Street, Chelsea – the London home of Oscar and Constance Wilde – and perfectly illuminated two figures sitting close together at a small window table, apparently holding hands.

One was a woman, a widow, in her early forties, with a pleasing figure, well-held, and a narrow, kindly face – a little lined, but not care-worn – and large, knowing eyes. She was dressed all in black silk and on her head, which she held high, she wore a turban of black velvet featuring a single, startling, silver and turquoise peacock's feather. The colour of the feather matched the colour of her hair.

The other figure seated at the table was quite as striking. He was a large man, aged thirty-seven, tall, over-fleshed, with a fine head of thick deep-chestnut hair, large, slightly drooping eyes, and full lips that opened to reveal a wide mouth crowded with ungainly teeth. His skin was pale and pasty, blotched with freckles. He was dressed in a sand-coloured linen suit of his own design. At his neck, he sported a loose-fitting linen tie of Lincoln green and, in his buttonhole, a fresh amaryllis, the colour of coral.

The woman was Mrs Robinson, clairvoyant to the Prince of Wales, among others. The man was Oscar Wilde, poet and playwright, and literary sensation of the age.

Slowly, with gloved fingers, Mrs Robinson caressed Oscar Wilde's right hand. Repeatedly, she brushed the side of her little finger across his palm. With her right thumb and forefinger she took each of his fingers in turn and, gently, pulled it straight. For a long while, she gazed intently at his open hand, saying nothing. Eventually, she lifted his palm to her cheek and held it there. She sighed and closed her eyes and whispered, 'I see a sudden death in this unhappy hand. A cruel death, unexpected and unnatural. Is it murder? Is it suicide?'

'Or is it the palmist trying to earn her guinea by adding a touch of melodrama to her reading?' Oscar withdrew his hand from Mrs Robinson's tender grasp and slapped it on the table, with a barking laugh.

'You go too far, dear lady,' he exclaimed. 'This is a tea party and the Thane of Cawdor is not expected. There are children present. You are here to entertain the guests, Mrs Robinson, not terrify them.'

Mrs Robinson tilted her bird-like head to one side and smiled. 'I see what I see,' she said, without rancour.

Oscar was smiling also. He turned from the table and looked beyond the pool of sunlight to a young man of military bearing who was standing alone, a yard away, observing the scene. 'Come to my rescue, Arthur,' he called. 'Mrs Robinson has seen "a sudden death" in my "unhappy hand". You're a medical man. I need a second opinion.'

Arthur Conan Doyle was then three weeks away from his thirty-third birthday and already something of a national hero. *The Adventures of Sherlock Holmes* was one of the most popular books in the land. Doyle himself, in appearance, was more Watson than Holmes. He was a handsome fellow, sturdy and broad-shouldered, with a hearty handshake, beady eyes and a genial smile that he kept hidden beneath a formidable walrus moustache. He was the best of men, and a true friend to Oscar, in good times and bad.

'I'm no longer practising medicine, Oscar, as you know,' he said, moving towards the window table, 'but if you want my honest opinion, you should steer well clear of this kind of tomfoolery. It can be dangerous. It leads you know not where.' He bowed a little stiffly towards Mrs Robinson. 'No offence intended, Madam,' he said.

'None taken,' she replied, graciously. 'The creator of Sherlock Holmes can do no wrong in my eyes.'

Doyle's cheeks turned scarlet. He blushed readily. 'You are too kind,' he mumbled awkwardly.

'You are too ridiculous, Arthur. Pay no attention to him, Mrs R. He's all over the place. I'm not surprised. He's moved to South Norwood – wherever that may be.'

'It's not far,' Doyle protested.

'It's a world away, Arthur, and you know it. That's why you were late.'

'I was late because I was completing something.'

'Your sculpture. Yes, I know. Sculpture is your new enthusiasm.'

Conan Doyle stood back from the table. 'How do you know that?' he exclaimed. 'I have mentioned it to no one – to no one at all.'

'Oh, come now, Arthur,' said Oscar, getting to his feet, smiling and inclining his head to Mrs Robinson as he left the table. 'I heard you telling my wife about the spacious hut at the end of your new garden and the happy hours you are intending to spend there, "in the cold and the damp". Only a sculptor loves a cold, damp room: it's ideal for keeping his clay moist.'

'You amaze me, Oscar.'

'Mrs Robinson would have uncovered your secret too – by the simple expedient of examining your fingernails. Look at them, Arthur. They give the whole game away!'

'You are extraordinary, Oscar. I marvel at you. You know that I plan to include you in one of my stories – as Sherlock Holmes's older brother?'

'Yes, you have told me – he is to be obese and indolent, as I recall. I'm flattered.'

Conan Doyle laughed and slapped Oscar on the shoulder with disconcerting force. 'I'm glad I came to your party, my friend,' he said, 'despite the company you keep.'

'It is not my party, Arthur. It is Constance's party. The guests are all alarmingly respectable and the cause is undeniably just.'

The party – for about forty guests, men, women and children – was a fund-raiser in aid of one of Constance Wilde's favourite charities, the Rational Dress Society. The organisation, inspired by the example of Amelia Bloomer in the United States, was dedicated to promoting fashions for women that did not 'deform the body or

344

endanger it'. The Society believed that no woman should be forced to endure the discomfort and risk to health of overly tight-laced and restrictive corsetry nor be obliged to wear, in total, more than seven pounds of under-garments. Constance spoke poignantly of the plight of so many women – scores of them each year: young and old, serving girls and ladies of rank – who were either maimed or burned to death when their voluminous skirts, petti-coats and underpinnings accidentally caught on a candle or brushed by a hearth and were set alight.

Oscar and Arthur stood together looking about the room. Conan Doyle leant forward, resting his hands on the back of one of the Wildes' black-and-white bamboo chairs. 'The cause is indeed a good one,' he said. 'Rest assured: I have subscribed.' He smiled at Oscar, adding, 'I remain to be convinced, however, about the complete respectability of the guests. For example, who are those two?' He nodded towards the piano.

'Ah,' said Oscar, 'Miss Bradley and Miss Cooper.'

'They look like chimney sweeps.'

'Yes,' said Oscar, squinting at the ladies. 'They do appear to have come *en travestie*. I think the costumes are deliberate. They probably wanted to bring us luck. They are not chimney sweeps by trade. They are poetesses. Or, rather, I should say, "they are a poet". They write together, under a single name. They call themselves "Michael Field".'

'I observed them in the hallway, smoking cigarettes, and kissing one another, upon the lips.'

'Extraordinary,' said Oscar, shaking his head wanly, 'especially when you consider the amount of influenza sweeping through Chelsea this spring.'

'And what about the unhealthy-looking gentleman over there? He has the appearance of a dope-fiend, Oscar.'

'George Daubeney?' exclaimed Oscar. 'The Hon. the Reverend George Daubeney? He's a clergyman, Arthur, and the son of an earl.'

'Is he now?' replied Doyle, chuckling. 'Why do I recognise the name?'

'It has been in all the papers, alas. The Reverend George was sued for breach of promise. It was a messy business. He lost the case and his entire fortune with it.'

'He has a weak mouth,' said Conan Doyle.

'And a stern father who declines to bail him out, I'm afraid. I like him, however. He is assistant chaplain at the House of Commons and part-time padre to Astley's Circus on the south side of Westminster Bridge.'

'No wonder you like him, Oscar! You cannot resist the improbable.'

Now it was Oscar's turn to chuckle. He touched Conan Doyle on the elbow and invited his friend to scan the room. 'Look about you, Arthur. You are a man who has seen the world, the best and worst of it. You have journeyed to the Arctic in a whaler. You have lived in Southsea out of season. You are familiar with all types and conditions of men. Consider the assorted individuals gathered in this drawing room this afternoon and tell me which one of them, to you, looks to be the most incontrovertibly "respectable".'

Doyle was entertained by the challenge. He stepped back and stood, arms akimbo, fists on hips. He pursed his lips and narrowed his eyes and, slowly, carefully, surveyed the scene before him. Constance had gathered a motley crowd to her charitable tea party. 'What precisely am I looking for Oscar?'

'The acme of respectability,' said Oscar. 'The face, the figure, the demeanour, the *look* that says to you, "This chap is sound, no doubt about it."'

'Mm,' growled Doyle, taking in the faces around him, turn by turn. 'They all look a bit doubtful, don't they?' He looked beyond where the Reverend George Daubeney was standing, to the doorway, where Charles Brooke – the English Rajah of Sarawak, a particular friend of Constance – was holding court. 'Brooke has the look of a leader about him, doesn't he? I know him slightly. He's sound. He's a gentleman.'

Oscar raised his forefinger and waved it admonishingly. 'No, no, Arthur. Don't tell me about people you already know. I want you to make a judgement entirely on appearance. Look about this room and pick out the one person who strikes you as having about him an air of absolute respectability.'

'I have him!' cried Doyle triumphantly. 'There!' He indicated a sandy-haired young man of medium build and medium height who was standing with Constance Wilde at the far end of the room. Constance's older boy, her six-year-old, Cyril, was at her side with his arms clasped around her skirt. Her younger son, Vyvyan, then four-and-a-half, was seated happily on the young man's shoulders tugging at his hair.

'He's your man, Oscar,' said Conan Doyle. 'He's easy with children – and children are easy with him. That's a good sign.'

'He is Vyvyan's godfather,' said Oscar.

'I'm not surprised. You chose well. He has the air of a thoroughly dependable fellow. What's his name?'

'Edward Heron-Allen,' said Oscar.

'A sound name,' said Conan Doyle, with satisfaction.

'Indeed,' said Oscar, smiling.

'A respectable name.'

'Certainly.'

'And his profession, Oscar? He's a professional man – you can tell at a glance.'

'He is a solicitor. And the son of a solicitor.'

'Of course he is. I might have guessed. Look at his open face – it's a face you can trust. It's the face of a good-hearted, clean-living, *respectable* young man. How old is he? Do you know?'

'About thirty, I imagine.'

'And how old is the Hon. the Reverend George Daubeney, may I ask?'

'About the same, I suppose.'

'But Daubeney,' said Doyle, his eyes darting from Oscar to Constance, 'looks ten years the older of the two, does he not? Daubeney's face, I fear, speaks of a life of dissipation. My man's face speaks of the Great Outdoors. He has colour in his cheeks. His jaw is clean cut, his eyes sparkle, his conscience is clear.'

'My, my, Arthur, you are taken with him.'

Conan Doyle laughed. 'I'm only doing as you asked, Oscar – judging by appearance. Edward Heron-Allen's appearance is wholly reassuring. You cannot deny it. Look at his suit.'

'The tailoring is unexceptional.'

'Precisely. The man is not a dandy. He is a gentleman. His suit is sober – it's exactly the sort of suit you'd expect a solicitor to wear on a Sunday – and his tie, I think, tells us he went to Harrow.'

'He did indeed,' said Oscar, grinning broadly, 'and played cricket for the First XI.'

Conan Doyle caught sight of Oscar's wide and wicked smile and, suddenly, with a clenched fist began to beat his own forehead. 'Oh, Oscar, Oscar,' he growled ruefully, 'have I taken your bait? Have I fallen headlong into an elephant trap? Are you about to reveal to me that my supposed model of respectability is, in fact, the greatest bounder in the room?'

'No,' said Oscar, lightly, 'not at all. But we all have our secrets, Arthur, do we not?'

'What's his? Has he embezzled all his clients' money?'

'He is in love with Constance.'

Conan Doyle looked concerned. He was a loyal and conscientious husband. His own young wife, Louisa, known as 'Touie', was a victim of tuberculosis. Doyle went out and about without her, but she was never far from his thoughts. Arthur Conan Doyle was that old-fashioned thing, a man of honour. His marriage vows counted with him. He tugged at his moustache. 'This fellow, Heron-Allen, being in love with your wife, Oscar – does it trouble you?'

'No,' said Oscar, 'not at all.'

'And Mrs Wilde?' asked Doyle, 'How does she feel?'

'It does not trouble Mrs Wilde.' Oscar smiled. 'Mrs Heron-Allen, however, may find it a touch perturbing.'

'Ah,' said Arthur frowning, 'the fellow's married, is he? He doesn't look like a married man.'

'I agree with you there, Arthur. He looks totally care-free, does he not?'

'He looks quite ordinary to me,' said Conan Doyle. 'That's why I picked him when you started me off on this absurd game. I shouldn't have indulged you, Oscar.'

'Edward Heron-Allen is anything but ordinary, Arthur. He cultivates asparagus. He makes violins. He speaks fluent Persian. And he is a world authority on necrophilia, bestiality, pederasty, and the trafficking of child prostitutes.'

'Good grief.' Arthur Conan Doyle blanched and gazed towards Edward Heron-Allen in horror. The young solicitor was lifting Vyvyan Wilde from his shoulders. He kissed the top of the boy's head as he lowered him safely to the ground. 'Good grief,' repeated Conan Doyle.

'I've seated you next to him at dinner, Arthur. You'll find him fascinating. He's a chiromancer too Let him read your palm between courses and he'll advise you whether to plump for the lamb or the beef.'

'I'm speechless, Oscar,' said Conan Doyle, still staring fixedly in the direction of Edward Heron-Allen and Constance Wilde. 'I'm quite lost for words.'

'No matter,' said Oscar blithely, 'Heron-Allen can do the talking. He has a great deal to say and you'll find all of it's worth hearing.'

'Are you serious, Oscar?' Doyle protested. 'Is that man really joining us for dinner?'

Oscar chuckled. 'Why not? He looks respectable enough to me. In fact, he's my particular guest tonight. Sherard is bringing the Hon. the Reverend George Daubeney. Who is your guest to be?'

Conan Doyle was now blowing his nose noisily on a large, red handkerchief. 'Willie . . . Willie Hornung,' he said, hesitating to name the name. 'You don't know him. He's a young journalist, an excellent fellow, one of the sweetest-natured and most delicate-minded men I ever knew.'

'Hornung . . . Willie Hornung.' Oscar rolled the name around his mouth, as though it was an unfamiliar wine.

Doyle returned his handkerchief to his pocket and looked Oscar in the eye. 'Perhaps I should advise Hornung to stay away. Willie's not what you'd call a man of the world.'

'Don't be absurd, Arthur. How old is he?'

'I don't know. Twenty-six? Twenty-seven?'

'Keats was dead at twenty-six, Arthur. It'll do Mr Hornung good to live a little dangerously, take life as he finds it. It's the possibility of the pearl or the poison in the oyster that make the prospect of opening it so enticing. Besides, we have to have him or we'll be thirteen at table.'

'Is Lord Alfred Douglas coming?'

'Bosie? Of course.' Oscar threw his head back and brushed his hands through his hair. 'Bosie is coming, very much so. And he's bringing his older brother, Francis Douglas, Lord Drumlanrig, with him. You'll like Drumlanrig, Arthur. He's about the same age as your young friend, Hornung, and sweet-natured, too. I'm all for feasting with panthers, but it's good to have a few delicate-minded lambs at the trough as well. One can have too much of a bad thing.' He looked around the room. 'Where is Bosie? He should be here by now.'

The Wildes' drawing room was beginning to empty. Katherine Bradley and Edith Cooper, the poetesses dressed as chimney sweeps, were standing by the doorway blowing kisses towards Oscar. Miss Bradley, the taller of the two, had taken a huge bulrush out of a vase by the fireplace. She called to Oscar: 'I'm stealing this, dearest one. I hope you don't mind. Moses and Rebecca Salaman are coming to supper. This will make them feel so at home.' Oscar nodded obligingly. Charles Brooke was handing Constance a cheque and grandiloquently saluting her for her charitable endeavours on behalf of humankind in general and the Rational Dress Society in particular. His wife, Margaret, a plain and patient woman, was pulling at his arm. 'Will he ever stop talking?' she asked. 'Only if we start listening,' answered Constance, with a kindly laugh, kissing her friend on the cheek. 'Thank you both for coming. And thank you, Charles, for your generosity. Everyone has been so kind, so good.'

'It's you, Mrs Wilde,' said Edward Heron-Allen, stepping toward his hostess and lifting her hand to his lips. 'You inspire us.'

Conan Doyle spluttered into his handkerchief and whispered to Oscar, 'The man's intolerable.'

'You inspire our devotion,' Heron-Allen continued, still holding Constance's hand and looking into her eyes. 'We love you. It's as simple as that.'

'We love Oscar, too,' said a voice from the landing, 'but that's more complicated, of course.'

'Ah,' said Oscar, clapping his hands, 'Bosie is upon us.'

Lord Alfred Douglas appeared in the doorway of the Wildes' drawing room and held his pose. Bosie was an arrestingly good-looking boy. I use the word 'boy' advisedly. He was twenty-one at the time, but he looked no more than a child. Indeed, he told me that, later that same summer, a society matron was quite put out when she invited him to her children's tea party and discovered her mistake. Even at thirty-one, people would enquire whether he was still at school. Oscar used to say, 'Bosie contained the very essence of youth. He never lost it. That is why I loved him.'

Oscar did indeed love Lord Alfred Douglas and made no bones about it. Slender as a reed, with a well-proportioned face, gently curling hair the colour of ripe corn and the complexion of a white peach, Bosie was an Adonis — even Conan Doyle and I could not deny that. Oscar loved him for his looks. He loved him for his intellect, also. Bosie had a good mind, a ready wit — he liked to claim credit for originating some of Oscar's choicest quips — and a way with words and language that I envied. He was intelligent, but indolent. He left Oxford without a degree. (But so did I. And so did Shelley and Swinburne. Bosie's poetry may not rank alongside theirs, but, nonetheless, the best of it has stood the test of time.)

Oscar Wilde also loved Lord Alfred Douglas because of who he was. Though he made wry remarks to suggest otherwise, Oscar was a snob. He liked a title. He was pleased to be on 'chatting terms' with the Prince of Wales. He was happy that his acquaintance encompassed at least a dozen dukes. And he was charmed to find that Bosie Douglas (with his perfect profile and manners to match) was the third son of an eighth marquess — albeit a marquess with a reputation.

Even in 1892, Bosie's father, John Sholto Douglas, 8th Marquess of Queensberry, was notorious. Ill-favoured, squat, hot-tempered, aggressive, Lord Queensberry was a brute, a bully, a spendthrift and a womaniser. His one strength was that he was fearless. His one unsullied claim to fame was that, with a university friend, John Graham Chambers, he had codified the rules of conduct for the sport of boxing. He was himself a light-weight boxer of tenacity and skill. He was also a daring and determined jockey (he rode his own horses in the Grand National) and a huntsman noted for ruthlessness in the field. He was said to use his whip with equal ease on his horses, his dogs and his women. In 1887, Lady Queensberry, the mother of his five children, divorced him on the grounds of his adultery.

Bosie despised his father and adored his mother. In Bosie's eyes, Sybil Queensberry could do no wrong. 'My father has given me nothing,' he said. 'My mother has given me everything, including my name.' Lady Queensberry had called him 'Boysie' when he was a baby. Oscar called him 'my own dear boy' from the moment they met, early in the summer of 1891. They became firm friends almost at once. By the summer of 1892, they were near inseparable. Where Oscar went, Bosie came too. I liked him. Constance liked him, also. Conan Doyle had his reservations.

As he stood, posed, in the drawing-room doorway, with his head thrown to one side, like a martyred saint upon a cross, Bosie looked straight towards Constance. 'Mrs Wilde,' he cried, '*Peccavi*. I have missed your party and I didn't want to miss it for the world. Will you forgive me?' From behind his back he produced a small bunch of primroses tied together with blue ribbon. He stepped forward and presented them to her. She kissed him, as she might have done a child, and said, 'What a sweet thought, Bosie. Thank you. I'm glad you're here. I'm sure Oscar was getting anxious.'

Bosie, nodding to Edward Heron-Allen, went over to Oscar and Conan Doyle. George Daubeney and I joined them. 'I apologise, Oscar,' he said. I've had a damnable afternoon. Arguing about money. With my father. He's been through £400,000 you know and won't advance me fifty. The man's a monster. I'd like to murder him.'

Arthur Conan Doyle raised an eyebrow and sucked on his moustache.

'I mean it,' said Bosie seriously. 'I'd like to murder him, in cold blood.'

'Well, you can't, Bosie,' said Oscar, 'leastways, not tonight.'

'Why not?' demanded Bosie petulantly.

'It's Sunday, Bosie,' said Oscar, 'and a gentleman never murders his father on a Sunday. You should know that. Did they teach you nothing at Winchester? Besides, it's the first Sunday in the month and we are going to dinner at the Cadogan. You can't have forgotten, surely?'